SULLIVAN'S STING

SULLIVAN'S STING

Lawrence Sanders

G. P. PUTNAM'S SONS
New York

G. P. Putnam's Sons
Publishers Since 1838
200 Madison Avenue
New York, NY 10016

Library of Congress Cataloging-in-Publication Data

Sanders, Lawrence, date.
Sullivan's sting / Lawrence Sanders.
p.   cm.
I. Title.
PS3569.A5125S86   1990   89-70046 CIP
813′.54—dc20
ISBN 0-399-13542-1

Printed in the United States of America
1   2   3   4   5   6   7   8   9   10

This book is printed on acid-free paper.

SULLIVAN'S STING

1.

He was a perfect gentleman, attentive, eager to please. There was something balletic in his movements: a swoop to light Mrs. Winslow's cigarette with a gold Dupont, a bow to place the black mink stole about her fleshy shoulders, a pirouette as the maître d' came bustling up.

"Was everything satisfactory, Mr. Rathbone?"

"Everything was excellent, Felix," he said, and pressed a folded twenty into the waiting palm.

"The zabaglione was *divine*," Mrs. Birdie Winslow said. "Something extra, wasn't there?"

"Just a few drops of rum, madam. For flavor."

"Marvelous idea. We must come again."

"Please do," Felix said, escorting them to the door. "On Friday we shall have baked pompano with a champagne sauce."

Outside, they stood a moment staring up at a lucid sky sown with rows of stars. But the easterly wind had an edge, and Mrs. Winslow wrapped her stole tighter. Rathbone slipped an arm lightly about her thick waist.

"Chilly?"

"Not really."

He leaned closer. "Love your perfume. Obsession, isn't it?"

"Oh David," she said, "you know everything."

"Yes," he said solemnly, "I do." And then laughed, hugging her to share the joke. "All right, now let's test your sense of direction. We're in Boca Raton. Which way do we go to get back to Lauderdale?"

She looked around a moment, then pointed. "That way?"

"And end up in Palm Beach? Nope, we go south."

He handed the ticket to the waiting valet, and they stood in comfortable silence until the black Bentley was brought around.

"Thank *you*, Mr. Rathbone," the valet said, pocketing his tip. "You folks have a nice evening now, y'hear."

"Everyone in Florida is so polite," Mrs. Winslow said as they drove southward on A1A.

"Uh-huh," David Rathbone said. "The last outpost of civility. All you need is money. Birdie, I hope you don't mind dropping in at this party."

"Of course not. I'll be happy to meet your friends."

"Not friends—clients. I don't socialize much with them. I prefer to keep our relations on a professional level. But I thought it would give you a chance to chat with them, find out for yourself if they're satisfied with my services. That's the best way to select an investment adviser: talk to the man's clients and get their opinions."

"Are they all wealthy?"

"None of them is hurting. And Sidney Coe is *rich* rich. He keeps a yacht down at Bahia Mar that's just a little smaller than the *QE2*. Crew of five live aboard, but Coe never takes it out. Just uses it for partying."

"And you handle all his funds?"

"Oh yes. Up about forty percent last year. But all my clients have done as well. At that rate you can double your money in less than two years."

"I'd like that. Poor Ralph used to handle all our investments and after he died I just turned everything over to the bank."

"Banks are all right," Rathbone said, "but too conservative. They're so heavily regulated that there are a lot of aggressive investment opportunities they're not allowed to touch."

"How long will it take the bank to double my money?"

"Probably about ten years—if you're lucky."

"And you can do it in two?"

"Or less," he said. "You won't object if we only spend an hour at the party? Then I'll drive you home. I've got to get back to my office. I have a client in Madrid who's phoning at midnight."

"Madrid? Oh my. Do you have many foreign clients?"

"Five. One in Spain, two in England, one in France, one in Germany. I usually get over there several times a year and visit them all. And of course they frequently come to Florida. Especially in the winter!"

"I can understand that," Birdie Winslow said. "The climate is *divine*. I'm so glad I moved here."

"So am I," David Rathbone said, and placed a hand gently on her plump knee.

The home was on the Intracoastal Waterway at the Hillsboro Inlet. They parked on a circular driveway of antique brick, along with a Cadillac, BMW, and Jaguar XJ-S. They sat a moment, staring at the glittering mansion.

"David," she said, "it's *divine!*"

"Is it? Four bedrooms, three baths, marble floors, pool, sauna, private dock. It's listed, fully furnished. They're asking a million five. Interested?"

"Oh heavens, no! Too big for just little old me."

11

"Of course it is. You have better things to do with your money."

"But why are they selling?"

"They're building on the beach. A larger place with a guest house. Before we go in, let me brief you on what to expect. The host and hostess are Mortimer and Nancy Sparco. He was in sewer pipe in Ohio. Retired now. The guests will be Sidney Coe, the yacht owner I told you about, and his third wife, Cynthia. He made his money in natural gas. Oklahoma. The third married couple are James and Trudy Bartlett. He was a neurosurgeon. Then there's Ellen St. Martin. You already know her. A divorcée. And Frank Little, who may or may not be gay. He's an importer. Mostly sports equipment. The butler's name is Theodore, and the maid is Blanche."

"I'll never remember all that."

"Of course you won't," he said, taking her arm as they strolled up the chattahoochee walk. "But you'll sort them out eventually. Don't forget to ask what they think of the job I'm doing for them."

Mrs. Winslow was happy she'd worn her basic black and pearls, for all the women were in evening gowns and the men, like Rathbone, were spiffy in white dinner jackets and plaid cummerbunds. She was introduced around, and everyone was just as nice as they could be. Champagne was served in crystal flutes.

Rathbone drew aside and let Mrs. Winslow mingle with the other guests. They spoke of planned cruises, a new restaurant in Miami, the polo season at Wellington, and an upcoming charity ball in Palm Beach for British royalty. It was all easy talk, moneyed talk, and Mrs. Winslow was dazzled.

"If you don't mind my asking," she said to Cynthia Coe, "what do you think of David Rathbone? I mean as an investment manager. I'm thinking of going in with him."

"Do it," Mrs. Coe said promptly. "The man's a wizard. The best in the business."

"He's got the Midas Touch," James Bartlett said. "Doubled my net worth in two years. You can't go wrong."

"A financial genius," Mortimer Sparco said. "Absolutely trustworthy. He'll make you a mint."

"*Divine,*" Mrs. Winslow kept breathing. "*Divine.*"

The hour passed swiftly. Finally, goodbyes were said, with all the women vowing to call Birdie for lunch or a shopping tour of the malls. Then Rathbone drove her home to her rented condo.

"Nice people," he said, "weren't they?"

"*Very* nice. So friendly. Nothing standoffish at all. David, I've decided I'd like to have you manage my money."

"I think that's a wise decision," he said. "You won't have the nuisance of watching your investments every day. You'll get a monthly statement from me detailing exactly how much you've made. My fee will be deducted automatically from the profits. Suppose I stop by around eleven tomorrow morning with the papers. Just a simple power of attorney and a management contract. It won't take long. And then perhaps we could have lunch at the Sea Watch."

"I'd like that," Birdie Winslow said.

He stopped in front of the lobby, got out of the Bentley, came around and held the door open for her. Before they parted, he kissed her cheek lightly.

"Thank you for a lovely evening," he said. "I'm looking forward to a long and mutually profitable relationship."

"Friendship," she said with a tinkly laugh, touching his sun-bleached hair.

"Of course," he said.

He drove swiftly back to the house on the Hillsboro Inlet. The others were still busy cleaning up, wiping out ashtrays, plumping cushions, arranging the chairs precisely.

"Come on, gang," Ellen St. Martin was saying. "Everything's got to be spick-and-span. I'm showing this dump tomorrow."

They all looked up expectantly when Rathbone entered. He

lifted a hand, thumb and forefinger making a circle in the A-OK sign.

"Got her," he said, and they applauded.

He moved amongst them, taking out a gold money clip in the shape of a dollar sign. He gave each of them a fifty, not forgetting Theodore and Blanche, washing glasses in the kitchen.

"Now let's adjourn to the Palace," Rathbone said. "The booze is on me, but you guys will have to buy your own macadamia nuts."

Laughing, they all moved outside to their cars. Frank Little grabbed Rathbone's arm.

"Where did you find that mooch?" he asked. "My God, she's as fat and ugly as a manatee."

"Really?" Rathbone said with a smile. "I think she's *divine!*"

2.

His name was Lester T. Crockett, and he was an austere man: vested, bow-tied, thin hair parted in the middle. He raised his eyes from the open file on his desk, looked at the woman sitting across from him.

"Rita Angela Sullivan," he said. "Unusual name. Spanish and Irish, isn't it?"

"You've got it," she said. "Puerto Rico and County Cork."

He nodded. "That was a fine operation in Tampa," he said.

"I didn't get much credit for it."

"Not in the newspapers," he agreed with a frosty smile. "You can blame me for that. I didn't want your name or picture used. I wanted you down here for an undercover job."

"But it was me who roped the banker," she argued. "Without him, they'd have no case at all."

"I agree completely," he said patiently, "but I assure you that your work did not go unnoticed. That's why you're here."

"And where the hell is *here?*" she demanded. "All I know is that my boss in Tallahassee put me on a plane for Fort Lauderdale and told me to report to you. What kind of an outfit is this?"

He sat back, twined fingers over his vest, stared at her. "Let me give you some background. About a year ago it became obvious that the war against so-called 'white-collar crime' in Florida was being mishandled. I'm speaking now not of the drug trade but money laundering, boiler room scams, stock swindles, and tax frauds. There are a lot of elderly people in Florida, *rich* elderly people, and along with the retirees came the sharks."

"So what else is new," she said flippantly, but he ignored it.

"The Department of Justice sent me down to study the problem and make recommendations. I found that it wasn't so much a lack of money or a lack of manpower that was hurting law enforcement in this area, it was the number of agencies involved, overlapping jurisdictions, and a competitiveness that frequently led to inefficiencies and rancorous dispute."

"Everyone hunting headlines?" she suggested. "Big egos?"

"Those were certainly factors," he acknowledged. "The FBI, SEC, State Attorney's Office, IRS, and local police, to name just a few, were all involved. Investigators from those agencies were walking up each other's heels, withholding evidence from each other, and planning sting and undercover operations with absolutely no coordination whatsoever."

"I believe it," she said. "I heard of a case in Jacksonville where a local undercover narc set up a big coke buy. Only the seller turned out to be an undercover FBI narc."

"Happens more often than you think," Crockett said, not smiling. "My recommendation was to set up an independent supra-agency that would draw personnel from all the others, as needed, and work with absolutely no publicity or even acknowledgment that such an agency existed. My recommendation was approved with the proviso that such an organization would be allowed to function for only two years. At the end of that time, an evaluation would be made of the results, if any, and it would then be determined whether or not to allow the supra-agency to continue to exist. I was appointed to direct the agency's activities in south Florida."

"Lucky you," Rita Sullivan said. "What's the name of this agency?"

"It has no name. The theory is that if it's nameless it is less likely to attract attention."

"Maybe," she said doubtfully. "And where do I fit in?"

"You'll be working with a man named Anthony Harker. He's on loan from the Securities and Exchange Commission."

"A New Yorker?" she asked.

"Yes."

"That's one strike against him," she said. "He's my boss?"

Crockett gave her his wintry smile. "I prefer the word 'associate.' He's waiting in his office, down the hall. He'll brief you."

"If I don't like the setup, can I go back to Tallahassee?"

"Of course."

"But it'll go in my jacket that I bugged out. Right?"

"Right," Lester T. Crockett said, rising to shake her hand.

Instead of names painted on the doors, there were business cards taped to the frosted glass. She found one that read Anthony C. Harker and went in. The man seated behind the steel desk had an inhaler plugged up one nostril. He looked at her, blinked once, pocketed the inhaler.

"For an allergy," he said. "You might have knocked."

"Sorry."

"You're Rita Angela Sullivan?"

"That's right. Anthony C. Harker?"

"Yes." Then, stiffly, "You can call me Tony if you like."

"I'll think about it," she said and, unbidden, slid into the armchair alongside his desk.

"When did you get in?" he asked.

"Last night."

"Where you staying?"

"The Howard Johnson in Pompano Beach."

"Using your real name?"

"Yes."

"Good. What address did you give when you registered?"

"My mother's home in Tallahassee."

"That's okay. When you check out, pay cash. No credit cards."

"When am I going to check out?"

"We'll get to that. Have you got wheels?"

"No."

"Rent something small and cheap. By the way, I heard about the bust in Tampa. Nice work."

"Thanks."

"They were flying the stuff in from the Bahamas?"

"That's right. Using an old abandoned landing strip out in the boondocks."

"How did you get the banker to sing?"

She lifted her chin. "I persuaded him," she said.

Harker nodded. "This thing we're on isn't drugs. At least not the smuggling or dealing."

"Money laundering?"

"That may be part of it. The key suspect is a guy named David Rathbone. No relation to Basil."

"Who's Basil?"

"Forget it," he said. "You're too young. This David Rathbone is a wrongo. No hard stuff, but he's a con man, swindler, shark, and world-class nogoodnik. You hungry?"

"What?" she said, startled. "Yeah, I could eat something."

"Here's the subject's file. Read it. Meanwhile I'll go get us some lunch. Pizza and a beer?"

"Sounds good. Pepperoni and a Bud for me, please."

He was gone for almost a half-hour. When he returned, they spread their lunch on his desktop.

"No pepperoni for you?" she asked.

"No, just cheese. I've got a nervous stomach."

"I read the file on Rathbone," Sullivan said. "A sweet lad. Where did you get that photo? He's beautiful."

"From his ex-wife. If she had her druthers, she'd have given us his balls, too."

"What's he into right now?"

"He's set himself up as an investment adviser or financial planner—whatever you want to call it. I estimate—and it's just a guess—that's he's got at least fifteen mooches on his list, and he's handling maybe twenty million dollars."

"Oh-oh. Who are all these lucky victims?"

"Widows and divorcées plus a choice selection of doctors and airline pilots—the biggest suckers in the world when it comes to investments."

"What's his con?"

"He gets them to sign a full power of attorney plus a management contract. Then he's home free. His fee, he tells them, is three percent annually. If he's handling twenty mil like I figure, it would give him a yearly take of six hundred thousand. But I don't think he's satisfied with that. A greedy little bugger, our Mr. Rathbone. And with his record, he's got to be dipping in the till. But he sends out monthly statements, and no one has filed a complaint yet. About two months ago I convinced one of his clients, a divorcée, to demand all her money back from Rathbone, including the profits he claimed he had made for her. She got a teller's check for the entire amount the next day. She was so ashamed of doubting Rathbone that she returned the check and told him to keep managing her money."

"If Rathbone is looting the assets, how was he able to return the divorcée's funds?"

"Easy. The old Ponzi scam. He used other investors' money to pay off. He came out of it smelling like roses, and it made me look like a shmuck. Why are you staring at me like that?"

"How long have you been in south Florida?" Sullivan asked.

"Almost eight months now."

"How come you're so pale? Don't you ever hit the beach?"

"I'd like to but can't. I get sun poisoning."

"Allergy, nervous stomach, and sun poisoning," she said. "You're in great shape."

"I'm surviving," Harker said. "You look like you toast your buns every day."

"Not me," she said. "This is my natural hide. I can get a deeper tan just by walking a block or two in the sunshine."

"Count your blessings," he said. "Now let's get back to business. Rathbone hangs out with a crowd of wiseguys who are just as slimy as he is. I've only been able to make one of them: an ex-con named Sidney Coe, who did time for a boiler room operation in Kansas City. I don't know what the others are into, but you can bet it's illegal, illicit, and immoral. They all meet in the bar of a restaurant on Commercial Boulevard in Lauderdale. It's called the Grand Palace."

"Great," she said. "Now let me guess. You want me to start hanging out at the Grand Palace and try to cozy up to this gang of villains."

"That's about it," he agreed. "Especially David Rathbone. I'm the guy who racked him up on that insider trading charge in New York. But he waltzed away from that with a slap on the wrist. That's one thing to remember about this man: He's been charged three times, to my knowledge, and never spent a day in chokey. You know why?"

"He cut a deal?" Rita suggested.

"Right. By ratting on his pals. This is not a standup guy. The other thing to remember about him is that he's a womanizer. It helps him hook those female mooches, but he also plays around when there's no profit involved."

She stared at him a long moment. Finally: "I'm beginning to get the picture. You expect me to ball this guy."

Harker slammed a palm down on the desktop. "I expect you to do your job," he said angrily. "How you do it is up to you. I want to know how he's rolling his victims and I want to know what his buddies at the Grand Palace are up to. You want out?"

She considered for two beats. "Not yet. Let me make a few moves and see what happens. Do I call you here?"

"No," he said. "And don't come back to this building again. These people we're dealing with are bums but they're not stupes. You could be tailed. Here's a number you can call, day or night. Leave a message if I'm not in. One other thing: What are you carrying?"

"Thirty-eight Smith and Wesson. Short barrel."

"A cop's gun," he said, holding out his palm. "Let me have it."

She hesitated, then took the handgun from her shoulder bag and handed it over. Harker put it in his desk drawer and gave her a nickel-plated Colt .25 pistol. She examined it.

"What am I supposed to do with this peashooter?" she asked.

"Carry it," he said. "It's more in character. And leave your ID and shield with Mr. Crockett's secretary on your way out. Here's something else."

He withdrew a worn, folded newspaper clipping from his wallet and passed it to her. It was a two-paragraph story about Rita Angela Sullivan being arrested in a Tallahassee specialty shop for shoplifting. According to the clipping, charges were dropped for lack of evidence.

She read the story twice, then looked up at him. "How much did it cost to have this thing printed up?" she asked.

"Plenty," he said. "It looks like the real thing, doesn't it? Don't lose it. It might come in handy."

"How do you figure that?"

"If Rathbone goes through your purse, he'll find your dinky little gun and this clipping. It'll help you con the con man."

21

"Uh-huh," she said. "Pretty sure of me, weren't you?"

"I was hoping," Harker said.

She tucked pistol and clipping into her shoulder bag and stood up.

"Thanks for the lunch," she said.

"My pleasure."

She paused at the door. "You can call me Rita if you like," she said.

"I'll think about it," he said.

3.

The Grand Palace was located on the north side of Commercial Boulevard between A1A and Federal Highway in an area known to local law enforcement agencies as Maggot Mile. The restaurant advertised Continental Cuisine, which in south Florida might include broiled alligator and smoked shark.

The main dining room, decorated in Miami Hotel Moderne, attracted a regular clientele of well-heeled retirees and tourists during the season, October to May. The shadowy back room, called the Palace Lounge, had its own side entrance opening directly onto the parking lot. The Lounge was decorated with fishnets, floats, lobster traps, and a large preserved sailfish over the bleached pine bar.

David Rathbone left his black Bentley in the care of the parking valet in front of the Grand Palace, then walked around to the Lounge entrance. He was wearing a suit of raw white silk with a knitted mauve polo shirt, open at the throat. His white bucks were properly scuffed. His only jewelry was an identification bracelet of heavy gold links, a miniature anchor chain.

The Lounge was empty except for Ernie polishing glasses behind the bar. Ernie was an ex-detective of the NYPD, cashiered for allegedly shaking down crack dealers. In addition to his barkeeping duties, he booked bets and served as a steerer for pot and coke dealers. He could also provide the phone number of a young call girl who happened to be his daughter.

"Good evening, Mr. Rathbone," he said. "How you doing?"

"Surviving," Rathbone said, and removed a five-dollar bill from his money clip. "Will you do me a favor, Ernie?"

"You name it."

"Put this fin in your cash register. Later in the evening I'll ask you for a five. Be sure to bring me this one. Got it?"

Ernie examined the bill, running his thumb across the surface. "Queer?"

"No," Rathbone said, "it's the real thing."

The bartender stared at him. "Is this a scam?"

"Nah, just a little joke."

"Uh-huh. What's in it for me?"

"The five."

"Okay," Ernie said, "I'll play. You want the usual, I suppose."

"You suppose correctly. With a wedge of lime, please."

The Lounge had tables of fake hatch covers polyurethaned to a high gloss. Most of them seated two or four patrons comfortably. But in the most shadowed corner was a giant table set about with nine mate's chairs. This table bore a small card, RESERVED, and it was there Rathbone carried his vodka gimlet. He lighted his first Winston of the day and settled down.

He didn't wait long. Ten minutes later Mortimer and

Nancy Sparco came in, stopped at the bar, then brought their Scotch mists over to the big table. Rathbone stood up.

"Nancy," he said, "you look ravishing, and if Mort wasn't here, I would."

"Be my guest," Sparco said and flopped into the chair next to Rathbone's.

"Mort's in a snit," Nancy said. "He didn't win the lottery—again."

"You still playing that?" Rathbone asked. "It's a sucker's game; you know it. Look at the odds."

"Look at the payoff," Mortimer said. "Millions! It's worth a hundred bucks a week."

"What numbers do you play?" Rathbone asked idly.

"He plays anything with a seven in it," Nancy said. "Claims it's his lucky number. Some luck!"

"It'll hit," Mort said. "Seven has always been very good to me."

"That's where you're making your mistake," Rathbone said. "Look at the winning numbers over the past year. You'll find that most of them have five in them. Like five, fifteen, twenty-five, and so on."

Sparco looked at him. "You're kidding."

Rathbone held up a palm. "Scout's honor. I've studied random number frequency on my computer and believe me, five turns up more often than seven or any other number."

"I don't believe you," Mortimer said.

Rathbone shrugged. "It's even true for the serial numbers on five-dollar bills. You'll find that the digit five occurs most frequently."

"David, you're nuts."

"Am I? Would you like to make a small bet?"

"Mort," Nancy said, "don't do it."

"I'll make it easy on you," Rathbone said. "I'll bet you twenty bucks that the first five-dollar bill we examine will have more fives in the serial number than any other digit."

"All right," Sparco said, "I'll take your bet." Then, when he saw Rathbone reach in his pocket for his money: "Oh no, not your five! You've probably got a ringer all ready for me."

Rathbone shook his head. "What a suspicious bastard you are. You're my friend; I wouldn't cheat you. All right, we'll do it this way." He called over to the bar: "Ernie, you got any fives in the register?"

"Sure, Mr. Rathbone," the bartender said. "How many you want?"

"Just one. Pick out any five-dollar bill you like and bring it over here for a moment, will you?" Then, to Sparco: "Satisfied it's on the up-and-up now?"

"I guess so."

Ernie brought the bill to their table. They bent over it and examined the serial number.

"There you are!" Rathbone said triumphantly. "Three fives. Now do you admit I'm right?"

"Son of a bitch," Mortimer said, and handed a twenty to the other man. "You've got the luck of Old Nick."

"It's the science of numbers," Rathbone said. "You can't fight it."

"Mort, I told you not to bet," Nancy said morosely. "David always wins. I need another drink."

James and Trudy Bartlett joined them, and a few regulars came through the side entrance to sit at the smaller tables. A noisy party of four tourists entered from the dining room, headed for the bar. Sidney and Cynthia Coe arrived, and then Ellen St. Martin and Frank Little. More regulars came in; the tables filled up; someone fed the jukebox; the joint began to jump.

At the big table, the talk was all about a three-year-old filly, Jussigirl, who had won all her eleven starts. Then the conversation turned to the recent run-up in the price of precious metals. Sid Coe, who owned a boiler room on Oakland Park Boulevard, announced his intention of switching his yaks from gemstones to platinum.

Ernie came from behind the bar, leaned over Rathbone, whispered in his ear.

"That guy at the end of the bar, dressed like an undertaker, he says he's a friend of yours, wants to talk to you. Okay, or should I bounce him?"

Rathbone turned his head to stare. "Yes, I know him. Is he sober, Ernie?"

"He's had a few, but he's holding them."

Rathbone excused himself and joined the man standing at the bar. He was tall, skinny, almost cadaverous, wearing a three-piece black suit of some shiny stuff. The two men shook hands.

"Tommy," Rathbone said, "good to see you. When did you get out?"

"About a month ago."

"Hard time?"

"Nah. I can do eighteen months standing on my head. Just the cost of doing business."

"They sure as hell didn't fatten you up."

"The food in that joint is worse than hospital slop. The warden's on the take."

"Need some green?"

"No, thanks, David; I'm doing okay. I had a safe deposit box they never did find. You got anything going?"

"This and that."

"I got something that could be so big it scares me. But I don't know how to handle it. You interested?"

"Depends," Rathbone said. "What is it?"

Tommy leaned closer. His breath was 94 proof. "I shared a cell with an old Kraut who was finishing up five-to-ten. He was in for printing the queer. Not pushing it, just manufacturing fifties and hundreds and selling them to the pushers. He told me a lot about papers, inks, and engraving. The guy really knows his stuff. He claimed that when he was collared, he had just come up with an invention that could make a zillion if it was handled right. Well, you know how old lags talk, and I thought he was just blowing smoke. He got out a couple of months before I did and told me to look him up and maybe we could work a deal together. So when I was sprung, I decided to do it. Right now he's got a little printshop in Lakeland. We killed a jug one night, a bottle of schnapps that tasted like battery acid, and he showed me his great invention."

"And?" Rathbone said. "What was it?"

Tommy withdrew a small white envelope from his inside jacket pocket, lifted the flap, took out a check. "Take a look at that."

Rathbone examined it. It appeared to be a blank check printed with the name and address of a California bank. "So?" he said.

"Got a pen?"

Rathbone handed over his gold Montblanc ballpoint. Tommy made out the check to David Rathbone for a thousand dollars, dated it correctly, then signed "Mickey Mouse." He slipped the check back into the white envelope, sealed it, handed it to Rathbone.

"Keep it for a week," he said, "then open it. I'll come back here in ten days or so and we'll talk about it. Okay?"

"If you say so, Tommy, but why all the mystery?"

"You'll see. Just leave the check in the envelope for a week and then open it. David, this could be our ticket to paradise. See you around."

Tommy left a sawbuck on the bar, then went out the side entrance. Rathbone put the sealed white envelope in his side pocket and rejoined the crowd at the big table.

"Who was that?" Jimmy Bartlett asked. "The guy you were talking to at the bar."

Rathbone laughed. "You didn't recognize him? That was Termite Tommy."

"Never heard of him."

"He organized a great gig in south Florida. Guaranteed

termite extermination. Traveled around in a van offering free termite inspection to homeowners. He also carried a jar of live termites and a bag of sawdust. After he made his inspection, he showed the mooch how his house was about to collapse unless he signed a contract for total termite control. Then Tommy would pocket the up-front deposit and take off. He had a nice thing going for almost three years until the gendarmes caught up with him. He drew eighteen months. But as he said, it's just part of the cost of doing business."

"What's he up to now?" Cynthia Coe asked.

"Who knows?" Rathbone said. "Probably selling earmuffs to south Floridians. The guy's a dynamite yak."

Frank Little leaned across the table. "Hey, David," he said, "catch who just came in. Ever see her before?"

4.

Rita Sullivan figured that if she dressed like a flooze, Rathbone would make her for a hooker arrived in south Florida for the season, and he'd be turned off. At the same time she didn't want to look like Miss Priss. So she settled for a rip-off of a collarless Chanel suit in white linen with a double row of brass buttons. The newly shortened miniskirt showed a lot of her long, bare legs. Her white pumps had three-inch heels.

When she got out of her rented Honda Civic, the parking valet caught a flash of tanned thigh and said, in Spanish, "God bless the mother who gave birth to you."

"Thank you," Rita said and, chin high, marched into the Grand Palace.

The maître d' came bustling forward, giving her an admiring up-and-down. "Ah, madam," he said, "I am *so* sorry but the kitchen is closed."

"That's all right," she said. "I just wanted a nightcap. You have a cocktail bar?"

"But of course!" he cried. "The Palace Lounge. Through that back doorway, if you please."

The Lounge was jammed, noisy, smoky. Rita swung onto a barstool, turned sideways, crossed her legs. She ordered a vodka stinger from the baldy behind the bar. It was served in a glass big enough to float a carp. She took a sip.

"Okay?" Ernie asked.

"Just right," she said. "Busy night."

"It's always like this. On Saturday we have a three-piece jazz combo."

"I'll have to catch that."

"You can't go wrong," he told her.

"In that case I'll skip it," she said, and he gave her a knowing grin.

She turned and surveyed the Lounge casually. It wasn't hard to spot David Rathbone. He was seated at the head of a big table in the corner. He was even better-looking than his photograph, a golden boy, and he was staring at her.

She turned back, waited until baldy was down at the other end of the bar, then opened her shoulder bag and took out a pack of Virginia Slims. She kept rooting in her bag as if looking for a match. It was a corny ploy, but she reckoned if the guy was on the make he'd catch the signal and come running. He did. A gold Dupont lighter was proffered.

"May I?" he said.

She liked his voice. Deep, throaty, with a burble of laughter.

"Thank you," she said, and lighted her cigarette.

He looked at the pack. "You've come a long way, baby," he said.

"So they tell me," she said.

"Can I buy you a drink?" he asked.

"I've hardly touched this one."

"So? The night's young. May I join you?"

"If you like."

31

He took the barstool alongside her, not too close.

"First time here?"

She nodded.

"You'll like it. Good crowd. Big drinks."

"Uh-huh. And not exactly cheap."

"They're expensive," he acknowledged. "But there are a lot of fringe benefits." He gave her a dazzling smile. "I'm one of them."

She laughed and worked on her stinger.

"Where are you from?" he asked her. "I've been in Florida for years and I've never met anyone who was born here. Everyone's from somewhere else. I'm from Boston originally, then New York. You?"

"New Orleans originally, then Tallahassee."

"Work down here?"

"Hope to. I just arrived. I'm a schoolteacher."

"Oh? And what do you teach?"

"Spanish."

"*A otro perro con ese hueso.*"

Rita laughed again. "Do you know what that means?"

"Not really. But I once told a Spanish lady that I loved her, and that's what she said. I always thought it was the Spanish equivalent of 'And I love you, too.' "

"It's the Spanish equivalent of 'Tell it to the Marines.' "

Then *he* laughed. "I better stick to English. Ready for a fresh drink? I am."

"Sure," Rita said. "Why not."

Ernie brought them a vodka gimlet and a stinger and left them alone.

"I love your Chanel suit," Rathbone said.

"It's a cheap copy."

"You're joking." He examined one of the brass buttons. "It even has the insignia." He shook his head. "Those rip-off artists are really something. Do me a favor, will you?"

"What?"

32

"Never cut your hair. It's glorious."

"Thank you. But it's a pain in the ass to wash."

"I'll help," he said, and they stared at each other.

"My name is David Rathbone," he said.

"My name is Rita Sullivan," she said, and they shook hands.

"Where do you live, Rita?"

"I just got in a few days ago. I'm staying at the Howard Johnson in Pompano Beach."

"You want to go back to HoJo tonight?"

"Not particularly."

"You have a car?"

"Yes."

"So do I. I also have a town house on the Fourteenth Street Causeway. The drinks are free. Will you follow me there?"

"All right," she said, "I'll follow you."

They rose to leave. Ernie, watching covertly from the end of the bar, wondered who was hustling whom.

Rathbone's home was between A1A and the Waterway. They stood on the lawn and looked up.

"It's enormous," Rita said.

"Not really," he said. "Two bedrooms and a third I use as an office. Three and a half bathrooms. Florida room. Terrace. The pool is for the entire development, but no one uses it; they walk to the ocean."

"You live alone?"

"I have a houseman and a cook-housekeeper. Theodore and Blanche. Jamaicans. Nice people. But they don't live in."

The vaulted living room was all white, beige, gold. There was a forty-one-inch rear projection TV. The kitchen was white with black plastic panels on the appliances. A restaurant range, microwave, overhead rack of coppered pots and pans.

"You know how to live," Rita said.

"Everyone knows how to live," he said. "There's no trick to it. All you need is money. Want to stick to the stingers?"

"Please."

"I'll have one, too."

They took their drinks into the living room, sat on the couch, kicked off their shoes.

"What do you do to afford all this?" Rita asked. "Rob banks?"

"No," he said with a tight smile. "I manage O.P.M.—Other People's Money. I'm an investment adviser."

"I'd say you're doing all right," she said, looking around.

He shrugged. "I work hard. And I've been lucky. Luck is very important."

"It's been in short supply with me lately."

"Married? Separated? Divorced? Or widowed?"

"No, no, no, and no," she said. "Just a single lady. Disappointed?"

"Of course not."

"What about you?"

"Married," he said. "Once. And now divorced. Thank God."

"And never again—is that what you're saying?"

"That's what I'm saying. Today. Tomorrow I might feel differently."

"You might," she said, "but I doubt it. You know, if I was a man, I'd never get married. What for? Sex? Companionship? A nurse if you get sick? A housekeeper when you get old? You can buy all that."

"If you've got the money," he reminded her. "You have a very cynical outlook, Rita."

"Not cynical, just realistic. Am I going to spend the night?"

"I want you to, but it's your decision."

"The bedrooms are upstairs?"

"Yes."

"Mix us another and let's take them upstairs."

"Wise decision," he said.

"You want me out of here tomorrow morning before your servants show up?"

34

"That's the first dumb thing you've said tonight."

Upstairs, she looked around the master bedroom and whistled. "I like everything about it except for the engraving over the bed. Who the hell is *that*—your grandfather?"

Rathbone laughed. "Big Jim Fisk. I'll tell you about him someday. A romantic story. He was murdered at the age of thirty-eight."

"Oh? How old are you, David?"

"Thirty-eight."

"Whoops!" she said. "Can I use the john?"

She did, and then he did. When he came out, she was lying naked atop the silver coverlet, black hair spread over the pillows. He stood looking down at her long body, dusky, with raspberry nipples.

"Ah, Jesus," he breathed.

She watched him undress. "You really are a golden boy," she said. "Where did you get that allover tan?"

"Show you tomorrow," he said, and joined her.

He was very good. She was better.

The morning sun was hot, bright. She roused slowly, staring at the ceiling, wondering where she was. Then Rathbone was at the bedside, looking down at her without smiling. He tossed a yellow terry robe onto the coverlet.

"Breakfast on the terrace in fifteen minutes," he said, no laughter in his voice now.

She came out into the sunlight, wearing the robe, toweling her hair.

"Glorious day," she said.

"It may be," he said. He was wearing a short-sleeved shirt of cotton gauze, pale linen slacks belted with a neck tie, espadrilles.

She glanced around the terrace. Glass-top table and chairs of verdigrised cast iron. Canvas slings. Two redwood lounges with flowered mattresses.

"Now I know where you get your allover glow," she said.

"Right. The only ones who can see you are helicopter pilots."

Theodore served freshly squeezed grapefruit juice, honeydew melon with wedges of lime, hot miniature croissants with sweet butter and mango jam, black coffee laced with chicory.

"You eat like this every morning?" she asked.

"Uh-huh. Why do you carry a gun?"

She continued buttering her croissant. "Self-defense," she said. "Everyone in Florida carries a gun."

"Maybe everyone in Florida *has* a gun," he corrected. "I do. But not everyone *carries* a gun."

"Since you obviously tossed my bag," she said, looking at him directly, "you probably found the newspaper clipping, too. Why the search?"

"You know what Barnum said?"

"There's a sucker born every minute?"

"And two to take him. I prefer being a taker rather than a takee. I like to know the people I deal with. And you're no schoolteacher."

"So now you know: I pack a popgun and I was charged with shoplifting. You want me gone?"

"No, I don't want you gone," he said. "Do you want to move in?"

She was astonished. "For how long?"

"Until I want you gone."

She took that. "What do I do for walking-around money?"

He took out his gold clip, extracted five hundred in fifties, handed them across the table.

She took the bills, then looked at him with a crooked grin. "What's this for?" she said. "Fun and games?"

"Check out of your hotel," he told her. "You can take the guest bedroom. Then go buy some clothes and lingerie. That stuff you're wearing is a disgrace. Get things that are simple and elegant—whites and beiges, blacks and grays. Forget about the wild colors. Tone down."

"Yes, boss," she said. "You wouldn't be putting a hustle on me, would you?"

Then he smiled for the first time that morning, displaying his sharp white teeth. "Call it love at first sight."

"The L-word?"

"You got it," he said.

5.

The meeting ended precisely as 2:45 P.M. (Lester T. Crockett ran a tight ship), and the staff filed out carrying case folders and notebooks. The air was still fumy with cigarette smoke and the odors of hamburgers and french fries they had ordered in for lunch. Crockett switched his window air conditioner to Exhaust and turned back to his desk. Anthony Harker was still sitting in a folding metal chair.

"Fifteen minutes, chief?" he asked.

"Can't you put it in a memo?" Crockett said.

"No, sir."

"All right. Ten minutes."

Harker hunched forward. "Sullivan called yesterday and left a message on my machine. She's made contact with David Rathbone."

"Made contact?" Crockett said. "What does that mean?"

"She's moved in with him."

The chief laced fingers across his vest and stared up at the ceiling. "Yes," he said, "I would call that making contact. What else did she say?"

"Not much. He was in a unisex beauty salon getting his hair trimmed and styled, plus a shampoo, facial, manicure, and pedicure."

Crockett grunted a laugh. "He lives well."

"Anyway, Rita left him there while she did some shopping with money he gave her. That's when she made her call."

"So? What's your problem?"

"Communications. Chief, there were a lot of questions I wanted to ask, but she had to leave her message on my machine. I want to give her permission to call me here anytime during the day."

Crockett frowned. "Including from Rathbone's home?"

"Yes, sir."

"Chancy. She might be overheard. No, she's too smart for that. But he might notice the higher phone bills and ask for itemization of local calls. That could blow the whole thing."

"I realize that," Harker said. "What I'd like is an unlisted phone in my office for Sullivan's use only. We'd arrange with the phone company that all incoming calls on that line would be billed to us. That way she could call me here during the day and, in case of emergency, my motel at night."

"All right," Crockett said, "set it up." He unlaced his fingers, leaned forward over the desk. "Something else bothering you?"

"Chief, Rathbone and his pals are not tough guys. I mean they don't go around knocking people on the head or robbing gas stations. They live relatively normal lives; they're just nine-to-five crooks."

"Get to the point."

"Admittedly Rathbone isn't Billy the Kid, but if he finds out Rita is a plant, he might turn vicious."

"He might. But you spelled out the deal to her, didn't you? And she didn't back off. She's a cop, and a good one."

"Still . . ."

"Listen, Harker, you're accustomed to stock swindles and inside trading. White-collar crime. Sullivan's expertise is drug smuggling, homicide, and rape. So don't tell me she won't be able to handle a flimflam artist like Rathbone if he turns nasty." He paused a moment, then: "Worried about her, are you?"

"Yeah."

"Want to pull her off the case and go at Rathbone from a different angle?"

"No."

"Then stop worrying. If anything happens to Sullivan, I'll take the rap, not you."

Harker stood up. "This is the first time I've asked a woman to put out to help me make a case. I don't like this business."

"You'll get used to it," Crockett said.

6.

The door to David Rathbone's office was equipped with a Medeco lock and a dead bolt. Only Blanche was allowed in once a week to clean, and then Rathbone was always present.

It was an austere chamber with a tiled floor: black and white in a checkerboard pattern. The desk, chairs, file cabinets, coat tree, and glass-fronted bookcases were all oak. Even the Apple Macintosh Plus was fitted into an oak housing. The room was dominated by an old-fashioned safe, a behemoth on casters, with a handle and single dial, painted an olive green and decorated with a splendid American eagle.

Rathbone sat in his high-backed swivel chair, an antique that had been reupholstered in black leather with brass studding. He stared at the sealed white envelope Termite Tommy had given him, containing the thousand-dollar check.

He had known from the start that he'd never be able to wait the week Tommy had requested; he couldn't endure unsolved riddles, puzzles, mysteries. He took a sterling silver letter opener from his top desk drawer and slit the flap. He peered inside.

The check had disappeared. In its place was a fluff of white confetti, no piece larger than a quarter-inch square.

"Son of a bitch," Rathbone said aloud.

He dumped the confetti onto his palm. It felt slightly oily and smelled oily, too. That wasn't important. What counted was that a thousand-dollar check had disintegrated. That old German forger had developed a paper that self-dissolved into worthless chaff. Except, as Termite Tommy had said, if handled right, it could be a ticket to paradise.

He spun the dial of the big safe: 15 left, 5 right, 25 left. He heaved up on the handle and the heavy door swung silently open. He put the white envelope and confetti inside, closed the door, spun the dial. Then he left the office, locked up, went out onto the terrace.

Rita Sullivan was lying naked on one of the lounges, hair bound up in a yellow towel. On the deck alongside her were a bottle of suntan oil, a thermos and plastic tumbler of iced tea. Rathbone pulled a chair close to the lounge.

"You know how to live," he told her.

"I'm learning," she murmured.

"I have to go pick up my tickets," he said. "I'm flying to London tomorrow, then on to France, Germany, and eventually to Spain. I have clients over there and have to discuss their investments."

She raised up on an elbow, back arched, and he caught his breath.

"How long will you be gone?" she asked.

"Three days. I'll fly back from Madrid."

"Can I go?"

He smiled and handed her the tumbler of iced tea. "Not this time. Maybe next trip. I go four or five times a year. Clients need stroking."

"What airport are you leaving from?"

"Miami. Will you drive me down?"

"Of course."

She put the tumbler aside and lay prone again.

"More oil?" he asked.

"Please," she said. "My legs."

He loved it, and she knew it: smoothing the oil onto her hard, muscled thighs, onto the dark satin behind her knees, her smooth calves.

"Will you be faithful while I'm gone?" he said in a low voice.

"Uh-huh."

"I know you will be. Or I'll find out about it. My spies are everywhere. I thought we'd drive up to Boca tonight for dinner. Then meet some people at the Palace for a few laughs."

"Sounds good."

"Happy?" he asked her.

"If I was any happier I'd be unconscious."

He laughed, slapped her oiled rump lightly, and left to pick up his tickets.

That night, at a Spanish restaurant in Boca Raton, they had a pan of paella in the classic version, made with chicken, rabbit, and snails. And they shared a bottle of flinty muscadet. Then they drove back to Fort Lauderdale singing "I Can't Give You Anything But Love." They both had good voices.

The Lounge at the Grand Palace was bouncing: tables filled, the bar two-deep, and waitresses hustling drinks. David's friends were already at the big table, and Rita Sullivan was introduced around. No chair was available for her, but Frank Little offered his lap, and she accepted with great aplomb.

Rathbone excused himself and went over to the bar. He waited patiently and was finally able to grab Ernie's arm.

"That man I was talking to the other night," he said. "The

43

one dressed in black. If he comes in, tell him I'll meet him here Tuesday night. Got it?"

"Got it, Mr. Rathbone," the bartender said. "Tuesday night."

Rathbone slipped him a fin and went back to the gang. After he took his chair at the head of the table, Rita came and sat on *his* lap. She was drinking vodka gimlets now: the way David liked them, with a lime wedge and just a drop or two of Triple Sec.

After a while Ellen St. Martin waved goodnight and departed. Rita took her chair, sitting between Frank Little and Mortimer Sparco. She asked how long they had all known each other.

"Too long," Sparco said, laughing. "Years and years."

"We're a troop," Little proclaimed, "and David is our scoutmaster. Watch out for him, sweetie; he has merit badges for loving and leaving."

She listened to the idle chatter at the table for a while, then excused herself to go to the ladies' room. She made her phone call from there.

She returned to the big table, finished her gimlet, ordered another. She listened to the bright talk, marveling at how nonchalantly these people spoke of their swindles: of mooches taken, the naive conned, the gullible defrauded and plucked clean. David and his friends dressed nicely, drove Jaguars, and rarely used profanity. But they were a bestiary of thugs.

The gathering broke up shortly after midnight. Rita and David drove back to his town house, laughing at the new business card Frank Little had distributed. It read: "FL Sports Equipment, Inc. Baseball, Football, Basketball, Soccer, Softball, Volleyball." And at the bottom: "We have the balls for it."

Rathbone took a chilled bottle of Asti Spumante and two flutes from the fridge.

"Oh my," she said, "are you trying to get us drunk?"

"No," he said. "Just keep the glow."

They went up to the terrace. The moon was not full, but it was fat enough. A few shreds of clouds. A balmy easterly wind. Scent of salt sea and bloomy things.

"Be back in a minute," David said. "Don't go away."

He returned with a portable recorder, inserted a cassette, switched it on.

"I swiped this off a radio station that plays Golden Oldies," he told her. "I was born too late. I should have been around in the 1920s and '30s. Cole Porter. Fred Astaire. Gershwin."

They drank a little wine. They danced to "You're the Top." They drank a little wine. They danced to "I Get a Kick Out of You." They drank a little wine. They danced to "Let's Fall in Love." They drank a little wine. They danced to "Anything Goes," and stopped.

They went to his bedroom. The sheets were silk, and he couldn't get enough of her.

7.

Anthony Harker was living on the second floor of a motel on
A1A in Pompano Beach. It was on the west side of the highway, but his suite was in the rear so most of the traffic noise
was muted.

Rita Sullivan showed up a little after nine P.M. She was
wearing a pink linen jumpsuit, her long hair tied back with
a dime-store bandanna. There was a chunky silver bracelet
on her right wrist.

"I hope you didn't drive his Bentley," Harker said. "Someone might spot it parked outside."

"No," she said. "He bought me a Chevy Corsica. White."

"Oh?" Tony said, looking at her. "Generous scut, isn't he?"

"Yes," she said, "he is. I hope his flight to London got off
okay. If not, and he calls home and I'm not there, I'm in
deep shit."

"He took off," Harker said, "but he's not flying to England.
I had a CIA tracker standing by at the airport. But Rathbone

went to Nassau in the Bahamas. And from there he's going to the Cayman Islands, then on to Limón in Costa Rica, and returning home from there. We checked his ticket after he left, but it was too late to set up a tail."

Rita sighed and looked around. "Got anything to drink in this dump?" she asked.

"Some cold Bud."

"That'll do me fine. How're the allergy and nervous stomach?"

"I'm surviving. Mind drinking out of the can?"

"That's fine," she said. "Pop it for me, will you? The government can't afford better digs for you than this shithouse?"

"It suits me," he said. "I'm only on loan for a year. Then back to New York. I can stand it for a year."

"If you say so. Got a tape recorder?"

"Sure."

"Let me put my report on tape. Then we can talk."

Twenty minutes later she finished dictating the names and descriptions of Rathbone's friends, plus what little she had learned of their activities.

Harker switched off the recorder. "Nice job," he said. "Let's take them one by one. First, have you any glimmer of what Rathbone is up to?"

"Nope. He keeps his office double-locked. He claimed he had to go stroke clients in England, France, Germany, and Spain."

"Uh-huh. But he's heading for places where it's easy to hide money if you pay off the right people. Well, I'll start a search in Nassau, the Caymans, and Costa Rica, but he's probably using a fake name and phony IDs. What about this Ellen St. Martin?"

"Apparently a legit real estate lady," Rita said, "with a small-time scam going on the side. She owns a house-sitting outfit for rich clients who go north from May to November. She gets paid to inspect their homes or condos weekly and make sure the air conditioning is working and the place hasn't been trashed. What the owners don't know is that she's also renting out their homes to tourists. In fact, some of the places are probably hot-pillow joints. But she makes a nice buck."

"Beautiful. And Frank Little?"

"Here's his business card. Notice the last line."

Tony read aloud: " 'We have the balls for it.' It doesn't double me over with laughter. You think he's legit?"

"And playing around with that crowd? I doubt it."

"All right," Harker said, "I'll have him checked out. Sparco?"

"A discount broker on Commercial. I think he deals in penny stocks. He also handles Rathbone's Wall Street investments."

"Then he'll be registered with the SEC, and I can get a look at his books. Sidney Coe?"

"He's got a boiler room on Oakland Park Boulevard. Right now his yaks are pushing precious metals."

"We can't do much on that until someone files a complaint. But mooches are funny; they'll take a big loss and immediately fall for another sucker deal, trying to recoup. They never do. What about James Bartlett?"

"A pleasant roly-poly guy. Something to do with banking. He seems to know every bank in south Florida."

"Laundering drug money?"

"Could be," Rita said. "He and David had a long, whispered conversation last night before the party broke up. Bartlett was doing most of the talking. And that's all I've got so far. I should be able to fill in some of the blanks as I get to know these people better."

"What's your take on Rathbone?" Tony said. "The honcho?"

"Well, I get the feeling that they're all independent operators, but they do look up to him. He sits at the head of the table. 'Our scoutmaster,' Frank Little called him. They seem to respect his opinions, but I don't think he bosses them."

"Good start, Rita," Harker said. "You've given me enough to requisition some more warm bodies from Crockett and get the wheels turning. Now I suppose you want to go home."

"Why do you suppose that?" she asked. "Is the beer all gone?"

"No, I have another six-pack."

"Break it out, sonny boy, and let's kick off our shoes and Confess All."

They slumped with feet up on a scarred Formica cocktail table, sipped their beers, stared at each other.

"Listen, Tony," she said, "I want you to know you were right on target with that dinky little pistol and the fake newspaper clipping. Rathbone did go through my bag, and I think those decoys convinced him I was in the game."

Harker shrugged. "Con men are easy to con. Their egos are so big they just can't conceive of being diddled. But don't relax. I had a talk with the boss about you. I told him I was afraid that if Rathbone ever discovers you're a plant he might turn physical."

"What did Crockett say?"

"He said you can take care of yourself."

"He's right; I can."

"Just be careful, will you?"

"Yes, mommy. And I'll look both ways before I cross the street."

Harker stirred restlessly. "You never know how a rat is going to act when he's cornered."

"David's no rat; he's a pussycat. I can handle him."

Tony took the inhaler from his shirt pocket, turned it in his fingers. Then he put it away without using it. "There's something else."

"What's that?"

He sighed. "You might as well know. I don't like the idea of you—or any other woman—putting out just to help me make a case."

"Well, aren't you sweet," she said, and leaned forward to

pat his cheek. "Don't give it a second thought. I worked a
drug case in Gainesville last year. My partner was a local cop
everyone called King Kong. He was six-six and must have
weighed three hundred. He used to be a second-string line-
backer for the Dolphins. Anyway, when King Kong questioned a suspect, he'd never touch the fink with his hands,
but he'd crowd him, coming in close and pushing his big
chest against the guy. The suspect would look up and see this
monster towering over him, and he'd start singing. King Kong
was using his body to get the job done. I use my body in the
same way."

"Not exactly," Harker said in a low voice.

"Look, Tony, I don't have the muscle of a male cop, so I
use what I do have. If we rack up Rathbone and his pals, it'll
go into my jacket and eventually I'll get a raise or promotion.
I'm doing it for myself as much as I am for you."

"I don't know," he said, shaking his head. "It just doesn't
seem right."

"Right? What the hell is *right*? You're talking like a Boy
Scout."

"I suppose," he said. "Maybe I'm a closet puritan."

"Married?"

"No."

"Ever been?"

"No."

"Me neither," she said. "I've been too busy having fun."

"You call being a cop having fun?"

"It is to me. I like the challenge."

He looked at her directly. "And the danger?"

She thought a moment. "Maybe," she said finally.

She reached up and untied the bandanna. Shook her head
and let her long hair swing free. She toyed with the zipper
tab on her jumpsuit.

"I haven't got a thing on underneath," she said. "Interested?"

"Yes," Tony said.

"I'd be deeply, deeply wounded if you weren't. Does this dump provide clean sheets?"

"They were supposed to change them today."

She rose. "Let's go see if they did."

She sat on the edge of the bed, watched him undress.

"My God," she said, "you look like an unbaked breadstick."

"I know," he said. "A golden boy I ain't."

"That's all right," Rita said, inspecting him. "You've got all the machinery."

She stood, unzipped the jumpsuit, wriggled out of it. She flopped back on the bed, bouncing up and down a few times.

"Come on," she said, holding out her arms to him. "Everyone deserves a little joy."

"I suppose," he said.

8.

David Rathbone waved the valet away and parked the Bentley himself. "What time have you got?" he asked.

Rita held her new gold Seiko under the dash light. "About a quarter to eleven."

"Don't give me *about;* what time exactly?"

"Ten forty-three."

He consulted his own Rolex. "Okay, I've got it. Now you sit out here and don't come into the Lounge until exactly eleven o'clock. You've got to be on the dot. Understand?"

"Sure. What's this all about?"

"Tell you later."

He picked up his gimlet at the bar and sauntered over to the big table. Trudy and Jimmy Bartlett were there, and Cynthia and Sid Coe. They all waved a greeting.

"Where's Rita?" Trudy asked. "You haven't ditched her already, have you?"

"Not yet," Rathbone said, smiling. "She had some things

to do. Said she'd meet me here at exactly eleven." He glanced at his watch. "In seven minutes. She's very prompt."

Sid Coe rose to the bait.

"A prompt woman?" he said. "That's like a fast turtle. Ain't no such animal."

"Rita is prompt," David insisted. "If she said she'll be here at eleven, she will be."

"Ho ho ho," Coe said. "She'll be late; you can count on it."

"A little wager?" Rathbone said. "I'll bet you twenty Rita will show up here at eleven, within a minute either way."

"You're on," Coe said. "Easiest twenty I ever made. I know women."

They sat comfortably, smiling pleasantly at each other, occasionally glancing at their watches. At precisely eleven o'clock Rita came sailing through the side door of the Lounge.

"Hi, everyone," she said.

Rathbone held out his hand to Coe. "Twenty," he said. "Clean bills, please."

"Tell me something, dimwit," Cynthia said to her husband, "have you *ever* won a bet with David?"

"And no one else has either," Trudy Bartlett said. "Our David has the luck of the devil."

"You make your own luck in this world," Rathbone said.

"Ernie's waving at you, David," Rita said.

He turned to look. Ernie gestured toward the end of the bar where Termite Tommy was standing.

"Please excuse me," Rathbone said, rising. "Keep the party going. I'll be back in a few minutes."

He took Tommy out to the parking lot. They sat in the back of the Bentley and lighted cigarettes.

"You're right," David said. "It's got possibilities—but it needs managing."

"That's why I came to you."

"How much does that German printer want for the paper?"

"He wants a piece of the action. But I figure we can always cook the books. Besides, he's usually half in the bag."

"Uh-huh. That check you gave me dissolved in about four days. Is that the usual time?"

"Three days to a week. It's not exact."

"That's even better," Rathbone said. "I've been talking to Jimmy Bartlett. You know him?"

"No."

"He's in the game. He knows everything about banks. He should; he owned one up in Wisconsin until the examiners moved in. He did a year and nine, and he was lucky. Anyway, he knows how banks move checks. I asked a lot of questions—without mentioning the self-destruct paper, of course—and Jimmy gave me some good skinny on how to hang paper with minimum risk."

"How do we do that?" Termite Tommy asked.

Rathbone turned to look at him in the gloom. "I figure the best is to print up government checks."

"Holy Christ!" Tommy cried. "That's a federal rap."

"So is mail and wire fraud. No matter how you slice it— queer civilian checks or government checks—the bottom line is Leavenworth. But I think it can be fiddled. The risk-benefit ratio looks good to me. The big plus in using fake checks from Uncle Sam is that, according to what Jimmy told me, you can draw against them in one day. Sometimes immediately if the bank knows you."

"I don't get it."

"Look, if you write a forged check against someone who lives, say, in California, that crazy paper would be sawdust before the check clears. That means the California bank will never debit it to the mooch's account because all they've got is a handful of confetti. But if a local bank will credit a U.S. Treasury check within a day, then you can draw on it and waltz away whistling. By the time the blues catch up with the scam, that fake check is little bitty pieces of nothing, and they've got no evidence. No fraud. No counterfeiting. No forgery. Nothing."

"Yeah," Tommy said slowly, "I can see that."

"What I figure is this: We'll make a trial run. Have the Kraut make up a fake U.S. Treasury check, complete with computer code. Make it look like an IRS refund or something. Then we'll get the pusher to set up a checking account in a local bank. After the account is established, the fake government check is deposited. The next day the pusher takes out the money and disappears."

Tommy lighted another cigarette. "The way you explain it makes sense. Let's try it and see how it works. But don't expect me to do the pushing. I've done all the time I want to do."

"No," Rathbone said, "not you and not me. I think I've got the right player for the part. As soon as you have the check ready, let me know."

"How much you want to make it for?"

"Some odd number. Like $27,696.37. Not over fifty grand. We'll start small and see how it goes."

Termite Tommy nodded and got out of the car. Then he leaned back in. "You'll have to give me the name of the pusher. It's got to be printed on the check."

"I'll let you know," Rathbone said, and took a business card from his Mark Cross wallet. "Here's my front; it's legit. David Rathbone Investment Management, Inc. Call me there when you're set."

"Will do," Tommy said, and walked away.

Rathbone went back into the Grand Palace Lounge. All the gang had assembled, and everyone was laughing up a storm. David took his chair at the head of the table and winked at Rita. She rose and came behind him, leaned down and nuzzled his cheek.

"Where have you been?" she asked.

"Business," he said.

"Monkey business?"

"Something like that. How would you like a job?"

"I've got a job: keeping you happy."

"And you succeed wonderfully. This is just a little errand with a super payoff."

"Lead me to it," she said.

9.

Knowing the ways of officialdom, Harker asked Crockett for ten more warm bodies. He got four, which was one less than he had hoped for. They were reportedly all experienced investigators from agencies lending personnel to Crockett's operation.

Tony started with a local from the Broward County Sheriff's Office. He was a tall black named Roger Fortescue.

"That's an unusual moniker," Harker said. "English, isn't it?"

"Beats me," Roger said. "Could be. My folks come from tidewater Virginia. I got a grandpappy still alive. When he talks, I catch about every third word he says. What kind of an outfit is this?"

"Mostly white-collar crime."

"Nobody in south Florida wears white collars. We got red, green, yellow, all-colored golf shirts. Call it purple-collar crime and you'll be closer to the mark."

"I guess," Harker said. He passed Frank Little's business card across the desk. "This is your subject."

Fortescue held the card a moment without reading it. "What's his problem?"

"Unsavory associates."

"Sheet," the investigator said, "they could rack *me* up on that charge. I guess you want the inside poop on this guy."

"You've got it. He may turn out to be clean, but I want him checked out."

"No strain, no pain. I report to you?"

"That's right. Here's my night number. If I'm not in, you can leave a message."

"This Frank Little—is he a heavy?"

"You tell me."

Fortescue nodded and rose lazily. "I'll take a look at him. Keep the faith, baby."

Harker said, "They stopped saying that twenty years ago."

"Did they? Well, I still say, 'That's cool,' but I always was old-fashioned."

Fortescue ambled down to his four-year-old Volvo and took another look at Frank Little's business card. The guy was out on Copans Road. The snowbirds were beginning to flock down, and Federal Highway would be crowded. But the investigator figured he had all the time in the world. That Harker seemed laid-back; not the type to crack a whip.

He found FL Sports Equipment, Inc., sandwiched between a shed that sold concrete garden statuary and a boarded-up fast-food joint that still had a weather-beaten sign: OUR GRITS ARE HITS. Fortescue parked and eyeballed Little's place.

Not much to it. A cinderblock and stucco building, painted a blue that had been drained by the south Florida sun. Behind it was what appeared to be a warehouse surrounded by a chain-link fence with a locked gate. A wide blacktop driveway led from the road past the office to the warehouse. And that was it—except for an American flag on a steel flagpole in front of the blockhouse.

Roger locked the Volvo and shambled up to the office. The door was unlocked. The inside was as bare and grungy as the exterior. There was a cramped reception room with one desk, one chair, one file cabinet, one coat tree. No inhabitant. An open door led to an inner office.

"Hello?" Fortescue called. "Anyone home?"

A man came out of the inner office. He had hair as fine and golden as corn silk. He was wearing a sharp suit that Roger recognized as an Armani. His embroidered shirt was open to the waist, and he wore a heavy chain supporting a big gold ankh. It lay on his hairless chest.

"Yes, sir," he said briskly. "Help you?"

"Hope so," Fortescue said. "I'd like to buy a dozen base-balls."

The man's smile was cool and pitying. The investigator didn't like that smile.

"Oh, we don't sell retail," he said. "We're importers and distributors."

"I was hoping maybe you could sell me a dozen baseballs wholesale. Give me a break on the price."

"We don't even sell wholesale. As I said, we're distributors. We sell *to* wholesalers."

"Sheet," Fortescue said. "Well, can you tell me any local place that carries your stuff?"

"Sorry, we have no wholesale or retail outlets in south Florida. All our sports equipment goes north."

"You sure?"

The flaxen-haired man gave him that irritating smile again. "I'm Frank Little. I own the business, so I should be sure. I think your best bet would be Sears or any sporting goods store on the Strip in Lauderdale."

"I guess so," Fortescue said. "Thanks for your trouble. Sorry to bother you."

"No bother," Little said. "I wish I could help you out, but I can't. Tell me something: Why do you want a dozen baseballs?"

"I coach an inner-city Little League," the investigator said. "We haven't got all that many bucks. That's why I was trying to shave the price."

Unexpectedly Little took out a fat wallet and handed Fortescue a crisp fifty. "Here," he said. "For your kids."

"That's mighty kind of you," Roger said, "and I do appreciate it."

Back in the Volvo he slipped the fifty into his pocket and decided he liked the way this case was shaping up.

He drove to Federal Highway and stopped at a discount liquor store. He shot the fifty plus on a liter of Absolut, a bottle of Korbel brut and another of Courvoisier cognac. His twin sons were still awake when he arrived home, and he roughhoused with them awhile until Estelle packed them off to bed. She returned to the kitchen to find her husband had mixed a pitcher of martinis with the Absolut. The other bottles were on the countertop.

"What's the occasion?" she asked.

"A nice man gave me a tip," he said. "A nice, freaky man."

They each had two martinis and drank the champagne with a fine dinner of broiled grouper, corn on the cob, and creamed spinach. Then they took cognacs and black coffee into the living room to watch TV.

"I wonder what the poor folks are doing," Fortescue remarked.

"I don't want to know," his wife said.

It was close to midnight when he rose, strapped on a hip holster with a .38 Police Special, and checked a little two-shot derringer he carried in an ankle pouch. Estelle watched these preparations without asking questions.

"A little business," he told her. "Should be back in an hour or two. You go on to bed."

"You know I won't," she said. "Listen, you get yourself killed, and I'm not going to bury you, I swear it. I'll prop you up on the couch in front of the TV until you just turn to dust. Then I'll sweep you out—y'hear? You remember that."

"I surely will, mommy dearest," he said, grinning.

He drove back to Copans Road, past the FL Sports Equipment layout. He parked on the shoulder across the street and sauntered back. He stood in the shadow of a big bottle palm, watching the activity.

Floodlights were on, the gate of the chain-link fence was open, and a big white semi was parked alongside the warehouse. At least four men were carrying cardboard cartons from the warehouse and loading them into the trailer. Frank Little and another guy, a mastodon, stood to one side watching the loading. Little had a clipboard and was apparently keeping a tally.

Slumped against his tree, Fortescue observed the action for almost an hour. He counted at least fifty cartons. Then the truck doors were slammed and locked. Three men got into the cab, and the semi began to back slowly onto Copans Road. That's when Fortescue got a good look at the legend painted on the side: SIENA MOVING & STORAGE. NEW YORK–NEW JERSEY.

The investigator strolled back to his Volvo and drove home. Estelle was still awake, watching an old movie on TV. She looked up when he came in.

"You again?" she said. "Have a good time?"

"A million laughs," he assured her.

He went into the kitchen and called the night number. It was after two in the morning, but the phone was picked up almost immediately.

"Harker. Who's this?"

"Fortescue. Look, you're from New York, aren't you?"

"That's right."

61

"Ever hear of Siena Moving and Storage? They operate in the New York–New Jersey area."

There was a brief silence. Then: "I've heard of them. The outfit is owned by one of the Mafia families in Manhattan."

"My, my," Roger Fortescue said. "Those bentnoses must play a lot of baseball."

10.

It was starting out to be a great season: balmy days and one-blanket nights. The tourists lolled on the sand, groaning with content, and later showed up at Holy Cross Emergency with second-degree burns. That noonday sun was a tropical scorcher, but the snowbirds bared their pallid pelts and wanted more.

Rathbone took the sun in small, disciplined doses, before eleven A.M. and after three P.M. And he spread his body with sunblock. Rita Sullivan was out on the terrace every chance she got, slick with baby oil, getting darker and darker.

"The back of the bus for you," David said, laughing. But he loved it, loved the contrast between her cordovan and his bronzy gold.

Then, one day at breakfast, he said to her, "Ready for that little job I told you about?"

"I'll never be readier."

"We'll leave at ten-thirty."

She showed up in the same pink linen jumpsuit she had worn to Tony Harker's motel.

"Nice cut," Rathbone said, inspecting her. "But I told you I don't like those sorbet colors on you."

"Want me to change?"

"No. Where did you buy it?"

"At Hunneker's."

"How much?"

"About two hundred with tax," she said.

"You still have the sales check?"

"I guess so. Why? Are you going to return it?"

"Not exactly. How did they wrap it when you bought it?"

"What's this—Twenty Questions?"

"Come on," he said, "how was it wrapped?"

"In tissue paper and then put in a Hunneker's bag. A plastic bag."

"Still got the bag?"

"Yes."

"Get it and the sales check. I'll meet you downstairs and we'll get this show on the road. We'll take your car."

They drove over to Pompano Fashion Square and found a slot in the crowded parking lot.

"Stay in the car," Rathbone ordered, "but keep the doors locked. I shouldn't be more than twenty minutes or so. What floor did you buy the jumpsuit on?"

"The second. Sportswear."

He headed directly for Hunneker's, the plastic bag and sales check folded flat in his jacket pocket. The store had big plate-glass windows with gilt lettering: J.B. HUNNEKER'S. SATISFAC-TION GUARANTEED OR YOUR MONEY CHEERFULLY REFUNDED.

He took the escalator to the second floor and wandered about until he located the Sportswear department. It didn't take long to find a rack of jumpsuits exactly like the one Rita was wearing. He looked about casually. Then, finding himself un-observed, he took a pink jumpsuit off the rack, folded it into the plastic Hunneker's bag, and approached the service desk.

"I'm sorry," he said to the woman behind the counter, "but I bought this for a birthday gift, and my wife doesn't like the color."

"What a shame," she said. "Would you like to exchange it for another color?"

"No, I think I better let her come in and pick out what she wants. Could I get a refund, please. Here's my sales check."

He was back in the car in fifteen minutes. He told Rita what he had done, and she laughed.

"You don't miss a trick, do you?"

"Not if I can help it. I'm certainly not going to shell out two hundred for something I don't like."

"Do I get the money?"

"I think not," he said. "You keep your jumpsuit and I'll keep my money. It's a win-win game—the kind I like. Now move over and let me drive."

He maneuvered the Chevy out of the parking lot and turned northward on Federal Highway.

"We're going to a bookstore on Sample Road near I-95," he told her.

"Oh? Going to shoplift a couple of books?"

"No," he said, "I'm not into boosting. This is an interesting place. It's owned by a man named Irving Donald Gevalt. He deals only in rare books and antique manuscripts."

"And he makes a living from this?"

"He owns two motels, a fast-food franchise, and three condos on the beach. But he didn't get all that from pushing rare books; he's got a very profitable sideline. He's in the game, and all the sharks call him ID Gevalt. He's the best paperman in south Florida. Social Security cards, driver's licenses, military discharges, voter registrations, passports, visas—you name it and ID can supply it. That's why we're going to visit him, to fix you up with an identification package for that little job you're going to do for me."

She turned to look at him. "Hey, wait a minute. You didn't say anything about forged papers. I don't like that."

"They're not forged," Rathbone said. "Everything ID Gevalt handles is strictly legit. That's why he gets top dollar."

"So where does he get the documents—from stiffs?"

"Sort of. He's got freelancers working for him in a dozen cities. They go through old newspapers in their hometowns and clip out items about infants and little kids who died twenty, thirty, forty years ago. They send the name, address, and date of birth to Gevalt. He writes to the Department of Birth Records in those cities, requesting a copy of the dead kid's birth certificate. Costs him from two to ten bucks, and they never ask what he wants it for. So now he's got a legitimate birth certificate of someone who's been dead for years. The certificate is the key. With that Gevalt can get a Social Security card, voter's registration, even a driver's license, by hiring someone to take the test under the name on the certificate."

"A slick operation."

"Like silk. How old are you, Rita—about thirty-five?"

"That's close enough."

"So we'll buy you a package of identification for a white female about thirty-five years old."

"And what do I do with that?"

"Tell you later. Here we are."

The Gevalt Rare Book Center was located over a shop that installed domed plastic ceilings for condo kitchens and bathrooms. There was a steep outside staircase leading to the second floor. The center was a dusty jumble of books, magazines, newspapers. It was comfortably air-conditioned, but smelled mildewy.

"David!" the old man said, coming forward with an outstretched hand. "Good to see you again!"

"ID," Rathbone said, shaking the proffered paw gently. "You're looking well."

"Liar," the geezer said. "But I'm surviving. And who is this lovely lady?"

"A dear friend. Rita, meet the famous Irving Donald Gevalt."

The gaffer bent creakingly to kiss her hand. "Famous, no," he said. "Notorious, possibly. Rita, you are a sylph."

"I hope that's good," she said.

"The best," Gevalt assured her. "The very best. David, this is a social call?"

"Not exactly. I need a package for Rita. Birth certificate, Social Security, driver's license. And any extras you might have."

The old man pushed up his green eyeshade and stared at Rita through rheumy eyes. "Middle-thirties," he guessed. "Could be Hispanic. I think I have something that will just fit the bill. Excuse me a moment, please."

He shuffled slowly into a back room, closing the door carefully behind him.

Rita looked around at the stacks of books and journals. "Does he ever sell any of this stuff?"

"Occasionally," David said. "Mostly by mail order. It's a good front. And he knows the rare book business. I heard he's got the world's best private collection of Edgar Allan Poe first editions and original manuscripts."

Gevalt was back in a few minutes with a worn manila envelope. "Gloria Ramirez," he said, "from San Antonio, Texas. I think Gloria will do splendidly. Would you care to inspect?"

"Of course not," Rathbone said. "I know the quality of your work. The usual, ID?"

"Ah, I am afraid not. With this dreadful inflation, I have been forced, regrettably, to raise my fees. Two Ks, David."

Rathbone took out his stuffed money clip and extracted the two thousand in hundred-dollar bills. "A business expense," he said, shrugging. "I'll write it off as entertainment."

"Of course," Gevalt said with a gap-toothed grin. "That is what life is all about—entertainment. Am I right?"

The door to the back room opened, and a young blonde, no more than nineteen, stood posed, hip-sprung. She was wearing a tiny black bikini that seemed to be all fringe.

"Lunch is ready, daddy," she said.

"In a moment," Gevalt said, and led the way to the outside door. "Do come back again, David, and you also, Rita. Not only for business, but just to visit."

In the car, Rita looked at him with a mocking smile. "You certainly didn't miss the daughter," she said.

"I noticed her," David admitted. "But she's not his daughter; she's his wife."

"You're kidding!"

"Scout's honor. That's what life is all about—entertainment. Am I right?"

On the drive back to the town house, he explained to Rita what the first part of her new job would entail. She would drive up to Boca Raton and, at the Crescent Bank on Glades Road, open an interest-bearing checking account under the name of Gloria Ramirez, depositing the minimum required.

"The bank officer to see is Mike Mulligan," Rathbone told her. "Give him a phony home address in Boca and say you work at the Boca Mall. Jimmy Bartlett has this Mulligan on the pad, and he'll be tipped off to approve your application without investigating your references. Got it?"

"Sure," Rita said. "See Mike Mulligan at the Crescent Bank on Glades Road in Boca and open a checking account in the name of Gloria Ramirez. That's all?"

"For now."

"I don't suppose you want to tell me what this is all about?"

"You're right; I don't. But it's for your own protection. If the deal turns sour, you can always claim you know nothing about it and were just doing a favor for a friend."

"Uh-huh. Why do I have a feeling you're playing me for a patsy?"

"I'd never do that," David said. "If I thought there was

any real risk, I'd never ask you to do it. I want you around for a long time. And now I'm going to drop you at the town house and switch to the Bentley. I have a lunch date with a potential client."

"He or she?"

"He. A retired professor who I hear has more bucks than brains."

"David, how do you find these mooches?"

"I have steerers all over south Florida. Sometimes Jimmy Bartlett hears of a good prospect through his bank contacts. Sometimes Ellen St. Martin gives me the name of someone who's just moved down here and is looking to spend big money on a house or condo. If I land the fish, I always pay a finder's fee. What are you going to do this afternoon?"

"I don't know. Maybe I'll go down to the beach for a few hours."

"I wish you wouldn't," he said. "There are a lot of sleazes cruising the beach looking to score off a single woman."

"David! You're worried about me! Don't give it a second thought, honey; I can take care of myself."

"Just carry your gun—all right?"

"Okay, I'll carry my gun, and I won't talk to beach bums. I'll even wear a one-piece suit. Satisfied?"

"With your body it doesn't matter if you wear a bikini or a raincoat; you're still going to attract attention."

"David, do you think I have a better body than Gevalt's wife?"

"You make her look like a boy."

"Flattery will get you everywhere. Hurry back from your lunch and we'll have us a matinee."

"Yes," he said, "I'd love that."

After Rathbone took off in the Bentley, Rita went into the kitchen and had lunch with Blanche and Theodore. They all shared a big shrimp salad and drank beer. Theodore told her how David landed Birdie Winslow as a client by staging a fake cocktail party with the Palace Lounge crowd masquerading as richniks. Everyone had a good laugh.

Rita put on a white maillot and used one of David's shirts as a coverup. She took her beach bag and told Blanche she'd be back in an hour or so. She walked eastward, crossing A1A. But she didn't join the crowd heading for the beach. She went into a hotel lobby, bought a pack of cigarettes and asked for two dollars' worth of quarters.

She found a public phone and called her special number. Tony Harker answered and had her wait a moment until he connected a tape recorder to his phone. Then she started talking.

11.

Crockett gave the new man the orientation lecture on the need and purpose of the supra-agency. Henry Ullman, borrowed from the Treasury Department, listened politely, his meaty features revealing nothing. Then, when Crockett finished, he said, "Why me?"

"Because," the chief said, "the personnel computer spit you out. You did time with the Federal Home Loan Bank Board, didn't you?"

"That's right. Six years as examiner. Working out of San Francisco. But I got tired of crunching numbers and wangled a transfer to the Secret Service."

"Counterfeiting?"

"No," Ullman said with a sour grin, "jogging. I was assigned to the Vice President, and that guy never stops jogging. Rain, sleet, snow—he's out there at seven every morning, with me puffing along behind him."

Crockett stared at him. "You look like you could keep up. Ever play any football?"

"Nah. I was big enough but not fast enough. I'll be re-porting to you?"

"Not directly. Your immediate supervisor will be Anthony Harker. He's right down the hall. You better check in with him now; he's expecting you. Good luck."

"Sure," Ullman said, hauling his bulk off the little folding chair.

In Harker's office the two agents introduced themselves and shook hands. Tony looked up at the Treasury man.

"About six-four and two-fifty?" he guessed.

"More or less," Ullman said. "I call you Mr. Harker?"

"Tony will do."

"Hank for me. What's this all about?"

Harker took several clipped pages from his top desk drawer and handed them over. "Take a look at this. It's a transcript of a taped telephone conversation called in by an undercover agent, a woman, we planted with the main villain, a guy named David Rathbone."

Ullman scanned the pages swiftly, then tossed them onto the desktop.

"You read it?" Tony said, amazed.

"Yeah. I took a speed-reading course. It's a big help. You want me to get the poop on this David Rathbone?"

"No, he's covered. Your target is James Bartlett, a man who seems to know a lot about banks. I want a complete rundown."

"Shouldn't be too difficult. I still have some good contacts in the bank biz. Do I get an office?"

"Afraid not. We're cramped for space as it is. You'll have to settle for a desk and phone in the bullpen."

"I'll manage," the investigator said.

The first thing Henry Ullman did was to go shopping for clothes. He had come down from D.C. wearing a three-piece, navy blue, pin-striped suit, and he saw at once it might at-tract a lot of unwanted attention in south Florida. So he bought four knitted polo shirts in pink, lavender, kelly green, and fire-engine red; two pairs of jeans, khaki and black; and a polyester sports jacket in a hellish plaid.

He went back to his motel room to change and inspected himself in a full-length mirror. "Jesus!" he said. Then he went back to the office and started making phone calls. He worked until almost midnight, then found a steakhouse on the Waterway and treated himself to a twenty-four-ounce rare sirloin, baked potato, double portion of fried onion rings, and two bottles of Molson ale.

On the second day he looked up James Bartlett in the Pompano Beach phone directory. None listed. But there was one in the Fort Lauderdale directory and Ullman hoped that was his pigeon. To make sure, he changed back into his vested pinstripe and drove out to Bayview Drive in his rented Plymouth.

He whistled when he saw the homes in that neighborhood: big, sprawling places with a lot of lawn, palm trees, and usually a boat on a trailer sitting in front of a three-car garage. There were gardeners and swimming-pool maintenance men at work, and the parked cars Ullman saw were Cadillacs, Mercedeses, and top-of-the-line Audis. He figured no one who lived on that stretch of Bayview was drawing food stamps.

He parked, locked the Plymouth, and marched up to the front door of the Bartlett residence. When he pushed the button, there was no bell, but melodious chimes sounded out "Shave and a haircut, two bits."

The man who opened the door was a short roly-poly with a wispy mustache that didn't quite make it. He was wearing Bermuda shorts that revealed pudgy knees, and his fat feet were bare.

"Mr. James Bartlett?" Ullman asked.

He got no answer. "Who're you?" the guy said, giving him a slow up-and-down.

"Sam Henry from Madison, Wisconsin, sir. I'm with the First Farmers' Savings and Loan up there. I'm sure you don't remember me, but I met you at the Milwaukee convention years and years ago."

"Oh? The one where I gave the keynote speech?"

Ullman wasn't about to get tripped up by a trick question like that. "To tell you the truth," he said, laughing, "I was so smashed for the entire convention, I don't remember who gave the speeches or what they talked about."

The man smiled. "Yes," he said, "it was rather wet, inside and out. Sure, I'm Jim Bartlett. What can I do for you?"

"The wife's got arthritis bad, and the doc thinks she'd do better in a warm climate. So I came down to south Florida to scout the territory. I hear it's booming."

"It's doing okay. This year."

"Well, I heard you had relocated here, and I thought I'd look you up and chew the fat awhile."

"I'd ask you in," Bartlett said, "but the house is full of relatives down for the season."

"That's okay," Ullman said. "This won't take but a minute. If we move down here, I'll have to find a slot. I was wondering if you know of any local banks looking for experienced officers."

"What's your specialty?"

"Home mortgage loans."

Bartlett shook his head. "I don't know of anything open at the moment, but I'll ask around. If I hear of anything I'll let you know. How do I get in touch with you?"

Ullman fished in his pocket. "Here's the card of the motel where I'm staying. It's a ratty place, and I'm looking for something better. If I leave, I'll give you a call. All right?"

"Sure," Bartlett said, taking the card. "Sam Henry of the First Farmers' S and L in Madison—right?"

"You've got it," Ullman said.

Bartlett nodded and pumped the big man's hand. "Nice to see you again, Sam," he said, and closed the door softly.

Ullman drove back to the office and asked Tony Harker for

ten minutes. He related the details of his meeting with James Bartlett.

"He's a cutie," he said. "I'll bet he's on the phone right now calling First Farmers' in Madison. But that's okay; I set up my cover with them. They were happy to cooperate with the Secret Service. Here's what I've got on Bartlett so far: He did a year and nine for bank fraud. He's only been in south Florida for seven years, but his most recent tax return shows an adjusted gross of more than eight hundred thousand, and that house he lives in has got to go for a million, at least. He lists himself as a bank consultant, but no one in banking down here has ever heard of him. Or so they say. Something ain't kosher."

"Yeah," Tony said, and pondered a moment. Then: "Hank, that business of Rathbone having our agent open a phony account at the Crescent Bank in Boca—how do you figure that?"

"I don't. A scam of some kind, but it's hard to tell what's going down."

"So what's your next move?" Harker asked. "Tail Bartlett?"

"I don't think so," Ullman said. "In that neighborhood he'd spot my dusty Plymouth in a minute. How about if I take a different angle. According to that transcript, Bartlett has Mike Mulligan of the Crescent Bank in his hip pocket. Suppose I drive up to Boca and get a look at this Mulligan. I'd like to know what the connection is."

"Sounds good to me," Harker said. "Maybe you can turn Mulligan. The only way we're going to flush this gang is by getting someone to sing."

"I'll give it the old college try," Hank said, rose to leave, then paused at the door. "By the way, Bartlett is married. Three kids. The oldest, a girl of nineteen, OD'd on heroin about two years ago."

They stared at each other.

"You better get up to Boca as soon as possible," Tony said.

"I think so," Ullman said.

12.

He explained to her that once a month the five men in the Palace gang met for a night of poker. The party was held in their homes, on a rotating basis, and tonight was Rathbone's turn.

"It's strictly stag," he told Rita. "No women allowed. I had Blanche make up a dozen sandwiches, and we'll mix our own drinks. The guys will be over around six o'clock. The rule is that no matter who's winning or losing, or how much, the game ends promptly at midnight. So I want you to take off at six and don't come back until after twelve. All right?"

"And what am I supposed to do for six hours?"

"Go shopping. Have dinner at some nice place. Take in a movie. Spend! You like to spend, don't you? Here are two yards; go enjoy yourself."

"Okay," she said. "Have a good time and win a lot of money, hon."

"I intend to," he said.

After she left, he put all the bottles of booze out on the countertop in the kitchen, along with containers of lemon peel, lime wedges, pearl onions, and some fresh mint for Jimmy Bartlett, who had a fondness for juleps. Glasses were lined up, and there was a big bucket of ice cubes with more in the freezer.

The doorbell rang a little before six o'clock, and Rathbone put on a pair of rose-tinted sunglasses before he opened up.

"Good evening, girls," he said, giving them his high-intensity smile. "Thank you for being so prompt."

Their names were Sheila and Lorrie, and both were dancers at the Leopard II, a nudie joint on Federal Highway. They were in their early twenties. Sheila did two lines of coke a day, and Lorrie had a four-year-old dyslexic son.

David took two envelopes from the inside pocket of his suede sports jacket and handed one to each woman. "Payable in advance," he said, still smiling. "And a nice tip before you leave if you do a good job."

"But no push?" Lorrie said.

"Absolutely not. If you want to make dates with these guys to meet them later, that's your business. But not in my home. Now come with me and I'll show you where to undress."

The two women stripped down in the pantry and left their jeans and T-shirts in a jumbled heap on the floor. Rathbone led them back into the kitchen and showed them the bar, the sandwiches in the fridge.

"You told me you could mix drinks," he said, "but if you have any problems, ask me. Help yourself to a sandwich if you get hungry."

"How about a drinkie-poo?" Sheila said.

"Of course," Rathbone said. "Just don't get plotched. That I don't need."

Frank Little was the first guest to arrive. He immediately pointed at David's sunglasses. "What's with the shades?" he asked.

"A mild case of conjunctivitis," Rathbone said. "The doc says I've got to avoid bright light."

"Tough shit," Little said. "Hey, I could use a drink."

"Why don't we wait for the others to show up. I've got a surprise for all of you."

James Bartlett and Sidney Coe arrived together. Then Mortimer Sparco came bustling in. When they were all seated in the living room, Rathbone told them he was tired of serving himself food and mixing his own drinks at their monthly get-togethers, so he was going to try something new.

"Sheila!" he called. "Lorrie! You can take our drink orders now."

The naked women came smiling out of the kitchen. The guests, startled, stared at them, then looked at their host, burst out laughing and climbed awkwardly to their feet.

"Sit down," David said. "These ladies are here to wait on us."

"David," Frank Little said, "you're too much."

"What would you like, sir?" Lorrie asked, bending over Mort Sparco, her pointy breasts almost touching his beard.

"If I told you," he said, "you'd slap my face. So I'll settle for a Scotch mist."

Everyone gave their drink orders, interspersed with ribald comments.

"The hell with poker," Sid Coe said after the waitresses went back to the kitchen. "I know a better game."

"Not in my home," Rathbone repeated. "What you do after midnight is up to you."

"Hey, David," Jim Bartlett said, "what's with the cheaters?"

He explained again about his mild case of conjunctivitis and how he had to avoid bright light. Everyone bought the story.

After the second round of drinks, the men moved into the dining room and sat at a big round table of bleached pine covered with a green baize cloth. Rathbone had set out two new decks of Hoyle playing cards.

"Dealer's choice," he said, shoving a deck at Sidney Coe.

"Five-card stud," Coe said. "Jacks or better to open. And just to separate the men from the boys, spit in the ocean."

He took out his wallet and dropped a hundred in the center of the table. The others followed suit. Coe broke the seal on the deck of cards, discarded the two jokers, and shuffled, shuffled, shuffled. Then he slapped the deck in front of Sparco.

"Cut your heart out," he said.

The playing cards were a forged deck and so cleverly marked that it required rose-tinted glasses to read the code printed on the backs. Rathbone bought them from a talented artist in Miami who also supplied the sunglasses. David knew that with his wiseguy pals, it was strictly a one-time gimmick, but worth the risk. The naked waitresses were his edge—to keep his guests distracted enough not to question his incredible luck.

He played craftily, folding when he saw he couldn't win, plunging when he held a winning hand. He deliberately lost a few small pots, but as the evening progressed the stack of bills in front of him grew steadily higher.

Meanwhile, the naked girls hustled drinks and sandwiches and held lights for cigars. Their presence had the desired effect; even Mort Sparco, the best poker player of the group, found it difficult to concentrate on his game. And, Rathbone noted, his guests were drinking a lot more than usual.

The session ended at midnight with David ahead almost four thousand, and all the others losers.

"You did all right," Jimmy Bartlett said, watching him pocket his winnings.

"It's about time," Rathbone said. "I've been a loser all year. Now I'm just about breaking even."

The other three men went into the kitchen to schmooze

with the women. Bartlett and David stayed at the table, smoking cigars and sipping their drinks.

"How did you make out with Mike Mulligan at the Crescent in Boca?" Jimmy asked. "Any problems?"

"Not a one. Thanks for setting it up."

"I don't suppose you want to tell me what's going down."

"Not yet," Rathbone said. "If it works, I will. It could be a sweet deal, and I'll cut you in. Is Mulligan one of your laundrymen?"

"On a small scale—so far. Things are getting a little warm in Miami, so I've been trying to expand: Lauderdale, Boca, Palm Beach."

"Business good?"

"So-so. The demand is always there, but right now the supply is so plentiful that prices have dropped. One of these days my clients will get smart and set up a cartel like OPEC, just to stabilize prices."

"Is it all coke?"

"Coke, pot, heroin, hash, mescaline—you name it. I've even got one guy handling nothing but opium. With all the Asian immigrants in the country, he's doing all right. David, why are you staring at me like that?"

"I just had a wild idea," Rathbone said. "So crazy that it might work. Look, what you're talking about are commodities—right? The prices rise and fall just as they do with grains, metals, livestock, foods, and everything else they trade in the Chicago pits."

"That's correct."

"Well, what if we set up a commodity trading fund that would deal only with drugs, buying and selling futures and options?"

Bartlett drained his drink and set the empty glass down with a thump. "You're right: It is a wild idea. What are you going to do—advertise the fund in *The Wall Street Journal?*"

"Of course not. But what if we have Mort Sparco set up a

penny stock in the fund, and have Sid Coe push the shares in his boiler room."

Jimmy rubbed his chin. "Now it doesn't sound so crazy. You could organize it for peanuts, and there's a possibility it could actually turn a profit on the fluctuation of drug prices. Some of my clients would probably be willing to sell kilos for future delivery in three months or six months at a set price. David, let me think about this awhile and talk to a few people."

"If there's a Ponzi payoff up front," Rathbone pointed out, "you know the mooches will be fighting to buy stock. They don't have to know what the fund is dealing in; just that it's commodities."

"It might go," Bartlett agreed. "Don't say anything yet to Coe or Sparco. Let me figure out how we can finagle it."

"Don't take too long," David warned, "or some other shark will think of it and get it rolling. It could be a world-class scam."

"You're right," Jimmy said. "And the best part is that you're not dealing with the drugs themselves. Just with contracts: pieces of paper using code names for coke, heroin, and so forth. David, I'm beginning to think it's doable. Now I need a drink."

"Let's go in the kitchen and see how my waitresses are making out."

"How much did you pay them?"

"An arm and a leg," Rathbone said. "But it was worth it."

"That Sheila turns me on. Great boobs."

"Come on, Jimmy; you're married."

"My wife is," Bartlett said. "I'm not."

13.

They were walking on the beach, carrying their shoes. A gleaming crescent cast a silver dagger across the sea. The breeze was from the southeast, smelling strongly of salt. There were a few night swimmers splashing about, yelping in the chilly surf.

"He's having his pals over for a poker party," Rita reported. "Strictly stag. I can't go back till midnight so we have plenty of time. Did you eat?"

"I worked late," Tony said, "and had a pizza sent in. How about you?"

"I did some shopping at the mall and then grabbed a Caesar salad. Lots of garlic. Can't you smell it?"

"Smells good. These guys Rathbone's having over—the gang from the Grand Palace?"

"That's right. They're as thick as thieves, that bunch."

"Rita, they *are* thieves. Has he sent you back to the bank in Boca?"

"Not yet. I haven't the slightest idea what's going on there."

"Anything else?"

"Not much. He's got a new client, a retired professor with *mucho dinero.*"

"Damn!" Harker said. "I can't get a handle on how his swindle works. I had the SEC take a look at his accounts with Mortimer Sparco, who's a discount broker. Sparco runs a lot of penny stocks, but so far he's clean. Anyway, Rathbone has accounts for all his clients. But they're all holding blue chips like IBM and AT&T. But I know, I *know* Rathbone is skimming. I just don't know how."

She told him the story of how David got a refund from Hunneker's on a jumpsuit he didn't like. Tony laughed.

"A crook is a crook is a crook," he said. "The guy is making at least six hundred thousand a year, but he can't stand the thought of someone taking him, even for two hundred."

"In some ways," she said, "he's very generous."

"You already told me that."

"Well, he is! I bet if I asked him for a thousand, he'd hand it over and not even ask what I wanted it for."

"He's getting his money's worth," Harker said in a low voice.

She stopped walking, making him stop, and turned to stare at him. "That was a shitty thing to say. Let's you and I get something straight, buster. I'm not a total bubblehead, you know. I have very good instincts about people, especially men. I know David is a conniving thief and belongs in the pokey, but I happen to like the guy. Okay? I happen to think he's sweet."

"Sweet?" Harker said with an explosive snort. "He's a bum!"

"So he's a sweet bum. All right?"

They turned around and continued their stroll back to his motel.

"You claim you have a good instinct about men," he said. "What about me?"

"You? A straight arrow. Uptight. If you could learn to re-lax, you could be quite a guy."

"Well, if it'll make you feel any better, since I met you I've stopped using my inhaler and tonight I had a pepperoni pizza."

"Bed therapy. Stick with me, kiddo, and you'll be tanning your hide in the sun." She hugged his arm, adding, "We've got till midnight."

His bedroom window was open wide, and they could smell the sea. The ghostly moonlight was all the light they needed. Her body was a hot shadow on the white sheet.

"Hand and glove," she said dreamily.

"What?"

"That's how we fit."

He was enraptured, lost and gone. He surrendered totally. I must never lose this woman, he vowed. Never.

Later, she took his face between her palms. "You're getting there," she said.

"Thank you, Dr. Sullivan," he said. "Would you like a cold beer?"

"I'd love a cold beer."

They sat up in bed, sipping. She rested the dripping can on his belly, and he winced.

"Mama told me," she said, "that I should never talk to a man about another man—especially in bed—but this is part of our job, so I figure it's okay."

"What is?"

"David Rathbone. You said he's a bum, and he is. He cheats his friends; I know that for a fact. But I've had a lot of ex-perience with hard cases, and I've learned one thing about them: none are completely bad. A rapist can be devoted to a sick mother. A safecracker can help support his church. Even a murderer can drag a kid out of a burning house. None of us is one-dimensional. So when you call David a con man, a swindler, a thief, I know you're right. But he's more than that."

84

"If you say so," Tony said.

She left a little before midnight, and he went to sleep smelling the garlic on his pillow and smiling.

The next morning he gave Crockett an update. The chief listened intently, fingers laced across his vest. He looked as broody as an Easter Island statue. Harker knew he was bossing a half-dozen concurrent investigations; the man's brain must be churning.

Crockett stirred when Tony finished his recital. "Can't you move any faster on this?" he asked.

"No, sir. The two new men are coming in today. But I had to set up their legends first. I've established cover stories that'll back them up. I'll put one on Sidney Coe and one on Mortimer Sparco."

"Which on which?"

"I want to talk to them first."

Crockett nodded. "So all we've got at the moment is that paperman, Irving Donald Gevalt. You want to pull him in?"

"I don't think so, sir. He's small-fry. If we take him now, it might tip our hand and blow the whole investigation. We can pick him up anytime we want."

"I suppose so," Crockett said. "But Washington is screaming. They want to see some results from all the money they've been spending. Well, they'll just have to be patient. Like me. Anything else?"

"Yes, sir. I'd like you to authorize a black-bag job on Rathbone's town house."

"Tap his phone? We could do that at the central exchange if you think it would yield anything."

"I doubt if it would. He's too clever for that. What I had in mind was to bug the whole apartment. He had the whole gang over for a poker session. I would have loved to hear what they talked about."

Crockett shook his head. "Too risky. If he has the place swept electronically, and the bugs are discovered, there goes your ball game."

"I don't think he has the place swept. I don't think it would occur to him that he could be a target."

"What would you bug?"

"Everything, though we may have trouble getting into his office. But certainly the living room and bedrooms."

"Bedrooms? And would you tell Rita Sullivan about the bugs?"

"Oh no, sir. Why would we want to do that?"

"Why indeed," said Lester Crockett, staring at him. "I'll think about it, Tony."

14.

Manny Suarez was a feisty little man with a black walrus mustache and a habit of snapping his fingers as he walked. In fact, his walk was almost a dance step, and as he bopped along, he smiled at all the passing women. Most of them smiled back because he looked like fun.

Manny was with the Miami Police Department, where he was called "Bunko" Suarez because that was his specialty: breaking up flimflams and swindles, especially those preying on newly arrived immigrants. He spoke Spanish, of course, but a lot of his success was due to his warm grin and ingratiating manner. The bad guys couldn't believe he was a cop until he snapped the cuffs on them.

He bade an emotional farewell to his wife and six children in Miami and, following orders, drove up to Fort Lauderdale in his new Ford Escort for what he was told was a "special assignment."

In Lauderdale, he reported to Tony Harker and got a two-hour briefing. Manny thought Harker was a typical Anglo: cold, starchy, and not the kind of guy you'd want to have over for a pig roast and a gallon of Cuba Libres.

But he had to admit his new boss was efficient; Harker had already set up his cover: Manny had done eighteen months in a San Diego clink for an aluminum-siding fraud, and had decided to come east to put as much distance as possible between himself and his irate victims.

His target was a man named Sidney Coe, who ran a boiler room on Oakland Park Boulevard. Manny was to apply for a job as a phone salesman, a yak, and since yaks worked only on commission, the chances were good that Coe would take him on for a trial period to see if he could fleece the mooches.

Suarez knew all about bucket shops and assured Harker that, if he was hired, he'd be handed a script to follow. It really was an acting job, Manny said, and if he could deliver a convincing performance, he'd be in like Señor Flynn.

"What I want out of this," said Harker, "is an inside report on Coe's operation, what he's pushing right now, how much money you figure he's stealing. Also, Coe has a good friend, a man named David Rathbone. I want to know if Rathbone has a piece of Coe's action, or what his connection with Coe might be. Got all that?"

"Don't worry," Manny said, grinning. "I can do it. Tell me something—do I get to keep the moaney I make?"

Tony was startled. "I never thought about that," he admitted. "I'll have to check it out with the chief. Meanwhile you try to land a job at Coe's place. Here's the address."

"Hokay," Suarez said cheerfully.

He already had a place to stay: a room in the home of a nice Cuban lady, a friend of his aunt's, who was happy to have a cop in the house and someone to cook for. So he drove directly to Coe's boiler room on Oakland Park Boulevard.

It looked no different from the legit places on the wide boulevard. The sign over the door read: INSTANT INVEST-

MENTS, INC. The sign was on a board, hung on a chain from a nail pounded into the stuccoed wall, and Manny wondered how often that sign had been changed.

"Good morn'," he said to the receptionist, flashing his big white teeth.

"Good morning, sir," she said, returning his smile. "May I help you?"

"Could I speak to the boss man, pliz. I am looking for a job."

"Just a moment, sir. I'll see if he's in."

She spoke softly in a phone, listened a moment. Then, to Manny: "Please sit down, sir. He'll be with you in a few minutes."

The investigator sat in an orange plastic chair and picked up a month-old copy of *Business Week*. He read a short article on inside trading, then tossed the magazine aside. He stared at the receptionist, who was typing away busily. She had short brown ringlets, and Manny thought her ears were *exquisito*. The lobes were flushed and plump. He could go *loco* nibbling on one of those lobes.

Finally a skinny, suntanned guy came out of a back door and beckoned. Suarez followed him into an inner office. It was a square chamber, sparsely furnished. The desk, chair, and file cabinet looked ready to collapse, and the tiled floor was stained and scarred with cigarette burns. The man didn't sit down and didn't ask Manny to sit.

"Looking for a job?" he asked. Cold voice.

"Tha's right."

"How did you hear about this place?"

Suarez shrugged. "You know how word gets around. Maybe some of your yaks are mouthy guys. That's why they're yaks—am I right?"

"Uh-huh. Well, I'm Sidney Coe. I own the joint. What's your name?"

"Manuel Suarez."

"Cuban?"

"Mexican," Manny said, figuring this Anglo would never know the difference in the accents.

"You live in south Florida?" Coe asked.

"Now I do."

"Where you from?"

"San Diego."

"How come you left?"

"I had a little trouble."

"Yeah?" Coe said. "How little?"

Manny hung his head and shuffled his feet. "Eighteen months," he said in a low voice.

Coe nodded. "That's a little trouble, all right. What were the eighteen months for?"

"I was selling aluminum siding."

Coe laughed. "That scam will never die. You ever sell by telephone?"

"No, but I know I can do it. I can talk fast and hard."

"I don't know," Coe said doubtfully. "You *sound* Spanish. I'm not sure the mooches will go for that."

"Look, mister," Manny said, "you got Hispanic names on your sucker list—am I right? There are plenty of rich Cubans, Mexicans, Salvadorans, Nicaraguans in the country. Let me talk to the Hispanics in their own language. I ask how is their health, are their families well, how do they like the United Sta'. Hispanics like that: the personal touch. Right away they trust me. Then, when we're friends, *compañeros,* I give them the hard sell."

Coe stared at him a moment. "Yeah," he said finally, "that might work. Let's try it. Come with me."

"Wait, wait," Suarez said hastily. "How much you pay?"

"Strictly commish. Ten percent. The harder you work, the richer you get. Some of my yaks clear a grand a week. How does that sound?"

"Hokay," Manny said.

15.

Rathbone rose early and showered, shaved, dressed. He went downstairs where Blanche and Theodore were laughing in the kitchen. David had a small tomato juice and told them he'd be back soon to have breakfast on the terrace.

There was a heavy morning fog, but he knew that would burn off as the sun strengthened. He drove to a nearby mini-mall that included a drugstore selling out-of-town newspapers. He parked and noticed, on the other side of the mall, a newly installed line of newspaper-vending machines. One was the distinctive blue box of *The New York Times*' national edition.

Rathbone walked over, fishing two quarters from his pocket. He dropped them in the slot, pulled down the front lid. Glancing around to make certain no one was watching, he took two copies of the *Times* from the box and let the lid slam shut.

One newspaper he tossed onto the front seat of the Bentley. The other copy he carried into the drugstore.

"My wife bought this," he said, smiling at the clerk. "It's today's paper. But she didn't know I had already bought a copy. I wonder if I can get a refund."

"Sure," the young man said. "No problem."

He took the newspaper and handed David two quarters.

"Thank you very much," Rathbone said.

He drove home, noting the fog was already thinning. It promised to be a warm, sunny day, but maybe a little humid. Rita was still sleeping, so he breakfasted alone on the terrace. Theodore served California strawberries, a toasted bagel with a schmear of cream cheese, and black coffee. Rathbone read the Business Day section of his newspaper as he ate—paying particular attention to activities in the Chicago commodity pits—and had a second cup of coffee.

He was just leaving when Rita came straggling out, wearing his terry robe.

"I guess I overslept," she said.

"Not really," he said, kissing her cheek. "It's still early. But I'd better get to my office. Work, work, work."

"Rather you than me," she said, and yawned.

He sat before his computer screen and took a look at balances in his checking accounts. He maintained both personal and corporate accounts. But because the government provided deposit insurance of only $100,000, he used several banks with no account in excess of the cap.

He was working on a schedule of deposits and withdrawals when his phone rang.

"David Rathbone Investment Management," he said. "David Rathbone speaking."

"This is Tommy."

"How're you doing, Tommy?"

"Okay. Can we meet?"

"Sure. When?"

"Soon as possible."

"How about a half-hour. Same place we met before."

"Suits me," Termite Tommy said. "I'll be there."

Rathbone locked his office and went back to the terrace. Rita was finishing her breakfast and reading his newspaper.

"I have to run out for a few minutes," he told her. "Stick around for a while, will you? I may have a job for you later."

"I'll be here," she promised. "Knock us a kiss."

He bent to kiss her lips. "Last night was super," he said.

"They're all super," she said. "I love being pampered."

"Is that what you call it?" he said, laughing. "Slavery is more like it."

The Grand Palace hadn't opened yet; the parking lot was empty except for a decrepit pickup truck. Rathbone parked, and Termite Tommy got out of the pickup and came over to join him in the Bentley.

"Going to be a hot mother," he said.

"I guess," David said. "Got something for me?"

Tommy handed over a white envelope. "I hope we got the name spelled right," he said.

Rathbone examined the forged U.S. Treasury check. It was made out to Gloria Ramirez in the amount of $27,341.46. It looked very official, with seal, numbers, computer coding.

"A work of art," David said. "It still feels a little oily, but not so much that a busy teller would notice. How much time do we have before it dissolves?"

"Three days. Maybe four."

"I'll have the pusher deposit it today, and we'll draw on it tomorrow."

"You'll let me know?" Tommy asked.

"Of course."

"That crazy German wants a third."

"Let's wait till we see how this goes. When we have the money, we can talk a split. Except that the pusher wants her cash off the top. I promised her two grand. Okay?"

"Sure," Termite Tommy said. "If this goes off without a hitch, maybe we can use her again. Have a nice day."

"You, too," Rathbone said.

He drove home and found Rita in her bedroom, painting her toenails vermilion. David sat down on the bed next to her and held up the check for her inspection.

"Don't touch it," he warned. "You might get polish on it."

She stared long and hard at the check.

"Queer?" she asked.

"As a three-dollar bill. But it's beautifully done. It'll pass. As soon as your toenails dry, I want you to endorse it as Gloria Ramirez. Then drive up to Boca and deposit it at the Crescent."

"And then?"

"Tomorrow you go back to the bank. Draw this out plus your original deposit. Close out the account."

"What if they ask why I'm closing an account I just opened a few days ago?"

"Death in the family, and you've got to go home to San Antonio. Tell them anything. If you have any problems, Mike Mulligan will okay it."

She bent down to remove the wads of cotton from between her toes. Then she straightened up to stare at him.

"I don't like it," she said. "It's a federal rap. They'll lock me up and throw away the key. What if they lift my prints off the check?"

"They won't," he assured her. "Trust me."

She stood, naked, and began to pull on white bikini panties. "Seems to me you're asking for a whole bunch of trust. It's my ass that'll be on the line, not yours."

"In the first place," he said, "if I thought there was any real risk, I wouldn't ask you to do it. I don't want to lose you; I already told you that. In the second place, I want to find out just how much I can trust *you*. If you turn me down on this, I'll know."

"And then it's goodbye Rita?"

"You better believe it," he said, nodding. "But if you do

94

it, there will be other jobs, bigger jobs. So it's your future you've got to consider."

She looked again at the check he was still holding. "What's in it for me?" she asked.

"Now you're talking like a mature adult," he said, giving her his 100-watt smile. "A grand for this job. And much more to come if you play along."

"All right," she said. "I'm game."

"That's my girl," he said, pulling her close.

He watched her endorse the check "For deposit only" and the account number. Then he went back to his office. Rita dressed and drove her Chevy up to Boca Raton, where she deposited the Gloria Ramirez check at the Crescent Bank. Then she called Tony Harker.

"A counterfeit Treasury check?" he said. "I can't believe it. Most yobs are specialists. A bank robber does nothing but hit banks. A strong-arm guy mugs people. They very rarely go outside their field. Like a gynecologist doesn't do tonsillectomies. Now we've got David Rathbone, a con man, going in for forgery. It doesn't make sense."

"I'm just telling you what he told me."

"I know," Harker said. "All right, do exactly what he wants. Go back to Boca tomorrow and close out the account. I'll take it from there. We'll let the Ramirez check clear so we have evidence of counterfeiting and bank fraud."

"I suppose I'll have to testify."

"Of course," he said. "That doesn't scare you, does it?"

"No," she said.

"Listen," he said in a low voice, "when am I going to see you again?"

She laughed. "Anxious?" she asked.

"Not anxious," he said. "Eager."

"That's nice," Rita said.

16.

The fourth man assigned to Anthony Harker's staff came from the U.S. Attorney's office in Chicago. He had helped investigate and prosecute a stock-rigging fraud that had sent a half-dozen brokers and financiers to jail. His name was Simon Clark, and Harker disliked him on sight.

There was nothing wrong with Clark's appearance, although he could have lost twenty pounds, but he had a supercilious air about him and made no effort to hide a patronizing attitude toward Lester Crockett's supra-agency. Obviously, he thought Fort Lauderdale was no Chicago, and nothing that might advance his career could possibly come out of this rinky-dink operation.

He listened, expressionless, when Harker explained that his target was Mortimer Sparco, a discount broker with offices on Commercial Boulevard. Sparco was suspected of possible fraud and criminal conspiracy in the trading and manipulation of penny stocks, thinly traded securities that usually sold for less than $1 a share. In addition, Sparco was a close friend of David Rathbone, who called himself an investment manager but was quite possibly a con man swindling his clients with a variation of the Ponzi scheme.

"What I want you to do is—" Harker started.

"I know what you want," Clark interrupted. "You want me to pose as a new client, find out what Sparco is pushing and promising, and if this Rathbone is in on it."

The fact that he was completely correct didn't make his superior manner any easier to endure. "That's about it," Harker admitted, and couldn't resist adding, "Think you can handle it?"

The other man gave him a glare that might have chilled defendants in a courtroom, but had absolutely no effect on Tony.

"You don't need an assistant DA for a job like this," Clark said. "Any gumshoe could do it."

Harker shrugged. "You want out? Planes leave for Chicago all the time. It'll go in your file, of course."

That rattled the attorney. "I'll look into it," he said. "Besides, it's getting cold in Chicago." His smile was stretched.

"Uh-huh," Tony said. "Keep me informed. Calls every day, and a written report every week. I'll try to find you a desk and chair in the bullpen."

Cursing his luck at being dumped in what he considered a backwater, Clark returned to his hotel on the Galt Ocean Mile and changed from his heavy tweed suit to polyester slacks and a lightweight sports jacket. He stopped at the hotel bar for a quick gin and bitters, then got into his rented Olds Cutlass and drove back to Commercial Boulevard.

Sparco's place of business was located in a long, low building that also housed a unisex hairdresser, a real estate agency, a women's swimwear shop, and a store that sold and shipped Florida oranges "Anywhere in the World!"

The brokerage itself looked legit enough. There was a small

anteroom with wicker armchairs and a table piled with financial periodicals. There was also a TV set with the stock tape jerking across the screen. Two old geezers wearing Bermuda shorts and sandals stood in front of it, transfixed by the moving price quotations.

There was a receptionist's desk at the open doorway to a spacious room in which several men sat at littered desks equipped with computer terminals. Most of the brokers, Clark noted, were on the phone or busily writing on order pads. The place seemed prosperous enough, but so did betting shops and boiler rooms.

"May I speak to the manager, please," Clark asked the middle-aged receptionist. "I'd like to open an account."

"Just a moment, please, sir," she added, and spoke into her phone.

The man who came forward a few moments later was tall, stooped, and had a neatly trimmed beard so black and glossy that Clark figured it had to be dyed and oiled.

"I'm Mortimer Sparco," he said, smiling and holding out his hand. "How may I be of service?"

"Simon Clark," the attorney said, gripping the proffered hand briefly. "I'm in the process of moving to Fort Lauderdale from Chicago and thought I'd open a brokerage account."

"You're too young for retirement," Sparco said, still smiling. "Your company transfer you down here?"

"Not exactly. My parents live in Lauderdale, and I thought it would be nice to be closer to them. I'm a freelance writer for how-to magazines—you know, like *Home Mechanics*—and you can do that from anywhere."

"Fascinating," Sparco said. "Why don't you come back to my office and talk about your investment aims."

"My aim is to make money," Clark said.

"You've come to the right place," Sparco said. "This way, please."

The office was all leather, chrome, and glass, and smelled of cigar smoke. The entire rear wall was covered with a mural: a Florida beach scene with sand, palm trees, sailboats on the ocean, pelicans in the sky. The painted sun looked like a toasted English muffin.

The two men sat at either end of a tawny leather couch and turned to face each other.

"I'll be honest with you, Mr. Sparco," Clark said. "I've never bought a share of stock in my life. I know zilch about the market. But I've become dissatisfied with the rates I'm getting on my savings account and CDs."

"Completely understandable," the broker said.

"I've been doing some reading on stock investing and learned that discount brokers may charge as little as half the commissions of the big brokerage houses, but they don't provide a full range of services."

"Generally that's true. But at Sparco, while our fees are competitive with those of other discount brokers, we pride ourselves on offering services the others don't. Most of them are merely order-takers. But at Sparco we believe in personalized service, tailored to our clients' needs. Tell me, Mr. Clark, how much were you thinking of investing?"

"Well, I thought I'd start slow, sort of dip my toes in the water. I'm sure you'll think it's chicken feed, but I'd like to begin with ten thousand dollars."

The broker leaned forward, very earnest. "Let me tell you something: At Sparco we treat a client with ten thousand exactly the same way we treat one with ten million. We take our responsibility to *all* our clients very seriously, and provide the most up-to-date information and the best advice we possibly can. You say you are dissatisfied with the current rates on your CDs. Does that mean you're willing to assume a limited amount of risk to increase your yields?"

"Well . . . not *too* much risk."

"Of course not. Sparco wouldn't put you in anything where

the risk-benefit ratio is not in your favor. But occasionally we learn of special situations that demand fast decisions. I would advise you to open a discretionary account with us. That will authorize Sparco to buy and sell in your name, on your behalf. It relieves you of the need to watch your portfolio every day. After all, you're just interested in results. Am I correct?"

"That's right."

"And, with your approval, we can trade on margin in your account. That will give you a lot more leverage; your ten thousand can have the clout of fifteen or even more."

"Sounds good to me," Clark said.

Mortimer Sparco leaned closer and lowered his voice. "In addition," he said, almost whispering, "we help make the market in certain specialized stocks that are not listed on the exchanges. They customarily sell for less than a dollar a share and represent ownership in new companies with an enormous potential for growth. Sparco has a select group of clients who have done very well with these little-known equities. I think you'd be amazed at how fast your money can double, even triple, with stocks that most investors never even heard of."

"With no risk?" the attorney asked.

"There is risk in every investment, even government bonds. But in this case the risk is minimal and the possible profits simply unbelievable."

"Then let's do it."

"You're making a wise decision, Mr. Clark. Now if you'll just step over to my desk, there are a few documents I'd like you to sign."

17.

She loved to drive the Bentley.

"It's so *solid*," she said. "And it even smells of money."

So she was at the wheel as they headed up A1A to Boca Raton. Traffic was surprisingly light going northward, but out-of-state cars, jammed with vacationers, were flocking south.

Rathbone sat relaxed, smoking his first cigarette of the day.

"After you finish at the bank," he said, "let's have lunch in Boca, maybe do some shopping. We'll get back in time to catch some sun on the terrace."

"Sounds good to me."

"Nervous?" he said.

"Nah. You said it will be a piece of cake."

"Sure it will," he said. "Just sail in, pick up the money, and sail out. You'll do fine."

They parked in front of the bank. Rita got out, and David slid over behind the wheel.

"I'll be right here," he told her. "I'm not going anyplace."

She nodded and marched into the bank. Rathbone spent the next twenty minutes making "air bets," declaiming them aloud:

"I'll bet fifty that the next woman to come out of the bank will be wearing blue.

"I'll bet a hundred that the next man to come around the corner will have a mustache.

"I'll bet a thousand that the next car to park will be a white two-door."

And so on.

By the time Rita returned, he was two hundred dollars ahead, which he took as a good omen.

She opened the door on the passenger side, slid onto the leather seat. She tossed a fat manila envelope into his lap. "Bingo!" she said.

He smiled and leaned to kiss her lips. "Any problems?" he asked.

"Nope. They wanted to give me a bank check, but I told them I was flying home to San Antonio tonight and needed the cash. So they came across."

"Beautiful," he said.

He took a thousand in hundred-dollar bills from the envelope and handed them to her.

"Invest it wisely," he said.

"With you?"

"You could do worse," he said. "Now let's go eat. I know a place that makes a great chef's salad."

"Can I have a hamburger instead?"

"You can have anything you want," he said, and kissed her again. "Partner," he said.

They had a nice, relaxed lunch, did a little shopping at the Town Center, then headed home.

"Can we pull that bank dodge again?" she asked him.

"Oh-ho," he said. "Getting ambitious, are you?"

"It's so *easy*," she said.

"Sure it is. The problem is whether or not to use the Gloria Ramirez ID again, and if we do, hit another Boca bank or try somewhere else. I'll have to think about it."

"Who printed up that queer check?" she asked idly, staring out the side window.

"A genius," he said, and she didn't push it.

An hour later they were lying naked on the terrace lounges. The sun was behind a scrim of high cloud cover, but it was strong enough to cast shadows and hot enough to make them sweat. They drank iced tea from a thermos.

"I'm going to have to change my plans," he said.

"What plans?"

"A schedule I had mapped out. I was going to give it maybe another six months and then retire, get out of the game."

She raised her head to look at him. "What about me?"

"Not to worry," he said. "I'll take care of you; you know that. But this check scam changes things. The possibilities are tremendous if it's handled right. Also, something else came up the other night that could be a gold mine. So I think I'll stick around for a while."

"Where were you going?"

"Oh . . . there are a lot of places in this world I haven't seen yet."

"When you decide to go, can I go with you?"

"We'll see. Let's take another half-hour of sun and then go shower."

"And then what?"

"You know what," he said.

That night they dined at an Italian restaurant on Atlantic Boulevard, and David ordered a bottle of Dom Perignon to celebrate their triumph at the Crescent Bank. Then they drove to the Grand Palace and found the gang already assembled at the big table in the Lounge. Rita sat in one of the mate's chairs and watched as Rathbone beckoned James Bartlett over to the bar. The two men stood close together, talking with lowered heads.

"Jimmy, have you given any more thought to what I suggested on poker night?"

"The commodity trading fund? Yes, I've talked to several clients about it. You know, David, these guys are shrewd. They've got all the street smarts in the world, but they don't understand options and futures. Finally, I stopped trying to explain, and just told them it would mean money in their pockets. That, they could understand. Four of them definitely will sign contracts for delivery in three, six, nine, and twelve months at preset prices."

"They'll trust you?"

"On the first delivery. If I welsh, I'm dead; you know that."

"So actually we have three problems. One is to analyze the market for the coming year and determine prices that'll yield a profit. The second is to make sure funds are available to take delivery. And finally, we've got to line up markets and sign contracts with buyers."

"You've got it."

"Jimmy, I think now is the time to bring Sparco, Coe, and Little in on this. It's too big for the two of us to swing alone."

"I agree."

"Then let's talk to them. I think they'll go for it."

"They'd be idiots not to."

"Who were the four clients who agreed to play?"

"Three Colombians and one American. These are not men you'd want to introduce to your wife, David—if you had a wife."

"Hard cases?"

Bartlett rolled his eyes. "Last year one of the Colombians murdered his younger brother because the kid lost a shipment to the Coast Guard. You know how he killed him?"

"No, and I don't want to know. Let's get back to the table."

"Rita is looking especially sexy tonight, David. She's not beautiful, but she's striking."

"I know."

"You serious about her?"

"I don't know how I feel about her. All I know is that she's got me seeing pinwheels."

"That sounds serious. Does she know what you do?"

"I'm letting her in on it, little by little. It doesn't turn her off. I think she likes it. Maybe it's the risk, the danger."

"Uh-huh," Jimmy said, staring at him. "And maybe it's fear. With some women fear can be an aphrodisiac."

Rathbone laughed. "And what's an aphrodisiac to men?"

"Guilt," Bartlett said.

18.

"Mr. Harker," the secretary said on the phone, "will you come to Mr. Crockett's office, please."

Tony pulled on his jacket, straightened his tie, walked down the hall. There was a somber man seated alongside the chief's desk. He wore wire-rimmed spectacles with lenses so thick they made him look pop-eyed.

"Tony," Crockett said, "this is Fred Rabin from the Federal Reserve. Mr. Rabin, this is Anthony Harker, who spoke to your office."

Rabin didn't stand up or offer to shake hands, but at least he nodded. Tony nodded back. No one asked him to sit down, so he remained standing, looking down at the two men.

"Mr. Rabin," Crockett said, "will you please repeat what you told me."

The Federal Reserve man stared at Tony through those thick glasses. "You asked us to put a trace on a U.S. Treasury check in the amount of $27,341.46, issued to a Gloria Ramirez and deposited at the Crescent Bank in Boca Raton. Is that correct?"

"Yes."

"Why did you ask for a trace?"

"Because I had good reason to believe the check was counterfeit. Allowing it to clear the Crescent Bank and then recovering it would give me hard evidence of bank fraud. Did you find the check?"

"Oh, we found it," Rabin said. "Would you like to see it?"

He took a long glassine envelope from an attaché case and held it up for Harker to inspect. It appeared to be filled with greenish-blue confetti.

"What the hell is that?" Tony said, bewildered.

"That's the check you wanted."

"What happened? Did it get chopped up in a canceling machine?"

Rabin sighed. "The intact check was retrieved in Atlanta, on its way to Treasury. It was put aside to be mailed to you the next morning. But in the morning, this was all that was left of it. It just shredded away, disintegrated. We have our lab working on it now."

Harker turned to Crockett. "There goes our case," he said.

"Your case may be important," Rabin said, "but not as important as finding the source of this paper that self-destructs. Do you realize what this could do to the banking system? Chaos! We are now in the process of preparing a letter of warning to every bank and savings and loan in the country."

"Mr. Rabin wants the Secret Service to take over the whole investigation," Crockett said, lacing his fingers across his vest. "He feels they have more manpower and resources than we have."

"We already have a Secret Service man working on it," Harker said. "Henry Ullman, a good investigator."

Rabin shook his head. "One man is hardly sufficient to assign to a problem of this magnitude. I must ask that you turn over to us all the information you have in your possession, such as how you knew the check was forged, who deposited it, and any other evidence you may possess bearing on the case."

Silence in the room. Finally, Crockett shook his head.

"No, Mr. Rabin," the chief said, "I don't think so. I am sure you'll go over my head and file your request with my superiors. If they order me to turn the case over to you, then I have no choice. But at the moment I do have a choice, and I choose to have this organization retain control of the investigation."

Rabin looked at them, eyes blinking furiously. "I shall certainly inform Washington of your refusal to cooperate. You are making a very, *very* serious error of judgment."

He stood, gathered up hat and attaché case, stalked out. He didn't exactly slam the door behind him, but he didn't close it gently either.

"Thank you, sir," Tony said.

Crockett shrugged. "Calculated risk. I have some chits in Washington I'll have to call in on this, but I think we're safe for a time. I'll ask for six months. Can you do it?"

Harker drew a deep breath. "Sure," he said. He left the office and went directly to the bullpen. He found Henry Ullman at his desk, writing on a yellow legal pad.

"I know," Ullman said, looking up. "You want my report. You'll have it this afternoon."

"No, Hank," Tony said, "it's something else. Will you come to my office, please."

There he told the investigator about the disintegrating check.

"Son of a bitch," Ullman said. "That's a new one. Going to pick up Rathbone?"

"What for? The evidence is destroyed. And I want to give our plant a chance to track the source of the paper. Rathbone isn't the forger; he's the pusher, once removed. And I still

want to know what part Mike Mulligan is playing. He was
Rathbone's contact at the Crescent Bank. What have you got
on him?"

"Apparently a fine, upstanding citizen. No rap sheet. He's
clean with the IRS. Been with the bank almost thirty years.
Divorced. No children. Lives in a one-bedroom condo in a
plush development. Drives a two-year-old Buick. Goes to
church. Nothing in his lifestyle to indicate he's on the take."

"What kind of a guy is he?"

"You'd think, wouldn't you, that with a moniker like Mike
Mulligan he'd be a big, brawny, red-faced Irishman. Actually, he's a scrawny little guy, a real Caspar Milquetoast.
Elderly. White-haired. Wears horn-rimmed cheaters and
carries an umbrella on cloudy days. He's got a schedule during the week that never varies. People say they can set their
watches by him. For instance, every working day he leaves
the bank at precisely five o'clock, walks three blocks to a bar
called the Navigator. Mulligan sits in a back booth by himself
and has two extra-dry gin martinis straight up, no more, no
less. Then he goes home by cab. I got most of this personal
stuff from the barmaid, a mouthy broad. She says she's never
seen him drunk or with a woman."

"Have you been able to make contact?"

"Not yet. I've been hanging out at the Navigator, so now
I'm considered a regular. But the guy sits by himself way in
the back and doesn't talk to anyone. I'm afraid a direct approach might spook him. I've got a way to get to him, but
I'll need a partner. You have anyone I can borrow for an
afternoon?"

"Sorry," Harker said, "all my guys are out. What's your
idea?"

Ullman described it to him. "It's a neat scam," he finished.
"A variation of the good cop–bad cop routine. I've used it
before, and it works. But I need someone who can put on an
act."

"I think I could do it," Tony said.

"You sure?" Hank said. "If you blow it, I never will be able to get close to the guy."

"I won't blow it," Harker said. "Come on, let's do it today."

"Okay," Ullman said. "We both better take our cars because if this thing goes down, we won't be coming back together."

They discussed the details, and the Secret Service man drilled Tony on the role he was to play. Then they went out for hamburgers and fries before heading up Federal Highway.

They got to Boca Raton about three-thirty, Ullman leading the way in his dusty Plymouth. He pulled up in front of the Navigator Bar & Grill, signaled by waving an arm out the window, then drove away. Harker parked nearby, locked up, and walked back to the bar.

It was a long, narrow room, bar on the right, booths on the left. There were no customers. When Tony entered, the tall, rawboned barmaid put down the supermarket tabloid she was reading and gave him a gap-toothed smile.

"Am I ever glad to see *you*," she said. "I was beginning to wonder if we had a quarantine sign on the door."

As instructed by Ullman, Harker went to the rear and took the last barstool.

"Want to be by your lonesome, huh?" the barmaid said, coming down to stand before him. "What can I get for you, honey?"

"Vodka on the rocks. Splash of water."

"Any special brand?"

"Nah," he said. "The house vodka will do. They're all alike."

"If you say so," she said, made his drink, and put it on a cork coaster in front of him.

He drank it off in four deep swallows and set the empty glass down.

"Another," he said.

"Hoo, boy," she said, "someone was thirsty. Take it easy, honey; the day is young."

He made no reply and she gave up on him, going back to her tabloid. After he finished his second drink, he deliberately knocked over the glass, spilling ice cubes onto the bar.

"Clean this up, will you?" he said.

"Sure," the barmaid said, mopping up. "Happen to anyone. Another?"

"Yeah," Harker said. "Make it a double. This lousy vodka's got no kick." He threw a twenty on the bar.

"You're the boss," she said, but she was no longer smiling.

As he worked on his drink, patrons began to straggle in, taking seats at the bar. Two couples arrived and took a booth. At four-thirty Henry Ullman came in and stood near the center of the bar.

Harker signaled the barmaid. "Another double," he said in a loud voice. "You sure you're not watering this booze?"

She didn't reply but poured him a refill. Then she went back to where Ullman was standing. She leaned across the bar and whispered to him, jerking her head in Tony's direction.

At five after five, precisely, a white-haired man entered the Navigator. Harker figured he had to be Mike Mulligan. He was small, skinny, in a three-piece suit of gray tropical worsted. And he was wearing horn-rimmed specs. He went directly to the last booth and slid in. The barmaid was at his side almost instantly with a martini in a stemmed glass.

In about fifteen minutes, Tony glanced at Henry Ullman, and the big man nodded once. Tony got off his barstool and staggered slightly. He didn't have to fake that. He looked around a moment, then carried his drink over to Mike Mulligan's booth.

"Mind if I join you?" he said in a voice he hoped was suitably drunken.

"Yes, I would," Mulligan said. "I prefer to enjoy my drink alone."

"What're you, a goddamn hermit or something?" Harker said boozily. "Wassamatter, I'm not good enough for you?"

"Please," Mulligan said, staring straight ahead. "I just want to be left alone. All right?"

"Well, screw you, buster," Harker said in a loud voice. "I could buy and sell you any day of the week."

Now the bar had quieted, and all the customers were looking in their direction.

"I have to go now," Mulligan said, and tried to get out of the booth. But Harker blocked his way.

"I don't like your looks," he said. "You look like a real wimp to me."

The barmaid was heading toward the booth, hefting an aluminum baseball bat. But Henry Ullman got there first. He put a meaty hand on Tony's shoulder, spun him around.

"Okay, buddy," he said, facing Harker toward the door. "Out!"

"What?" Tony said, wavering on his feet. "Who're you to—"

"You heard what I said. *Out!*"

Tony hesitated, then looked up at the big man. "Lissen," he said. "I was only—"

Ullman pushed him toward the door. "On your way," he said. "Go sober up."

Harker stumbled toward the street, mumbling to himself, not looking at the people he passed. The joint didn't relax until he was gone.

"Thank you, sir," Mike Mulligan said to Ullman. "What a nasty fellow that was."

"He's drunk," Hank said. "But there's no excuse for acting like that."

"You're absolutely right," Mulligan said, "and I appreciate your assistance. May I buy you a drink?"

"Only if you let me buy the next round."

"Why not?" said Mike Mulligan.

19.

The best thing about this job, Roger Fortescue decided, was that his boss, Tony Harker, was letting him run free. None of this "Call me every hour on the hour" bullshit. Harker seemed to feel Roger was capable of figuring out what had to be done and then doing it. The investigator appreciated that. Maybe he moved slowly, but sooner or later he got there.

The *worst* thing about the job was that Estelle kept busting his balls about the hours he was keeping.

"I never know when you're coming home for dinner," she complained. "Or if you're coming home at all."

"It's my job, hon," he explained patiently. "It's what puts bacon on the table."

He looked up Frank Little's home address. It was way out in the boondocks, in Parkland north of Sample Road. Roger drove by slowly, but when he saw a sign on the fence, UN-LEASHED PIT BULLS, he decided not to stop. It was flatland with no cover or concealment, and Fortescue knew a stakeout would be impossible.

Little's home was really a ranch with a separate garage, outbuildings, and what looked big enough to be a three-horse stable. Roger figured the spread for maybe five acres. There was a guy on a sitdown power mower working one of the fields, and another guy with a long-handled net fishing dead palm fronds from the surface of a big swimming pool.

"Two million," Fortescue said aloud. "Sheet, *three* million!"

He drove back to Copans Road and cruised by the FL Sports Equipment layout. No activity. Just a car parked outside the office. And what a yacht that was! A 1959 white Cadillac convertible that appeared to be in mint condition. That grille! Those tailfins! Roger's Volvo seemed like a pushcart.

He noted again the boarded-up fast-food joint next to Little's place. That would be it, he suddenly decided; his home away from home.

He was right on time for dinner that night, bringing a five-pound boneless pork loin as a peace offering to Estelle. They put the pork in the fridge for the next day because she had already baked up a mess of chicken wings with hot barbecue sauce. They had that with home fries and pole beans. Beer for the adults, Cokes for the kids.

After dinner, Roger went upstairs, kicked off his loafers, and crashed for almost two hours, sleeping as if he had been sandbagged. Then he rose, changed to dungarees, checked his armament, and began assembling his Breaking & Entering kit: small crowbar, set of lockpicks, penlight, bull's-eye lantern, a shot-filled leather sap, binoculars, small transistor radio, and a cold six-pack of beer.

At about nine P.M. he drove back to Copans Road, past FL Sports Equipment, looking for a place to park. He finally located a likely spot, alongside a darkened garage that did muffler and shock replacements. He loaded up with his gear and trudged back to the deserted fast-food joint.

Traffic on the road was light, but he tried to stick to the shadows during his amble. In the rear of the derelict restaurant he found a weather-beaten door secured with a rusty hasp and cheap padlock. He could easily have wrenched it away with his crowbar but didn't want to leave evidence of an illegal entry. So he spent five minutes picking the lock, holding the penlight between his teeth. Then he pushed the creaking door open.

It was unexpectedly warm inside, and smelly. He heard the rustle of wildlife which he hoped was just rats and not snakes. He made a lantern-lighted tour through what had been the dining area, kitchen, lavatory, and a small chamber that had probably served as an office.

It was this last room he selected for his stakeout because it had a boarded-up window facing FL Sports Equipment, Inc. Prying two of the boards farther apart gave him a good view of the blockhouse, driveway, and warehouse. He dragged a rickety crate in from the kitchen to use as a chair, turned on his radio with the volume low, and popped a beer. Then he settled down to wait.

He was still waiting at four in the morning, peering out the window every few minutes and walking up and down occasionally to stay awake. The beer was finished, and his favorite radio station had gone off the air. He packed it in then, and lugged all his gear back to the Volvo. He left the padlock in the hasp, seemingly closed but actually open. He drove home, and when he went up to the bedroom, Estelle roused and said sleepily, "When do you want to get up?"

"Never," he answered, undressed, and rolled into bed.

But he was back at his hideout the following night, and for three more nights after that. Estelle stopped complaining about his crazy hours, and his sons seemed to like the idea of Daddy being home during the day.

By the time he decided to end his vigil, he had compiled four pages of notes on ruled paper he swiped from one of the kids' notebooks. He read over his jottings on what he had observed and tried to make some sense out of it all.

1. Deliveries were made to FL Sports Equipment, usually well before midnight, by trucks and vans with familiar names lettered on the sides. They were carriers working out of Port Everglades and the Fort Lauderdale–Hollywood Airport.

2. These deliveries were packed in wooden crates, some secured with steel bands. The boxes were long enough to hold smuggled AK-47s or other weapons, Roger reckoned, but he doubted if they did; each crate was handled easily by two men.

3. Pickups were made after midnight by an assortment of trucks, flatbeds, and vans, all with out-of-state license plates. Most of them were unmarked, although once the big Siena Moving & Storage semi showed up.

4. The pickups were cardboard cartons, and there was little doubt what they contained; one of them broke open and white baseballs went rolling all over the place. The loaders carefully collected every ball, and Frank Little, standing nearby with his clipboard, seemed to be verifying the count.

Fortescue, reading over his notes, concluded that for some reason the big wooden crates of baseballs were unpacked in the warehouse and their contents repacked into the smaller cardboard cartons.

One thing he couldn't understand was why the pickups, presumably by those wholesalers Frank Little had mentioned, were always made at godawful hours like two, three, and four o'clock in the morning. And why weren't the wholesalers' trucks painted with their names and addresses?

Most perplexing were the deliveries of imported baseballs from Port Everglades and the Lauderdale airport. After all, baseball was the National Pastime, the Great American Game. Surely baseballs would bear the stamp MADE IN THE USA.

"Hey, hon," Roger called to his wife, "you know that girl-friend of yours who works in the main Broward Library. The lady with the big teeth."

"You talking about Claire?" Estelle said. "Her teeth aren't so big. She's just got a lot of them is all."

"I guess. Well, will you give her a call and ask if she can look up where baseballs are made. Tell her I need the information as part of a crucial law enforcement investigation."

"Oh sure," Estelle said. "Baseballs are real crucial."

But she went into the living room to make the call, leaving Roger reading his notes in the kitchen, trying to see if he had missed anything.

Estelle came back in a half hour. "Claire has a cold," she reported. "She's afraid it might be the flu."

"That's a shame," Fortescue said. "Did she say she'd look up where baseballs are made?"

"She didn't have to look it up," Estelle said. "She knew right off. Most baseballs are made in Haiti."

Roger stared at her. "Haiti?" he said. "That's amazing."

20.

Rita arrived with a chilled bottle of premixed strawberry daiquiris and two plastic glasses. Harker took a blanket from his bed, and they went down to the beach. They sat close together, knees drawn up. It was a cool night, but there was no wind and there were so many stars that the cloudless sky looked as if it had been ordered from Tiffany's.

"How come you got out tonight?" Tony asked. "Don't tell me he's playing poker again."

"No," she said, "he told me he had a business conference. I said maybe I'd stop by the Palace and have a drink with the gang, but David said no one would be there. So I guess he's meeting with the other sharks."

"You know that check scam at the Crescent Bank?" Harker said. "Well, you're off the hook. There's no case against Rathbone. No evidence."

He told her how the Treasury check had disintegrated.

"Son of a bitch," she said. "No wonder he told me there was no risk. What do we do now?"

118

"We're working a couple of angles," Harker said. "Starting with Mike Mulligan at the Crescent. Listen, do you think you could find out where Rathbone got the check? We need to find the source of that trick paper."

"I asked him straight out, but no soap, he wouldn't say. I'll try again, but he's awfully closemouthed when his own neck is on the block. Tony, it's going to be tough to rack up this guy; he's smart."

"I know," Harker said, "but I'll get him. Sooner or later his greed will trip him up."

"Maybe," Rita said. "Pour me another, will you, baby?"

"I like your white pants," Tony said, filling her glass. "Real leather?"

"You better believe it."

"Rathbone buy them for you?"

"That's right. Any objection?"

"No," he said, "you're entitled. Rita, I don't want you to push him so hard he gets suspicious, but could you suggest that maybe he needs a secretary? A private secretary. You. The aim is to get into that locked office, take a look at his records, find out exactly how he's clipping the mooches."

"I don't think he'll go for it."

"Look, the way to manipulate this guy is through his love of money. He's got a corporation. Suggest to him that he could put you on the payroll legitimately. The corporation will pay your salary, and it'll reduce his corporate tax. The cash you get won't come out of *his* pocket; Uncle Sam will be financing your relationship."

She was silent a moment. "Yeah," she said finally, "that might work. He surely does worship the green."

"Give it a try," Harker urged. "Don't make a big deal out of it; just throw him the bait and see if he bites. I think he will."

"But putting me on salary as a secretary is no guarantee that he's going to let me in on his secrets."

"No, but it's a start. Maybe he'll like the idea of having

someone answer the phone, do his typing, go to the banks and post office for him. It'll make him feel like a tycoon."

Rita laughed. "You know," she said, "you just may be right. He thinks he's pretty important people. Okay, I'll see if I can grift the grifter. Hey, I'm getting goose bumps. Let's go to your place."

Back at the motel, Rita climbed into bed fully clothed. Still shivering, she pulled sheet and blanket up to her chin. Tony made her a cup of black coffee and brought it to her with a pony of cognac.

"Can't have you getting sick," he told her. "You're too valuable."

He sat on the edge of the bed and watched as she sipped coffee and brandy.

"That's better," she said. "I'm beginning to thaw. I really got a chill. I've never been sick a day in my life, and I sure don't want to start now."

He leaned back against the footboard. "Rita, how come you joined the police? Was your father a cop, or maybe a brother?"

"Nah, I'm an only child. And my father was a carpenter. He died five years ago. What happened was that a girlfriend was going to take the police exam and talked me into going along with her and taking it, too. Well, she flunked, and I passed. So then I thought, why not? It sounded more exciting than a typing job or working at K Mart."

"Ever regret it?"

"Never. It's been a hoot. Something new and different every day. I love it. Honey, turn off the light, will you. It's shining in my eyes."

He switched off the overhead light. When the brightness faded, their voices lowered, almost becoming murmurs.

"Do you plan to get out of it someday?" he asked. "Marry, settle down, have kids?"

"Who can plan a life? Looking ahead is a drag. I just take it day by day. When it gets routine, maybe I'll look around for a change. But right now I'm having a ball. How about you?"

"I like what I'm doing, and I happen to think it's worthwhile. There are worse ways to earn a living than putting crooks behind bars. Listen, Rita, I'd like to ask you something, but I'm afraid you'll get angry."

"Why don't you ask and find out."

"You're not falling for Rathbone, are you?"

She finished coffee and cognac, and leaned out of bed to put cup and glass on the floor. "I honestly don't know how I feel about him," she admitted. "Sometimes he can be so sweet and considerate that I have to keep reminding myself that he's an out-and-out thief. Also, he knows how to treat a woman. He washes my hair, gives me a super massage, goes shopping for clothes with me. And he's always giving me unexpected gifts. It's hard to hate a guy like that."

"I can imagine," Tony said.

"But I know I've got a job to do," she went on. "If I ever get to the point where the way I feel about him interferes with that job, I'll tell you and ask you to pull me out. Okay?"

"Sure," he said. "And not only for the sake of the job. Getting involved with that guy could be dangerous for you."

"I can handle it," she said. "Hey, I'm all warmed up now. So what I'm going to do is get undressed. And let nature take its course. How does that grab you?"

Just before nature took its course, she held his face between her palms, peered closely into his eyes.

"Are you sure you're not jealous?" she whispered. "Of David?"

"Maybe," he said. "Maybe I am. Because he spends so much more time with you than I can."

"That's sweet," she said. "Which means we'll have to make the most of the time we do have. Right?"

"Right," he said, and gently pulled her closer.

"Don't be afraid, honey," she said. "I bend, but I don't break."

21.

The living room of Frank Little's ranch was decorated in *faux* Texan: Indian rugs on the polished wood floor; deer antlers on the whitewashed walls; exposed beams overhead; a gun rack; sling chairs covered with pony hides. Looking at this set for a Western movie, and then inspecting Little in his silk slacks and sports shirt unbuttoned to the waist, hairless chest festooned with gold chains and amulets, David Rathbone could only think of the classic definition of a would-be Texan: "All hat; no cattle."

The five men were served drinks and cigars by Jacques, Little's Haitian houseboy. Jacques was nineteen, olive-skinned, sloe-eyed. He would last a year. Little replaced his houseboys annually, all clones of Jacques.

Rathbone waited until all five had drinks and Jacques had left the room. Then he said, "Here's what this is all about."

He outlined the proposed commodity trading fund, dealing only in "controlled substances," meaning marijuana, cocaine, heroin, and other illicit drugs. The fund would buy and sell options and futures, making a profit by the spread between buy and sell orders, and from the investors, who would, of course, be unaware of the true nature of the commodities being traded.

Bartlett would sign buy contracts with his clients. Little would sign sell contracts with his customers. Mort Sparco would organize the fund and peddle shares of the penny stock to his local accounts. Sid Coe would push the shares in his boiler room. Rathbone would serve as comptroller and chief executive officer.

"But none of us risks his own money," he said. "Start-up cash comes from Mort's suckers and Sid's mooches. We start out small and see how it goes. If it looks like a winner, we tie up with bucket shops all over the country and with penny stock brokers in Denver, giving them a piece of the action. All profits are split evenly five ways. How does it sound?"

"Let me get this straight," Frank Little said. "You want me to get my customers to sign contracts to buy?"

"Right," Rathbone said. "The drugs will be given code names, and you'll set a price for delivery in three, six, nine, and twelve months. Jimmy will do the same with the imports. The only way this is going to work is by analyzing what the future market will be like: how big the supply, how big the demand."

"I think you got a hot idea," Sparco said. "But take my advice and forget about trying to push options and futures. My pigeons just don't understand them. Buy low and sell high—that they can understand. But not the mechanics of future and option trading."

"Ditto the suckers on my lists," Coe said. "My yaks have a limited time to close a deal. They've got to keep their pitch short and sweet."

"That's what I told David," Bartlett said. "My clients work on a simple business principle: make a sale, get cash on delivery. They're willing to sign contracts at preset prices, but they know nothing about options."

"All right," Rathbone said, "then let's stick to basics. We set up the fund financed by sucker money. We pull a Ponzi to keep the early investors eager. But we invest the bulk of the cash in purchases for future delivery. Jimmy, can you trust your clients to honor signed contracts?"

"Some of them, sure. I know which ones we can trust. But buying the stuff is less a risk than selling it. Frank, will your customers honor a signed contract if, say, the price drops before you deliver? You follow? I mean if you promise H at 18K a kilo in six months, and then in six months the going price falls to 16K a kilo, will your guys ante up the 18K or will they renege?"

"Some of them will welsh," Little said. "But some I deal with have this big macho honor thing; they'll pay what they agreed on even if they have to take a bath."

They all fell silent as Jacques padded in with a tray of fresh drinks. They waited until he left the room before resuming their discussion.

"What about timing on this?" Rathbone asked. "Mort, how long will it take to set up the fund and get the shares printed?"

"A week or ten days. No more than that. My paperman works fast, and he turns out beautiful stuff. Old engravings on the shares. They really look legit."

"And what about you, Sid?" David said. "It shouldn't take long to write a script for your yaks on the new fund."

"I could do it tonight," Coe said, "if I knew what the name was. What are we going to call this thing?"

They stared at each other a moment.

"How about the Croesus Commodity Trading Fund?" Bartlett suggested.

Rathbone shook his head. "It won't fly," he said. "The mooches aren't going to know who Croesus was."

"How about this," Frank Little said. "The Fort Knox Commodity Trading Fund."

Everyone smiled.

"A winner," Sparco said. "And if the suckers think we're dealing in gold, so much the better."

The name decided, they then discussed their first deal. Bartlett urged that they start small with limited contracts for the purchase and sale of cocaine in three months' time.

"You've got to remember that I've never bought on my own," he said. "I just provide banking services. Being an importer is new to me, and I want to go easy at first."

"Same with me," Little said. "I'm just a transshipper and live off fees. My customers do their own buying."

"But if you can shave the price and deliver high-quality stuff," Rathbone said, "they'll buy from you, won't they?"

"No doubt about it. These are bottom-line guys."

"Good," David said. "I'll get to work on a standard contract and draw up a list of code names for the commodities we'll be handling. I'll also get some new software for my computer. Maybe a spreadsheet. If we're going to do this thing, let's do it right."

"The way I figure is this," Mort Sparco said. "What's the worst thing that could happen? That we lose all our money— right? Only it's not our money. So we've really got nothing to lose, and everything to gain. If we call the prices right and make a nice buck, we'll just pay the investors enough to keep them coming back—and pocket the rest. This could be a sweet deal."

"Yeah," Coe said, "even better than the Gypsy Handkerchief Drop." And they all laughed.

They had another round of drinks and discussed where and how to set up a checking account for the Fort Knox Commodity Trading Fund. They talked about the advisability of renting a small office, hiring a secretary, and having letterheads and business cards printed. Then the gathering broke up. Before they separated, they all shook hands as serious entrepreneurs starting a daring enterprise with exciting possibilities.

Rathbone had picked up James Bartlett at his home and had driven him to Frank Little's. Now, on the ride back to Bayview Drive, the two men briefly discussed the meeting.

"I was surprised at how easily it went," Rathbone said. "I didn't have to use the hard sell at all. Well, they're shrewd guys and could see the potential. Jimmy, it could be a bonanza if we have luck analyzing the future market."

"I think I know the man who can evaluate the supply and demand picture for us," Bartlett said. "He knows the drug scene inside out, from Bogotá to the South Bronx."

"Sounds good," David said. "Is he a dealer?"

Bartlett laughed quietly. "No," he said, "he's a federal narc who turned sour about four years ago. Now he's got accounts in Switzerland and the Cayman Islands I helped him set up. He'll be happy to help us."

"You sure? If he turned once, he can turn again."

Jimmy shrugged. "That's a risk we'll have to take. But I don't think it'll happen. He's in too deep."

"Well, tell him what we need and see what he comes up with. If he works out, we can always cut him in for a point or two. Jimmy, there's something else I want to talk to you about. You'll love it."

"Will I?" the other man said. "Try me."

Rathbone told him all about Termite Tommy, the old German printer in Lakeland, the self-destruct paper, and how he had passed a forged check at the Crescent Bank.

Bartlett didn't speak for a moment after David finished. Then: "You saw Termite Tommy's sample check after it had disintegrated?"

"With my own eyes. Believe me, it turned to confetti in about four days."

"No way he could have pulled a switch on you?"

"Come on, Jimmy; I'm no rube. That check just fell apart."

"And since Rita deposited the fake Treasury check, you've heard nothing about it? No cops knocking on your door at midnight?"

126

Rathbone rapped his knuckles on the walnut dash of the Bentley. "So far, so good," he said. "We got the cash, and Treasury has a handful of fluff."

"So what's your problem?"

"How to capitalize on this. I could keep buying new ID for Rita—or anyone else—and pulling the same scam on other Florida banks. But the take wouldn't be big enough. I thought of franchising the whole operation: selling pads of blank checks to paperhangers all over the country. But that wouldn't work; the checks would destruct before they got through the mail. You got any ideas?"

"I know a little about counterfeiting," Bartlett said, "and I can tell you one thing: That German never *made* the paper. Making paper is just too difficult and complex an operation for one guy. It would take forever. So counterfeiters buy standard grades of paper and doctor them to suit their needs. A lot of them soak paper in black coffee to give it a weathered look, like their fake bills have been handled. I knew a hustler who spent hours with a one-hair brush painting his paper with those tiny threads you see in U.S. currency."

"Well, if the German didn't make the paper himself, how did he get the checks to fall apart?"

"My guess is that he bought paper of Treasury check weight and stiffness, and then treated it with chemicals. Probably an acid. You know, David, the wood-pulp paper used in most books and magazines is acidic and will crumble to dust in about thirty years. I think the Kraut found a chemical that speeds up the process."

"Well, all I know is that it works, and I've been racking my brain trying to figure how to make the most of it."

"David, why did you use the trick paper in a check?"

"Why? I guess because Termite Tommy gave me a sample of the stuff in check form, and that got me thinking of how to turn a profit from self-destructing checks."

Bartlett sighed. "You know, you're one of the best idea men in the game. You've got a lot of creative energy. Like that commodity trading fund you came up with. But sometimes you go sailing ahead without thinking things through. You're so eager to cash in, you don't stop to wonder if there might be a less risky or more profitable way. One of these days your love affair with lucre is going to do you in."

"I don't see you passing up any surefire rackets, old buddy."

"I don't—if they *are* surefire. But I spend a lot more time than you do calculating the risk-benefit ratio. Look, David, you can go on hanging queer checks, hiring more pushers, buying more fake ID, but as far as I'm concerned, the risk outweighs the benefit. The banks are sure to be alerted by the Federal Reserve, and sooner or later they'll get to you."

"So you think I should just drop it?"

"I didn't say that. But there's a better way. You said this Lakeland printer did time for counterfeiting?"

"That's what Termite Tommy told me. He met the guy in the pokey. The German was doing five-to-ten. Tommy said he had been printing and wholesaling the queer, not pushing it."

"Well, there's your answer. Get him back to making twenties and fifties, using the self-destruct paper. Then anyone— you, me, the man in the moon—can deposit the queer cash in any bank account. If it gets by the teller, you're home free because in a couple of days those bills are going to be gone, and there'll be nothing to point to who made the deposit. How are they going to arrest you for pushing forgeries if there's no evidence? The only things left will be your deposit slip and the credit to your account."

Rathbone lifted one palm from the steering wheel to smack his forehead. "Now why didn't I think of that? It's a great idea. But maybe we should wholesale the stuff instead of pushing it ourselves. How do you feel about that?"

"Wholesaling is what put the Kraut behind bars, and he might be a little gun-shy about trying it again. There's another possibility that occurs to me. You know, in my laundering deals, the cash is brought to the banks' back doors in shopping bags or suitcases. Sometimes the banks don't even bother counting; they weigh it. And they certainly don't inspect every bill to make sure it's legit."

By that time they were parked in the brick driveway of Bartlett's home. Rathbone switched off the engine and turned to stare at the other man.

"Jimmy," he said, "let me guess what you're thinking. If we wholesale the queer self-destruct bills, we'll be lucky to get twenty percent of the face value. But if you can switch the fake bills with your clients' genuine bills, we'll get full face value."

"That's right," Bartlett said, "and so will my clients. They'll be credited for the correct total deposited. It's the banks that'll take the loss when the queer turns to dust."

"But won't the banks scream when their twenties and fifties fall apart?"

"Scream to whom?" Jimmy asked. "If they call in the law, they'll have to explain why they were accepting shopping bags full of cash at the back door. No, they'll take the loss and keep their mouths shut. They'll figure it's just the cost of doing business, and the profits are so enormous they'll keep on dealing. So it really ends up a win-win game."

"Brilliant," Rathbone said.

22.

The bullpen was on the second floor of Sidney Coe's office building, and although the ceiling and walls were sound-proofed, the place was bedlam.

Almost twenty yaks worked in that madhouse, their splintery desks cramped side by side. On each desk was a telephone, script, sucker list, and overflowing ashtray. The air conditioner was set at its coldest and operated constantly, but the smoky air in that crowded room rarely got below 80°, the humidity was a fog, and some of the men stripped to the waist.

The yaks were currently hawking platinum, selling ounce bars of the metal with "free insurance and storage" included in the sales price. At the moment, the price was $500 per troy ounce (ten ounces minimum purchase), and any mooch could consult the financial pages and see he was buying at $23 per ounce under the market price.

"Because we have an exclusive source of supply that's liable to dry up any minute, the demand is so great. Now's the time to get in on the greatest money-making opportunity we've ever offered. Here's the chance of a lifetime, but you've got to get in on it NOW! Tomorrow may be too late. How much can I put you down for? Mail in your check today, and then go shopping for a new Cadillac because you're going to be rich, *rich*, RICH!"

Twenty yaks made this pitch, talking into their phones as rapidly and loudly as they could so the mooch was confused, didn't have time to think, heard only the shouted NOW! and RICH!, and decided he better get in on this bonanza before the exclusive source of cheap platinum was exhausted.

Checks arrived daily from all over the country, so many in fact that Sid Coe made two trips to the bank every day, hoping the checks would clear before the mooches had second thoughts and stopped payment. Few did. Even more remarkable, suckers who had lost money with Instant Investments, Inc., on precious gems, uranium, rare coins, and oil leases, sent in checks for platinum, hoping to recoup their losses.

"They like to suffer, Cynthia," Sid opined to his wife. "I tell you it's pure masochism. For some reason they feel guilty and want to be punished."

"Thank you, Doctor Freud," she said.

Coe stalked the boiler room like a master lashing on his galley slaves. "Close the deal!" he kept yelling. "Close the deal, get a meal! Get the cash, buy the hash! Get the dough or out you go!"

He hung over their sweaty shoulders, nudging them, spurring them on. Occasionally he grabbed the phone from their hand and demonstrated his version of the hard sell: raucous, derisive, almost insulting.

"Go ahead," he'd shout. "Put your money in CDs and savings accounts. Take your lousy eight percent. Haven't you got the *guts* to be rich? Does it scare you to make real money? I'm offering you a chance to get out of that rut you're in. Do you want to live like a man or do you want to play kids' games all your life?"

Invariably he closed the deal.

Manny Suarez loved the place, couldn't wait to get to work in the morning. It was eight to twelve hours of noisy action, right up his alley. Coe assigned him one of the few vacant desks, gave him a script and sucker list, and turned him loose. Manny imitated the other yaks, with a few significant changes.

He picked out the Hispanic names on his list, and although he made the pitch rapidly in Spanish, he never shouted. Instead, his voice was warm, friendly. Their health? The health of their family? And how did they like the United Sta'? Then, after a few moments of his intimate chitchat, he launched into the spiel.

He discovered he had a real talent for bamboozling. He closed the deal on almost half his calls, a percentage that rivaled that of the most experienced yaks. And during the second day he was on the job, he sold $25,000 of nonexistent platinum to a mooch in Los Angeles, a coup that impelled Sid Coe to give him a $500 bonus on the spot.

Payday was Saturday afternoon. The yaks filed into the ground-floor office, one by one, and were paid their commissions in cash from a big stack of bills on Coe's desk, alongside a brutal .45 automatic. For his first week's work, Manuel Suarez earned over $900, including his five-yard bonus.

"You're doing real good," Coe told him. "You like the job?"

"It's hokay," Manny said. "But I need more Hispanic names."

"You'll get them," the boss promised. "I buy our sucker lists from a guy in Chicago who supplies most of the boiler rooms in the country. I called him, and he's going to run his master list through a computer and pull every Spanish-sounding name for us. He says it's a great idea, and he's also going to get up an Italian list, a French list, and a Polish list.

Apparently no one ever thought of ethnic sucker lists before. It could help the whole industry."

Suarez pocketed his earnings and drove down to head-quarters. It was then late Saturday afternoon, but Anthony Harker was still at his desk, working on a big chart that he covered up when Manny came into his office.

"Hey, man," Suarez said, flashing a grin, "I got a small problem."

"Yeah?" Tony said. "How small?"

"I just got paid at Coe's boiler room. Do I gotta turn in the moaney to this organization or what?"

"I asked Crockett. He says you'll have to turn in the money. Sorry."

"Hokay," Suarez said.

"By the way," Harker said, "how much did you make?"

"Almost three hundred," Suarez said, and bopped out to his car, snapping his fingers and smiling at all the women he passed.

He stopped at a few stores before returning to the home of the Cuban lady where he was staying. She was nicely put together. And she seemed *muy simpática*. Manny bought five pounds of barbecued ribs, a liter of light Puerto Rican rum, and drove homeward whistling "Malagueña."

On Monday morning there were new scripts on all the yaks' desks. They were no longer peddling platinum. Now they were to push shares of stock in something called the Fort Knox Commodity Trading Fund. One dollar per share; 1,000 shares minimum. Suarez picked up his phone and went to work.

23.

On his way to Birdie Winslow's condo, David Rathbone stopped at a florist on Atlantic Boulevard. The place was crowded, with two clerks trimming and wrapping flowers at a back counter.

Just inside the door was a display of lavender mums. They were bunched by the dozen with maidenhair, each bouquet held by a rubber band. The sign read: $20 PER DOZEN. Glancing at the busy clerks to make certain he was unobserved, Rathbone selected a bouquet, then slipped a single mum from another bunch and added it to his selection. He took the thirteen flowers to the desk, had them wrapped in green tissue, paid the $20 plus tax, and was on his way.

Mrs. Winslow met him at the door of her apartment clad in a paisley muumuu that hid her lumpish body. David proffered his bouquet.

"A dozen mums!" she cried. "How *divine!*"

"Baker's dozen," he said, smiling. "About an eight-point-four percent return on investment."

"What?" she said, puzzled. "Well, they're lovely, and I thank you for them. But you've been a naughty, naughty boy. You haven't called me once, and I thought you had just forgotten little old me."

"No chance of that," he said, touching her cheek. "But I've been to Europe since I saw you last and came home to a deskful of work."

She motioned toward the couch, then took the mums into the kitchen. She returned with the flowers in a crystal vase half-filled with water.

"Don't they look *divine?*" she said. "Lavender is one of my favorite colors. Now where shall I put them?"

He glanced around. He couldn't blame her for the way the apartment was furnished since it was a rented condo, but the decoration was really horrendous, the upholstery and wallpaper all fuchsia poppies and bilious green palm fronds.

"Perhaps on top of the TV set," he suggested.

She placed the vase there and stood back to admire the effect. "Sooo pretty," she murmured. Then: "I made a pitcher of your favorite—vodka gimlets."

"Just what I was hoping for."

She brought him a warm drink in a small glass with one lone ice cube. He sipped and decided it had to be the worst vodka gimlet he had ever tasted, so limey that it puckered his lips.

"Delicious," he said. "Aren't you having any?"

"A diet cola for me," she caroled. "I've been trying so hard to lose weight."

"Oh Birdie," he said, "you're not too heavy. You're like my gimlet—just right."

"Thank you, kind sir," she simpered, brought her drink and sat close to him on the couch.

He lifted his glass in a toast. "Here's to health and wealth," he said.

"And love," Mrs. Winslow said, looking at him through her false lashes. "Don't forget love."

135

He set his drink on the glass-topped cocktail table. "Birdie, I hope you've been getting your statements regularly."

"Yes, I have, and that's something I want to talk to you about."

"Is anything wrong?"

"Well, my next-door neighbor has an account with Merrill Lynch, and he says that every time he buys something or sells something he gets a confirmation slip. Should I be getting confirmation slips, David?"

"None of my clients ask for them, but you can certainly have them if you wish. I just didn't want to flood you with a lot of unnecessary paper. After all, the purchases and sales I make on your behalf show up every month on your statement."

"That's true. So you don't think I need confirmations?"

"Not really. Just more paper to file away and forget."

"I suppose you're right. I can't tell you how pleased I am with the way my money has grown."

"And it's going to do even better," he said. "Why, just this morning I got a tip from a friend on Wall Street about a new commodity trading fund that's being organized. If we get in on the ground floor, I can practically guarantee a fifty-percent return."

"Oh David, that *is* exciting!"

He finished his drink manfully. But it did him no good; she brought him another.

"Now let's forget about business for a while," she said, "and just relax. It's been so long since we've been together. I hope you don't have to rush off."

"Not immediately," he said. "But I do have an appointment in about an hour."

"Plenty of time," she assured him. She rose, held her hand out to him. "I bought a new clock-radio for the bedroom," she said. "Would you like to see it?"

She was naked under the muumuu and smelled of pa-

136

tchouli. But in situations like this—and he had experienced many—he resolutely closed his mind to physical stimuli, or the absence thereof, and concentrated only on the profits this suppliant woman represented. Then he was able to perform competently, his mind detached and calculating.

He left her lolling on the rumpled sheets. He dressed swiftly, kissed her cheek, and murmured, *"Divine!"* Then he drove home, windows open, gulping the salty sea air. Back in the town house, he gargled, brushed his teeth, and showered. He hoped he merely imagined that the scent of patchouli still clung to him.

He mixed a decent vodka gimlet, a double in a tall tumbler with plenty of ice and fresh lime. He carried it upstairs to the terrace. It was a warm day but cloudy, with rumblings of thunder westward. He hoped for a driving rain that might wash everything clean and leave the world shining.

He was still on the terrace, a few fat drops beginning to splatter, when Rita returned.

"You're going to get soaked," she warned. "It was pouring at the Pompano Mall."

"I won't melt," he said. "Did you ever walk through puddles when you were a kid?"

"No, and I never toasted marshmallows. I had a deprived childhood. I'm going to take a shower."

"I'll mix us drinks and bring them to your bedroom."

"That's a good boy," she said.

When he brought the drinks up from the kitchen she was still in her bathroom, the shower running. He sat on the edge of her bed, sipped his gimlet. He knew that in a few moments he would be the suppliant, a reversal of the roles he and Mrs. Winslow had played, and he wondered idly if love might be a lose-lose game.

Rita came out of the bathroom dripping, wiping her shoulders and arms. She handed him the towel and turned. Obediently he dried her back, with long, slow strokes.

"Guess what," she said. "I was wandering through the Mall, just looking around, and I bumped into an old girlfriend I haven't seen in years. Claire McDonald. We used to party together in Tallahassee. We had lunch together and talked over old times."

She took the damp towel from his hand and tossed it onto the floor. Then she sat down next to him on the bed, picked up her drink, took a sip.

"Claire looked like she had won the lottery: dressed to kill, her fingers covered with rocks. The real stuff, too. She told me this older guy was sponsoring her. 'Sponsoring.' I never heard it called that, did you?"

"Never did," Rathbone said, smiling.

"Anyway, her guy owns two restaurants in the Orlando area, so I guess he's got *mucho dinero.* They drove down to scout a location in Lauderdale for a new restaurant. She says he put her on the payroll of his company as a secretary; the corporation pays her salary. So the money he gives her doesn't come out of his pocket, it just reduces his corporate income tax. David, could you do that? Make me a secretary in your company? That way you wouldn't have to give me your own money. It would just be a business expense."

"Well, that's one way of looking at it," Rathbone said. "But by paying her a salary, he's also reducing his corporation's after-tax income. So one way or another, she's costing him."

"So you don't want to hire me as your private secretary?"

"Afraid not," he said, laughing. "But I'm willing to sponsor you."

They put their drinks aside. He took off his robe and they slid into bed. The thunder was closer, then overhead, then dwindling away. But it was raining heavily, streaming down the windows. The room was filled with a faint ocher light, dim and secret.

She let him do all the things that she knew pleasured him.

She lay almost indolent, staring at the fogged windows, until her body roused. Then she closed her eyes, listened to the rain and the sounds he was making. Finally she heard nothing but the thump of her own heart, and cried out. But he would not stop, or could not, and she suffered him gladly.

At last he emerged panting from under the sheet, his hair tousled, a wild, frightened look in his eyes.

"Are you all right?" he asked anxiously.

She smiled, took his face in her hands, kissed his smeared lips.

"Let's do it again, lover," she said.

He managed a small smile, then got out of bed and stalked naked about the darkened room, hands on his hips.

"I thought I might die," he said.

"Die? From what?"

"It was too much. I couldn't stop."

"No one dies from too much love."

"I was afraid I was hurting you."

"You didn't. I'm a tough girl."

"I know. Do you need anything?"

"Like what?"

"Kleenex? A washcloth?"

"Nope. I like the way I feel. Now, stop pacing and come over here."

He stood alongside the bed. She leaned to him.

"Now it's my turn," she said.

Within minutes he was shuddering and sobbing. She was tender-cruel and would not let him move away until he surrendered, his mouth open in a silent scream. Then he collapsed facedown across the bed.

"I died and I was born again," he said. "And then I died and was born again."

"That's the way to do it," she said. "Don't ever stop halfway."

He reached under the sheet, grasped her left foot, pulled

it to his lips, kissed the instep. Then he looked up at her. "Don't ever leave me, Rita."

"Why should I do that? It's hard to find a sponsor like you." She saw the focus in his eyes change. "Why are you looking at me like that? A penny for your thoughts."

"They're worth more than that. I just had a great idea. I don't want to put you on my payroll, but I know how you can make a steady salary."

"Pushing your queer checks?"

"No, that scam's on hold. But the Palace gang and I are starting a new business, and we'll need a secretary."

"Yeah? What kind of business?"

"It's an investment company. Ellen St. Martin is looking for office space for us. We'll need someone to answer the phone and type a few letters. You can type, can't you?"

"Oh sure. Hunt and peck."

"Good enough. How about it? Would you like an office job?"

"Does it mean I'll have to sit behind a desk eight hours a day?"

"Nah. We'll get you an answering machine, so you can come and go as you please."

"Sounds good," she said.

"To me, too. Because your salary won't be coming out of my pocket; just one-fifth of it."

"You think the other guys will go for it? Hiring me, I mean."

"Sure they will. We'll have an office and a secretary; everything on the up-and-up."

"What's this new business called?"

"The Fort Knox Commodity Trading Fund. Like it?"

"Love it," she said.

24.

Simon Clark still resented what he considered a demotion to Florida. In the Chicago office of the U.S. Attorney he had been an executive, a man of substance. He rarely had been personally involved in outside inquiries. He sat at a desk, collected and assimilated reports from detectives, analyzed evidence, prepared briefs, obtained arrest warrants, and finally represented the DA's office in court.

Now he was being called upon to assume the role of what he had scathingly called a "gumshoe." But to his surprise, he found he was enjoying it. The investigation of Mortimer Sparco's discount brokerage required the talents of an actor, and nothing in Clark's education or experience had prepared him for the job. But his ego was not small, and he grudgingly accepted the fact that to nail Sparco, he had to prove himself the more accomplished liar.

There was no difficulty in obtaining sting money from Lester Crockett's office. The $10,000 was deposited in a local bank suggested by Crockett. It took less than a week to obtain a book of blank checks imprinted with Clark's name.

Meanwhile, he had another meeting with Sparco, and on his recommendation bought two different dollar stocks, neither of which was listed on any exchange. One company, according to the broker, had developed an electronic booster for solar cells, and the other, Sparco claimed, was about to market a revolutionary remedy for baldness. The purchase of the two stocks almost depleted Clark's bank account.

Then Sparco called his hotel and asked him to drop by to hear "some really sensational news." When Clark arrived, the broker took him into his private office and announced he had sold out both stock positions, and Clark had a profit of slightly more than $3,000.

"Why, that's wonderful!" the investigator said. "You're certainly doing a bang-up job. I had no idea I could make so much money so quickly. I hope you have more suggestions as good."

Sparco looked about cautiously, then lowered his voice. "I have a special deal I'm restricting to a select list of clients. Even my account executives don't know about it. Look, there's a restaurant across the street called the Grand Palace. It has a bar in the back that should be deserted this time of day. Why don't we go over there for a drink and a private talk. This investment opportunity is so hot I don't even want to mention it in the office. The walls have ears, you know."

Sparco told the receptionist he'd be right back, and then they dodged through traffic on Commercial Boulevard and entered the Palace Lounge through the side door. They were the only customers, and Ernie brought their drinks to a rear table tucked into a shadowed corner.

"Do you know anything about commodities?" Sparco asked in a conspiratorial whisper.

"Commodities?" Clark said. "You mean like corn, wheat, soybeans?"

"Exactly. Well, about a week ago, a new, SEC-approved

142

investment vehicle was organized on Wall Street. It's called the Fort Knox Commodity Trading Fund. I heard about it through a close friend. The man running the Fund is a genius in commodity trading. A *genius!* He's made a lot of people multimillionaires, and now he's decided to do the same thing for himself. He's keeping a controlling interest, of course, but through my friend I was able to tie up a limited number of shares. Not as many as I wanted because when this fund is announced publicly, the share value will double overnight. At least! It's your chance to get in on the ground floor."

It was an impressive spiel and, Simon Clark reflected, shattered at least three regulations governing the sale of securities.

"The only problem," Sparco went on, "is that because of the limited number of shares I was able to get at the initial offering price, I had to set $50,000 as a minimum investment. I have one package left. Do you think you can swing it?"

"Gee, I don't know," Clark said. "I really don't have that much ready cash."

"Uh-huh," Sparco said, glancing at his watch. "Didn't you tell me your parents live down here?"

"That's right. They have a home in Plantation."

"Think your father would be willing to loan you the money? Just for a short time until you take your profits."

"To tell you the truth, I don't think he has that much cash available. Everything he owns is tied up in his home and long-term government bonds."

"He could get a home-equity loan," Sparco said, looking at his watch again. "The bank doesn't have to know what it's really for. He can tell them home improvements, and they'll accept that."

"I can ask him," Clark said. "You're positive this is a sure thing?"

"Can't miss," Sparco said. "I've been in business fifteen years, and this is the hottest—"

The side door of the Lounge banged open, and a short,

stout man came bustling in. He paused until his eyes became accustomed to the darkness. Then he looked around, spotted the two men at the rear table, and rushed over.

"Mort," he said, "you've got to get me another 50K of that commodity fund. I just heard that the price of shares in the secondary market is already up thirty percent and—"

Sparco rose and put a finger to his lips. "Shhh, Jimmy," he said. "Not so loud. Mr. Clark, this is James Bartlett, a valued client. Jimmy, this gentleman is Simon Clark. We were just discussing the Fund."

"Grab it," Bartlett said to Clark, shaking his hand. "And if you don't want it, I do. Mort, you've got to get me more."

"I'll do my best," Sparco said. "Call me in the morning and I'll let you know."

"I'm depending on you!" Bartlett cried. "Nice to have met you, Mr. Clark." And he scurried out.

Sparco smiled. "Jimmy's a banking consultant and knows a good deal when he sees one. How about it, Mr. Clark? Think you can get your father to take out a home-equity loan? It's the last package of Fund shares I have available, and I'd hate to see you miss out on a dynamite opportunity like this."

Clark considered a moment. "I'll convince my father," he said finally. "Can I call you later today?"

"Anytime before five o'clock. If you haven't called by then, I'll have to give it to someone else. Bartlett isn't the only client begging for more."

They left the Palace Lounge, shook hands, and separated. Sparco returned to his brokerage. When he walked into his office, James Bartlett was seated on the leather couch smoking a fat cigar.

While the two men had a drink from Sparco's office bottle of Chivas, Simon Clark sat in his rented Cutlass, pausing a moment before he drove to headquarters to request additional sting money.

He found it hard to believe the crudeness of south Florida swindlers. Sparco's claiming a profit on Clark's first two investments was an ancient technique used by con men of all stripes, from pool hustlers to bait-and-switch retailers: Let the mark win, or *think* he's winning. Then, when he plunges heavily, overcome by greed, cut his balls off.

Even more primitive was Sparco's use of a shill. That Jimmy Bartlett was no more a legitimate investor than Clark himself. The two slickers had staged the scene in the bar, confident it would convince the pigeon that he *had* to invest in a get-rich-quick deal and do it *now*.

Compared to the sharks on Wall Street and in Chicago's commodity pits, these south Florida chiselers were pilot fish. And yet, for all their dated tricks, they seemed to be thriving. Probably, Clark decided, because they were preying on an ever-growing population of financially unsophisticated retirees trying desperately to augment their Social Security and pension incomes during a time of horrendous inflation.

But if mutts like Sparco and Bartlett could flourish, Clark thought, what might an operator do who knew all the latest methods of duping money-hungry suckers? There was a fortune to be made, and if you knew the law, as Clark did, the risk was negligible.

It was, he decided, a prospect he'd have to consider seriously. The climate of south Florida was super, and there were more than oranges to be plucked.

25.

"What exactly *is* the Fort Knox Commodity Trading Fund?"
Lester T. Crockett asked. "Do you know?"

"Negative, sir," Harker said.

They were standing in Tony's office, looking down at the
chart spread across his desk. It was an organization diagram
with a box at the top labeled David Rathbone. Straight lines
led to four smaller boxes: Mortimer Sparco, Sidney Coe,
James Bartlett, Frank Little. The boxes also contained the
names of the assigned investigators: Rita Sullivan, Simon
Clark, Manuel Suarez, Henry Ullman, Roger Fortescue.

Within each box was written the subject's ostensible occu-
pation and his relationship with any of the other suspects.

"Here's what we've got so far," Harker reported. "Rathbone tells Sullivan that he and the guys from the Palace are
organizing a new business, the Fort Knox Commodity Trading Fund. They've rented a small office on Federal Highway.
Sullivan goes to work there tomorrow as a secretary, the Fund
paying her salary.

"Suarez says Coe is pushing shares of the Fund in his boiler room, and Clark says Sparco is doing the same thing in his brokerage. Clark also confirms that Bartlett is in on it. The only one whose connection remains iffy is Frank Little, but I'm betting he's a partner, too.

"And that's about all I've got so far, sir. It's possible, of course, that the Fund is an out-and-out swindle, it really doesn't exist, and they're selling shares in soap bubbles."

"But you don't believe that?" Crockett asked.

"No, sir. If the whole thing is just one big goldbrick, why go to the bother of renting an office and hiring a secretary?"

"Just as a front?"

"Maybe," Harker said, "but I think there's more to it than that. They're having letterheads and business cards printed up, like this is a company that's going to be in business for a while."

"Registered?"

"Not with the SEC, the Chicago Board of Trade, the Chicago Mercantile Exchange, or the State of Florida. They may have offshore registration, but I've been unable to find any evidence of it. I'm hoping Sullivan will be able to tell us more about the nature of the Fund after she's been working in their office awhile."

Crockett thrust his hands in his pockets, hunched his shoulders, stared down at the chart. "Of course," he said, "we could pick up the entire mob right now, on charges of security fraud, mail fraud, and conspiracy. And maybe throw the RICO book at them for good measure."

Harker stared at him. "You don't really want to do that, do you, sir?"

"No," Crockett said, "because the moment we put the cuffs on Rathbone, he'll clam up about the source of that self-destructing check. Have you learned anything more about it?"

"According to Sullivan, Rathbone said that scam's on hold."

"Do you believe that?"

147

"No—but no more of those queer checks have been reported."

"Ullman is still working on the bank officer?"

"Yes, sir. He's become very buddy-buddy with Mike Mulligan. So I'm expecting a break there."

"Soon, I hope," Crockett said. "The Washington brass keep pushing me. All I can do is keep pushing you. And all you can do is keep pushing Ullman."

"I intend to," Tony said.

"Good. Anything else?"

"Yes, sir. Have you come to any decision about bugging Rathbone's town house?"

"No," Crockett said, "not yet. I'll let you know." And he tramped out of Harker's office.

Tony sat down behind his desk, bent over the chart. He felt aswirl in swindles, and not all of them by the crooks: The good guys, in the course of their investigations, were pulling their share of cons, too. Harker was troubled by it, couldn't convince himself of the need to "fight fire with fire." His distress went deeper than that.

He presumed that if you were forced to live in a slum, eventually the ugliness of your surroundings would seep into your nature. Maybe without even being aware of it, you'd begin to think ugly thoughts, say ugly things, act in ugly ways.

Similarly, he now found himself in an environment where everyone lied, schemed, cheated. He had done it himself in the Navigator Bar in Boca. He wondered if, over time, this atmosphere of connivance might corrupt him to such an extent that deceit became normal and he would palter as naturally as he breathed.

He stared down at his chart, at the name of Rita Sullivan. She was a good cop, his most valuable operative, and he appreciated the job she was doing. But he wondered if he had become so tainted by this world of deception that he was now capable of conning himself.

26.

Henry Ullman took it easy with Mike Mulligan, playing him slowly and not asking too many personal questions. The bank officer seemed to enjoy meeting Ullman for drinks every evening after work. Once he invited the investigator to his home for dinner. His condo looked as if it had been decorated by a department store, and was so spotlessly clean that it was difficult to believe anyone lived there.

Ullman told him the same cover story he had given James Bartlett: His name was Samuel Henry, and he was a mortgage loan officer at First Farmers' Savings & Loan in Madison, Wisconsin. He had come to south Florida to see if he and his wife could relocate. Mulligan accepted this fiction without question, especially since the two men spent a lot of time talking shop, and Ullman was obviously knowledgeable about banking procedures.

They were in the back booth of the Navigator on Friday evening when Mulligan said, "Sam, how about dinner at my place tomorrow night?"

149

"You've already fed me once," Ullman protested. "Now it's my turn."

"No, no," Mulligan said, smiling. "Maybe some other time, but tomorrow is going to be a special occasion. I'll send out for Italian food, and after dinner a couple of guests are going to drop by."

"Oh? Friends of yours?"

"Sort of," Mulligan said. "I think you'll like them."

On Saturday night, Ullman arrived at Mulligan's apartment bearing two cold bottles of Chianti, having learned that practically everyone in south Florida preferred their red wine well chilled. The food had already been delivered and was being kept warm in the oven. Mulligan had ordered antipasto, veal piccata, spaghetti all'olio, and arugula salad.

They each had two martinis before sitting down to eat. They finished a bottle and a half of Ullman's Chianti during dinner. Then Mulligan served big snifters of brandy. By that time the little man was feeling no pain, blinking rapidly behind his horn-rimmed glasses and occasionally giggling. He tried to tell a joke about an Englishman, a Frenchman, and an American, but forgot the punch line. Ullman wondered if his host would still be on his feet when his guests arrived.

They showed up around ten-thirty: two tall, thin women who appeared to be in their late thirties. They were introduced to Ullman as Pearl and Opal Longnecker, sisters, who worked at a Crescent Bank branch in Deerfield Beach.

Both women were rather gaunt, with lank hair and horsey features. They were drably dressed except for their shoes: patent leather pumps; kelly green for Opal, fire-engine red for Pearl. They sat primly on the couch and politely refused the offer of a drink. They spoke little, but answered questions in a heavy southern accent.

Ullman made them for a couple of rednecks and hoped, for the sake of Crescent Bank's public relations, their jobs—

maybe data entry work—were in a back room where their speech patterns and appearance were unimportant. He couldn't understand what staid, respectable Mike Mulligan had in common with these unattractive and uncommunicative women.

After about ten minutes of desultory conversation, Opal rose and announced, "I gotta use the little girls' room."

"I'll come with you," Pearl said, standing.

Ullman noted they went directly to the bathroom without asking directions.

"What do you think of them, Sam?" Mulligan asked.

Ullman took a sip of his brandy. "They seem very nice," he said. "But quiet."

The host had a fit of giggling. "You'll see," he said, spluttering, "you'll see. You're the guest, so you take the bedroom. I'll make do on the couch."

"What?" the investigator said, bewildered. "What are you talking about, Mike?"

"You'll see," the little man repeated, and sloshed more brandy into his glass.

The Longnecker sisters came out of the bathroom about fifteen minutes later. They were laughing, holding hands, practically skipping.

"Whee!" Opal cried.

"It's party time!" Pearl shouted, eyes glistening. "Time for all good men to come to the aid of the party. Let's go, big man." And she held out her hand to Henry Ullman.

He turned to look at Mulligan. The bank officer had taken off his glasses and pulled Opal onto his lap. His hand was thrust beneath her skirt. He saw Ullman staring at him.

"Go ahead," he urged. "Pearl will do you good."

Henry followed her into the darkened bedroom, but then she turned on all the lights.

"I like to see what I'm doing," she said.

"Shall I close the door?"

"What the hell for? Wait'll you hear Mike huffing and puffing. It's a scream!"

She undressed so swiftly that he was still taking off his socks when she was naked, lying on the bed and kicking bony legs in the air.

"C'mon, hurry up," she demanded. "I been waiting all week for this, and I'm hot to trot. Oooh, look at the big man. What a sweet cuke!"

He had never had a woman like her before and wasn't certain he'd live to have another. She was demented, insatiable, and wrung him out. She was still at it twenty minutes later, long after he had collapsed, drained. Suddenly she stopped, jumped out of bed.

"Little girls' room," she said, panting. "Don't go away."

Ullman lay in a stupor, thinking this was above and beyond the call of duty, and wishing he might find the strength to rise, dress, and stumble out of that madhouse. But then naked Opal came bounding into the lighted bedroom.

"Turnabout's fair play!" she yelled, and he saw in her eyes what he expected to see.

It was another half-hour before he could get away from her, stagger to his feet, go reeling into the bathroom. He soaked a washcloth in hot water and swabbed off his face and body.

Then he started looking for it.

He checked all the boxes, jars, and bottles in the medicine cabinet, but it wasn't there. It wasn't behind the frosted glass doors of the bathtub. Then he did what he should have done in the first place: lift the porcelain lid of the toilet tank.

There it was: a watertight mason jar containing at least a dozen little glassine envelopes filled with a white powder. He took out the jar, unscrewed the lid, removed one of the envelopes. Then he tightened the lid, replaced the jar in the water-filled tank.

Ullman opened the door cautiously. There was talk and

laughter coming from the living room. He heard the voices of the two women and, as promised, the huffing and puffing of Mike Mulligan. He slipped into the bedroom, put the glassine envelope deep in the breast pocket of his jacket.

Then he went back to the living room. Mulligan, his body fish-belly white, mouth smeared, eyes bleary, was sprawled on the couch, and both women were working on him. They all looked up when Ullman entered.

"Party time!" he bawled.

27.

A new discount drugstore had opened on Federal Highway and had quickly become a mecca for every hustler in Broward County. All because the owner was using peel-off price labels on his merchandise and wasn't yet aware of how he was being taken.

David Rathbone stopped by to stroll through the crowded aisles. He selected Halston cologne for himself and Chanel dusting powder for Rita. He casually switched the price labels with those from a cheap after-shave and an even cheaper face powder, and brought his purchases to the desk where a harried clerk was trying to cope. She rang up the sale without question, and Rathbone carried his bargains out to the Bentley, reflecting on the credo of con men everywhere: "Do unto others before others do unto you."

He drove to the office of the Fort Knox Commodity Trading Fund, north of Atlantic Boulevard. He parked and carefully removed the incorrect price label from the box of Chanel dusting powder. Then he entered the office. Rita was listening to a transistor radio, sandaled feet on her desk. He leaned to kiss her cheek.

"Hi, boss," she said. "What's going on?"

"A present for you," he said, handing her the powder. "Just for the fun of it."

"Thanks a mil," she said, sniffing at the box. "Hey, this stuff is expensive."

"Only the best for you," he said, touching her cheek. "We travel first class."

"Oh? Are we going to travel?"

"Maybe," he said. "Someday. Any excitement around here?"

"Oh sure," she said. "A real hectic morning. The stationery store delivered the letterheads and business cards."

"Let me take a look."

She showed him the five boxes of business cards bearing the name, address, and phone number of the Fund, plus the names of the Palace gang in elegant script.

"No titles," Rita pointed out. "Are you president, or what?"

"We're all equal partners," he said. "No titles. I like these letterheads and envelopes. Very impressive. Listen, I have a little work to do here, and then I've got to go visit a client."

"Yeah? Man or woman?"

"A widow lady named Birdie Winslow. Every now and then she gets antsy about her investments, and I have to hold her hand."

"Make sure that's all you hold. Honey, I'm bored. This is a real nothing job."

"Hang around until I'm finished, then turn on the answering machine, lock up, and go get some sun. It's a super day."

He went into the inner office and closed the door. Rita took a single business card from each of the five boxes and slipped them into the top desk drawer. Then she fished an emery board from her shoulder bag and went to work on her nails.

David came out of the inner office in less than twenty minutes.

"That was quick," she said.

"I've had my fun, and now I'm done. Maybe I'll take those business cards along with me. If we see the gang for drinks tonight, I'll hand them out. They'll get a kick out of them."

"You guys are like kids with a new toy. Are we eating at home tonight?"

He thought a moment. "Why don't we have dinner at the Palace? Then we can have drinks later in the Lounge."

"The Palace? I've never eaten there. How's the food?"

He flipped a palm back and forth. "So-so. They have a double veal chop that's edible. But I don't eat there very often. It's the kind of restaurant that never throws out unused butter, half-eaten rolls, or unfinished steaks. They recycle everything."

"Isn't that illegal?"

He laughed. "Come on," he said, "you know better than that. So they make beef bourguignonne out of leftover steak. Who's to know?"

"I'm not sure I want to eat there," she said.

"Don't tell me you're a straight arrow," he said. "If you found a wallet on the street with a hundred bucks in it and the owner's phone number, would you return it to him?"

"Probably not. I'd keep the money and drop the wallet in a mailbox."

"So would I. So would anyone with an ounce of sense. If the owner is dumb enough to lose his wallet, he's got to pay for his stupidity. Would you steal a towel from a hotel?"

"I might."

"Not me. It's not a class act."

"What's boosting a hotel towel got to do with eating other people's garbage at the Palace?"

"I'm just proving to you that everyone cuts corners. I wouldn't swipe a hotel towel, but I'd clip a mooch for every cent he's got. I enjoy outwitting suckers, but I'd never bash one over the head in a dark alley. I have my standards."

"I guess you do at that."

"Just remember the Golden Rule: He who has the gold, rules. See you later, honey."

She watched him drive away, then went into the inner office. She had to admit they hadn't stinted on the furnishings: new steel desks and file cabinets, leather-covered chairs and Simbari prints on the freshly painted walls.

There was nothing in the unlocked desk except a few scratch pads and pencils. She wondered what "work" David had been doing in there. Then she saw three pieces of crumpled paper in the shiny brass wastebasket. She scooped them out, went back to her own desk, and examined them. They seemed to be three lists of words, five on each list:

1. Machines, melons, mousetraps, mittens, mangoes.
2. Chairs, computers, cherries, corkscrews, catalogs.
3. Hammers, hubcaps, honeydews, heels, hats.

Three of the items had little checkmarks next to them: melons, chairs, and hammers.

She phoned Tony Harker.

"Where are you?" he asked.

"In the office. David was here for a while but he's gone now. I'm taking off in a few minutes. I'm going to hit the beach and tan my buns."

"That I'd like to see," Tony said. "Anything going on?"

"*Nada.* Except they delivered the business cards and letterheads. I lifted one card from each box and figured I'd mail them to you."

"Good idea. Is there one for Frank Little?"

"Yep."

"Bingo. That ties him up with the Fort Knox Commodity Trading Fund—whatever that is. Now we know they're all in on it."

"Something else," Rita said, and told Harker about the

crumpled pieces of paper she had found in the wastebasket. She read the three lists to him.

"Mean anything to you?" she asked.

"Not a thing. Just a collection of nouns."

"Three words have little checkmarks next to them: melons, chairs, and hammers."

"It still means nothing to me," Harker said.

"Maybe I'll mail the lists to you along with the business cards. You might be able to make sense out of them if you see them."

"No," Tony said quickly, "don't do that. Rathbone might come back looking for them. Make copies of them as exactly as possible. Mail me the copies. Then crumple up the original lists and toss them back in his wastebasket."

"You don't miss a trick, do you?"

"I miss *you*," he said in a low voice. Then: "Did Rathbone say where he was going?"

"To visit a client. A widow named Birdie Winslow. That's the first time he's mentioned the name of one of his mooches."

"I'm making a note of it. Is her first name spelled with a *y* or *ie?*"

"Beats me. He just said Birdie Winslow."

"Okay. I'll try to get some skinny on her. Anything else?"

"Nope."

"Then go toast your tush."

"Hey, I like that," she said. "I really do think you're beginning to lighten up. My therapy is working."

"Thank you, nurse," he said. "What would I do without you?"

She smiled and hung up. But a moment later she had forgotten about Tony; she was thinking about David, wondering if he really was going to see a client or if he had another bimbo on the side and was planning a matinee. As he had said, everyone cuts corners, and she couldn't believe fidelity was one of his virtues.

She was right; David didn't visit Birdie Winslow. But an assignation with another woman was not on his agenda. Instead, he met with Termite Tommy in the parking lot of the Grand Palace.

The two men sat in the Bentley and cut up the proceeds from the dissolving check scam.

"Gross was 27K plus," Rathbone said. "The pusher drew two thousand as I told you. That leaves 25K plus in the kitty."

"Manna," Tommy said. "How do you want to split?"

David turned sideways to stare at him. "Thirds," he said, "You, me, and the printer."

"You crazy?" Tommy cried. "I thought we were going to stiff the Kraut."

Rathbone put a soft hand on the other man's arm. "Don't you trust me, Tommy?" he asked.

"Remember that old sign in saloons. 'In God We Trust. All others pay cash.' "

"There'll be more cash than you can count if you go along with me on this. First of all, the Treasury check went through without a hitch. But Tommy, how many times can we pull that dodge? We'd have to find a different pusher for every operation, and you know as well as I do that the more people you let in on the action, that's how much your risk increases. There's a better way of using that queer paper. And giving the printer a third will tickle his greed."

"Yeah? What's on your mind?"

"Persuade the German to use the paper for making fake twenties and fifties."

"He'll never go for it," Tommy said. "That's what put him behind bars the last time."

"No, it wasn't," David said. "What put him behind bars was that the feds caught him selling and grabbed the queer. But if he prints on self-destruct paper, where's the evidence?"

"The feds won't have any evidence, but the customer won't have any money either. They'll have paid for a bag of confetti. It'll shred away before they have a chance to push it. Then they'll come looking for us."

"Just listen a minute, will you? The German prints up the fake bills on that freaky paper. But we don't try to sell the bills for the reason you just said. Instead, you and I open bank accounts with phony ID and make cash deposits. It's credited to our accounts. Then who cares if the cash dissolves three days later? The bank takes the loss. And we withdraw clean money whenever we want."

Termite Tommy looked at him. "Nice try, David, but how much cash can we deposit before the banks get suspicious?"

"They're not going to ask questions if we keep each deposit under ten grand. And what if they do? We can always say we sold our car for cash. We each open maybe a dozen accounts so all the queer doesn't go to one bank."

"I don't like it."

"Tommy, my scam will have two big advantages. First of all, it cuts out the need to use pushers. There's a saving right there. Second of all, we'll be getting face value for the queer. How much was the German making before he was nabbed? Twenty percent? Thirty?"

"About that."

"There you are! We do it my way and we make twenty on a twenty and fifty on a fifty."

Tommy was silent. He had turned his head away and was staring out the window.

"Now what's bothering you?" David asked.

"It means I'd have to become a pusher," the other man said in a low voice. "I'm not sure I've got the balls for it. Ten years ago I'd have jumped at the chance. But that time I did in stir did something to me, David. I never want to go back in there again. Never!"

"All right, Tommy," Rathbone said, "I can understand that. Look, you brought me this deal; it's only right that I pay my way. I'll do all the pushing. I'll open accounts in a dozen banks. You get the cash to me as quickly as you can. I'll stick it in the banks as fast as I can, while the money is still fresh. I'll take all the risk."

"You'll really do that, David?"

"Of course I will. Because that's how positive I am that this thing is going to work."

"I'm not sure I can talk the German into printing bills again."

"Why don't you let me meet him? I'll convince him that this is the way to go."

"And we split three ways? On the face value?"

"Absolutely."

"Yeah," Tommy said, "maybe that's the way to handle it. I'll go back to Lakeland and set it up. Then I'll give you a call, and you drive over. Now what about the payoff on the fake Treasury check?"

"I'll bring it to you and the German when I come to Lakeland."

Termite Tommy nodded and got out of the Bentley. "I'll be in touch," he said. "Goodbye, David."

Rathbone lifted a hand in farewell. Then, watching the other man walk back to his battered pickup, he said softly, "Goodbye, Tommy."

28.

A black man from the Drug Enforcement Administration had a desk in the bullpen next to Roger Fortescue's. His name was Hiram Johnson, and he was working a case involving a ring peddling a new laboratory drug called "Rapture" to schoolkids in Dade and Broward counties. The two investigators— the only blacks in the room—discovered they were both graduates of Howard University, and whenever they had the chance, they had lunch together, or a few beers, and talked shop.

They were scoffing fried fish in Long John Silver's on Federal Highway when Fortescue brought up the subject of Haiti.

"A lot of drugs coming in from there?" he asked.

"Indubitably," Johnson said, which was the way he talked. "But you must realize, my dear confrere, that very limited quantities of controlled substances *originate* in Haiti. Like Panama, Haiti is a transshipping point. Because it's closer to the U.S., y'see. Heavy shipments of la dope come in on freighters or flights from Colombia, or Bolivia, or wherever, and are packaged in Haiti for delivery in bulk to Miami or New York."

"Is the stuff flown here or brought in by boat?"

"Both. And smuggled through in hollowed-out lumber, under false bottoms in furniture, in cans of flea powder—a thousand different ways. A few years ago we intercepted a shipment of toothpaste, each tube filled with heroin."

"Toothpaste?" Roger said. "Unreal."

"The villains are extremely clever," the DEA man went on. "Every time we uncover one subterfuge, the rascals come up with another. Just last year the Spanish police intercepted a million dollars' worth of cocaine concealed in a shipment of coconuts. A neat little plug had been drilled out of the shell of each nut, the meat and milk removed, the coconut filled with coke, and the plug replaced. A lot of arduous labor involved there, but justified by the profits, I do assure you, bro."

"Coconuts," Fortescue repeated. "That's cool."

After he left Johnson, Roger drove to a locksmith's shop on Dixie Highway. It was owned by Louis Falace, an ex-con. After spending almost thirty of his seventy-four years in the clink on several burglary raps, Falace had decided to go straight and had opened Be Safe, Be Sure, a successful store where he sold locks, bolts, chains, peepholes, window guards, alarms, and other security devices designed to thwart the kind of Breaking & Entering artist he had once been.

Fortescue, who had helped send Falace away on his last trip to the pokey, stopped by occasionally to see how the old man was doing. There was no enmity between crook and cop; they were both professionals.

"Lou," Roger said, "I need your advice. There's this place I want to get into, but it's surrounded by a high, chain-link fence. The gate faces a street and is usually lighted, so I don't want to go in that way. I figure I've got to cut a hole in that fence or take a ladder along and go over it. Which do you think is best?"

The old man smiled. He had new dentures, and they glistened like wet stones. "No cutta hole," he said. "No climba over."

"No?" Fortescue said. "Then how do I get in?"

Falace went into a back room and returned in a moment carrying a folding entrenching tool with a khaki cloth over the blade: standard U.S. Army issue.

"Go *under*," Falace said. "Dig just deep enough to wiggle beneath the fence. When you come out, fill in the hole, make it nice and neat. Everyone says, 'How did he get in?' "

"Lou, you're a genius," Roger said. "I'll return your little shovel."

"Don't bother," Falace said. "I don't go digging anymore."

Fortescue's next stop was at a sporting goods store. He bought a baseball. It cost $7.99 plus tax. He carried his purchase (in a little plastic bag with handles) out to the car and before he examined it, he entered "$7.99 (baseball) and 48 cents (tax)" on the page of his notebook where he recorded his out-of-pocket expenses.

The ball was in a small box marked "Official Major League Baseball." It came from a company in Missouri, but in fine print it stated: "Contents assembled in Haiti." Fortescue smiled.

Then he inspected the ball itself. It had a white leather cover stitched in red, and it felt as hard as a rock. On the side of the baseball was printed: "Cushioned cork center." Roger had no idea what the rest of the ball contained and didn't want to cut the cover open to find out.

He drove home with his baseball and folding shovel. Estelle was out—probably shopping—and the kids were at school, so Papa went to bed and had a fine nap.

That night, just before twelve o'clock, he assembled all his gear.

"You better not wait up," he said to Estelle.

"I wasn't going to," she said. "What's that you're carrying?"

"A baseball."

"Oh? A night game?"

"Something like that," he said.

He went back to his hidey-hole in the deserted fast-food joint and took up his position at the window facing the FL Sports Equipment warehouse. The gate was open, floodlights were on, an unmarked van was being loaded with cartons. Frank Little, as usual, stood to one side keeping a tally.

The van didn't leave until almost one-thirty A.M. Then Little closed the gate and locked it. He went into the block-house, and a moment later the floodlights went off. But there was a light in the rear of the office. Fortescue waited patiently. Finally the light was extinguished. Frank Little came out, locked up, and drove away in his snazzy Cadillac convertible. The investigator waited in the darkness another half-hour. Then, when it seemed likely that Little wouldn't return, he went outside and got to work.

He picked a spot at the rear of the warehouse where he couldn't be seen from Copans Road. He unfolded his little shovel, locked the blade into place, and started digging. The Florida soil at that spot was sandy and loose, and the hole went swiftly. The only trouble was that displaced dirt kept sliding back into the excavation, and Roger had to shovel it farther away.

It took him about thirty minutes to scoop out a trench deep enough so he could lie down and roll under the chain-link fence. But first he went back to the restaurant to get the baseball, bull's-eye lantern, and set of lockpicks. Then he squeezed under the fence, rose, dusted himself off, and started exploring.

What concerned him most was that there might be an alarm system: electronic or infrared. The last thing in the world he wanted was to be poking around and suddenly have the floodlights blaze and a siren go "WHOOP-WHOOP-WHOOP!" He was well aware that he was engaged in an illicit enterprise and whatever he found could not be used as evidence. Still, as every cop learns early in his career, there are many ways to skin a cat.

He made a cautious circuit of the warehouse, using his lantern sparingly, and finally decided his best means of entry was through one of the small, fogged windows in the rear. Locked, of course. It would have been easy to take off his dungaree jacket, wrap it around his fist, and punch out a pane of glass to get at the rusted window lock. But he didn't want to leave such an obvious sign of a break-in. So, mumbling angrily at his own lack of foresight, he went back to his trench, rolled under the fence, fetched the little crowbar from his hideaway, rolled under the fence again, and went to work on the locked window.

It took almost ten minutes of prying before the lock snapped and the window slid up with a loud squeal. He waited awhile, and when he heard no shouts of "Stop, thief!" or the sound of approaching sirens, he climbed through the window and looked around the warehouse, using his lantern with his fingers spread across the lens to dim the glare.

It was a cavernous place, smelling of damp. But all the cartons and crates were stacked on pallets close to the front entrance, which made his job easier. Even better, one of the top cartons was unsealed, and when Roger lifted the flaps he saw at least fifty white baseballs piled in there.

He slipped one of the balls into his jacket pocket, replaced it with the baseball he had bought that afternoon, then began his withdrawal. Out the window. Lower the sash carefully. Check to make certain he had all his gear. Wiggle out under the fence. He filled in the trench and tamped it down, leaving it "nice and neat," just as Lou Falace had instructed.

He was home within an hour, the house silent, family sleeping peacefully. He sat down at the kitchen table and examined the stolen baseball. It looked just like the one he had left in its place: white leather cover, red stitching, printing on the side: "Official Major League Baseball. Cushioned cork center."

He found a sharp paring knife and very, very carefully slit open a few of those red stitches. He began squeezing the hardball with both hands, gripping it with all his strength. After a while white powder began to spurt out of the cut and pile up on the tabletop.

He put the ball aside. He licked a forefinger and touched it cautiously to the white powder. He tasted it, made a bitter face.

"Bingo," he said.

29.

Simon Clark considered writing a letter home to his wife, merely to tell her he was alive, well, and living in Fort Lauderdale. But then he thought better of it; she'd have absolutely no interest in his health or whereabouts. Their childless marriage had deteriorated to the point that while they occupied the same domicile, they communicated mostly by notes stuck on the refrigerator door with little magnets in the shape of frogs and bunnies.

This sad state of affairs had existed for several years now, exacerbated by the long hours he had to work and her recent employment at a Michigan Avenue boutique. That resulted in her making many new friends, most of whom seemed to be epicene young men who wore their hair in ponytails.

So rather than write a letter, Simon mailed his wife a garishly colored postcard showing three young women in thong bikinis bending over a ship's rail, their tanned buns flashing in the south Florida sunlight. He wrote: "Having a fine time;

glad you're not here," and didn't much care if she found it amusing, offensive, or what.

He had a gin and bitters at his hotel bar and decided to drive over to Mortimer Sparco's discount brokerage and check on the status of his investment in the Fort Knox Commodity Trading Fund. It wasn't listed anywhere in *The Wall Street Journal,* and Clark didn't expect it ever would be.

As he was about to enter the brokerage, a woman was exiting and he held the door open for her. She was a very small woman, hardly five feet tall, he reckoned, and seemed to be in her middle thirties. She swept by him without a glance or a "Thank you," and he had the distinct impression that she had been weeping.

Old men in Bermuda shorts were still watching the tape on the TV screen in the waiting room, and there was one geezer, presumably a client, sleeping peacefully in one of the wicker armchairs. His hearing aid had slipped out and was dangling from a black wire.

"Could I see Mr. Sparco, please," Clark said to the receptionist. "My name is Simon Clark."

"Oh, I know who you are, Mr. Clark," she said warmly. "But I'm afraid Mr. Sparco is in a meeting. He won't be free for at least an hour."

"All right," Simon said. "Maybe I'll try to catch him this afternoon."

He went outside, wondering if he should drive to headquarters and work on his weekly report to Anthony Harker. Then, realizing he really had nothing to report, he decided to goof off for a few hours, perhaps have some lunch, and return to the brokerage later.

He left his rented Cutlass where it was parked and crossed Commercial to the Grand Palace. He walked through the empty dining room to the Lounge at the rear. There was a table of four blue-haired women, all laughing loudly and all drinking mai tais, each of which had a plastic orchid floating

169

on top. There was a single woman seated at the bar, the small woman Clark had seen leaving Sparco's brokerage. He stood at the bar, not too close to her, and ordered a gin and bitters.

As he sipped his drink, he examined the woman in the mirror behind the bar. If she had been weeping when he first saw her, she certainly wasn't now. In fact, she was puffing on a cigarette, working on a boilermaker, and chatting animatedly with the bartender. Simon thought her attractive: a gamine with a helmet of short blond hair.

He waited until the bartender was busy making fresh mai tais. Then he stepped closer to the woman.

"I beg your pardon," he said, smiling, "but I believe I saw you at Sparco's brokerage, and I wondered if you're a client."

She looked at him, expressionless. "No," she said, "I'm not a client. I'm Nancy Sparco, the schnorrer's wife."

"Oh," Simon said, startled. "Sorry to bother you."

"You're not bothering me. Bring your drink over and talk to me. I hate to booze alone. People will think I'm a lush, which I'm not."

He took the barstool next to her.

"You've met my husband?" she said.

He nodded.

"A prick," she said. "A cheap, no-good, conniving prick. But that's neither here nor there. What's your name?"

"Simon Clark."

"Where you from, Simon?"

"Chicago."

"Nice town. Greatest shopping in the world. Married?"

"Yes," he said, "but I'm not working at it. Neither is my wife."

"I know exactly what you mean. My marriage isn't the greatest either."

"May I buy you a drink?" he asked.

"Why not. Where are you staying, Simon?"

"At a hotel on the Galt Ocean Mile."

"Good," she said. "As long as it's not the YMCA."

Two hours and two drinks later they were in his hotel room. He thought her the wittiest woman he had ever met: vulgar, raunchy, with a limitless supply of one-liners, some of which went by too fast to catch.

When she undressed and took off her cork wedgies, she was positively *tiny*.

"My God," he said, "this is like going to bed with a Girl Scout."

"A Brownie," she corrected. "You'll notice my collar and cuffs don't match. But the lungs aren't bad—right? The best silicone money can buy. I'll never drown."

She showed him how they could manage, with her sitting atop him. He was amenable, but she wouldn't stop talking, and he was laughing so much he was afraid he couldn't perform. Finally he told her to shut up, for five minutes at least.

"May I groan?" she asked, but then was reasonably quiet while she rode him like a demented jockey.

When they finished, she took his wrist and lifted his arm into the air. "The winner and new world champion!" she proclaimed. "When's the rematch?"

"In about twenty minutes," he said. "Shall I call down for drinks?"

"Please," she said. "A whiskey IV. Mommy needs plasma."

Later in the afternoon, when they were just lazing around and sipping sour mash bourbon, she said, "Don't go back to Chicago, Simon. Not just yet."

"It depends," he said.

"You got any money?" she asked suddenly.

He wondered if she was a pro, and she caught his expression.

"Not for fun and games, dummy," she said. "I'm no hooker. I mean real money."

"I'm not rich, but I get by."

She sighed. "I've got this great idea for a new business. It would be profitable from Day One. So I go to my dear hubby for start-up cash, and the asshole stiffs me. He's loaded, but it's all for him, none for me."

"Maybe he wants to keep you dependent on him."

"Yeah, that's probably it. He knows if I ever had my own income, it'd be goodbye Mort."

"What's this new business you want to start?"

"An escort service," she said. "Covering the Miami-Lauderdale area. Listen, next to drugs, tourists are Florida's biggest cash crop. Men and women come down here on vacation and want a good time. But they don't know anyone. They don't know where to go, what to see. I'd provide escorts—young, good-looking guys and dolls—they could hire for an hour, an evening, a day, a week, to show them around, best restaurants and so forth. Keep them from getting lonely. What do you think?"

"Sex?" he asked.

She shrugged. "It wouldn't be in the contract, but if the escorts want to make a private deal, it would be up to them. As long as my agency gets its fee. I pay the escorts a percentage and pocket the rest. The escorts can keep the tips, if any."

"You know," he said, "it just might go."

"Can't miss," she said. "I could even arrange boat charters and things like that. And I'd screen the escorts carefully. All clean, tanned kids. South Florida is full of beach bums, male and female. I'd recruit a choice staff who have table manners, know how to dress and talk and dance and show the tourists a good time."

He poured them more bourbon. "What do you figure your start-up costs would be?"

"Twenty-five thousand at least. Possibly more. Because I want this to be a class operation. And listen, there are a lot of ways to make an extra buck. Like getting kickbacks from restaurants and nightclubs for steering clients there. Ditto for jewelry stores, hotels, and expensive boutiques. It could be a gold mine. You got twenty-five grand to spare?"

"I wish I did," he said. "As a matter of fact, I did have it a week ago. But then I met your husband."

"Mooch!" she jeered. "You can kiss those bucks goodbye. What'd he put you in—penny stocks?"

"For starters. But those made money."

"The old come-on. Did you see any of the money he said you made?"

"Well . . . no. It was reinvested, plus more."

"Uh-huh, that sounds like Mort. What are you in now?"

"Something called the Fort Knox Commodity Trading Fund."

"Yeah," she said, "I heard him talking on the phone about that. I don't know what it is, but all his buddies are in on it so it's got to be a scam. I call them Captain Crook and his Merry Crew."

"Your husband is Captain Crook?"

"Nah, he's just one of the crew. The Captain is a guy named David Rathbone, a handsome devil who hasn't got a straight bone in his body."

Clark did some heavy thinking. "Maybe I can get my money back from your husband," he said.

"Fat chance! Once he's got his paws on your green, it's his, to have and to hold till he croaks."

"If I *could* get it back," he persisted, "maybe we could talk some more about your escort service."

"Hey," she said, "that would be great."

"Tell me something," he said. "If I could come up with the money you need, would you leave your husband?"

"Is the Pope Catholic?" she cried. "I'd be gone so fast all he'd see would be palm trees waving in my wind."

"And move in with me?" Clark asked, staring at her.

She didn't blink. "I learned a long time ago, you don't get something for nothing in the world. You bankroll my business, and I'll do whatever turns you on."

"Okay," he said, "then we've got a deal. Give me your home phone number so I can reach you if anything breaks.

173

You can always call me here at the hotel. Leave a message if I'm out."

She nodded, rose, and began dressing. "How soon do you think it'll be?"

"It may take weeks," he said. "Even a month. Try to be patient."

"I'm good at that," she said. "Meanwhile we can be getting to know each other better."

"It couldn't be much better than this afternoon."

She left, and he showered and dressed. Then he went downstairs to drive to headquarters. Now he had something to put in his report.

Something, but not everything.

30.

They started for Lakeland early in the morning, David driving the Bentley.

"We should be there by noon," he said, "if the traffic isn't too heavy. My meeting will take an hour or so. Then you and I'll have lunch and do some sightseeing before we head back. We should be home around eight o'clock."

"Whatever you say, boss," Rita said, yawning. "I think I'll grab a little shut-eye. You didn't let me get much sleep last night. Where did you learn those tricks?"

"Mommy taught me," he said, laughing.

"You've never mentioned your parents, David. You did have parents, didn't you? I mean you weren't just found in a cabbage patch?"

"Oh, I had parents," he said, keeping his eyes on the road. "Plus two brothers and a sister. All of them so straight they were practically rigid. I was the Ebony Sheep, in trouble since the age of seven when I was caught playing doctor and

175

nurse with the little girl next door. I knew even then I'd cut loose from that family as soon as I could."

"You ever hear from them?"

"Hell, no! And that's just the way I want it."

"Don't you have an urge now and then to write or phone them? After all, they *are* your family."

"Go to sleep," he said, and she did.

It was a hot, hazy day with not much breeze stirring. They drove northward on U.S. Highway 27, through part of the Everglades, around Lake Okeechobee. The scenery kept changing: dense woods, arid patches of scrub pine, condo developments, lakes and canals, swamps, golf courses, somnolent little towns, and roadside diners that advertised alligator steaks. Everyone they saw was moving slowly in the heat. Some of the women carried parasols, and in every patch of shade, no matter how small, a hound lay snoozing.

They stopped once to gas up and gulp a cold Coke. Then they pushed on and were in Lakeland a little after noon. It looked like any other whitewashed Florida city with elderly tourists rocking on the verandas of ancient hotels. But there were a lot of out-of-state cars, and the souvenir shops were doing a brisk business in carved coconut masks, shell picture frames, and necklaces of shark teeth.

"What do the people who live here do besides clip the tourists?" Rita asked. "I mean, how do they make a living?"

"Probably take in each other's laundry," Rathbone said. "I hope I remember the directions. Yep, here's the street, and there's the church. Now I make a right, go five blocks and hang a left. We dead-end at a park."

"You're going to have a meeting in a *park?*"

"That's the way the printer wanted it," David said. "I wasn't about to argue. Ah, here we are."

He pulled into a turnaround and stopped the car. Ahead lay a broad spread of flat lawn, nicely manicured, and trimmed palm trees surrounding a stretch of clear water, more pond than lake. There were meandering walkways, benches, clumps of scarlet hibiscus. Lovers were strolling, a family was picnicking on the grass, two small boys were trying to get a kite aloft on a windless day. It was a painted scene, artfully composed, gleaming with sunlight.

"Nice place for a do-or-die meeting," David said. "I'll wander around, and my guys will see me or I'll see them. You take the car, drive downtown, do some shopping, have a drink. Just remember to be back here in an hour. Don't forget me."

"I won't forget you," Rita said. "Maybe I'll look for a place where we can have a decent lunch."

"Good idea," he said. He took a manila envelope from the glove compartment, and she recognized it as the same one that had contained the Crescent Bank money. He kissed her cheek and got out of the car.

"Don't talk to any sailors," he warned.

"In the middle of Florida?" she said, laughing. "That would be some trick."

She drove away without looking back. It took her less than twenty minutes to find a reasonably modern hotel. At least it was air-conditioned and had a public phone in the lobby. She called Anthony Harker in Lauderdale, collect.

"What the hell are you doing in Lakeland?" he asked. "No ocean there."

"He's got a meeting in a public park, if you can believe that."

"Oh? With whom?"

"Beats me. But he talks of 'guys,' so it must be more than one. He took the envelope of cash I got from the Crescent Bank in Boca. And he let something slip. I asked him how come he was having a meeting in a park, and he said that's the way the printer wanted it."

"The *printer?*" Tony said, voice excited. "You sure he said printer?"

177

"That's what he said."

"Beautiful. The first good lead we've had on that phony check. No way you can get a look at the printer?"

"Nope. Not without risking my cover."

"Then play it cozy. I'll take it from here. How many first-class counterfeiters can there be in Lakeland? I'll find him. Nice work, Rita. When am I going to see you?"

"I'll try to finagle something. An afternoon or evening."

"Try," he urged. "I went to the beach over the weekend."

"You did? Great! Did you get a tan?"

"No," he said, "I got a red. But at least I didn't break out or peel."

"Good for you," she said. "Now go for the bronze."

She hung up and wandered about the hotel. She found a little restaurant and bar tucked into one corner. It was decorated in Key West style, with overhead fans and planked tables scrubbed white. Not a soul in the place except for the bartender, who looked to be one year younger than God and was reading a romance paperback titled *Brazen Virgin*.

Rita ordered a frozen daiquiri and it turned out to be excellent, not too tart, not too sweet.

"Kitchen open?" she asked him, looking around at the empty room.

"I can open it," he offered.

"You're the chef?"

"And bartender. And waiter."

"I'd like to bring a friend back for lunch in about an hour," she said. "Could I see a menu, please."

"I'm also the menu," he said. "Today I can fix you some eggs, any style; a hamburger I wouldn't recommend for a nice lady like you; or homemade lentil soup."

"How about a salad?"

He thought a moment. "Would you settle for canned shrimp? I got all the greens; they're fresh. And I make my own dressing."

"You've got a deal," she said. "How about some white wine to go with it?"

He rummaged in a cupboard and dragged out a dusty bottle of Pouilly-Fuissé. "Here's some pooly-foos," he said. "Will that do?"

"Just fine. Put it on ice to chill. Okay?"

"I think I got a corkscrew," he muttered. "Somewhere."

She had a second daiquiri, then drove back to pick up David. When she reached the turnaround, she saw him out on the lawn with the two boys, trying to launch their kite. He was running like a maniac, but the kite just kept bumping along the ground behind him. Then he saw the Bentley, waved, handed the string to one of the kids.

He came over to the car, grinning. He really was a beautiful man, she decided: blond hair tousled, flashing smile, everything about him alert and active, taut body bursting with energy. The golden boy at play.

"I couldn't get it up," he said.

"That's the first time you've had that problem. How did the meeting go?"

He made the A-OK sign. "Couldn't have been better. We're going to be *rich* rich."

"Good," she said. "That's better than *poor* poor. Let's go eat."

On the drive back to the hotel, she told him about the ancient bartender-chef-waiter-menu, and the lunch they were going to have.

He laughed. "I love that pooly-foos," he said. "But who cares what he calls it as long as it's cold. I could drink the whole bottle myself."

"My God, you're wired," she said. "That meeting was a real upper."

"It went great," he said. "One little drawback, but I know how to get around that."

They were the only diners in the restaurant, and the old

man fussed about them anxiously. He poured their wine with a trembling hand and beamed at their approval. He brought the salad in a big wooden bowl, enough for four, and let them help themselves. The shrimp were undeniably canned, but there were a lot of them, and everything else was fresh and crisp.

"You picked a winner," Rathbone said to Rita. "I wonder why this place isn't mobbed."

"No chrome, no plastic, no chili dogs or french fries. By the way, he also makes the world's best frozen daiquiri."

"For dessert," David said.

They sat sprawled for almost an hour after they had finished lunch and the table had been cleared.

It was getting close to three o'clock, and the bartender had disappeared into the kitchen. There were occasional muted sounds from the lobby and outdoors, but quiet engulfed the room, and they spoke in hushed voices, not wanting to shatter the spell.

"About our being rich," David said, "I meant it. I have two deals in the works that are shaping up as winners, plus my investment service. I figure to give it another year and cash in."

"And then?"

"Off we go, into the wild blue yonder."

"Both of us?"

He lifted her hand, kissed her fingertips. "Yes," he said. "Both of us."

"You won't have to hustle anymore?"

"Not if the payoff is as big as I figure. I don't mean we'll be able to light our cigarettes with hundred-dollar bills, but we'll be able to live very comfortably indeed. We won't have to count pennies."

"You'll really take me with you?"

He kissed the palm of her hand. "You remember the morning after our first night together?"

"When you told me to move in?"

180

"Right. I said it was love at first sight. You thought I was conning you, and maybe I was. Then. But I'm not conning you now. I love you, Rita. More than that, I *need* you. You're the most important thing in my life."

"That's heavy," she said.

"It's the truth. It's why I'm getting into these new deals. To make enough for *both* of us to have the good life. You like all the perks that money can buy. So do I. Neither of us wants to live like a peasant."

She looked down at their linked hands. "You're right," she said in a low voice. "I've never had as much as you've given me. Have I ever said, 'Thank you'? I'll say it now: Thank you."

"You don't have to thank me. I don't want your gratitude; I want your love. And besides, you've paid me back just by being there when I need you. Did I tell you I'm addicted to you? Well, I am. But what about you? I've never really asked if you'd be willing to spend the rest of your life with me. It would mean leaving the country and probably never coming back. Could you do that?"

She gave him a twisted smile. "I don't know. When you talked before about cashing in and taking off, I thought that's all it was—talk. But now you're serious, aren't you?"

He nodded.

"I don't have to give you an answer right now, do I, David?"

"No, of course not. Maybe my deals will go sour. And then I'll have to change my plans. Or postpone them. But you'll think about it?"

"Yes," she said, "I will."

"Good. Now let's go home."

"Are we going to the Palace tonight?"

"I'd rather not," he said. "Let's spend it together. Just the two of us."

"I'd like that," she said.

31.

Anthony Harker's office was jammed. He had brought in folding chairs so his crew had a place to sit, but it was shoulder-to-shoulder and everyone was smoking up a storm. The air conditioning wasn't coping. But Harker wasn't having an allergic reaction.

"Okay," he said, "here's what we've got. Roger, we'll start with you. That stuff in Frank Little's baseball tested out as high-grade cocaine."

"Thought it might," Fortescue said.

"You figure he's importing and selling?"

"I'd guess not. I think he's just a trafficker. His customers make their own buys. The stuff comes to Little's warehouse in baseballs from Haiti, and the dealers pick it up there. It's like a distribution center. He charges a fee for providing a service. But he's not pushing the stuff himself."

"That reads," Harker said, nodding. "I've persuaded Mr. Crockett to hold off raiding the warehouse until we learn more about Little's operation. If we get called for stalling the

182

raid, we can always say we were trying to track the source and the guys making the pickups—which is the truth."

"That would take an army of narcs," Fortescue said.

"Maybe not," Tony said. "We're trying to get more bodies assigned to us. They'll tail those vans and trucks you spotted to their eventual destinations. It looks to be a big, well-organized distribution system, and we'll hold off busting the warehouse until we know the identity of Little's customers."

"That coke I found in Mike Mulligan's toilet," Henry Ullman said, "you figure it came from Frank Little's baseballs?"

"The lab says no," Harker said. "It was high-grade cocaine all right but had a different chemical signature—whatever that is from the stuff Fortescue found. Henry, you think Mike Mulligan is snorting?"

"I don't think so. I've become close pals with the guy and he shows no signs of it. He loves the sauce, but I think he just uses the coke to get women. Some of them are young and attractive, too. He pays off with the dust, and it's party time every Saturday night."

"Where's he getting it? Does he buy it?"

"I doubt it. Not in that quantity. If he was paying for it, he'd have been dead broke a long time ago. According to your snitch, David Rathbone said that James Bartlett claimed Mulligan was on the pad. How's this for a scenario: Bartlett is laundering drug money through the Crescent Bank, and Mike Mulligan is his contact. Mulligan is a bank officer; he could fiddle the deal. And Bartlett pays him off with coke."

"That's possible," Tony said. "Likely, in fact. You know, we started out tracking a gang of con men and swindlers, and now it's beginning to look like they're up to their ass in dope. Suarez, Clark, have you heard anything about Coe or Sparco pushing any kind of drugs?"

"Not me," Manny Suarez said. "Coe smokes a joint now and then, but all he's pushing right now is that crazy commodity fund."

"The same with Sparco," Simon Clark said. "He's selling

shares in the Fund like there's no tomorrow. I checked all my contacts in Chicago, and no one in the commodity pits ever heard of the Fort Knox Fund and there's no record of any trades under that name."

Harker sighed. "All right," he said, "just keep on doing what you're doing, but try to dig a little deeper. That Fund may be an out-and-out fraud or it may be a front for something bigger. I think it is, but can't pin it down. That's all for now."

They rose and began folding chairs so they could get out of the office.

"Wait a minute," Tony said. "I want the four of you to take a look at something and tell me if it means anything to you."

He opened his desk drawer, took out copies of the lists Rita Sullivan had fished from David Rathbone's wastebasket. He handed them to Ullman.

Henry read them, shook his head. "They don't make any sense to me," he said, and handed them to Suarez.

Manny read them over twice. *"Nada,"* he said. "Just words." He passed them along to Clark.

Simon scanned them quickly, shook his head, gave them to Fortescue.

Roger read them, shrugged, returned them to Harker. "Means nothing," he said. "Just—" He stopped suddenly. "Wait a minute. Let me have another look." He took the lists back from Tony and studied them again. "Uh-huh," he said, grinning. "Five words beginning with C, five with H, five with M. C, H, M. Put them all together and they don't spell Mother. But they could be code words for cocaine, heroin, and marijuana."

Harker stared at him, then took a deep breath. "Thank you very much," he said.

After they left, Tony called Lester Crockett's secretary. "Five minutes," he said. "That's all I need."

"Hang on a moment," she said. "I'll check with him."

He waited, took his inhaler out of his shirt pocket, tossed it into the bottom desk drawer.

She came back on. "All right, Mr. Harker," she said. "Five minutes. Right now."

"On my way," he said.

He stood in front of Crockett's desk and told him about the lists of words from Rathbone's wastebasket. He handed over the copies.

"I couldn't make any sense out of them, sir," he said.

Crockett read the lists slowly. Then again. "Nor can I," he said.

"I showed them to my men. Roger Fortescue caught it. The lists start with C, H, and M. Standing for cocaine, heroin, marijuana."

Crockett looked at him and nodded. "Possible," he said.

"Probable, sir," Tony said. "And if so, Rathbone, his pals, and that Fund are involved in drug dealing. Those lists are potential code words. The nouns with checkmarks are the ones Rathbone selected. I guess they need code words for messages, documents, and telephone conversations concerning their deals."

Crockett nodded again.

"It's all supposition," Harker said. "Smoke and mirrors. But I think there's a good chance the Fort Knox Fund is trading commodities all right: coke, shit, and grass. Now can I put central-office taps on Rathbone's phones and bugs in his town house?"

"All right," Crockett said, "you win. Draw up a detailed plan of how all this is to be accomplished and the evidence justifying it. We'll have to get a court order."

"Will do," Tony said.

"And you're still determined not to tell Sullivan about the bugs?"

"She has no need to know," Harker said stubbornly.

Crockett didn't say anything. Tony turned to leave, then stopped.

"I was supposed to be covering white-collar crime," he said. "As I told my men a half-hour ago, it now looks like the sharks we're tracking are into drug dealing. And Rathbone is dabbling in counterfeiting. It's unusual for criminal leopards to change their spots. How do you account for it, sir?"

The chief clasped his fingers across his vest, stared up at the ceiling almost dreamily. "The something-for-nothing syndrome," he said. "Con men depend on human greed for their livelihood. If it wasn't for greed, swindlers would have no victims. What do they call them—mooches? Most people have get-rich-quick dreams. How else can you explain the popularity of lotteries? The sharks exploit that dream and profit from it. But their defeat is inevitable. Because they themselves are not immune to the dream. Your swindlers and sharpers see the enormous profits being made in the drug trade, and they can't resist trying to get a piece of the action. They are just as unthinkingly greedy and vulnerable as their mooches. In fact, they are mooches, too."

Tony Harker laughed. "Maybe we all are mooches."

Lester Crockett brought his gaze down from the ceiling and stared at him. "Maybe we are," he said. "Greedy in irrational ways. Not only for money, but for fame, pleasure, power." He paused. "Perhaps even for love," he said. "Your five minutes are up."

32.

A few of the yaks in Sid Coe's boiler room worked till midnight, culling their lists for West Coast suckers.

But Manny Suarez and most of the others quit work around six or seven o'clock. Ten hours in that noisy sweatbox were enough; they had to unwind, have a cold beer, replenish their store of nervous energy for the next day's wheeling and dealing.

"Suarez," one of the yaks called as Manny was heading for his Ford Escort, "do you have a few minutes?"

"Yeah, sure. You wanna go have a coupla brews?"

"Not at the moment," the man said, coming up close and lowering his voice. "I have a private matter I'd like to discuss with you. Let's sit in my new Porsche. I just took delivery."

It was a midnight-blue 928S4 model, and Manny could believe the talk that the owner was the highest-paid yak at Coe's, averaging a reported two grand a week in commissions. His name was Warren Fowler. He was an older man who dressed like an investment banker and never removed his jacket no matter how steamy it got in the boiler room. Suarez thought he talked "fancy."

"Nice car," Manny said, stroking the leather upholstery. "I even like the smell."

"It's advertised as capable of doing one-sixty," Fowler said, "but I haven't let it out yet. Would you like one just like it?"

"Oh sure," Suarez said, "but I don't rob banks. Not my shtick, man."

"You won't have to. Tell me something: Do you enjoy working for Coe?"

"It's hokay. The moaney's good."

"Good? Compared to what Coe is netting, it can't even qualify as peanuts. Ten-percent commission—that's obscene!"

"Yeah, sure, but he's taking all the risk. The feds move in, and he's liable for fraud, and he goes to the slam. You and me, we can cop a plea and maybe get off with probation or a slap on the wrist. But Sid would do hard time."

Fowler shrugged. "I doubt if he'd get more than a year or so. Just the cost of doing business. And when he came out, I'm sure he'd still have all his profits in overseas accounts."

Suarez turned sideways to stare at him. "What's on your mind? You want us to go on strike for more dough?"

"Don't be absurd. But about six months ago a gentleman came to me with a proposition that sounded too good to resist. I've tried it, and it's turned out to be just as good as it sounded. This man wanted me to talk to a selected few of the other high-producing yaks to see if they'd be interested in doubling their income. I've spoken to four so far, and they've all joined up. Now I'd like to lay it out for you. I should tell you immediately that I get a bonus for every yak I bring into the scheme. But my bonus is nothing compared to the money you'll be making."

"So now you've given me the buildup. Let's hear the rest of the script."

"It's simplicity itself. Here's how it works: This man has

established a small office in West Palm Beach. It's really just a mail drop. Now suppose I close a deal for five thousand. My regular commission would be five hundred. But if Coe isn't hanging over my shoulder, I tell the mooch to mail his check to that office in West Palm Beach. When the money arrives, I get seventy-five percent or a sweet $3,750. How do you like that? The man running the mail drop takes twenty-five percent for renting the office, cashing the checks, and the risk."

"It's a rip-off."

"Of course it is. But there's poetic justice there. Coe is sweating his peons and paying a ridiculously small commission for our hard work. Now the clipper is getting clipped. Nothing wrong with that, is there? But of course you can't do it with all your deals or Coe's income would fall off drastically, and he'd smell a rat. I usually limit myself to one big sale a week, and I've advised the other four yaks to do the same. The important thing is not to get too greedy. Coe will never notice if you're skimming one deal a week. Just make it a biggie."

"And you've been pulling this for six months?"

"That's correct. And our esteemed employer doesn't have a glimmer of suspicion that he's being royally rooked."

"If he ever finds out, he'll have your kneecaps blown away."

"How can he possibly find out? The man who devised this scheme is very insistent that we keep our take modest. Even at that, I estimate the five of us are costing Coe close to a hundred grand a month. Serves him right."

"This guy who's running the chisel," Suarez said, "what's his name?"

"You have no need to know that," Fowler said. "Just take my word for it that he pays off promptly. He's content with his cut."

"He should be," Manny said. "With five yaks nicking for him, he's probably clearing twenty-five big ones a month."

"He's entitled. After all, old boy, it was his idea. Well, what's your decision? Coming in with us? You'd be a fool not to. And if I thought you were a fool I would never have solicited you."

"Lemme think about it tonight," Suarez said. "Hokay? I'll tell you tomorrow."

"Excellent," Fowler said. "If you decide to join us, you get the address of the West Palm Beach office and can begin doubling your income."

Manny drove home in a thoughtful mood. Since working at Instant Investments, Inc., he had been turning in his weekly take to Anthony Harker—but not all of it. He had been skimming two or three yards a week and sending mail orders home to his wife in Miami. He figured the government would never miss the money, and if the boiler room was raided, Suarez was confident that Coe kept no records of commissions he had paid his yaks.

But this chiseler in West Palm Beach was an unknown. If he got busted, the feds might find records detailing all his transactions, and then, conceivably, Manuel Suarez would be in the *sopa*. He decided that as a matter of self-preservation, he'd better play this one straight.

Later that evening he got out of his hostess' bed and stumbled into the living room. He called Harker's night number and when Tony came on, Suarez told him all about the proposition from Warren Fowler.

Harker laughed. "Beautiful," he said. "The screwer gets screwed. And I'll bet it's one of his Grand Palace buddies who's doing the screwing. Probably David Rathbone. Swindling friends is his style."

"What do you want I should do?" Suarez asked.

"Go for it. And try to find out for sure who's running the scam."

"Hokay," Manny said.

33.

Lester Crockett tried to get additional personnel to do the job on Frank Little's warehouse, but Washington reminded him that he was already over budget; he would have to make do with the men he had. So he did the next best thing: He cut a deal with the local office of the Drug Enforcement Administration.

"I don't like it any more than you do," he told Harker. "But we'll have to live with it."

The deal took a long afternoon of often rancorous argument to arrange, but eventually an agreement was hammered out that had as many compromises as the Treaty of Ghent.

The DEA would take over surveillance of FL Sports Equipment, Inc., and responsibility for tracing the Haitian source of the coke-filled baseballs and trailing the vans and trucks that picked them up at the warehouse. In return, the DEA agreed not to bust the operation or collar Frank Little with-

191

out Crockett's prior notification and approval. Hiram Johnson, one of Crockett's men and Roger Fortescue's buddy, was assigned to liaise with the DEA's investigative team.

So it happened that on a blustery night in late November, Fortescue conducted Johnson to his hideaway in the deserted fast-food joint adjacent to Little's warehouse. The hurricane season had ended, but the weather had turned mean and brutal. A northwest wind was driving gusts of cold rain, and both men were drenched before they could duck into the restaurant, Roger leading the way with his lantern.

"Loverly," Johnson said, peering around. "Perfect for weddings and bar mitzvahs."

Fortescue showed him the office where boards covering the window could be moved apart to provide a clear view of the goings-on at FL Sports Equipment.

"All the comforts of home," Roger pointed out. "I even dragged in this swell crate so your guys will have a place to sit while they peep."

"Primitive," Johnson said. "Definitely primitive. But as they say in real estate circles, the only three things that count are location, location, and location."

Within a week, the DEA, working through a dummy corporation, had leased the empty building and were ostensibly converting it into a new restaurant. A sign went up—FINNY FUN—and underneath a promise that read "Coming Soon: Fresh Fish."

The exterior renovation went slowly; the outside of the building showed little change. But inside, in the small office, DEA specialists built a fully equipped command post with telephones, two-way radios, video cameras, bunks for two men, a hot plate, and enough canned provisions to feed a regiment. The toilet was put back into working order, power was restored, and the kitchen faucets flowed.

The cameras were the first equipment installed, and were put into use immediately with hypersensitive film to record nighttime activities. The arrival and departure of vans and trucks taking delivery of Little's baseballs were radioed to teams of agents parked along Copans Road, and the shadowing began.

Having played his role, Roger Fortescue ambled into Anthony Harker's office.

"I guess I'm out of a job," he said.

"Not quite," Tony said. "How would you like to go to Lakeland?"

34.

The rain ended during the early morning hours. The air smelled of fresh-cut grass, salt sea.

Theodore mopped up puddles on the terrace and turned the cushions. Rita and David had breakfast out there: grapefruit juice, toasted raisin bread with guava shells and cream cheese, coffee laced with cinnamon.

"I forgot to tell you," Rita said. "I came home early, and the phone in your office was ringing. Why don't you put your office phone on the regular line so someone can take messages when you're out."

"I don't want to mix my private life with business," he said, smiling at her. "If it's important, they'll call back. Probably one of my clients."

"That Birdie Winslow you mentioned?"

"Oh, did I mention her? Yes, it probably was. She demands a lot of attention. Really more trouble than she's worth. I may have to drop her."

"How old is she?"

"Older than you, believe me. And heavier. Much, much heavier."

"Pretty?"

He fluttered a hand back and forth. "So-so. Passable, but not my type."

"Who is your type?"

"You. How many times do I have to tell you?"

"I never get tired of hearing it," she said, squeezing his arm. "What're your plans for today?"

"I have to see my travel agent. I've got to go to England for a few days. Tomorrow if I can get a flight."

"Me, too?"

"Nope. Not this time."

"That's what you said last time."

"You'll get your chance," he assured her. "Maybe sooner than you think. We'll have to visit Irving Donald Gevalt and get you fixed up with ID and a passport."

"Why can't I use my real name?"

"I don't think that would be wise," he said.

He spent the morning in his office, reviewing the accounts of his clients and drawing up a schedule of investments each would make in the Fort Knox Commodity Trading Fund. Birdie Winslow called shortly before noon.

"I phoned you all day yesterday," she complained. "I suppose you were gallivanting around."

"I wish I had been," Rathbone said. "But I had to attend a seminar in Boca on zero-coupon bonds. Very dull stuff."

"Can we have lunch today?"

"Oh, I'm so sorry," he said. "I have a luncheon appointment with a Palm Beach banker. He's probably on his way here right now, so I can't cancel."

"Then how about dinner?"

"I'm sorry," he repeated. "I'm flying to Germany tonight. Just for a few days. Maybe we can get together when I get back."

"David, you're not avoiding me, are you?"

"Of course not. It's just that I've been so busy. Making money is hard work, you know."

"Uh-huh. Well, I have something *very* important to talk to you about. I could come over to your office."

"Oh, it's in such a mess right now," he said, "I'd hate to have you see it. Tell you what: I have to stop at my travel agent after lunch to pick up my ticket. Suppose I come by your apartment for a short time at about three o'clock."

"*Divine!*" she said. "I'll have your vodka gimlet all ready for you."

"Wonderful," he said.

He had lunch with Jimmy Bartlett at an outdoor café on the Waterway. They sat at an umbrella table and watched the big boats coming south for the winter.

"I had a visit from Termite Tommy," Rathbone said. "He claims the German doesn't want to engrave new plates for the bills. Says his hands aren't steady enough. Which is probably true; the old guy was half in the bag when I met him in Lakeland."

"So the deal is off?"

"Not yet. The printer wants to buy one of those new color laser copiers, an office machine. He says it does beautiful work. Sharper than the original. If he can use his self-destruct paper to pick up copies of twenties and fifties, we're in business."

"Worth a try," Bartlett said. "Even if it's a half-ass reproduction. We're going to salt it in with the drug cash anyhow. And from what you say, it'll disintegrate before anyone has a chance to spot it as queer."

"Right. But I told Tommy to bring me a sample before I go ahead on this."

"He still thinks you're going to deposit the funny money in bank accounts?"

"That's what he thinks. Which brings me to our big problem. To get this thing rolling, I had to promise Tommy Ter-

mite a third and the printer a third. But that would leave
only a third for you and me to split. Not enough, considering
the risk we're running."

"I agree. And the idea was ours."

"Yours. The German is the producer and worth a third.
But Tommy is just a go-between, a messenger. He's not con-
tributing anything. So the problem is how to cut him out of
the loop."

"Finished your lunch?" Bartlett said. "Then let's move to
the bar and have a real drink."

They sat close together at the thatched bar and ordered
margaritas.

"What kind of a guy is this Tommy?" Bartlett asked.

"A boozer," Rathbone said. "A natural-born loser. I
thought he was out on parole or probation, and it would be
easy to set up a frame and send him back to the clink for a
while. But now I find out he served his full time. So, as they
say, he's paid his debt to society and he's home free."

"He could still be framed," Jimmy observed. "It doesn't
have to be anything heavy; just get him sent back for a year
or two. Our operation isn't going to last any longer than that."

"I know," David said, "but there's another factor. The
guy's psychopathic about going back behind bars. I'm afraid
that if he's even arrested for speeding, he'll rat to save his ass.
Then I'm down the tube."

Bartlett looked at him with a crooked smile. "And if you
go, I go—is that what you're saying?"

"Something like that," Rathbone admitted.

From where they sat they could watch an enormous yacht
moving slowly toward the Atlantic Boulevard bridge. There
was a small helicopter lashed to the top deck, and on the
afterdeck two older men in white flannels and blue blazers
were horsing around with three tanned young women in bikinis. They all had drinks, and their laughter carried across
the Waterway.

"From the way you describe it," Bartlett said, "there's only one solution."

The bridge rose, the shining yacht disappeared down the Intracoastal.

The two men turned to stare at each other.

"Let me ask around," Jimmy said.

"How much would it cost?" Rathbone asked in a low voice.

"Not much," Bartlett said.

They finished their drinks in silence, rose, lifted hands to each other, and separated. Rathbone returned to his car and lighted a Winston. He was startled to see that his fingers were trembling slightly. He smoked slowly, and by the time the cigarette was finished, his jits had disappeared. He drove two blocks to his travel agent.

He could have saved money by flying directly to San José from Miami. But he elected to go first to San Juan, then to Panama City, and finally to Costa Rica. He reasoned that if, for some reason, he was dogged, it would be easy to spot a tail making the same plane changes he did. He had learned to trust his instincts, and right now they were telling him to play it cozy.

"Need a hotel room in San José?" the agent asked.

"No," Rathbone said, "I'm staying with friends."

He glanced at his gold Rolex, saw it was time to be heading for Birdie Winslow's apartment. He considered bringing her a gift, then decided not to; it would be smart to chill that relationship.

She met him at the door wearing lounging pajamas in psychedelic colors that made him blink. She threw her meaty arms about him in a close embrace that stifled him.

"You bad boy!" she cried. "Never home when I phone. Never come to see me."

"I've really been busy, Birdie," he said. "And then this trip to Spain came up unexpectedly."

"I thought you said you're going to Germany."

"Spain *and* Germany. And I haven't even started packing yet. So I'm afraid I can't stay very long. You said you had something important to talk about."

"Something *very* important," she said. "But first you sit yourself down, and I'll serve you a vodka gimlet just the way you like it."

This one had two ice cubes, but he postponed tasting it, fearing the worst.

"Now then," he said, "what's this all about?"

"Come over here and sit near me," she said, patting the couch cushion. "You're so far away."

Obediently he heaved himself out of the armchair where he had hopefully sought refuge and sat next to her. She put a heavy hand on his knee.

"David, you told me you live in this cramped one-bedroom apartment, and today you mentioned how messy your office is. I really don't like this apartment all that much, and my lease will be up in a few months. So my wonderful idea is this: Why don't the two of us take an apartment together? A really big place with enough room for your office and a nice living room and terrace where we could do a lot of entertaining. I think it would be fun, don't you?"

He lifted his drink slowly and swallowed half, not tasting it.

"Birdie," he said, "that's a heavy decision to make. You know, we're the best of friends now, but living together is something entirely different. I've known couples who have tried it, and within a week or so they're at each other's throat."

"I just know that could never happen with us because we get along so well together. David, you're not involved with anyone else right now, are you?"

"Oh no," he said. "No, nothing like that."

"Well, there you are! You're by your lonesome and so am I—which is really silly when you think about it. I mean paying two rents and keeping two kitchens and all. If we lived together, we could share the rent and have this fabulous big apartment we could decorate just the way we want it. What do you think?"

He finished his drink. "Birdie, first of all I want to thank you for suggesting it. It's quite a compliment to me. But I'm not sure we could make a go of it. Sometimes I work till midnight and even later. I have clients visiting and business meetings in my office. I even—"

"Oh, I'd respect your privacy," she interrupted. "You don't have to worry about that. And we could have all your friends over for cocktail parties and dinners. I thought we might get a place right on the beach, with a terrace. And sometimes I'd make a nice, home-cooked meal when we didn't feel like going out. I'd even keep your office neat and all tidied up so you wouldn't be ashamed of it."

"You make it sound very attractive," he said, trying to smile. "But as I said, it's a big decision, and I think we should both consider it very carefully and talk more about it before we make up our minds."

"Oh, I've already made up my mind," she said gaily. "I think it would be *divine!*"

"Well, I promise you I'll give it very serious thought."

"And you'll let me know?"

"Of course."

"When?"

"Suppose we do this: When I get back from Europe, we'll get together and discuss it in more detail. Meanwhile, I promise you, I'll be thinking about it very, very carefully. Neither of us wants to rush into something we might regret later."

She swooped suddenly to kiss his lips. "I'd never regret it," she said breathlessly. "Never!"

He drove home recklessly, speeding, jumping lights, cutting off other cars. And steadily cursing as he frantically devised scenarios to finesse his way out of this outrageous complication.

He went directly to his office and revised his plan so that Birdie Winslow's total wealth would be invested in the Fort Knox Commodity Trading Fund. Then he sat back and tried to figure out how this new development would affect his schedule.

When Rita came home from work, he was seated on the terrace working on a big iced gimlet and staring out over the ocean.

"Where's *my* drink?" she demanded.

He looked at her a moment without replying. Then: "Remember this morning you asked when you were going on a trip with me, and I said it might be sooner than you think."

"Sure, I remember," Rita said. "So?"

"I was right. When I get back, we'll go to Gevalt and get you new ID and a passport."

"Whatever you say, boss," she said. "Now can I have a kiss and a drink, in that order?"

"Whatever you say, boss," he said, and felt better.

35.

The rip-off of Sidney Coe's boiler room went pretty much the way Warren Fowler described it. Manny Suarez closed a deal with a mooch in Little Rock, Arkansas, for $2,000 in the Fort Knox Fund stock. He told the sucker to mail his check to the West Palm Beach office. Then he informed Fowler of the sale.

"When do I get my moaney?" he asked. "And who pays me?"

"You'll get paid as soon as the check clears," Fowler assured him. "Then I'll give you your seventy-five percent."

"The check will be made out to Instant Investments, Inc. So how does your friend cash it?"

Fowler shrugged. "That's his problem. Maybe he peddles the checks to another goniff at a ten-percent discount. That would still leave him fifteen percent clear. But I suspect he may have opened an account in an out-of-state bank in the name of Instant Investments. In any event, you'll get your money from me."

"Just don't go out-of-state," Manny said, and both men laughed.

Suarez took Saturday off and drove up to West Palm Beach. He had never been there before and it took him a half-hour to locate the office. It was in a grungy neighborhood, on the second floor over a gun shop. There was a card thumbtacked to the locked door. All it said was "Instant Investments. Please slide mail under door."

Manny went downstairs to the gun shop and waited patiently while a clerk sold a semiautomatic rifle to a pimply-faced youth with a banner, *Death before dishonor,* tattooed on his right bicep.

When the kid left, carrying his rifle in a canvas case, Manny approached the clerk. He was an oldish guy, heavy through the chest and shoulders. He was wearing a stained T-shirt that had printing on the front: GUNS DON'T KILL PEOPLE. PEOPLE KILL PEOPLE.

"The owner around?" Suarez asked.

The beefy guy looked at him. "Who wants to know?" he demanded.

Sighing, Suarez took out his shield and ID from the Miami Police Department. The clerk inspected them carefully.

"You're outside your jurisdiction, ain'tcha?" he said.

"Cut the crap," Manny said. "Where can I find the owner?"

"I'm the owner," the guy said, "and I got all my permits and licenses, and you can look at my books anytime you want."

"I'm not interested in your guns," Manny said. "Who owns the building?"

"I do."

"You rent the upstairs office?"

"That's right."

"Who rents it?"

"Some outfit that does mail order."

"What kind of mail order?"

"I don't know and I don't care."

"What's the name of the guy running it?"

"Who the hell knows? I don't."

"You must have some name. The name on the lease for the office."

"There ain't no lease. It's rented month to month."

"Who signs the rent checks?"

"There ain't no rent checks. I get paid in cash."

Manny stared at him. "You keep jerking me around," he said, "and you're in deep shit. I'll visit the locals and see what we can do about closing you down. Like is the fire exit clearly marked, is the toilet clean, do the sprinklers work, how do you handle your garbage, and so forth. Is that what you want?"

"The guy's name is Smith."

"Don't tell me it's good old John Smith."

"Robert Smith. I got his home address writ down on a piece of paper somewhere."

"Find it," Suarez commanded.

It took him another half-hour to locate the address, or rather where it should have been. It was a weedy vacant lot next to a small factory that made novelties such as whoopee cushions, dribble glasses, and plastic dog turds. Manny drove back to the gun shop.

"You again?" the owner said.

"Me again," Manny said. "This Robert Smith, does he come to his office every day?"

"Nah. Two, three times a week."

"To pick up his mail?"

"I guess."

"What does he drive?"

"A black BMW."

Manny whistled. "The mail order business must be good," he said. "Tell you what: I'm going to phone you every day next week. I want you to get the license number of that

BMW. I'll keep calling until you get it. Hokay? I know you want to cooperate with your law enforcement officers."

"Oh yeah," the guy said. "Sure I do."

"Uh-huh," Suarez said. "Well, here's your chance."

"This Robert Smith, what's he wanted for?"

"He's been cheating on his girlfriend. She claims he's been sleeping with his wife."

He called the gun shop on Monday. Robert Smith hadn't shown up. But he was there on Tuesday morning, and the owner gave Manny the number on the BMW's license plate. Suarez phoned Tony Harker.

"The guy who has that office in West Palm Beach," he said. "The one who's ripping off Sid Coe. He calls himself Robert Smith and he drives a black BMW. Here's the license number."

"Got it," Harker said. "I'll check it out with Tallahassee. Call me back tonight."

Manny phoned him at his motel, a little before midnight.

"Well?" he said. "Is it David Rathbone?"

"No," Harker said, sounding disappointed. "It's Mortimer Sparco."

36.

They were slouched in armchairs in Harker's living room, bare feet up on the shabby cocktail table. They were nursing beers. It was cool enough to turn off the air conditioner and open the windows. They heard the scream of a siren speeding by on A1A.

"That's the 911 truck," Rita said. "You know what they call this stretch of road? Cardiac Canyon."

"I'm liable to have one," Tony said, "if I don't get a few days off to unwind."

"So?" she said. "Take them."

"Can't," he said. "Too much happening. Things are really heating up. Right after you called I put a man on Rathbone at the Miami Airport, and we got a look at his ticket. He thought he was being cute, going to Costa Rica by way of Puerto Rico and Panama. So I had to arrange for a different agent to pick him up in San Juan, and another at Panama City. So he wouldn't spot the tail. A lot of phone calls, a lot of work to coordinate all that in a short time."

"And he's in Costa Rica now?"

"The last I heard. He got off the plane in San José, where a fourth agent took up the trail. This is costing Uncle Samuel a mint."

"He can afford it. What do you suppose David is up to?"

"You want me to guess? I'd guess he's preparing to make a run for it sometime soon. He probably has fake ID from that Gevalt guy, and he's been building up his offshore bank accounts. Maybe he's bought a house or hacienda, whatever they call it, in Costa Rica, and he's planning his retirement. Taking all his loot with him, of course. Has he said anything to you about leaving the country?"

Rita took a swallow of her beer. "Not a word," she said.

"Well, I'll bet he's working on it. If he follows the pattern, he'll stick around long enough to make one final killing, then take off. We'll have to move in on him before that. The agent tailing him right now in San José will try to find out what name he's using. Then we'll be able to check other property and bank accounts in the Bahamas and Cayman Islands. If we can nail him under RICO, we'll take everything but the fillings in his teeth."

"Have you discovered what the Fort Knox Fund is?"

"Working on it. I think it's got something to do with drugs, but I haven't pinned it down yet."

She slumped farther down in her chair. "Drugs? David wouldn't have anything to do with drugs. He's strictly small-time."

"Don't kid yourself. If there's easy money to be made without too much risk, he'll be dealing and pushing like all the other punks. And drugs are only half of it. There's a good chance he's also working some kind of counterfeiting scam. I should know more about that next week. Rita, you've got to get rid of the notion that your Prince Charming is just a naughty boy clipping widows and divorcées for a few bucks. This man is a vicious criminal, and he's dangerous. Do me a favor, will you?"

She looked up at him. "What?"

"Get out. Now. I won't pull you because it'll look like you weren't doing your job. But if you request reassignment, Crockett will find another slot for you; I know he will. And no one will blame you."

"No," she said. "I signed on for this particular job, and I want to be in on the kill. You have no complaints about the way I've handled it, do you?"

"No," he said in a low voice. "No complaints."

"Then let's have another beer and go to bed. And no more bullshit about taking me off the case. Okay?"

"Okay," he said. "If that's the way you want it."

Her tanned body was a smooth rope and entwined about him, her long hair making a secret tent for them both. The heat of her flesh made him wonder if he could be scorched by her intensity.

He heard himself making sounds he didn't recognize and couldn't stop. And then she was crying out, grasping him. It was only later, when he reached to caress her face, that he felt the wet and wondered if it might be tears.

"Better than a few days off," he murmured. "To unwind."

"That afternoon I met you," she said. "In your office. I thought you were nerdy."

"Did you? I suppose I was."

"*Was*," she said. "Not now."

"The nerd turns," he said. "No more inhaler, no more allergies, no more nervous stomach. Marry me."

She laughed.

He propped himself on an elbow, peered down at her in the gloom. "I'm serious," he said. "Marry me."

She reached up to touch his cheek. "Tony," she said softly.

"That's really why I want you off the job," he said. "I want you out of his bed. I want you to resign. I want you to marry me."

"Oh darling," she said, "you want, you want, you want.

It's very nice to hear, but I want, too. To be independent. Do it my way. I like my job, and I'm good at it; I know I am."

"Listen," he said, "I composed this speech. Can I recite it to you?"

"Sure. Go ahead."

"You're the only woman I've ever met who can lighten me up. When I'm with you, I grin. If it's not on my face, it's inside. When you're away from me, I work nights and weekends and I don't know what I'm killing myself for. But when I'm with you, my life makes sense. It has meaning. I'm not only jealous of the time you spend with Rathbone, I'm jealous of the time you spend alone, doing your nails or sleeping or whatever. I want us to be together every minute. Obsessive? I guess. What it all boils down to is that I love you and want to spend the rest of my life with you. End of speech."

She sat up in bed, hugged her knees. "Thank you," she said huskily. "You really know how to puff up a girl's ego. But you're talking about a big decision, Tony."

"I didn't expect you to yell, 'Yes, yes, yes!' But will you think about it? Consider it carefully and seriously?"

"Of course," she said. "This is my first proposal. Plenty of propositions, but only this one proposal. So I don't really, honey, know how to handle it. You're right; I better think long and hard about it."

"Do that," he said, leaning forward to kiss her knee. "Please. Don't just reject me out of hand. I've got some money—not a lot but some—and I make a good living; you know that. Also, if I can put Rathbone behind bars, that'll help my career. I just want you to know that I can support you, but if you want to keep on working, that's okay, too. But preferably not as a cop."

"Wow," she said, "you've really tossed me a fastball. I don't know what to do. Yes, I do."

She was so loving he wanted to shout his rapture. Her

warm mouth drifted, tongue flicked, prying fingers tugged him along to ecstasy.

"Rita," he said, gasping, "I can't take this."

"Yes, you can," she said, and wouldn't stop.

She pleasured him as if she had a debt to pay, and only his gratification would wipe it out. Her ministrations became increasingly rapid; she seemed driven by a wildness that calmed only when he was drained of sense and vigor.

Then she slid out of bed, went into the bathroom, and didn't emerge for at least ten minutes. By that time Harker was standing shakily and gulping a fresh brew. She took the can from his hand and finished it.

"I've been thinking," she said, speaking rapidly. "Not about you and me but about business. Earlier tonight when we were talking about the case, and I said I wanted to be in on the kill, I meant I want to be around when the whole thing is wrapped up. But I don't want to be there when you take Rathbone. After all, I've led the lamb to the slaughter, haven't I? So I'd appreciate it if you could give me plenty of advance notice of when you intend to bust everyone and I'll make myself scarce. You can understand that, can't you?"

"Oh sure," he said.

37.

Harker told Roger Fortescue about the self-destruct paper and how Rathbone pushed a counterfeit Treasury check made of the stuff through a Boca bank.

"Rathbone went to Lakeland and met with a man he referred to as the printer," Tony said. "That's the only lead I've got. It's all yours."

"Sheet," Fortescue said. "I better get some more skinny before I go up there or I'll just be spinning my wheels."

So he spent almost two days at his desk in the bullpen, making phone calls and requesting assistance from strangers. It took that long because invariably they stalled until they could check his bona fides. Then sometimes they'd call back, but usually he had to make a second or third call. But he never lost his temper, figuring to catch more flies with honey than with vinegar. And he was properly apologetic for the extra work he was causing and grateful when his inquiries yielded results.

He started with the Secret Service and was shunted from

office to office until he was connected with a cranky agent who finally agreed to ask his computer if there was any record of a counterfeiter working out of Lakeland, Florida.

The computer spit out the name of Herman Weisrotte, German-born but a naturalized citizen. He had just completed a stay in stir for wholesaling twenties and fifties. Quality stuff, too. The computer even provided a physical description and his last known address in Lakeland.

So far, so good.

Then, because he had the smarts of a street cop, Fortescue called the warden's office in the prison where Weisrotte had done time and asked a very nice lady for the name of the forger's cellmate. It turned out that during the last year in jail Herman had shared living quarters with a convicted swindler named Thomas J. Keeffringer, recently released, who had committed his depredations over a five-state area, but mostly in south Florida.

This time Roger phoned a friend, Sam Washburn, an old bull who had spent most of his working life in the Detective Division of the Fort Lauderdale Police Dept. Then he had retired to spend his remaining years making birds and animals from shells his wife picked up on the beach. Sam had given Fortescue a shell owl which Estelle had promptly given to her mother who gave it to her minister who, at last report, was desperately seeking someone who would accept it.

The moment Fortescue mentioned Thomas J. Keeffringer, Washburn started laughing. "Termite Tommy!" he said, and told the investigator about the con man's scam using bottled bugs and sawdust to convince mooches to sign on for costly termite control.

"Is he a heavy?" Roger asked.

"Nah, he's a pussycat. Likes the sauce. A dynamite salesman. I heard he's out. What's he been up to?"

"I'm not sure. Maybe counterfeiting."

"That's a switch. Boosting mouthwash is more his style."

So now Fortescue had two names and an address in Lakeland. He went home to pack.

"How long will you be gone?" Estelle wanted to know.

"It depends," he said.

"Thank you very much," she said. "I may not be here when you get back. The bag boy at Publix has eyes for me."

"Lots of luck," Roger said.

He arrived at Lakeland late in the evening and checked into a motel with a neon sign that advertised TV—HAPPY HOUR—POOL PARTY ON SAT. Fortescue's room smelled of wild cherry deodorant and had a framed lithograph of the Battle of Shiloh on the wall over the bed. He wasted a few hours watching television.

In the morning he checked in with the locals as a matter of professional courtesy. He talked to an overweight detective who was working on an anchovy pizza and drinking Jolt for breakfast.

"Yeah, we brace the Kraut every now and then," he said, his mouth full. "He looks to be straight. He's got this little store where he prints up letterheads, business cards, and stuff like that."

"He wouldn't be printing the queer again, would he?"

The dick wiped his smeared lips with a paper napkin. "That I doubt very much. First of all, the guy's an alkie. Talk to him later than four in the afternoon, he just don't make sense. Second of all, he never seems to go nowhere. So how can he be pushing?"

"No funny money showing up in town?"

"Now and then. Nothing big. And most of the queer is spent by snowbirds who don't know what they got. Some of it is miserable stuff."

"Ever hear of Thomas J. Keeffringer, known as Termite Tommy?"

"Nope. That's a new one on me. Why all the interest in Weisrotte and this Termite Tommy?"

"Beats the hell out of me," Fortescue said. "They just sent me up here to see if these guys are behaving themselves."

"They could have done that with a phone call."

"Sure they could," Roger agreed, rising. "Well, I'll nose around and see if anything smells. If I find anything, you'll be the first to know."

"Uh-huh," the detective said, starting on his second slice of pizza. "When pigs fly."

Fortescue looked up the address of Weisrotte's Print Shop in the telephone directory and located it without too much trouble. He parked two blocks away and walked back. It was a dilapidated place with a dusty plate-glass window cracked across one corner. The interior was more of the same: a long, littered room crammed with cartons of stationery; presses of all sizes, some of them rusty and obviously unused; yellowed, flyspecked samples of business cards, letterheads, and envelopes pinned to a corkboard above a scarred sales counter.

The only piece of equipment that looked modern and new was a big white-enameled machine on casters. It had plastic shelves protruding from both ends, and in front was a push-button control panel that looked as complex as the dash on a 747.

An old man was working a small treadle press in the rear of the shop. When he saw Fortescue standing there, he came shuffling forward, wiping his palms on his ink-stained apron. He looked to be pushing seventy, with the suety face of a heavy drinker, bulbous nose a web of burst capillaries.

"Mr. Weisrotte?" Roger asked.

"Yah," the printer said, peering at him through inflamed eyes.

"You print business cards?"

"Yah."

"How much?"

"Thirty dollars a thousand."

"Wow," Roger said, "that's stiff."

"Iss quality work," Weisrotte said. "Any color ink. Iss thermographed. Raised printing. Six lines of type. Take it or leave it."

"I'll ask my boss," Roger said, and turned to leave. Then he paused and pointed at the gleaming white machine. "What the hell is that thing?" he asked.

Weisrotte came alive. "Iss color laser copier," he said proudly. "The latest. Iss beautiful, no?"

"Yeah, that's some piece of machinery. What'll they think of next."

As he exited from the shop a bozo was climbing out of a dented pickup truck parked at the curb. He was tall, skinny, and dressed like an undertaker. He headed for Weisrotte's door.

It's not enough to be a smart cop; you also need luck. Fortescue decided to try his.

"Hey, Tommy!" he cried. "How you doing, man?"

The guy stopped, turned slowly, stared at the agent. "Do I know you?" he asked in a toneless voice.

"Sure you do," Roger said cheerily. "Leroy Washington. I just got out a couple of weeks ago."

Keeffringer shook his head. "I don't make you," he said.

"I know," Fortescue said, laughing. "All us smokes look alike. I was in Cellblock C."

"Yeah? Where did you work?"

"They had me all over the place, but mostly in the kitchen."

"That was lousy food," Tommy said, relaxing.

"I know, but we did the best we could with what they gave us. You live in Lakeland?"

"For a while."

"Yeah," Roger said, "me, too. I just stopped by to visit an old girlfriend. Then I'm going down to Lauderdale. More action."

"Lauderdale?" Termite Tommy said. "I'm heading there later this afternoon. Need a lift?"

Fortescue jerked a thumb at the battered pickup. "Not in that clunker," he said, grinning. "Thanks anyway, but the girlfriend is fattening me up so I think I'll stick around a few days. Hey, it's been good talking to you, man. Maybe I'll bump into you again on the Lauderdale Strip."

"Maybe you will," Tommy said. "Nice seeing you again, Leroy."

Fortescue ambled slowly down the street in case Keeffringer was watching. But the moment he turned the corner, he walked quickly to his parked Volvo. He reckoned this was too great to pass up; he'd probably do better with Termite Tommy in Fort Lauderdale than tailing the Kraut around Lakeland.

He packed swiftly and checked out of the motel. He drove back to Weisrotte's shop and was gratified to see the mangled pickup still in front. Fortescue found a place to park about a half-block away where he could watch the action. Keeffringer had said he was heading for Lauderdale later that afternoon, so Roger left his car and found a fast-food joint not too far away. He bought a meatball submarine, a bag of fries, and a quart container of iced Coke. He returned to his stakeout and settled down.

It was almost three o'clock before Termite Tommy came out. And in all that time, Fortescue hadn't seen a single customer enter the shop. Which probably meant the German wasn't buying his schnapps with the income from printing business cards.

He gave the pickup a head start, then took off after it. He didn't stick too close, figuring Keeffringer would probably cut over to take Highway 27 south, and even if he lost him at a light he could always pick him up later; that decrepit truck would be breathing hard to do fifty mph.

But he never did lose Termite Tommy, even as traffic heavied south of Avon Park and Sebring, and even when they drove through a couple of heavy rainsqualls that darkened

216

the sky and cut visibility. They hit Fort Lauderdale a little after nine o'clock, and Fortescue decided that if Tommy had driven all this way for a shackup with some bimbo, he himself would have a hard time explaining to Tony Harker why he had deserted his assignment in Lakeland.

Keeffringer seemed to know exactly where he was going. He cut over to Federal Highway, turned onto Commercial, and pulled into the parking lot of the Grand Palace Restaurant.

"Welcome home," Roger said softly, feeling better.

He parked a block away and sauntered back. He returned in time to see Termite Tommy come out of the side entrance to the Palace Lounge. With him was a blond guy wearing a white suit. When they passed under the restaurant's outdoor lights, Fortescue thought the newcomer might be David Rathbone. But he couldn't be sure, having seen only that photograph Harker had.

Roger watched as the two men climbed into a parked car, a big, black job that, from where he stood in the shadows, he guessed was either a Rolls or a Bentley. They were together less than five minutes, then got out of the car. They shook hands. Rathbone, if that's who it was, went back into the Palace Lounge. Termite Tommy returned to his truck and pulled away. Fortescue could have taken up the tail again but didn't.

"The hell with it," he said aloud.

He drove home, and when he walked in carrying his suitcase, Estelle looked up from her sewing and said, "Have a nice vacation?"

But she rustled up a great meal of cold chicken, spaghetti with olive oil and garlic, and a watercress and arugula salad. She also warmed up a wedge of apple pie and topped it with a slice of cheddar, just the way she knew he liked it.

She watched him wolf all this down and asked, "Didn't you have any lunch today?"

"Oh I did, I did," he said. "Instant ptomaine."

He opened his second bottle of Heineken before he called Harker at his motel. He gave Tony a brief account of meeting Weisrotte and how he tailed Termite Tommy back to Lauderdale.

"He met a man in the parking lot of the Grand Palace," he reported. "I think it was probably David Rathbone, but I can't swear to it. A good-looking blond guy wearing a white suit. They sat together in a car that was either a Rolls or a Bentley."

"Rathbone drives a black Bentley," Tony said. "It was probably him and his car. Find out anything about that self-destruct paper?"

"Sheet," Fortescue said, "I barely had time to turn around. But while I was in the German's printshop, I spotted something interesting. He's got a brand-new color laser copying machine."

"Oh-oh," Harker said.

38.

"When's this guy going to show up?" Rathbone demanded.

"Hey, take it easy," Jimmy Bartlett said. "You've been awfully antsy lately."

"You're right," David said. "I'm getting impatient. And when you get impatient, you make mistakes. I'll try to slow down. But did we have to meet in a crummy place like this?"

Bartlett shrugged. "He picked it, and at the last minute. Look, the guy is playing a double game. If his agency finds out he's turned sour, he'll draw ten, at least. And if the Colombians even suspect he might be a plant—which he isn't—he's dead meat. So can you blame the guy for being paranoid? He's just meeting us as a personal favor to me. He'll show up—after he's made sure the place isn't staked out."

They were sitting in the bedroom of a motel far west on Atlantic Boulevard. The room smelled of roach spray, and the wheezing air conditioner in the window was no help at all. Bartlett had brought along a bottle of Chivas and a stack of plastic cups. They got a tub of ice cubes from the machine in the lobby, and were working on strong Scotch and waters.

"Before he shows," Jimmy said, "let's talk a little business. That queer twenty you got from Termite Tommy is a gem. *Was* a gem. I went to dig it out just before you picked me up, but it wasn't there. Just a pile of confetti."

"I told you," Rathbone said.

"David, this is the greatest invention since sliced bread. The possibilities are staggering. We'll start with a deal I've got coming up in a week or so: a big deposit at the Crescent Bank in Boca."

"Mike Mulligan covering for you?"

"Oh sure; he's true blue. The deposit will run at least a hundred grand. Probably more. I suggest we begin by salting it with thirty thousand of the queer and taking out thirty Gs of genuine bills."

"Whatever you say, Jimmy."

"If it goes okay, we'll increase our take from future deposits. Can you get thirty grand of those color prints from Tommy?"

"In twenties?"

"Better make them fifties and hundreds, half and half. Twenties will be too big a bundle."

"All right. I'll let him know."

"And if Tommy is out of the picture, you'll be able to deal directly with the printer?"

"Absolutely. He—"

But then there was a single knock on the door, and both men stood up. Bartlett put the door on the chain, opened it cautiously, peered out. He saw who it was, closed the door, slipped off the chain, then opened the door wide.

"Hiya, Paul," he said. "Glad you could make it."

The man who entered was tall, broad-shouldered, with a confident grin. His madras sports jacket and linen slacks didn't come off plain pipe racks. He moved smoothly and, before saying a word, walked into the bathroom and out again, opened the closet door and looked in, even went down on one knee to peek under the bed.

He rose, dusting his hands. "No offense," he said to Bartlett, "but I'm alive and mean to stay that way. Who's this?"

"David. He's in the game. Paul, meet David. David, meet Paul."

They nodded. No one shook hands.

"Warm in here," Paul said. "Why don't we all take off our jackets."

"Paul," Bartlett said gently, "we're not wired; take my word for it."

"Sorry," the newcomer said, still grinning. "Force of habit. Hey, Chivas Regal! That's nice."

"Help yourself," David said. He sat on the bed, let the other two men take the spindly armchairs.

"So?" Paul said, taking a gulp of his drink. "What do you want to know?"

"An overall view of the world market," Jimmy Bartlett said. "What's going to happen in the next year. Your opinion, of course. We know you don't have a crystal ball. We just want your informed guess on the future fluctuation of the product price. Cocaine especially."

"Okay," Paul said, "but all this is just between us. Right now there's a product surplus. That should evaporate within three months. Demand will hold steady; supply will contract."

"How do you figure that?" David asked. "Government raids? Interception of shipments?"

Paul laughed. "Forget it," he advised. "Washington claims they stop ten percent at the borders. The truth is, if they're grabbing two percent they're lucky. No, the reason for the coming shortfall is more basic than that. The U.S. is saturated, all markets covered, no possibility of any great expansion. So the cartels are turning to the European Community. What's the market over there right now? Modest for heroin and marijuana, underdeveloped for cocaine. There are a few wealthy snorters, no one is free-basing, and they don't even know about crack. Plus you've got to realize that by 1992, the borders between countries in Western Europe will be a sieve; it'll be no problem at all to move the product. So the cartels' merchandising and sales managers have planned an all-out campaign to flood the whole continent with coke. It's already started in a small way, but eventually the European demand should be as strong or stronger than the American. That has got to mean reduced shipments to the U.S. and higher prices. You asked for an educated guess; that's mine."

"How high do you think it'll go?" David said.

Paul pondered a moment. "Assuming general inflation remains at its present level, I can see a wholesale price increase in the U.S. to 30K a kilo within a year. That may eliminate one social problem because the price has got to be about 10K before it's economically feasible to produce five- and ten-dollar vials of crack. But at the same time the price is rising in the U.S., it'll be reduced dramatically in the European Community. The Colombian marketing experts know there's a two- or three-year wait before a strong consumer demand develops. Cocaine addiction takes that long. Heroin and crack work much faster, of course. But the cartels have the money to invest and the patience to wait for the market to build. And cutting the wholesale price is the quickest way to open up Western Europe, but it'll mean a higher price per kilo in this country. Yes, I think it'll go to thirty grand within a year, and I wouldn't be surprised to see it hit fifty thousand in two or three years as more production goes overseas."

"Paul," Bartlett said, "who knows about this decision to target the European Community for coke? Do the domestic dealers know about it? The retailers?"

"I doubt that," the drug agent said, pouring himself another drink. "They're only interested in today's profits. They know from nothing about long-term planning and international marketing strategies. But the Colombian cartel executives realize they've got to develop worldwide demand if their growth is to maintain its current rate of increase. And after Western Europe, of course, there is always Russia, Japan, China. These men may not be Harvard MBAs, but they recognize the reality of the global economy and their need to expand their international trade. And price manipulation is one way of achieving that."

"Thank you, Paul," Jimmy Bartlett said. "You've given us exactly what we wanted. Can we contact you for an update in a month or so?"

"Whenever you like," Paul said, finishing his drink and rising. "I don't care how you use the information, as long as I'm not named as the source. By the way, this was a freebie, Jimmy. I owed you one for tipping me about that rat from Panama. Now we're even. If you want updates, it'll cost."

"Understood," Bartlett said. "Thanks again."

"Nice meeting you, David," Paul said.

"Nice meeting you, Paul," David said.

After he departed, the door locked and chained, Rathbone and Bartlett mixed a final drink.

"You believe him?" David asked.

"I trust his judgment and inside knowledge of the industry. He deals with some very important men. If he says the kilo price of coke is going to rise in the U.S., then it will. He'd have no reason to con us."

"I'll take your word for it. So we can plan purchases and sales by the Fort Knox Fund on that premise, that prices are going up because of a coming scarcity?"

"I think so. Let's start out on a small scale, wait a month or so, and then see if Paul's predictions are on the money."

"Okay," Rathbone said, "I'll contact Frank Little and set up a meet with his biggest client. We'll try to sell for eighteen to twenty thousand a kilo. How does that sound?"

"About right. Ask for more than twenty, but fight anything lower."

"What quantity?" Rathbone asked.

"How much is in the Fund's kitty right now?"

"About a quarter-mil."

"Then let's try to peddle fifteen kilos. We'll have enough cash from Sid and Mort's mooches before we make the buy."

"Suits me," David said. "How much should we offer on the buy?"

"Say 12K per kilo. We may have to pay more and sell for less. But let's aim for a net of 100 Gs. Now to get back to Termite Tommy . . . I talked to two professionals, the Corcoran brothers, well qualified to handle our problem. Their price is ten thousand. But they're going to be up in Macon on assignment for a few weeks. I could get the job done cheaper, but I'd feel better if we waited for these men to return from Georgia. They're really the best in the business."

"Ten grand?" Rathbone said. "I thought it would be less."

"Oh hell," Bartlett said, "you can buy a kill for fifty bucks if you want to trust a hophead. Do you? I don't."

"I don't either. You're right; this is not something we want to chisel. All right, we'll wait until the Corcorans are available. Meanwhile I'll get that thirty thousand in queer from Tommy. Now let's get out of this shithouse."

They rose, finished their drinks, looked around to make certain they were leaving nothing behind.

"Hey," Jimmy Bartlett said, "did I tell you my younger son won a catamaran race off Key West?"

"No kidding?" David Rathbone said. "That's great!"

39.

Simon Clark was aware of one of the basic tenets of con men, corporate raiders, and investment bankers: Never gamble with your own money. Although he was not ultra-rich, his net worth was sufficient to bankroll Nancy Sparco's new business if he chose to. He did not so choose.

The sting money he had invested with Mortimer Sparco's discount brokerage, if it could be recovered, would be more than enough to get Nancy started. Thus, in effect, the U.S. Government (actually the taxpayers) would finance her escort service in south Florida.

The puzzle was how to reclaim the money before the boom was lowered on Sparco and all his assets seized. Clark thought he might be able to finagle it if he could be present when the bust went down. Sharks like Sparco invariably kept a heavy stack of currency on hand for bribes and getaway insurance. It wouldn't be the first time a law enforcement officer had glommed onto a criminal's money during the confusion of an arrest.

But Clark decided that robbing the robber was just too risky; there had to be a better way of regaining the cash that had presumably purchased shares in the Fort Knox Commodity Trading Fund.

He put that problem aside temporarily and concentrated on his own future and the path it might take. While stealing Sparco's poke during the arrest had its dangers, there would be much less peril in lifting a list of the broker's clients. With that in hand, Clark would have a strong base for starting his own discount brokerage, pushing the same penny stocks that had made Sparco a wealthy man.

But running a brokerage, even semi-legitimately, required many registrations, licenses, and permits. And the SEC was always looking over your shoulder. Clark preferred a simpler swindle, with the risk-benefit ratio more in his favor. He decided his best bet might be to follow David Rathbone's example and become an investment adviser or whatever you wanted to call it.

With a limited number of wealthy clients with deficient money smarts, Clark reckoned he could do very well indeed. His background as a U.S. ADA would inspire confidence, he had an impressive physical presence, and his courtroom experience had taught him that when sincerity is demanded, style is everything.

So when he wasn't on the phone to Denver and Chicago, learning more details of Sparco's price manipulation and market domination of certain worthless securities, Clark went looking for permanent housing and an office location. He figured that by using leverage he could hang out his shingle for about a hundred thousand tops. He could do it for less, of course, but recognized the value of front in a business based on clients' faith in his probity.

The only opportunities he had to relax and enjoy south Florida came when Nancy Sparco visited his hotel room, two or three afternoons a week. Then they drank too much, talked too much, loved too much and, as she said, "told the whole world to go screw."

She showed up one afternoon when rainsqualls from the southwest had driven all the tourists off the beach and flooded the streets. Clark saw at once, despite a heavy layer of pancake makeup, that she was sporting a black eye. He embraced her, then held her by the shoulders and stared at the mouse.

"Who hung that on you?" he asked.

"Who?" Nancy said bitterly. "It wasn't the Tooth Fairy. My shithead hubby."

"Does he do that often?"

"No," she admitted. "Maybe a couple of times since we've been married."

"Was he drunk?"

"Nah. Just pissed off when I told him he couldn't screw his way out of a wet paper bag. I guess I shouldn't have said it, but I can't stand the guy anymore. I pray for the day when I can give him the one-finger salute and walk out. Pour me a drink, will you, hon. I've got to take off my shoes; they're soaked through."

He mixed bourbon highballs, and they slumped in armchairs and watched rain stream down the picture windows.

"I never belted a woman in my life," Clark said.

"I know you haven't, sweetie, because you've got class. But I don't have it so bad. A friend of mine, Cynthia Coe—her husband, Sid, runs a boiler room—is a real battered wife. Sid has a rotten temper and he's a mean drunk. When he's crossed, he takes it out on Cynthia. Really slams her around. Once he actually broke her arm."

"Why does she put up with it?"

"Why? M-o-n-e-y. After he beats the shit out of her, he starts crying, apologizes, swears he'll never do it again, and gives her cash, a rock, a gold watch, a string of pearls. Then a month later he's at it again. She says that when she's got enough money and jewelry put aside, she's going to give him the broom. But I doubt it."

"Maybe she enjoys it, too."

"Maybe she does," Nancy said. "A lot of nuts in this world, kiddo. I'm glad you and I are normal." She pulled off her dress and the two of them fell on the bed.

Afterward, Nancy asked, "Listen, you haven't forgotten about my new business, have you?"

"Of course not. I'm working on a couple of angles. You'll get your funding."

"When?"

"A month or so."

"Promise?"

"Yep. Nancy, I'm thinking about moving down here."

She sat up on the bed. "Hey, that's great! I love it! But what about your wife?"

He shrugged. "She'll be happy to see the last of me."

"Divorce?"

"Or separation. Whichever is cheaper. I'll leave it to my lawyer to cut a deal, but it's going to cost me no matter what."

"You plan to get a job down here?"

He didn't answer her question. "Tell me something, Nancy: Does your husband keep a list of his clients at home?"

She stared at him. "Oh-ho," she said, "you do have a plan, don't you? Thinking of joining the game?"

"I might," he said. "I'm tired of being a spectator."

"Well, I never saw Mort's client list. He probably keeps it in the office."

"Probably."

"But he does have a personal list of people he calls Super Suckers. Lots of loot and not much sense. That guy I told you about, Sid Coe, has his own list, and so does David Rathbone, another shark we know. They all have a Super Sucker list. Sometimes they get together and trade names like kids trade baseball cards."

"That's interesting," Clark said. "You think you might be able to get me a copy of your husband's list? It's worth a grand to me."

"In addition to the money for my escort service?"

"Of course. Two different deals."

She thought a moment. Then: "Five thousand," she said. "Those names are valuable. Money in the bank."

"How many names?"

"At least twenty. Maybe more. Widows, divorcées, senile old farts, and some younger swingers whose brains are scrambled. But all rich."

"Twenty-five hundred?" he asked.

"You got a deal," she said, and reached for him.

40.

"Look," Frank Little said to the man from New York, "I'll introduce this guy to you by his first name only. That's the way he wants it. Okay?"

"Sure," Lou Siena said. "I like a man who's careful. But who *is* he?"

"His full name is David Rathbone, and he runs an asset management company down here. But that's just a front. He spends most of his time in Colombia and Bolivia, advising the cartel bosses on how to launder their money, what legit investments to make, and how to move their cash around to take advantage of currency fluctuations. He's one smart apple, buddy-buddy with the cartel big shots. The only reason he agreed to this meet was that about a year ago I tipped him to a rat in Panama who could have caused a lot of trouble. David passed the guy's name along to the Colombians, and they handled it. So David owes me one."

"Uh-huh," Siena said, glancing at his watch. "I just hope he's on time. I got to get down to Miami by five o'clock."

"He'll be here," Little assured him. "Have another belt and relax."

They were in the back room of the blockhouse office of FL Sports Equipment, Inc., on Copans Road. And next door, in the deserted fast-food restaurant, the DEA agents in their command post had filmed the arrival of Lou Siena in his silver Lincoln Town Car. And they made a written record of the license number on his New York plates.

Little's office was strictly utilitarian, with a steel desk, steel chairs, and filing cabinet. There was a small safe disguised as a cocktail table, and on it were arranged a bottle of Chivas Regal, a tub of ice cubes, a stack of paper cups, and a six-pack of small club sodas.

"I still don't see the need for a signed contract," Siena said, pouring more Scotch into his cup.

"Lou," Frank said, "how long have we been dealing? Five, six years?"

"Something like that."

"And never a hassle. Which means we trust each other—right? I'm asking you to trust me on this. I want to expand my business. All I've been doing is transshipping. You make your own buys. It's delivered here, and you pick up. I've just been a go-between, a middleman, and you know I'll never make it big on my cut. So now I want to simplify the whole operation and become a distributor to wholesalers like you. I'll make the initial buy, get it put into the baseballs in Haiti just like before, bring it in, and you'll buy directly from me. That'll save you time and trouble, won't it?"

"I guess."

"Sure it will. And you can't blame me for wanting a bigger cut, can you? Now about the signed contracts. . . . You know the cartels are strictly COD. But where am I going to get the cash to make a fifteen-kilo buy? I've lined up a broker who'll make me a loan with very low vigorish, but first he wants to see some proof that I'm good for the money. And what better evidence could he want than a signed contract stating you're

231

willing to pay X number of dollars for those fifteen kilos in three months. Lou, you're a big man. Your name means more to the broker than mine. That's the reason for the signed contract. We'll use a code word for the coke, of course."

"You said X number of dollars for the fifteen kilos. What's X? How much you asking per kilo for delivery in three months?"

"That's why I asked David to come over and give us the lowdown on where the market is heading. I don't want to cheat you, and I don't want to cheat myself. I just heard a car pull up outside. That must be him. Excuse me a minute."

And next door, the DEA agent operating the TV camera reported to his partner: "A black Bentley just pulled up. One guy getting out. Caucasian male, five-ten or -eleven, one-eighty, blond, good-looking, wearing a vested black suit, white shirt, maroon tie. Take a look at the Bentley through your binocs and let's phone in the license number, along with the plates on the silver Lincoln. Headquarters can get started on the IDs."

"Lou, this is David," Frank Little was saying. "David, meet Lou. Mix yourself a drink and sit down."

"I'll have one," Rathbone said, "but only one. I've got to make this short. A heavy exporter is flying in from Mexico City, and I promised to meet his plane. What do you want to know?"

"Your overall view of the market," Little said. "Coke especially. Where's it going—up or down? What'll the kilo price be three months from now? Six months? A year?"

"Right now there's a product surplus," David said. "That will disappear within three months. Demand will remain steady or increase; supply will contract. In the U.S., the price per kilo will go up, up, up."

"How do you figure that?" Siena said.

Then, demonstrating almost total recall, Rathbone repeated the words of the renegade narc. But while Paul had merely reported, David used his words in a hard sell, leaning forward, staring steadily at Lou Siena, an easy enough trick if you concentrated your gaze on the space between a man's eyes.

He was a dynamite yak, very earnest, very sincere, very convincing. He spoke authoritatively of the global economy, the internationalization of trade, the significance of 1992, the decision of the drug cartels to concentrate their main marketing efforts in the European Community. He explained how they planned to reduce the kilo price to lure consumers in Western Europe, which would, inevitably, lead to higher prices in the U.S.

Lou Siena listened closely, fascinated. This was the first time he had heard such detailed financial information about his industry from a man who was obviously knowledgeable about the big picture and yet had enough street smarts to recognize how the relaxation of border regulations between European countries would facilitate drug trafficking.

"There's no doubt about it," David concluded firmly. "You'll see the wholesale price of high-quality cocaine hit 30K per kilo within three to six months, and I wouldn't be a bit surprised to see it go to 50K within a year. Any questions?"

"Yeah," Siena said. "How do I know you're giving me the straight poop?"

David stiffened, narrowed his eyes, looked coldly at the New Yorker. "What possible reason would I have to scam you? I'm meeting you today for the first time. I don't know what kind of deal you and Frank are cooking up, and I don't want to know. You asked for my opinion, and I gave it to you as honestly as I know how. And I resent the implication that I'm involved in some kind of a con game."

"Okay, okay," the other man said hastily. "I guess you're leveling."

Rathbone nodded, finishing his drink, and stood up. "I

don't care how you use what I told you, but just don't quote me as the source. I wouldn't care to have it get back to my close friends in Bogotá that I'm leaking inside information."

"Don't worry about it, David," Frank Little said. "You can depend on Lou and me. Thanks for your help."

"Now we're even," Rathbone said. "I wish you luck. See you around." Then he was gone.

"What did you think of him?" Little asked Siena.

"I guess he's straight. Like he said, what possible angle could he have?"

"Right. So let's figure coke will be up to 30K within three to six months. How about taking those fifteen kilos at 25 per?"

Then they started haggling.

An hour later Rathbone phoned Little from the office of the Fort Knox Fund. Rita was perched on his desk, filing her nails, bare legs crossed. As he talked, David stroked her knee.

"How did you make out?" he asked.

"Nineteen-five," Frank said.

"Not bad."

"I did my best, but he wouldn't come up. It's about five Gs more per kilo than he's been paying."

"So he bought my spiel?"

"Definitely. Very impressed. Said he'd like to meet with you again."

"Fat chance. Did he do the contract?"

"Signed, sealed, and delivered. Fifteen thousand chairs at nineteen-five per thousand. And the guy won't welsh, David. He's very hot on personal honor."

"Honor?" Rathbone said, laughing and leaning forward to kiss Rita's knee. "What's that? You did a good job, Frank. See you at the Palace tonight to celebrate?"

"I'll be there."

Rathbone hung up and grinned at Rita.

"Good news?" she asked.

"The best. We're going to be rich."

"I thought we were."

"You know what they say: You can never be too thin or too rich."

"I'll take care of thin," she said. "Rich is your department."

"I'm getting there," he said. "Now let's pick up a bottle of something cold and dry, and then go home and get some sun."

"Beautiful," she said. "I like this life."

41.

Mr. Crockett had become increasingly tetchy of late, and Tony Harker could only conclude the man was under increasing pressure from Washington to show some results. And because the chief was feeling the heat, his lieutenants were, too, and in turn were leaning on their subordinates.

Harker sat on one of those uncomfortable folding chairs in front of Crockett's desk and flipped through a sheaf of messages, telexes, and photographs.

"Here's what we've got so far, sir," he reported. "David Rathbone, using the name Dennis Reynolds—same initials you'll note; so he doesn't have to throw away his monogrammed shirts, I guess—has purchased a home about twenty miles west of Limón in Costa Rica. Our man down there says it's a big ranch-type place with about ten acres of orchards and a vegetable garden. Plus a swimming pool. Right now there's an old couple living there, taking care of things."

"Mortgage?" Crockett asked.

"No, sir, he paid cash. Reportedly about a hundred thousand American. And under the name of Reynolds, he has a balance of about twenty thousand in a San José bank. We're still looking for Dennis Reynolds bank accounts in the Bahamas and Caymans."

"He's getting ready to run?"

"Not quite yet, sir. I questioned Sullivan, and she says Rathbone has mentioned nothing about leaving the country. I figure he's waiting to make a big kill with his counterfeiting scam and the Fort Knox Commodity Trading Fund before he skedaddles."

"Tony, what *is* that Fund?"

"Drug trading," Harker said promptly. "Got to be. What a ballsy idea—to organize a commodity fund that trades only in controlled substances. And then to sell shares to the public to finance the business! If that's not chutzpah, I don't know what is. Anyway, the DEA traced those two cars parked outside Frank Little's office. The Bentley belonged to David Rathbone, as I figured, and he fits the agents' description of the driver. The other car, a Lincoln, is registered in New York to a nephew of Lou Siena. He owns Siena Moving and Storage and is currently under investigation by the Manhattan DA for allegedly running one of the biggest cocaine operations in the city."

"Interesting," Crockett said, drumming his fingers on his desktop. "You believe that links Rathbone and Little with the drug trade?"

"Definitely. The DEA is getting a court order to tap Little's office and home phones."

The chief frowned. "They're certainly moving swiftly on this, aren't they? I trust they'll remember their agreement to consult with us before making any arrests."

"I think we better keep up with them," Harker said. "Rathbone was seen meeting with a suspected drug dealer. That's additional evidence to justify tapping his home phones, wouldn't you say?"

Crockett nodded.

"And the office of the Fort Knox Fund?"

"All right," Crockett said. "Let's go for broke."

"And can we tape conversations in Rathbone's home?"

The other man stared at him. "You never give up, do you? How do you propose to do it?"

"At first I thought it would have to be a black-bag job. Our man would break in when no one's home and place mikes and transmitters. But that's too risky. Rathbone lives in a development where there are a lot of people around. If our agent was spotted, the whole operation would go down the drain. I talked to some phone people, and here's what they came up with: It'll be easy to tap incoming and outgoing calls at the central office. But to pick up other conversation inside the apartment, Rathbone's phones will have to be fitted with a special bug. It's a small, sensitive mike that picks up talk within about twenty feet and transmits it over the phone lines. It doesn't interfere with the normal functioning of the phone. In other words, Rathbone's line will be continually open to carry conversation taking place inside the apartment as well as incoming and outgoing calls."

"And how do you suggest we place these bugs?"

Harker grinned. "I'm going to scam the scammer. The phone people can feed interference into Rathbone's lines. All his calls will be jammed with static and crackling. He'll call the phone company to complain, and they'll send a man— *our* man—out to inspect his phones. That's when they'll be equipped with the bugs. Rathbone's static will clear up, and he'll be none the wiser."

Crockett made an expression of disgust. "I don't like all this," he said. "Whatever happened to privacy in this country? I find the whole concept of bugging and taping repugnant."

"Yes, sir," Tony said, "I agree. But can we go ahead with it?"

Crockett sighed. "Yes, go ahead. I'll have our attorney file for a court order with a friendly judge. And you're not going to tell Sullivan what we're doing?"

"No, sir, I'm not."

"Tony," his boss said in an almost avuncular tone, "I hope you know what you're doing."

"I hope so, too," Harker said, gathered up his papers, and left.

Simon Clark and Manny Suarez were waiting in his office. Tony dropped into his swivel chair and began drumming his fingers on the desktop, just as Crockett had done.

"Fortescue is back in Lakeland," he told the two men, "keeping tabs on the printer. And Ullman is up in Boca playing games with Mike Mulligan. But I didn't want to wait for your weekly reports. Things are beginning to move, and I'm trying to stay on top of them. Clark, what's happening at Sparco's brokerage?"

"The guy's into penny stock fraud up to his eyeballs," the agent said. "At the very least, I've got enough for the SEC to bring civil charges. And with a little more digging, I think we can rack him up on criminal charges, too. This shark and his Denver pals are breaking every securities law on the books and getting rich doing it."

"Yeah?" Suarez said, interested. "How they do that?"

"They've got a dozen gimmicks, but basically what they do is organize a shell company or find some rinky-dink outfit that doesn't have a prayer of success. One of the broker-dealers underwrites a stock offering at maybe a couple of bucks a share. They each buy a block of stock for themselves. Then they get busy high-pressuring suckers, usually by phone, touting the stock at inflated prices. Since it's not listed anywhere, they charge whatever the traffic will bear. When the price is inflated high enough, the promoters sell out to their customers. But if the suckers try to sell, there are no buyers. The most Sparco and his merry band of thieves will do is roll over the suckers' money into another fraudulent investment.

239

LAWRENCE SANDERS

And the suckers, hoping to recoup, send in *more* money. The whole dirty deal is a cash cow.'"

"We'll hold the penny stock swindle as an ace in the hole," Harker said. "What I really want to do is tie Sparco to the Fort Knox Fund. That outfit was organized to deal drugs. Sparco's brokerage is selling Fort Knox stock, so we've got him on umpteen conspiracy charges."

"Plus mail fraud and wire fraud," Clark added.

"Right. What I think will happen when we collar all these crooks is that one of them will cut a deal. Take my word for it, these are not standup guys."

"Which one do you think will rat?"

Harker thought a moment. "My guess would be James Bartlett. He's already done time for bank fraud, and an ex-con will sell his mother to keep from going back into stir. Manny, what's going on at Sid Coe's boiler room?"

Suarez shrugged. "We're still pushing shares in the Fort Knox Fund, but now Coe has added postage stamps. We tell the mooches they can make a killing on commemoratives."

Clark laughed. "No way," he said. "Most commemoratives of the last thirty years are selling for less than face value. The only way to break even is to stick them on letters."

"All I know," Suarez said, "is that I pitch stamps, and the moaney keeps rolling in."

"One thing I've been thinking about," Harker said, "is that when we eventually get these villains in court, we'll score a lot of points with the jury if we can enter as evidence a thick file of complaints from mooches who have been taken by Coe and Sparco. Manny, can you get me a copy of Coe's sucker list? Then I'll contact all of them with a form letter asking for details of their dealings. That should touch off a flood of weeping and wailing."

"No chance," Suarez said. "Coe treats the sucker lists like moaney in the bank. He says he pays a guy in Chicago big bucks for those names. He gives you the list when you get to work. When you leave, you turn it in. And he's right there to make sure you do. I guess he don' wanna yak to swipe a list and start freelancing."

"Could you call me from work and give me names and addresses on the phone?"

Manny shook his head. "Coe walks that boiler room like a tiger. Always leaning over our shoulder, listening to our spiel. If he ever heard me giving out his sucker list over the phone, he'd try to kill me. I mean it. The man is mean."

Harker pondered a moment. Then: "Do you ever go out to lunch?"

"Sometimes. Or to grab a beer."

"How about this . . . You go out for lunch or a beer and take the sucker list with you. I'm parked nearby with a photographer. We photograph every page on the list. It shouldn't take too long. Then you go back to work and turn in the list as usual when you leave."

"I guess," Suarez said slowly. "Maybe it'll work if he don' notice the list is gone while I'm out. Hokay, I'll take the chance."

"Good," Harker said. "I'll line up a photographer and let you know when this little con is scheduled. Are you still clipping Coe for Mort Sparco?"

"Oh sure," Manny said. "At least a coupla big sales a week."

Simon Clark straightened up in his chair. "What's that all about?" he asked. "Sparco is clipping Sid Coe?"

Harker laughed and told him the details of how the discount broker had turned several of Coe's yaks and was taking the boiler room operator for a hundred grand a month.

"That's what friends are for," Tony said.

Clark's smile was chilly. "An interesting story," he said.

42.

Rita Angela Sullivan switched on the answering machine and left the office early, bored out of her skull with that stupid job. David insisted on opening the mail himself, and the few times the phone rang it was usually a wrong number or someone trying to sell a timeshare in a Port St. Lucie condo.

So she locked up, headed for home, and her spirits rose. Christmas was only a week away, but you'd never know it from the weather: a dulcet afternoon with burning sun and frisky breeze. The holiday decorations along Atlantic Boulevard seemed out of place, and the white foam sprayed in the corners of shop windows looked more like yogurt than snow.

She had already mailed her cards and sent her mother a nice blouse from Burdines. She had bought a bottle of Courvoisier for Tony Harker. It came in a plush-lined gift box with two crystal brandy snifters. For David, she had shopped long and hard, and had finally settled on a slim black ostrich wallet with gold corners. It cost almost $500, but she didn't begrudge that. After all, it was his money, and she was certain it was a gift he'd love: elegant, expensive, and showy.

She went directly to the kitchen when she arrived home. Blanche and Theodore were there, preparing an enormous bouillabaisse that Rita would reheat for dinner. They were also working on a chilled jug of California Chablis, and Rita had a small glass. It tasted so tangy that she filled a thermos to take up to the terrace.

"Still having trouble with the phones?" she asked.

"Is worse," Blanche said. "So much noise!"

"I told Mr. Rathbone," Theodore said. "He called the phone company, and they're sending a man out to check the lines."

Rita carried her thermos upstairs and undressed slowly. Then she collected beach towel, sunglasses, oil, radio, and went out onto the terrace. The westering sun was unseasonably florid, and heat bounced off the tiles. If it hadn't been for that lovely breeze, she would have been lying in a sauna.

She oiled herself, wishing David were there to do her back, and then rolled naked onto the towel-covered chaise. She lay prone, lifting her long, thick hair away from the nape of her neck.

Whenever she tried to concentrate on the decisions facing her, that passionate sun made her muzzy and melted her resolve. She found her thoughts drifting, just sliding away, until her mind was a fog, and all she could do was groan with content and let the sun have her. But this time, determined not to become muddled, she sat up again, feet on the hot tiles. She turned off the radio and leaned forward, forearms on thighs, and reviewed her options as rationally as she could.

She had no doubt that Tony Harker was speaking the truth when he said he loved her and wanted to marry her. That dear, sweet man could cleverly deceive the black hats he was hounding, but she was convinced that his dealings with her were frank, honest, open.

No question about it: The guy would be a great husband. He'd work at it and do his damnedest to make a marriage succeed. He could be stuffy at times, but he wanted to change and was changing. Rita took some credit for that, but mostly it was Tony's own efforts that were making him less uptight. More *human*.

But despite the thaw, he still represented Duty, with a capital D. He was a straight arrow and would never be anything else. If a conflict ever arose between his personal pleasure and the demands of his job, Rita knew which path he'd take.

If Tony was good malt brew, David was champagne. It made Rita smile just to reflect on what a rogue he was. She knew all his faults, but she knew his virtues, too. He was generous, eternally optimistic, attentive to her needs, and loving. He was also the most beautiful man she had ever known, and that counted for something.

She admitted he was a swindler, but did not agree with Harker's harsh condemnation of Rathbone as a sleazy crook, a shark, and possibly a drug dealer and counterfeiter. Those were heavy crimes and, Rita decided, totally out of character for David.

It was also out of character for him to propose; she knew marriage played no part in his plans. The guy lived by his wits and had the typical con man's aversion to commitments. After his divorce, he was free, unencumbered by legal responsibilities, and he intended to stay that way.

Both men were good in bed, but in different ways. Tony was all male. He was always *there*, solid and satisfying, if predictable. With David, she didn't know what to expect. Kinkiness was the norm with him and sometimes, during their lovemaking, he feverishly sought role reversal as if he needed desperately to surrender and be used. Punished?

Rita lay back upon the chaise. She had sense enough to admit that neither man was totally or even mainly fascinated by her mental prowess or scintillating personality. She propped herself on her elbows, looked down at her tight, tawny body, at the sleek, black triangle, and wondered how long she could depend on *that*.

43.

Termite Tommy climbed into the Bentley and put a battered briefcase on the floor.

"Thirty grand in fifties," he said. "Queerest of the queer. Want to count it?"

"Of course not," Rathbone said. "I trust you."

"Going to stick it in banks?"

"I've already opened four different accounts," David said. "I've got to keep each deposit under ten thousand. By the way, I had to make initial deposits of my own money to cover the minimum on checking accounts. My expenses come off the top. Okay?"

"Sure. David, I think you better get this stuff in the banks as soon as possible. That nutsy German can't swear to how stable this batch of paper is."

"How long do I have?"

"Better figure two days tops."

"All right, I'll deposit it first thing tomorrow morning."

Termite Tommy lighted a cigarette. "How soon do you plan to cash in?"

Rathbone shrugged and opened the windows. "A week or two."

"That long?"

"Tommy, I can't put money in one day and draw it out the next. Even a brainless banker would wonder what the hell was going on."

"The problem is I need cash in a hurry. Legit cash. There's a payment due on that color laser copier, and the German and I have the shorts."

"How much do you need?"

"Ten grand."

"By when?"

"Yesterday. We've been stalling the guy who sold us the machine, but now he's threatening to repossess."

"Ten thousand?" Rathbone repeated. "I'd advance it out of my own pocket if I had it, but right now I'm in a squeeze. Look, let me see if I can hit a couple of friends. If I can raise the ten, I'll give you a shout and you come down and pick it up."

"I'd appreciate it," Tommy said. "I hate to put you in a bind, but I don't want to lose that copier."

"Neither do I," David said. "Leave it to me; I'll raise the loot somehow."

"Soon," the other man said, climbing out of the car. "The sooner the better."

Rathbone watched him get into his pickup truck and drive away. Then he opened the briefcase and inspected the money. Tommy and Herman Weisrotte had done a good job weathering the bills, and none of the serial numbers were in sequence.

He drove to the home of James Bartlett on Bayview. Jimmy opened the door wearing a lime-green golf shirt, lavender slacks, pink socks, white Reeboks.

"You're a veritable rainbow," David said and held up the briefcase.

"Got it?" Bartlett said. "Good. Let's go out to the pool. I have a pitcher of fresh lemonade and a bottle of port. Ever try port in lemonade?"

"Never have."

"Refreshing, and it's practically impossible to get stoned."

They sat at an umbrella table, the briefcase on the tiles. Bartlett mixed them drinks in tall green glasses.

Rathbone took a sip. "Nice," he said. "A little sweetish for me, but I like it."

Jimmy kicked the scarred briefcase gently. "All there?" he asked.

"I didn't count it, but I don't think they're playing games. The bills look good to me, but Tommy says the Kraut isn't sure how long the paper will last. He gives it two days."

"No problem," Bartlett said. "My deposit at the Crescent in Boca is scheduled for tomorrow morning. After it's in the bank, I don't care what happens to it."

They sat comfortably, sipping their drinks, watching sunlight dance over the surface of the pool. They could hear the drone of a nearby mower, and once a V of pelicans wheeled overhead.

"By the way," Bartlett said, "the Corcoran brothers are back in town. They're ready."

"Price still ten thousand?"

Jimmy nodded. "They'll make it look good. Guy gets drunk, ends up in a canal. But we've got to figure a way to get him down here from Lakeland and finger him for the Corcorans."

Rathbone stared at him. "I've got a way," he said. "Tommy needs a fast 10K. Says there's a payment due on the copying machine. You'll have the legit cash by tomorrow?"

"Noon at the latest. The courier from Miami is coming tonight. Almost two hundred thousand. I sign for it. He leaves. I take out thirty grand in legit bills and replace them with this 30K of queer. Tomorrow morning I drive up to Boca and deliver the package to Mike Mulligan. He gives me a signed deposit slip. That's it."

"All right," David said. "I'll call Tommy and tell him I've raised the ten thousand he needs. He comes down to Lauderdale, meets me at the Palace, and I hand over the ten grand. That's when the Corcorans pick him up and do their job. Their fee will be in Tommy's pocket. How does it play?"

"Like *Hamlet*," Bartlett said. "I'm glad you're on my side. But what happens when Tommy doesn't return to Lakeland? The German will wonder what happened to him and worry about losing the machine."

"I'll drive up there and snow him," David said. "I'll tell him Tommy got drunk, messed up, and is in the clink. He'll buy it. I'll give him ten grand for the machine and promise more to come. And I'll get him started on a new batch of the queer. Okay?"

"Sounds good to me. Order fifty thousand in fifties and hundreds. I have a feeling this deal is going to work out just fine."

"Can't miss."

"Then why do you look so down?"

"I guess it's because I've got to finger Tommy for the Corcorans."

"It has to be done."

"Sure," Rathbone said. "When are we going to Miami to make a buy for the Fund?"

"I'm working on it. The dealer I want to use is in Peru right now, but he's due back in a week or so."

"How much do you think we'll have to pay?"

"I'm hoping to get it for 13K per kilo. That would give the Fund a profit of ninety-seven thousand, five hundred on our first deal."

"Beautiful," David said. "Will your guy take a check?"

"I don't see why not; we're not asking immediate delivery. We have enough in the Fund's account to cover it, don't we?"

"More than enough. Will he sign a contract?"

"I think he will. We don't have the muscle to enforce it, but he doesn't know that. But contract or not, he'll make delivery. He's an honorable man."

"We're all honorable men," Rathbone said, and they both laughed and poured more lemonade.

44.

Henry Ullman was sticking close to Mike Mulligan in Boca. Four evenings a week he met the banker for drinks at the Navigator Bar & Grill. And on Saturday nights, Ullman took a bottle or two to Mulligan's pad, and they hoisted a few while waiting for the guests to arrive.

Ullman figured the mousy banker had about a dozen women on the string. Some showed up alone, there were a few duos, and one trio: all reasonably clean and attractive, not too old, and marvelously complaisant after dipping into the toilet tank in Mulligan's bathroom.

Henry wondered if, in the line of duty, he should be banging women zonked out of their gourds on high-quality coke. It was an ethical dilemma, and it bothered him for at least thirty seconds.

He didn't have drinks at the Navigator with Mulligan on Friday evenings because on Fridays the Crescent was open till seven P.M. to cash paychecks and take deposits. Mike worked late, and Ullman spent the evening writing out his weekly report for Tony Harker. It was usually a brief, uneventful account, although Henry included the names of Mulligan's female guests and their addresses if he could discover them.

Then, one Saturday night, just two days before Christmas, he showed up at Mulligan's apartment with two bottles of Korbel brut, and the weekly orgies came to a screeching halt.

When the banker opened the door, he looked like death warmed over. His poplin suit had obviously been slept in, there were food stains on his vest and gray stubble on his chin. Even worse, the man was crying; fat tears were dripping down his cheeks onto his wrinkled lapels.

"Mike," Ullman said, closing the door quickly behind him, "what in God's name is wrong?"

Mulligan shook his head, said nothing, but collapsed onto the couch. He leaned forward, face in his hands, shuddering with sobs. Ullman took his champagne into the kitchen. The place was a mess: unwashed dishes, encrusted pans, a broken glass. The agent found a bottle of bourbon in the freezer. He poured a healthy jolt into a clean tumbler and brought it to the banker.

"Come on, Mike," he said gently, "take a sip and tell me what's wrong."

Mulligan took the drink with trembling hands and gulped it down. Then coughed and coughed. Ullman waited for the paroxysm to subside, then asked again, "What's wrong?"

The other man wouldn't look at him; he just stared dully at the carpet. "I'm thirty thousand short at the bank," he said in a low voice.

"And that's what knocked you for a loop? It's just a bookkeeping error, Mike; you'll find it."

Mulligan shook his head. "It was a cash deposit. I signed for it without counting it. Then, last night, I discovered it was thirty thousand short."

"I don't understand," Ullman said, but beginning to. "How much was the total deposit?"

"Almost two hundred thousand."

Ullman whistled, then put an arm across the man's thin shoulders. "Tell me all about it," he said softly. "I may be able to help."

"I was just doing a favor for a close friend. I swear that's all it was."

"So you accepted cash deposits over ten thousand and didn't report them?"

"So much paperwork," Mulligan said. "Besides, we only held the funds for a short time and then they would go out in drafts."

"But Crescent profited while the money was in the bank— right? Short-term paper? Overnight loans?"

"Yes."

"Who authorized the drafts? The depositor—your close friend?"

"No. The president of the corporate account authorized the drafts."

"Who was that?"

"Mitchell Korne. It was just a name to me. I never met the man."

"Who were the drafts paid to?"

"Another bank."

"Where?"

"Panama."

"How long has this been going on, Mike?"

"Two years. At least."

"You knew it was drug money?"

Mulligan stared at him with the wide-eyed, innocent look of a guilty man. "I suspected but I had no proof. It could have been the cash proceeds from a real estate sale."

"Oh sure," Ullman said. "Or a yacht. Let's get back to your shortage. When was the deposit made?"

"Yesterday morning."

"In the lobby of the bank? Over the counter?"

"No. Back door."

"So the tellers didn't know about it?"

"No."

"Someone else in the bank must have known. Vice president? President?"

"They knew, but they let me handle it."

"I can imagine. All right, the two hundred grand was deposited at the back door of the bank yesterday morning and you signed for it without counting it."

"It would have taken a long time. It was Friday and I was busy. Besides, previous deposits had always been accurate to the dollar."

"How was the deposit made? I mean how was the cash delivered? In a shopping bag?"

"A suitcase. A cheap vinyl suitcase."

"What did you do with it—put it in the vault?"

"No. I brought it home."

"You did *what?*"

"I couldn't leave it in the bank. The examiners are coming in first thing Tuesday morning, the day after Christmas."

"Good enough reason. Where is the suitcase now?"

"In the bedroom, under the bed."

"No wonder you've got the jits. Mike, why don't you just tell your friend he was thirty thousand short and he'll have to come up with it."

"He won't believe me. He'll say all his previous deposits were accurate. He'll say I signed for the total amount. He'll say I have to make up the loss."

"So? You have thirty thousand in liquid assets, don't you? And if you don't, the bank does. If Crescent's top brass is in on this, they won't squeal too loud."

"Don't you think I've thought of that? But what if we keep getting shortchanged on the deposits?"

"There's an easy answer to that: Tell your friend to get lost."

Mulligan lowered his head. "I can't do that."

"Why not?" Ullman said. "Because he's got you by the short hair? Because for two years he's been paying you off with that white stuff you keep in your toilet tank?"

The banker's head snapped up. His mouth opened; he stared at Ullman, horrified. "You're from the police, aren't you?" he said.

"Sure I am," the agent said cheerfully. "But that doesn't mean I don't like you. I really want to help you."

"You just want to put me in jail."

"Nah. You're more valuable out. Look, if you cooperate maybe we can cut a deal. You'll get a fine and probation. Your career as a banker will be over, but you won't be behind bars with all those swell people. That's worth something, isn't it?"

"When you say cooperate, I suppose you want me to name my friend, the man who made the deposits."

"James Bartlett?" Ullman said casually. "No, you won't have to name him."

Mulligan gasped. "How did you know?"

"You just told me. What do you say, Mike? Will you play along?"

"I don't have much choice, do I?"

"Not much. Now you go take a quick shower, shave, and put on fresh clothes. Then I'm going to drive you down to Fort Lauderdale to meet a couple of men you can deal with."

"It'll be late," Mulligan objected. "They'll probably be asleep."

"I'll wake them up," Ullman promised.

"Am I under arrest?"

"Let's just call it protective custody. Now go get cleaned up."

"May I have another drink?"

"No. You'll want a clear head when you start talking to save your skin."

Mulligan went stumbling into the bathroom. Ullman went into the bedroom and dragged the vinyl suitcase from under the bed. He snapped it open and took out all those lovely bundles of twenties, fifties, and hundreds bound with manila wrappers. He stacked them neatly on the bed, then peered into the emptied suitcase. What he saw made him happy: a layer of confetti that felt oily to the touch.

He left the fluff there, repacked the currency, and closed the suitcase. Mike Mulligan, showered and shaved, came into the bedroom to dress. Ullman took the suitcase into the living room. Then he went into the bathroom and lifted the jar of glassine envelopes from the toilet tank. He took that into the kitchen and found a shopping bag under the sink. He put the cocaine in the bag and added his two bottles of champagne. He went back into the living room, poured himself a shot of bourbon, and sipped slowly.

They were ready to leave a half-hour later. Mulligan carried the shopping bag, and Ullman lugged the suitcase of cash. The banker carefully locked his front door, and then they waited for the elevator. The door slid open. Pearl and Opal Longnecker got out and stared with astonishment at the two men.

Ullman smiled at the sisters. "The party's over, ladies," he said.

45.

They spent a quiet New Year's, recovering from the noisy party at the Palace Lounge the previous night. It was a gray, sodden day; there was no sunning on the terrace. They read newspapers and magazines, watched a little television, lunched on cold cuts and potato salad. Both were subdued, conversing mostly in monosyllables, until finally David said, "The hell with resolutions; let's have a Bloody Mary."

"Let's," Rita said, and they did.

After that they perked up and began discussing all the outrageous things that had happened at the New Year's Eve party. Frank Little had dragged Trudy Bartlett under the table, and Nancy Sparco had to be restrained by her husband from completing a striptease atop the table.

"Great party," David said. "I'm going to miss those people."

"Miss them? Are you going somewhere?"

"Eventually," he said, smiling. "And so are you." He

glanced at his watch. "But right now I have a business meeting. Shouldn't be gone for more than an hour or so."

"You'll be home for dinner? Blanche made a veal casserole for us."

"I'll be back in plenty of time," he assured her.

"If you're going to be late," she said, "give me a call. The phones are working fine now."

"What was wrong—did the repairman say?"

"A short at the junction box, or so he claimed. Whatever it was, he fixed it and checked all the phones."

"Good. Lend me your car keys, will you? The Bentley's low on gas and nothing will be open today."

He drove Rita's white Corsica. It was only five o'clock, but the waning day was gloomy, and he had to switch on the wipers to keep the windshield clear of mist. He had deliberately picked this particular day and this particular time, figuring the gang would be home recovering from the party. And when he walked into the Palace Lounge through the side entrance, he was happy to see only Ernie, behind the bar and washing glasses used the night before. David swung onto a barstool.

"Happy New Year, Mr. Rathbone," Ernie said. "I'm surprised you're still alive. I didn't think you'd wake up for a week."

"Happy New Year, Ernie, and I feel fine. Mix me the usual, please. That was a dynamite party."

"I should do that much business every night," the bartender said.

He went back to his chores. Rathbone reached into his inside jacket pocket to make sure the envelope was there. Then he lighted a cigarette and sipped his vodka gimlet. Now that the time had come, he found he was calm, acting normally, hands steady.

He had just started his second gimlet when two men came in through the side entrance. Rathbone inspected them in the bar mirror. They matched Bartlett's description of the Corcoran brothers: short and burly with reddish hair cut in Florida flattops. Both were wearing cotton plaid sports jackets over black T-shirts. They took a corner table, and one of them came over to the bar.

"Beer," he said curtly.

"They almost cleaned me out last night," Ernie apologized. "All I got left is Miller's."

The man nodded. "Two bottles," he said.

He paid, then carried the bottles and glasses back to the table. The brothers sat stolidly, drinking their beers, not conversing. Rathbone finished his drink.

"More of the same," he called.

When Ernie started mixing his drink, David slid off the barstool and went into the men's room. He checked both stalls. Empty. He glanced at himself briefly in the mirror over the sink, then waited, not looking in the mirror again. In a few minutes one of the Corcoran brothers entered. He stared at Rathbone.

"From Jimmy Bartlett?" David asked.

The man nodded.

"The guy should be here any minute. He'll come through the side door. He's tall, skinny, and may be wearing a black suit. He'll join me at the bar, and we'll have a drink together. I'll slip him a white envelope. He'll probably take off first, but if he doesn't, I'll take off and leave him alone. He drives an old pickup truck. It'll be parked outside in the lot."

"Our fee's in the envelope?" Corcoran asked. His voice was unexpectedly high-pitched, fluty.

"That's right."

Corcoran nodded again, stepped to a urinal and unzipped his fly. David left hurriedly, went back to the bar, took a gulp of his new drink.

It was almost fifteen minutes before Termite Tommy showed up. He saw Rathbone at the bar and came over to stand next to him.

"Hey, Tommy!" David said heartily. "Happy New Year!"

"Same to you. And many of them."

"What're you drinking?"

"Jim Beam straight. Water on the side."

"If you had the kind of night I had, you better have a double."

"Yeah," Tommy said, "it was kinda wet."

David ordered the bourbon and another gimlet for himself. "Sorry you had to make the trip today," he said.

"That's all right. You got the dough?"

"Uh-huh."

"Good. We make the payment on the machine, everything's copasetic."

Rathbone took the envelope from his jacket pocket and handed it over, making no effort to hide the transfer. In the mirror, he saw the Corcoran brothers finish their beers, rise, and leave.

"Ten K," he said to Tommy. "Legit hundreds."

"I appreciate it, David. Everything go all right at the banks?"

"No problems. I'll start withdrawing next week and give you a call when you can pick up the balance due. Listen, I've got to split. My lady is expecting me home for dinner."

"That's okay; I'm leaving, too. Got a long drive ahead of me."

Rathbone stood, took his new black ostrich wallet from his hip pocket as if he was about to pay the tab.

"Thanks again," Termite Tommy said.

"Keep in touch," David said lightly.

Tommy took a swallow of water, then left. David put his wallet back in his pocket and sat down again.

"Another, Ernie," he called.

The bartender shook his head. "You're a bear for punishment, Mr. Rathbone," he said.

When he brought the drink, he leaned across the bar. "Did you see those two guys?" he asked in a low voice.

"What guys?"

"At the corner table. They had a beer, then went out."

"I just glanced at them. Why?"

"A couple of hard cases," Ernie said.

"You're sure?"

"Sure I'm sure. Wasn't I a cop for too many years? You wouldn't want to be caught in a dark alley with those yobs, believe me."

People entered, stayed for a drink or two, departed. Others took their place. The Lounge was quiet, jukebox stilled, conversation muted. David knew none of the customers, which was just as well; he didn't want to talk to anyone. He had another drink. Another. Another.

He floated in a timeless void, the room blurred, Ernie wavered back and forth. He could not concentrate, which was a blessing, but stared vacantly at the stranger in the mirror and watched the glass come up, tilt, pour out its contents. The throat constricted, the stranger grimaced and gasped.

" 'Nother," he said in a loud voice.

Ernie looked at him but said nothing. He was mixing the gimlet, taking his time, when he saw David fall forward onto the bar. He just folded his arms and his head went down. He sat there hunched over, not moving.

The bartender sighed, put aside the drink. He dug out his little red address book and looked up Rathbone's home phone number. He called from the phone behind the bar.

"The Rathbone residence."

"Rita?"

"Yes. Who's this?"

"Ernie. At the Palace Lounge."

"Oh. Hiya, Ernie. Happy New Year."

"Same to you. Listen, Mr. Rathbone is here, and he's a little under the weather. I hate to eighty-six him, but he's in no condition to drive. He'll kill himself or someone else."

Silence a moment, then: "I'll call a cab. I should be there

in twenty minutes, half-hour at the most. Don't give him any more to drink and try to keep him from leaving."

"Okay."

"And thanks for calling, Ernie."

When she hurried in, raincoat slick with mist, David was still sprawled over the bar. Rita stood alongside and looked down at him.

"How many did he have?" she asked Ernie.

"Too many. And fast. Seemed like he just couldn't stop. It's not like him."

"No," Rita said, "it's not. What's the bill?"

"Don't worry about it. I'll catch him another night."

"Thanks, Ernie. The valet brought the car around to the side entrance. Will you help me get him out?"

Ernie came from behind the bar. Rita shook David's shoulder, first gently, then roughly until he roused.

"Wha?" he said groggily, raising his head.

"Come on, Sleeping Beauty," she said, "we're going home."

She and Ernie got him to his feet and supported him, one on each side.

"All right, all right," he said thickly. "I can navigate."

But they didn't let go of him until he was outside, leaning against the Corsica, his face pressed against the cool, wet roof.

"Let me get some fresh air," he said.

"Thanks again, Ernie," Rita said. "I can take it from here."

The bartender went back inside. Rita opened the car door. But suddenly David lurched away, staggered several steps, and vomited all over a waist-high sago palm. He remained bent over for five minutes, and Rita waited patiently, listening to him retch.

Finally he straightened up, wiped his mouth with his handkerchief, and then threw it away. He came back to the car slowly, taking deep breaths.

"Sorry about that," he said huskily.

"It happens," Rita said. "Get in the car and I'll drive us home. Have a cup of black coffee, you'll feel better."

"I don't think so," he said.

When they arrived at the town house, he went directly upstairs to take off his spattered clothing. Rita sat on his bed and listened to the shower running. He was in there such a long time she was beginning to worry. But then he came out in a white terry robe, drying his hair with a towel.

"I'd like a cognac," he said. "Just an ounce, no more, to settle my stomach."

"You're sure?" she said.

"I'm sure."

"All right, I'll bring it up here for you."

"No, I'll come downstairs."

In the kitchen, he measured out an ounce of Courvoisier carefully. He took a cautious sip, then closed his eyes and sighed.

"You okay?" she asked anxiously.

"I will be. Let me mix you something. A brandy stinger?"

"Just right," she said.

They took their drinks into the living room and sat on the couch.

"I don't suppose you feel like eating that veal casserole."

"Jesus, no!" he said. "I never want to eat again. But you go ahead."

"I can wait. Maybe you'll feel like it later."

He stared at her, then picked up her hand, kissed her knuckles. "Know why I love you?" he asked.

"Why?"

"Because not once, at the Palace, on the ride back, or since we've been home, have you hollered on me or asked why I made such a fool of myself."

"I figured if you wanted to tell me, you would. I don't pry; you know that."

"It was that business meeting I had."

"It didn't go well?"

"It went fine."

"I don't understand."

"Forget it. I'm going to. Oh God, what would I do without you? You're my salvation."

"Don't make a federal case out of it, baby. You got drunk and I brought you home. No big deal."

"You were there when I needed you; that's what counts. Rita, I swear to you I'll never do that again."

"Even Ernie said it wasn't like you."

"Did you pay my bar tab?"

"He said he'd catch you another night."

"He's a good man. He called you?"

"Yep."

"And Florence Nightingale came running. Thank God. Listen, hon, I've been thinking; maybe we should take off sooner than I planned. Say in about six months."

"Whatever you say; you're the boss."

"On that drive home tonight, I got the feeling that things were closing in. Waiting around for just one more big deal is a sucker's game. Let's take the money and run."

"Where to?"

He grinned. "A secret. But believe me, you'll love it. Plenty of hot sun."

"A beach?"

"Not too far away. But a big pool."

"A private pool?"

"Of course."

"That's for me," she said.

"Will you have a lot of preparations to make?"

"Nope. Just pack my bikinis. I'll write my mother and tell her I'll be traveling awhile and not to worry."

He kissed her hand again. "You think of everything. You're not only beautiful, you're brainy." He raised his glass. "Happy New Year, darling."

46.

She called Tony Harker a little before noon and told him that Rathbone had driven up to Lakeland and wouldn't be back until late that night. Tony locked up his office and ran. He was at his motel with a cold six-pack of Bud by the time Rita arrived. Ten minutes later they were in bed, blinds drawn, air conditioner set at its coldest.

She had never been more impassioned, but now he had the confidence of experience and her ardor didn't daunt him. They coupled like young animals eager to test their strength, and if there was no surrender by either, there was triumph for both.

When finally they separated, they lay looking at each other wildly. It had been a curious union, so glowing that it frightened both for what it might promise. It exceeded the physical, gave a glimpse of a different relationship that, if nurtured, might remake their lives.

"What happened?" he asked wonderingly, but Rita could only shake her head, as confused and fearful as he.

The real world intruded, and they laughed and pretended it had merely been a dynamite roll in the hay and sexual pleasure was all that mattered.

But having experienced that epiphany, they desired to know it again, despite their dread, if only to prove such rapture did exist. So after a time they made love again, slowly and deliberately, and waited for that unequaled ecstasy to reappear. But it did not, leaving them satiated but conscious of a loss.

"Have you been taking lessons?" Rita asked him.

"Yes," he answered. "From you. My God, your tan is deeper than ever." His forefinger stroked the fold between her thigh and groin. "You're not worried about skin cancer?"

"Ahh," she said, "life's too short. And I drink too much, smoke too much, and pig out on fatty foods. It's stupid to give up all the pleasures of life just to squeeze out a few extra years. That's for cowards."

"Dying young doesn't scare you?"

"Sure it does. But what scares me more is living a dull, boring life." She sat up. "Let's talk business for a while," she said. "Have your guys come up with anything on David and the Palace gang?"

"Lots of things. I really think we're going to rack up the whole crew. Rita, why did Rathbone go to Lakeland?"

"He didn't say, and I didn't want to push."

"Has he mentioned anything about taking off permanently? Leaving the country?"

"Not really. A couple of times he's complained about how hard he works and how he'd like to retire. But it all sounds like bullshit to me. He's making a nice buck; he'd be a fool to cash in. And David's no fool."

"Don't be so sure of that. He's making a lot of mistakes."

"Like what?"

"Oh, this and that," Harker said vaguely. "Has he ever mentioned the names Herman Weisrotte or Thomas Keeffringer?"

266

"Nope. Never heard of them."

"How about Mitchell Korne?"

She shook her head. "No again. Who are all these guys?"

"Their names came up in our investigation. I'd like to tie them to Rathbone."

She drained her beer, got out of bed, began to dress.

"Hey," he said, "where you going?"

"You're itching to get back to the office," she said. "I can tell."

"Well, yeah, I've got a lot to do. Things are beginning to move."

"You're really after his balls, aren't you, Tony?"

"Rathbone? You betcha! I want him stuck out of sight for ten years at least. Maybe more."

"What'd he ever do to you?" she said in a low voice.

He stared at her. "What the hell kind of a question is that? I'm in the crook-exterminating business. Rathbone is a crook. So I'm going to exterminate him. Logical enough for you?"

"All right, all right," she said hastily. "Don't get steamed. It's just that you seem to have a personal feud with the guy, even if you've never met him."

"I know what he's done. Is doing."

"But it's more than just a cop doing his job. It's like a crusade. You're never going to let up until you nail him."

"You've got it. But screw Rathbone. What about us?"

She stood in front of the dresser mirror, combing her long black hair. "What about us?"

"You promised to think over what I said. Marriage. Have you?"

She whirled suddenly, hair flying. "Yes, I've thought about it. I think about it all the time. Don't lean on me, Tony, please don't. I told you it's a heavy decision, and it is. Right now I don't know what I want to do."

He came over to her and held her in his arms.

"Don't be angry with me, darling," he said. "I don't want

to pressure you, but you mean so much to me that I get anxious. I don't even want to think about losing you."

She reached up to stroke his cheek. "I'm not angry with you, baby. It's just that I'm trying to figure things out, and it's going to take time."

"How much time?"

She pulled away. "Six months. Tops. How does that sound?"

He blinked once. "All right," he said. "Six months."

47.

Roger Fortescue went home for Christmas Day and New Year's Eve. The rest of his time was spent in Lakeland, keeping a loose stakeout on Herman Weisrotte's printing shop and occasionally tailing Thomas J. Keeffringer just for the fun of it.

He hadn't uncovered a great deal. The German slept in a little room behind his shop, and Termite Tommy kipped in a motel even more squalid that Fortescue's. The two men spent a lot of time together, and the fact that Weisrotte rarely had a half-dozen customers a day convinced Roger that these two villains were engaged in some nefarious scheme that enabled them to get plotched almost every night at the Mermaid's Tail, a gin mill only a block away from the printshop.

It was, Fortescue decided, just about the dullest duty he had ever pulled, and only his nightly phone calls to Estelle enabled him to keep his sanity. But then, a few days into the new year, things started popping, and what had been a boring grind became a fascinating mystery.

It began when the agent realized he hadn't seen Termite Tommy around for three or four days. He didn't come to the printshop, and when Roger checked his motel, the surly owner said he hadn't been there since New Year's Day, and if he didn't show up soon with his weekly rent, the owner was going to chuck his sleazy belongings into the gutter.

Fortescue, sitting in his Volvo and keeping an eye on Weisrotte's shop, wondered if Tommy had split with the German and decided to try his larcenous talents elsewhere. But it didn't make sense that he'd take off without emptying his motel room. It could be, of course, that he was shacked up with a ladylove somewhere and would soon reappear.

While Roger was trying to puzzle out what had happened, he saw a black Bentley pull to a stop, and he straightened up in his seat. A handsome blond guy got out of the car, glanced around, and then sauntered into the German's shop. The agent made him for David Rathbone, but jotted down the license of the Bentley to double-check later.

Rathbone was in there almost two hours. Then he and Weisrotte came out and headed for the Mermaid's Tail, Rathbone talking a mile a minute.

The agent figured it was safe enough for him to move in. Rathbone had never seen him before, and if Weisrotte recognized him—so what? He was just a guy who had dropped by once to price business cards. So Fortescue entered the saloon, ordered a beer at the bar, and looked around casually. His targets were in a back booth, Rathbone still talking nonstop and the German downing shots of straight gin like there was no tomorrow.

This went on for almost an hour while Roger nursed a second beer. Then the two men got up, and Rathbone paid the tab. They started for the door, and as they passed, Fortescue noted the diamond ring on Rathbone's left pinkie. At least a three-carat rock, he estimated, and wondered how many mooches had contributed their life savings to the purchase of that sparkler.

Rathbone got the printer back to the shop and went in with him for a few minutes. Then he came out, lighted a cigarette, and got into the Bentley. By that time Fortescue was in his Volvo, and he tailed Rathbone until it became obvious the man was heading south, probably returning to Fort Lauderdale. Then the agent turned back and drove to his motel, trying to figure out the significance of what he had just witnessed.

He came up with zilch and decided maybe he'd give Tony Harker a call, report what had happened, and let him chew on it awhile. But before he did that, he made his nightly call home. He jived with his sons awhile, got their promises that they were doing their homework and weren't planning to rob a bank, and then Estelle came on.

"Guess who called you this morning," she said.

"Elizabeth Taylor?"

"Even better. Sam Washburn."

"Yeah? What'd he want?"

"Didn't say. But he claims it's important and said to call him."

"Probably got another owl made of shells he wants to unload on me."

"Don't you take it! Don't you dare!"

"Trust me," he said.

He hung up, found Washburn's number in his notebook, and called the old retired cop.

"Roger Fortescue," he said. "How you doing?"

"Hey, old buddy!" Sam said. "Your wife said you were out of town."

"I am. I'm calling from Lakeland."

"What the hell are you doing there—picking oranges?"

"Something like that. What's up, Sam?"

"You remember the last time we talked you asked me about Thomas J. Keeffringer, aka Termite Tommy?"

"Sure. What about him?"

"Well, he showed up down here."

"No kidding. What's he up to now?"

"Not a whole hell of a lot," Washburn said. "At the moment he's occupying an icebox in the morgue."

Silence. Then: "Sheet," Roger said, "how did you find that out?"

"There was a short article in the *Sun-Sentinel* this morning. I called to ask if you had seen it, but then Estelle told me you were out of town, so I figured you hadn't. Anyway, according to the story a kid was testing his new scuba gear in a canal out near Coral Springs. He spotted an old pickup truck on the bottom. Nothing unusual about that. You know how many people ditch their clunkers in the canals and then claim the insurance, saying it was stolen."

"I know, Sam," Fortescue said patiently, "I know."

"But when this kid got close to the pickup, he saw there was a guy sitting behind the wheel. So he got out of the water, called the cops, and they drug the truck out. The guy behind the wheel was Termite Tommy himself."

"Cause of death?"

"They're not sure yet. I phoned Jack Liddite at Homicide, but he doesn't think it'll be their baby. He said the ME's report isn't complete yet, but it looks like Tommy got smashed, didn't make a curve, and just drove into the canal. They found an empty liter of juice in the cab of the truck. That's all I got. But you sounded like you were working the guy so I wanted to make sure you knew about it."

"Thanks, Sam," Fortescue said. "I really appreciate it."

"Glad to help, old buddy. By the way, I got a shell penguin for you. It's a beaut."

"That's great," Roger said faintly. "Love to have it."

Then he called Tony Harker. He told him about Keeffringer's disappearance, the meeting between David Rathbone and Herman Weisrotte, and the discovery of Termite Tommy's body in the Coral Springs canal.

Harker didn't hesitate. "Get back as soon as possible," he

said. "The printer's not going anywhere; he'll be there when we want him. You schmooze with your buddies down here and see what you can pick up on the homicide."

"They're not even sure it *was* a homicide."

"I think it was," Harker said. "Don't you?"

"Yes," Fortescue said.

48.

They rehearsed their roles on the drive down to Miami. Both men were quick studies, and it didn't take long to cobble up a scenario and decide how it was to be played.

"Korne is not a megadealer," Jimmy Bartlett said, "but big enough. Most of his stuff goes to New Jersey and New England. He isn't in New York, but the last time I spoke to him, he was talking about expanding into Montreal and Toronto. He's an ambitious lad."

"Lad?" David Rathbone said. "Just how old is he?"

"Mitch? I don't think he's thirty yet. He's come a long way in a short time."

"Do you call him 'Mitch' to his face?"

"I do, but I suggest you address him as Mr. Korne. He likes it when older men use Mister."

"How did he get so far so fast? Is he a hard case?"

"Not personally. But he hires very dependable muscle and pays them well. I think the secret of his success is his business sense. He's a Harvard MBA, you know, and treats drugs like any other consumer product. That's what he calls dopers—consumers. He talks about his product line, distribution network, the need to maximize profitability, and so forth. Bribery of officials he calls Public Relations. His only regret is that he can't advertise. But he's considering putting a brand name on all his products as a guarantee of quality."

"I'll snow him with Wall Street lingo," David said. "The smarter they are, the harder they fall."

"By the way," Bartlett said, "how did you make out with the German in Lakeland?"

"In like Flynn. I could have sold him the Brooklyn Bridge. He bought the story of Termite Tommy being in the slammer. He promised to get started on our 50K of queer fifties."

"And he agreed to accept twenty percent of the face value?"

"He did after I got half a jug of Beefeater in him. That guy must have a liver as big as the Ritz."

"Who cares," Bartlett said, "as long as he does the job."

The offices of Mitchell Korne Enterprises, Inc., were located in one of the raw, pastel-colored towers jazzing up downtown Miami. The firm was registered as an importer of South and Central American furniture, lamps, and decorative accessories. This business showed an annual profit apparently sufficient to justify a lavish suite of offices that doubled as a showroom for the company's legitimate imports.

Cocaine, marijuana, heroin, hashish, and other illicit substances were imported and marketed by another division with its own financial structure, personnel, and distribution. Both divisions, overt and covert, were controlled by the CEO, Mitchell Korne, although it was rumored that Mitchell Korne Enterprises, Inc., was actually a sub rosa limited partnership with several investors who financed the operation in return for an enormous quarterly cash distribution.

Korne's private office had none of the carved wood and Aztec-patterned upholstery of the reception room. It was severely modern: glass, chrome, leather, and built-in bookcases of polished teak. There were Japanese prints framed on the walls, and behind Korne's high swivel chair was a plate-glass picture window with a startling view of the Miami skyline and a small patch of blue water sparkling in the January sunshine.

After the introductions, they sat around a cocktail table: a single sheet of stainless steel supported on black iron sawhorses. There were no ashtrays in the room, no family photographs, mementos, or anything else that might yield a clue to the occupant's background and character. The office was as impersonal as an operating theater, and as sterile.

Korne was a tall, scholarly-looking young man with a hairline mustache and glasses framed in gold wire. Rathbone made him for a cold fish but was impressed by the dealer's three-piece suit of dove-gray flannel.

"How was Peru, Mitch?" Jimmy Bartlett asked.

"Impressive. I saw one huge valley that was almost totally coca shrubs. Very reassuring. Supply won't be a problem for the foreseeable future."

"Which means, Mr. Korne," Rathbone said, "that distribution and marketing will be the keys to your bottom-line profitability."

Korne looked at him with interest. "Yes, I think that's a reasonable assumption."

"David," Bartlett said, "why don't you make your presentation now. Mitch is a busy man."

"Of course," Rathbone said. "I'll keep it as brief and ontarget as possible. Mr. Korne, I'm from Indianapolis, and a number of associates and I have formed an ad hoc organization that is exploring a variety of ways in which undeclared income might be invested."

Korne nodded. "I understand," he said.

"The associates I speak of are from Indiana, Illinois, and Iowa plus Ohio and western Pennsylvania. We have come up with a concept we feel has high upside potential and limited downside risk. In our home states are an enormous number of small colleges and universities. I can't quote the exact figure, but I assure you it's in the high hundreds. We feel the educational institutions in this area represent an exciting untapped market for your products. We propose to establish a network of distributors that would initially consist of one sales representative in each college and university. If initial results validate our optimistic computer analysis, we would eventually attempt to place a retail salesperson in every fraternity, sorority, and dormitory in every college throughout the target area."

Mitchell Korne straightened up in his suede director's chair, then leaned forward intently. "A very interesting game-plan. What specific product did you have in mind? Crack?"

Rathbone shook his head. "I don't think so. You must remember that these college students are relatively wealthy. Crack is consciously or unconsciously linked with poverty. But cocaine is considered daring, glamorous. Look at all the movie stars and rock singers who have admitted frequent use."

Korne nodded again. "Yes, I think your decision to avoid crack is wise. It is certainly not a recreational product. Tell me, Mr. Rathbone, have you done any market research?"

"No, sir, we have not," David said. "Which is the reason I am here today. We—my associates and I—have decided to conduct a test in a limited number of demographically selected markets. We feel it will take three months to have trained sales personnel on station. We would like to purchase fifteen kilos of high-quality cocaine to be delivered in three months. As proof of our dependability and serious intent, I have been authorized to pay the agreed-upon price immediately."

"I see," Korne said, sitting back. "And what price did you have in mind?"

"Ten K per kilo."

The dealer smiled coldly. "I'm afraid not. It is far below the present market price, and the weight involved would not justify such a heavy discount."

"I realize," Rathbone said, "that the sale of fifteen kilos hardly represents a significant transaction to a man in your position, Mr. Korne. But I want to emphasize that this initial purchase is merely for a market test. If our computer predictions prove viable, I have every expectation of requiring a vastly increased and regular delivery of the product in the future. What I am suggesting, Mr. Korne, is that if you are willing to take a chance on us in the formative period of our operation, you will find us a grateful and loyal customer in the years to come."

"Another consideration, Mitch," Bartlett said softly, "is that you will have the use of a hundred and fifty thousand dollars for the three months prior to delivery. Surely the profits from investing those funds, even for a period of ninety days, will help offset the difference between what David is prepared to pay and the going rate."

Korne stared at Rathbone a long time while the other two men remained silent. Finally Korne said, "I like your idea of direct distribution to the colleges. Of course, a great deal will depend on the personality of your local salespersons, but I'm sure you are aware of the need for cheerful service and customer satisfaction. Very well, I'm willing to take a flier. If you'll accept delivery in Miami in three months, you may have fifteen kilos at 10K per kilo."

"Thank you, Mr. Korne," Rathbone said.

"Call me Mitch," the other man said.

On the drive back to Lauderdale, still astounded by their good fortune, they calculated the take on the fifteen kilos. Sold for $19,500 per kilo to Lou Siena. Purchased at $10,000 per kilo from Mitchell Korne. Profit: $142,500.

"Amazing!" Bartlett said. "He didn't haggle a bit. I thought sure we'd have to up the ante to 12K per kilo."

"And he signed the contract for chairs and accepted the Fort Knox Fund check," Rathbone marveled. "Jimmy, we've got to get another, bigger deal in the works immediately. Different buyer, different seller, but let's stick to the same plot. It worked once, it'll work again."

"Fine with me," Bartlett said. "Let's have a meet with Sparco, Little, and Coe. We'll tell them the good news and figure ways to build up the Fund's working capital. It's a marvelous con, David."

"Only it isn't a con," Rathbone said. "Not really. The scenarios might have been a swindle, and maybe we're clipping the marks who bought shares in the Fund, but essentially the deal is legitimate. We're buying low and selling high. That's the religion of Wall Street, isn't it?"

49.

The tape clicked off, and Tony Harker switched it to fast rewind. Then he went into the cramped kitchenette and made himself a sandwich. The tape had rewound by the time he returned to the living room, and he settled down to listen again, reflecting that in the distant future his son might ask, "What did you do, Daddy, when your world was falling apart?" And he might reply, "I ate a bologna on rye with mustard."

He heard Rita Sullivan and David Rathbone, apparently on New Year's Day, discuss a party they had attended the previous night. He heard Ernie call Rita to come to the Palace and take care of Rathbone, who was "under the weather." He heard the subsequent conversation inside the town house during which Rathbone made it obvious that he was planning to leave the country in six months, and Rita practically promised to go along.

It was possible, of course, that she had been playing her

assigned role, trying to lure Rathbone into revealing his destination. But that was hard to believe; a few days later Rita, seated in the chair now occupied by Harker, had assured him that Rathbone had spoken of leaving only in general terms. She had been vague about that, but definite in promising Tony to answer his marriage proposal in six months. That would be after Rathbone had skedaddled. And Rita with him?

There were other things she should have told him but hadn't: the description of Rathbone's intended hideaway, a place in the sun, not too far from the beach, with a big private pool. That matched Rathbone's ranch in Costa Rica. And she mentioned nothing of his business meeting on New Year's Day, probably at the Palace, that "went fine" but resulted in Rathbone drinking himself into insensibility.

All those lapses were worrisome enough, but it was the content and tone of her conversations with Rathbone, obviously in a bedroom, that shattered Tony Harker. He could not believe that she was such an accomplished actress that she could fake the passion in the things she said and, presumably, did.

The intimacy and fervor of the pillow talk between David and her was at once arousing and depressing. He listened to it, feeling like a sick voyeur but unable to turn off the machine, knowing that even if he did, the hurt would not end.

When, finally, the tape ran out, he still heard the moans of delight. And he sat alone in a shoddy motel room, trying to puzzle out reasons for her possible duplicity. It was easy to say Rathbone was handsome, wealthy, loving, and she had succumbed to his charms. But Tony had to believe there was more to it than that. Rita was a hardheaded cop who could spot a phony a mile away. Yet here she was apparently embracing phoniness and willing to risk her future with an insubstantial man whose entire life was based on sham.

What were Harker's options in response to what he had

heard? He could confront Sullivan with the tapes. Her defense, he reckoned, was that she was doing her assigned job. She had delivered information on the Fort Knox Fund, hadn't she? And on Rathbone passing the forged Treasury check. And on the activities of Irving Donald Gevalt.

She could claim that she had done what she was ordered to do. But how she accomplished her assignment was her business, not Harker's. And how could he answer that? He could not, but the worm still gnawed.

He might take the actual tapes to Lester Crockett rather than submitting an expurgated précis, and let the boss decide where the truth lay. But that, Harker decided, would be surrender of his responsibility. Sullivan was *his* agent, and if he was willing to profit from her work, he should be willing to accept the blame if she turned sour.

He was convinced that the entire case was progressing well and nearing its denouement. Pulling Rita out might well rob the investigation of vital intelligence. He needed her as much as he needed Clark, Fortescue, Suarez, and Ullman.

And there was always the possibility—slim though it might be—that she *was* acting a role with Rathbone. And that she would deliver David's head to Tony Harker as soon as she had the evidence.

He hoped with all his heart that might be true. But he was tied in knots, felt the familiar pressure, and began searching frantically for his inhaler.

50.

He put it off as long as he could, answering her importunate phone calls with "Birdie, I can't talk right now; I have people in my office." Or, "Birdie, I have to go up to Palm Beach on business; call you when I get back." Or even, "Birdie, I have a miserable case of the flu, and I don't want to risk giving it to you."

But finally her calls took a nasty tone, and he decided to get it over with. The last thing he wanted at this stage of the game was a scorned woman blowing the whistle on him.

He bought a gold-plated compact for her and had it engraved with a cursive monogram, B.W. He paid for the gift with a stolen credit card, one of many that Ernie sold to trusted customers for fifty bucks a pop. The name on David's card was Finley K. Burden, and they hadn't yet redlined his account.

Mrs. Winslow met him at the door of her apartment with a glacial smile and a greeting that was barely civil. She waved him to an armchair. No snuggling on the couch and no offer of a vodka gimlet just the way he liked it—for which he was grateful.

"Birdie," he said, "that's an absolutely smashing suit you're wearing. Donna Karan, isn't it?"

"No."

"Well, I think it's divine. Birdie, I want to apologize sincerely for not having gotten back to you sooner. I just can't begin to tell you how sorry I am. But I've never been so busy in my life. The goods news is that your investments are doing wonderfully; so far your net worth has increased almost forty percent, and I think it'll do even better this year. I realize that's no excuse for my neglecting you, but I want you to know that I have been working very hard to increase the value of your account."

"Thank you," she said faintly.

He stood, went over to the couch, sat down close to her. He took the gift-wrapped package from his jacket pocket and presented it to her with his dazzling smile.

"For you," he said. "A peace offering."

She held the gift but made no effort to open it. "You know, David, I'm very angry with you. You never came to see me over the holidays, and I didn't even get a Christmas card from you, and you've been almost rude to me on the phone."

He looked at her, shocked and outraged. "You didn't get my card? That's terrible! My secretary said she mailed it a week before Christmas."

"Maybe you need a new secretary."

"Maybe I do," he mourned. "It was a special card I picked out just for you. I'm so sorry, Birdie, but I assure you I didn't forget you."

"I'll take the thought for the deed," she said primly. "But I must tell you honestly that I was so furious at the way you were treating me, I came very close to taking my account away and demanding all my money back."

He was instantly solemn. "First of all, you have every right to do that. The money is yours, and anytime you want to end our business relationship, the assets will be returned to you without delay."

"I'm happy to hear that."

"But before you do it, all I ask is that you consider your financial future carefully. What would you do with your investments? Who would handle them for you? There is an enormous amount of paperwork and very specialized expertise required. Birdie, I don't wish to brag, but I doubt very much if you'll find another asset manager able to provide the kind of return I've been earning for you. Do think it over carefully before you make a decision you may later regret."

"I thought we had more than a business relationship, David, but I guess I was wrong."

"No," he said firmly, "you are not wrong. Of course it is more than a business relationship; we both know that."

She looked at him challengingly. "Well then, what about our taking an apartment together? You never have given me a definite answer."

He rose and paced slowly back and forth in front of the couch. He had contrived a scenario he thought would fly.

"Birdie, I've considered it long and hard. I still feel the risks are tremendous. We know how we feel about each other, and I'd hate to do anything that might jeopardize that feeling. You honestly believe we could make a success of living together. I'm more cautious and conservative than you, just as I am in handling your money. But I've come up with a solution I think is reasonable, and I hope you'll agree."

"What is it, David?"

"Right now I'm heavily involved in a dozen business negotiations for you and my other clients. The pressures are enormous, requiring every bit of my energy and time. At the moment, I couldn't possibly think of moving. But I think I'm beginning to see light at the end of the tunnel. I estimate that

in six months I'll have things organized and running
smoothly. Then you know what I'd like to do?"

"What, David?"

"I'd like to take a vacation. I haven't had a real one in
years—just business trips. I'd like to take at least two weeks
off, maybe a month, and travel through Europe, Russia, maybe even Japan and China. A long, leisurely vacation that'll
enable me to unwind and recharge my batteries. I'd like you
to come with me—at my expense, of course. Not only will
we have a wonderful time, seeing all the sights, visiting Paris,
London, Rome, Moscow, Tokyo, but we'll be living together
for at least two weeks. It'll be like a trial run. If we find we
enjoy each other's company twenty-four hours a day, then
that will certainly be proof that we can make a success of
living together when we come back home. What do you say?
Will you be willing to make the trip with me in six months?"

She tossed the wrapped gift aside, heaved off the couch,
rushed to him, enfolded him in a suffocating embrace.

"Divine!" she cried. "Of course I'll go with you, David.
We'll have the time of our lives, you'll see, and really get to
know each other better."

"And you're willing to wait six months?"

"Of course, you silly boy, because I'm positive, just *positive*, that we'll come home closer than ever and eager to get
our own place—together. Oh, I'm so excited! I'm going out
tomorrow and start shopping: dresses and shoes and maybe
new luggage. There's so much, I've got to make a list of all
the things I'll need."

"You do that," he said with a tender smile, "but meanwhile look at your gift."

She ripped away the fancy wrapping, opened the box, removed the engraved compact, and stared at it with widened
eyes.

"Oh David, it's beautiful! Just what I wanted."

"I thought it would be," he said.

51.

It had been a frustrating morning for Manny Suarez. He and the other yaks were hawking the Fort Knox Commodity Trading Fund, commemorative postage stamps, and pork bellies, but it was one of those days when the mooches just weren't biting. Sid Coe was in a vile mood, stalking up and down the boiler room and screaming, "Close the deal or there's no meal! Get the buck in or get the fuck out!"

Finally, a little after noon, he went stomping downstairs, muttering and cursing. The yaks figured they were safe for a while because it was common knowledge that Coe was humping the comely receptionist in his private office during his lunch hour. Manny Suarez folded up the sucker list, stuck it in his hip pocket, and ducked out.

Just as he had promised, Tony Harker was parked a block away in a white Chevy van. Harker sat behind the wheel. In the back, a bearded young black waited with a classy Leica camera and a battery-powered floodlight. Suarez slid in next to Harker and handed the sucker list to the photographer. He put the list on the floor, turned on his light, adjusted the lens and started snapping.

"How's it going, Manny?" Tony asked.

Suarez flipped his hand back and forth. "*Comme çi, comme ça*. Moaney is tight today. The boss is goin' nuts."

"Stick with it," Harker said. "I don't think it'll be much longer. Ullman brought in a canary who's singing his heart out. We're going to nail the whole bunch, including your boss."

"I wanna be there when you take him," Manny said. "Hokay?"

"Sure, I was planning on it. I guess you'll be glad to get back to Miami."

"Oh, I don' know," Suarez said, thinking of the Cuban lady and the cash he was skimming from his commissions. "It's good duty. Maybe you can use me again?"

"Could be," Harker said. "After this case is closed, there'll be something else. It never ends."

"Have gun, will travel," Manny said.

The photographer tapped Tony's shoulder. "Finished," he said. "I took two of each page, different exposures. We're covered."

"Good," Harker said. "Here's your list, Manny. I hope there's no hassle."

Suarez shrugged. "He don' even know I'm gone."

But he did. When Manny walked into Instant Investments, Inc., Sid Coe was waiting for him, his face twisted with fury, and the agent knew he was in trouble.

Coe jerked a thumb toward his office. "In there, bandido," he said, his voice gritty.

Suarez followed him inside, and Coe slammed the door.

"Where you been?" he demanded.

"Having a beer," Manny said. "Hokay?"

"Where's your sucker list?"

"Right here," Manny said, taking it from his hip pocket.

"What the fuck you taking it out of the office for?"

"So no one swipes it. I got this list marked with all my best mooches. Why should I let another yak make deals with my pigeons?"

"Yeah? Let me see it."

Suarez handed over the pages. Coe scanned them swiftly.

"You're lying, you little shit," he said. "All you got marked are Hispanic names. You stole my list that I paid good money for. You sneaked it out of the office against what I told you and had it copied. You're figuring on going into business for yourself."

"Not so," Manny said, spreading his hands. "Ask up and down the street. Where could I have it copied in twenty minutes?"

Coe stared at him angrily. "No one messes with Sid Coe. You're fired. Get your ass the hell out of here."

"Sure," Suarez said, "as soon as you pay me commissions for three days' work. You owe me."

"I owe you shit," Coe said. He opened his desk drawer, took out the heavy .45 automatic, and placed it on the desktop. He turned it with his forefinger until the muzzle was pointing at Manny.

"Look what I got," Coe said. "Now get out."

Suarez lifted the tail of his white guayabera shirt to reveal the short-barreled .38 Special holstered on his hip. "Look what I got," he said. "You wanna see who's the fastest draw in the East?"

Coe looked up at his face, his eyes. Then he took out his wallet, extracted two hundred in fifties and threw them on the desk.

"You fuckin' spic," he said. "You're all alike."

"Yeah, I know," Manny said, picking up the bills. "We wanna get paid for the work we do. Un-American—right? See you soon, Mr. Coe."

"Not if I can help it."

"You can't," the agent said, smiling. "Too late."

He left Coe trying to figure that and went out onto Oakland Park Boulevard. He found a phone kiosk and called Tony Harker. But he wasn't back in his office yet, so Manny drove to a place that served Tex-Mex and had a big bowl of peppery chili and two icy bottles of Dos Equis. Then he called Harker again.

"I got canned," he reported.

Tony took it in his usual laid-back style. "Too bad," he said. "Any heat?"

"Some. He's a mouthy guy. But nothin' I couldn't handle."

"Good. Well, come on in; I've got another job for you."

"Yeah? What is it?"

"Roger Fortescue could use some help. He's investigating a homicide."

"No kid?" Suarez said. "Sounds inarresting."

52.

A real estate agent found Simon Clark a nice two-bedroom condo on the Waterway down near Las Olas. It was completely furnished and had a terrace facing east. He signed a year's lease and moved in. He figured that eventually he'd have to go back to Chicago and pack up clothes, law books, and personal belongings, and have them shipped down. But that could wait; he had bought enough Florida duds to dress like a native, and the condo was equipped with linens and kitchen stuff, so he was all set there.

He inspected possible office space on Commercial, but he really didn't want to be located there, so he kept looking. The agent, Ellen St. Martin, was helping him, and the last time they spoke, she reported she had a lead on a small but elegant office up near Boca Raton. That would be a long daily commute, especially during the tourist season, but Simon didn't plan on a nine-to-five job, and it was important to have a flash front.

Nancy Sparco had delivered a copy of her husband's Super Sucker list, and it looked good to Clark: twenty-four names, addresses, and telephone numbers with notations on net worth, personal peccadilloes, and the kind of scams they bought: oil wells, grain futures, computer leasing, real estate, even fish farms and Arabian mares.

His Chicago checking account was getting low, and it hurt him to run up unpaid balances on his credit card accounts, considering the usurious interest those bastards charged, so Clark figured it was time to hit Mort Sparco. He thought about buying a gun—God knows it was easy enough in Florida—but decided against it. With the ammunition he had, a gun just wasn't necessary.

He arrived at the discount brokerage a little after one P.M., but had to cool his heels in that ratty reception room for almost a half-hour because "Mr. Sparco is busy with a client right now." Clark doubted that, but waited patiently until the summons, "Mr. Sparco will see you now," like the guy was a brain surgeon or something.

The broker was Mr. Congeniality, greeting Clark warmly, shaking his hand, getting him seated in a low club chair alongside his desk.

"Well now," he said briskly, "I suppose you want a progress report on your investment in the Fort Knox Fund. I can sum it up in one word: *dynamite!* Let's see, you put in a total of about sixty thousand, didn't you?"

"About that."

"What would you say if I told you the value of your stock now is close to seventy-five? Is that a barn-burner or isn't it?"

"Mr. Sparco," Clark said, "I'd like to cash in. I've decided to move back to Chicago. But first, of course, I have to pay off my father's home-equity loan. So if you'll sell my stock as soon as possible, I'd appreciate it."

He had to admire the broker. Sparco didn't seem shocked or startled, and his affable smile didn't fade. Instead, he leaned back in his swivel chair, took a cigar from his desk drawer, bit off the tip and spat it into his wastebasket. Then he lighted the cigar with a wooden kitchen match scratched on the underside of his desk. He blew a plume of smoke at the ceiling.

"Now why would you want to do that, Mr. Clark?" he asked pleasantly. "The fact that you're moving back to Chicago needn't make any difference; you can keep your account open here. We have a number of active clients who go north eight months out of the year. They phone collect whenever they want to trade or ask a question."

"I don't think so. I'd like to sell my Fort Knox Fund and close out my account. How soon can I get the money?"

"But why should you want to unload such a money-making investment? You're already showing a twenty-five-percent profit, and that stock has nowhere to go but up."

"I want to sell," Clark repeated stubbornly. "I want my money. Immediately."

Sparco showed the first signs of discomposure, tapping his cigar frequently on the ashtray rim, blinking rapidly. He licked his lips a few times, leaned toward Clark, tried a smile that didn't work.

"That might present some difficulties," he said. "As I'm sure you've noticed, the Fort Knox Fund is not listed on any of the exchanges. That means we'll have to negotiate a private trade for you. It may take some time."

"You mean I can't get my money?"

"Oh no," Sparco said. "No, no, no. Your investment is perfectly safe. It's just not as liquid as you might have thought."

"How long will it take to sell it?"

"Well, that's hard to say. We'll certainly make a best-faith effort to unload it, but I can't guarantee you'll get top market price."

"That's all right," Clark said. "I'll forget about the profit. I'll be satisfied if I just get my sixty thousand back."

"Mr. Clark," Sparco said earnestly, "one of the first things I learned about this business is that a broker should always try to fit the investment to the client. It's not always a matter of dollars and cents; it's frequently an emotional thing. The client should be *comfortable* with his investments. If he's not, then I'm not doing my job."

Clark listened closely to this spiel, wanting to remember the phraseology since it might prove valuable in his new career as a shark.

"Now it's obvious to me," the broker continued, "that you are not comfortable with the Fort Knox Fund, regardless of how well it's doing. All right, I accept that. Around here, the client calls the shots. Now what I suggest is this: Instead of closing out your account, you roll over your funds, including your profit, into another investment. I can suggest a number of equities as good or better than Fort Knox. I see no reason why you can't double your money in six months or less."

Simon Clark was silent, staring steadily at the other man. The silence went on so long that the broker began to fidget, relighting his cigar with fingers that trembled slightly.

Clark sighed, leaned back in the armchair, crossed his legs. "Mr. Sparco," he said quietly, "I want sixty thousand dollars from you. Cash, not a check. And I want it now."

"That's ridiculous!" the broker burst out.

"Do you know Sidney Coe?" Clark asked suddenly.

"What?"

"Do you know a man named Sidney Coe?"

"No, I've never heard the name."

"He runs a business on Oakland Park Boulevard."

Sparco shook his head. "Don't know him."

"He has a really rotten temper," Clark said. "Alleged to be a wife-beater. A dangerous, violent man."

"What's that got to do with me?"

"Well, since I've been in Florida I've had the time to poke

around a little. I've talked to some interesting people and found out some interesting things."

"So?"

"So one of the interesting things I discovered is that office you rent up in West Palm Beach."

The cigar dropped from Mortimer Sparco's mouth onto the desktop. He made no effort to retrieve it but sat rigidly, gripping his chair arms.

"I also discovered," Clark went on, "that you've succeeded in turning several of Sid Coe's yaks. Although from what I understand about the man, it probably didn't take much persuasion. My informant tells me you've been clipping Sid Coe for about a hundred grand a month."

"What the hell's going on here?" Sparco cried.

"It's called blackmail," Clark said tonelessly. "I'm sure you've heard of it. Either I get my sixty thousand immediately or I leave your office, go directly to Coe's boiler room, and show him the evidence of how you've been jobbing him."

"What evidence? You've got no evidence!"

"A signed statement from your landlord in West Palm Beach who copied the license number on your black BMW. A Polaroid photo of the sign on the door of your office up there. It says Instant Investments, the name of Coe's business. And I can finger the yaks who've been working this scam with you. I figure all that'll be enough to convince Sid Coe. Ten minutes after I leave him, he'll come busting in here with steam coming out his ears. What do you think he'll do to you, Mr. Sparco? I hear he carries a gun."

Sparco gnawed furiously at his thumbnail. "Suppose I pay," he said. "Just suppose I give you back your sixty grand. How do I know you won't hit me again?"

"Easy," Clark said. "You pay me. Then you close down that West Palm Beach office. Tell the yaks the picnic is over. Drop the steal and figure a new way to cheat your friends. I'll be up in Chicago and won't know a thing about it."

"I haven't got 60K in the office."

"Sure you have. All you chiselers keep bribe and getaway cash available."

"I've got maybe thirty grand. No more than that. I'll have to go to the bank."

"That's okay," Simon Clark said cheerfully, rising. "I'll go with you."

53.

David Rathbone had a long, tiring day. He drove to Lakeland in the morning, picked up the fifty thousand in queer from Herman Weisrotte, then turned around and drove back to Fort Lauderdale. On the trip home he stopped for a club sandwich and a bottle of Rolling Rock.

He delivered the cash to Jimmy Bartlett, then dropped in at the Palace Lounge to pay his tab for New Year's Day.

He had one vodka gimlet at the Palace, then started home. On impulse, he pulled off Atlantic Boulevard on the east side of the Intracoastal and parked in the concrete area under the bridge. There were a few other cars there, a few night fishermen dipping their lines in the glimmering channel.

Rathbone lighted a cigarette and tried to unwind. He knew Rita was waiting for him, but at that moment he wanted to be alone, watch the boats moving up and down the Waterway, and think about where he had been, where he was, where he was going.

It had been in his early teens that he had suddenly realized, almost with the force of a religious experience, how stupid most people were. They were just dumb, dumb, dumb, and nothing in his life since that revelation had changed his conviction that the great majority of Americans had air between their ears.

Why, there were people who believed wearing a copper bracelet would prevent arthritis, people who believed they could beat a three-card-monte dealer, people who believed in astrology, flying saucers, and the power of crystals. There were even people who believed professional wrestling was on the up-and-up. How could you respect the intelligence of the populace when a con woman could travel the country collecting contributions by claiming to be the penniless widow of the Unknown Soldier?

Rathbone came to regard this mass stupidity as a great natural resource. Just like oil in the ground, gold nuggets in a stream, or a stand of virgin forest, it was there to be exploited. The ignorance and greed of most people were simply inexhaustible, and a man would be a fool not to harvest that bounty. It was no sin to profit from the mooches' need to believe what they *wanted* to believe, ignoring reason and common sense.

Now he was in south Florida, a paradise for con men and swindlers. Frank Little had once said that Ponce de León was looking for the Fountain of Youth but had found the Golden Mooch. The phrase had caught on with the Palace gang; they referred to Florida as The Land of the Golden Mooch. And best of all, hundreds of marks arrived every day, to live in a sunlit, semitropical climate, play shuffleboard, and listen to the siren song of the sharks—the human variety.

There just seemed to be no limit to the credulity of Florida mooches. They eagerly gulped the most rancid bait, and the saying amongst Florida sharpers was, "If the deal is so lousy that even a doctor won't bite, take it to a dentist." Deluding

Floridians, Rathbone decided, was shooting fish in a barrel, and he questioned if he was doing the smart thing to leave the state in six months.

But he recalled the advice of an old slicker he had met when he first arrived in south Florida. This guy had been on the con for fifty years and had accumulated a nice pile for his old age, mostly by wholesaling counterfeit brand-name perfumes he concocted in his bathtub. But he had retired and now, just to keep himself busy, he was running a magic shop in Miami, selling tricks and illusions.

"Remember kid," he had rumbled to David, "Easy Street goes two ways. You're young now, and you think it'll last forever. It never does. The swindles don't die—the old ones work as well as ever—but eventually you'll get tired of the game. Too much stress, too much pressure, never knowing when a mark might turn nasty and cut you up. Do what I did: Save up a stake, and then take the money and run. The game is really for young guys with balls and energy. But after a while you get to the point where you want to live a straight life, quit looking over your shoulder, and start smelling the roses."

There was probably some truth in that, Rathbone acknowledged, but he couldn't buy it all because it meant the way he was living now would eventually prove to be unsatisfying.

In six months he might cash in, but he knew that moving to Costa Rica wouldn't be the end of his plots. He'd be a bamboozler till the day he died simply because that's the way he was.

And the opportunities never seemed to end.

Like the fifty thousand in funny money he had just delivered to Jimmy Bartlett, to be salted into a deposit at a Palm Beach bank.

"The German gets twenty percent of the face value?" Bartlett had asked.

"That's right," Rathbone said. "I had to lean on him—he wanted thirty—but he finally agreed after I told him there'll be bigger jobs coming."

"Good," Bartlett said. "You're an A-Number-One yak."

Actually, Rathbone had conned the printer into accepting fifteen percent of the face value of the queer. David planned to skim that extra five percent for himself.

But Jimmy Bartlett, friend and partner, didn't have to know that.

54.

Mike Mulligan would have confessed to being Jack the Ripper if they had asked him. They read him his rights, but he said he didn't want an attorney present during his questioning. Lester Crockett gently suggested it might be a wise thing to do, but Mulligan insisted: No lawyer.

So they had him sign a statement that he understood his rights but didn't wish any legal assistance. Just to make sure, they videotaped the reading of the rights and the banker's disclaimer.

Then he started talking.

Crockett did the questioning, with Anthony Harker and Henry Ullman as witnesses. The entire session was video-taped, and later Mulligan read the typed transcript and signed it. All this took place over the Christmas weekend.

Mulligan confessed that as an officer of the Crescent Bank of Boca Raton, he had accepted deposits of cash in excess of $10,000 from James Bartlett for the account of Mitchell Korne

Enterprises, Inc., of Miami. In return, he had been supplied with cocaine by Mr. Bartlett. Mulligan had never used the drug himself—he was insistent on that—but had given it away to "friends."

He described how the deposited funds were eventually moved out of the Mitchell Korne account to a bank in Panama. He named the other officers of the Crescent Bank who were aware of these deals. But he bravely accepted complete responsibility for the money-laundering scheme and stated his intention to take his punishment "like a man."

"I think, Mr. Mulligan," Crockett said gravely, "that your punishment may prove to be milder than you anticipate. It all depends on your cooperation."

"You mean I won't have to go to jail?"

"Possibly not. What we want you to do is return to your job at the bank and carry on as before. Do not—I repeat, *do not*—inform your co-conspirators at the bank of your arrest. What we require is that you inform us promptly when James Bartlett calls to arrange for another deposit. Is that clear?"

"Yes."

"You will agree to accept that deposit, and then tell us the date and time. Meanwhile, Mr. Ullman will move into your apartment temporarily. He will also accompany you to and from work. In other words, Mr. Mulligan, you will be under constant surveillance. Understood?"

The banker nodded.

"Good," Crockett said with a bleak smile. "We appreciate your assistance."

Ullman and Mulligan left the office, with the agent's arm about the banker's thin shoulders.

Crockett waited until the door was closed, then shook his head softly. "No fool like an old fool," he said. "But at least he seems determined to make amends."

"Yes, sir," Harker said, "but we may have a king-size problem. When we nail Bartlett making the deposit, we'll have to scoop up all the other perps at the same time. Otherwise they'll hear of Bartlett's arrest, and the roaches will disappear into the woodwork. I think we better start working on the logistics of the crackdown right away. We'll have to make sure every suspect is covered, plus have enough men to confiscate the records of Rathbone, Coe, and Sparco. We'll also want to arrange for a coordinated DEA raid on Frank Little's warehouse, and pick up Herman Weisrotte and Irving Donald Gevalt. Then there's the problem of Mitchell Korne in Miami."

"I'll inform the Miami DEA office about that gentleman," Crockett said. "I presume they'll want to initiate their own investigation. Yes, I think you'd be wise to begin planning the roundup immediately. Then when we get the word on the Bartlett deposit, we'll be able to move quickly." He paused, stared at the other man, then asked curiously, "What role do you have in mind for Rita Sullivan?"

"I don't know," Tony said. "I'll have to think about it."

Simon Clark came into Harker's office and dumped a thick file on his desk.

"That's it," he said. "Everything I've been able to dig up on Mortimer Sparco's penny stock swindles. I can't do more without subpoenas."

"Got enough for an indictment?"

"More than enough. But it's all raw stuff. It really needs a staff to organize it and follow the leads."

Harker thought a moment. "I've got plenty on my plate without this," he said. "Besides, as I told you, this penny stock scam is a sideshow. I want to nail Sparco for dealing drugs. He'll do heavy time on that."

"Good," Clark said. "He's a slimy character."

"What I think I'll do," Harker went on, "is ship this file up to my old buddies in the SEC. They've got the manpower and contacts to handle it."

"That makes sense," Clark said. "Can I go back to Chicago now?"

Tony looked at him in surprise. "In the middle of winter?" he said. "That *doesn't* make sense. Don't you like Florida?"

The agent shrugged. "It has its points, I guess, but I prefer the big city."

"Well, I have another job for you before you cut loose. There's an old guy named Irving Donald Gevalt involved in all this. He claims to be a rare book dealer, but he's really a paperman. He's supplied David Rathbone with phony ID, and I suspect the others in the gang use him, too. See what you can find out about his past history and present activities."

"You want me to try making a buy?"

"It wouldn't do any harm. And if Gevalt gets spooked and tells Rathbone, it might make him sweat a little. I'd like that."

"All right," Clark said, "I'll see what I can do. When are you going to bust everyone?"

"Soon," Harker said. "I'm working on the details right now. I'll probably want you to lead the team that takes Sparco."

Clark did a good job of covering his shock. "Whatever you want," he said casually. "Meanwhile I'll get to work on Gevalt."

"He's supposed to have a wife one-third his age," Harker said, smiling. "I hear she wears the world's smallest bikini."

"I couldn't care less," Simon Clark said. "I'm a happily married man."

They sat around a littered table in the Burger King and worked on double cheeseburgers, french fries, coleslaw, and big containers of cola, using up a stack of paper napkins.

"Jack Liddite is handling the file," Roger Fortescue said, "and he's not happy about our nosing around."

"You're a smoke and I'm a spic," Manny Suarez said. "Why should he be happy?"

Harker grinned at both of them. "Screw Jack Liddite," he said. "Whoever he is."

"A homicide dick," Fortescue said. "And he wanted to know what our interest was in Termite Tommy. I mumbled something about his being involved in pushing queer, but I don't think he believed me."

"Homicide?" Tony said. "So it *was* murder?"

"Well, Tommy had enough alcohol in him to put the Foreign Legion to sleep, and when he went into the canal, he smacked his head a good one on the dash. But what actually killed him was that someone stuck a sharpened ice pick into his right ear. It took the medical examiner awhile to find it, but that's what did the job."

Suarez started on his second cheeseburger. "It would be nice," he said, "if he was out cold from the booze before he got stuck."

"Yeah," Roger said, "that would be nice. So where do we go from here?"

Harker slopped ketchup on his french fries. "You said Tommy left Lakeland on New Year's Day?"

"That was the last his motel owner saw him."

"Could he have been murdered that night?"

"Possible," Fortescue said. "It falls within the ME's four- or five-day time frame. He couldn't be more exact than that. After all, the guy had been marinating in canal water awhile."

"Let's figure he drove down here from Lakeland and got it that night," Tony said slowly. "The last time he came down he went to the Palace Lounge on Commercial."

"Right," Fortescue said. "Met David Rathbone."

"Well, on the evening of New Year's Day, Rathbone got smashed in the Palace Lounge. So drunk that the bartender had to call Rathbone's woman to come collect him."

The agents didn't ask how he knew that. They munched their burgers in silence.

"It's theen stuff," Manny said finally.

"Sure, it's thin," Harker agreed. "But what else have we got?"

"Okay," Fortescue said, "so let's figure that before Termite Tommy ends up in the canal, he goes to the Palace Lounge and meets with David Rathbone. Then he leaves, and Rathbone stays and gets plastered. If that holds, then someone at the Palace might remember Tommy being there on New Year's Day. Maybe the parking valet. Maybe the bartender."

"The bartender's name is Ernie," Harker said.

"Ernesto," Manny Suarez said. "I like it. Roger, let's you and me go talk to Ernesto."

"Let's run a trace on him first," Fortescue said. "I like to know who we're dealing with."

"This is fun," Suarez said. "Better than selling pork bellies."

Tony said, "Just be sure to ask Ernie if David Rathbone met with Termite Tommy on New Year's Day."

Roger stared at him. "Regardless of how Ernie answers that, he's going to call Rathbone and warn him the moment we leave."

"I know," Harker said happily.

55.

It had chilled off to 59°F overnight, but the morning of Friday, January 26, was sharp and clear, and the radio weatherman predicted the afternoon would be sunny and in the low 70s.

They decided it would be too nippy on the terrace, so they came down to the dining room in their robes. Theodore served a down-home breakfast of fried eggs, plump pork sausages, grits, and hush puppies.

"No office for you today," David said. "I think we'll pay a visit to Irving Donald Gevalt and get you fixed up with a passport."

"In my own name?" Rita asked.

He thought a moment. Then: "No, I don't think so. We'll use the ID of Gloria Ramirez you used at the Boca bank. You'll have to provide a photo, but that's no problem."

She glanced around to make certain Theodore was out of the room. "David, will Blanche and Theodore be going with us?"

He shook his head. "Unfortunately, no. Too many complications. Right now they've got fake green cards Gevalt provided. If I can work a deal, they may be able to join us later."

"What are you going to tell your clients when we leave?"

He grinned at her. "Nothing. They'll find out eventually. But by then we'll be long gone."

"Poor Birdie Winslow," Rita said. "She'll be devastated."

Rathbone laughed. "Did I tell you she wanted me to move in with her? Scout's honor. She had visions of the two of us sharing a big condo on the beach."

"What did you tell her?"

"I told her I already had a roomie."

They went upstairs to dress and, a little before noon, drove out to the Gevalt Rare Book Center. The old man seemed delighted to see them. He called into the back room, and a few moments later his wife, still wearing her fringed black bikini, came out with two wine spritzers for Rita and David.

"None for you?" Rathbone asked.

The gaffer shook his head sadly. "Even such a mild drink my stomach cannot stand. A glass of warm milk before I go to bed: That's my speed. This is a social visit, David?"

"Not entirely. You provided a package of paper for Rita in the name of Gloria Ramirez."

"I remember. Any problems?"

"None whatsoever. But now we need a passport in the same name. Something that looks used."

"Of course. Visa stamps and so forth. You have a photo?"

"We'll bring you one."

"Not necessary."

The young blonde went into the back room and came out carrying an old Nikon with an attached flashgun.

"The camera is ancient," Gevalt said with his gap-toothed grin, "but it does good work. Like me. David, could I speak to you a moment in private?"

His wife began to take close-ups of Rita while the two men moved away to a corner of the littered shop.

"Yesterday a man came in," Gevalt started. "He is wearing Florida clothes, but he talks like the Midwest. Hard and fast. A big-city man. He asks if I have a first edition McGuffey. I ask him what edition does he want? Is he looking for a reader, speller, or primer? He begins to hem and haw, and it is obvious to me he knows nothing about rare books. Finally he says he has heard I can provide identification papers. He needs a birth certificate and Social Security card and is willing to pay any price."

"You ever see this guy before?" Rathbone asked.

"No. Never."

"It's possible one of your clients talked, and this man overheard and really did need paper."

Gevalt shook his head. "If any of my clients talk, they wouldn't be my clients. I am very choosy, David; you know that. No, this man was law; I am convinced of it. Something about him: a clumsy arrogance."

"What did you say to him?"

"I became very angry. Told him I was a legitimate businessman making a living selling rare books, and I would never do anything illegal, and he should leave my shop immediately. He left, but it still bothers me. It is the first time anything like that has happened. David, do you feel I am in danger?"

"Of course not," Rathbone said. "Even if the guy was a cop—and you're not sure he was—it was just a fishing expedition. You handled it exactly right. If the law had anything on you, you'd be out of business already. You have nothing to worry about, believe me."

The old man looked at him, and his rheumy eyes filled. "Worry?" he said. "That's all I do—worry. About that stupid man with his first edition McGuffey. About one of my motels which is losing money because the manager is dishonest. *Dis-*

309

honest, David! And also I fear my wife has a lover. Oh yes, I have seen him lurking around. A muscular young man and he has—oh God, David, I hate to mention it but he has a tattoo on his right bicep. And you tell me not to worry!"

Rathbone put a hand lightly on Gevalt's shoulder. "It will all work out," he said soothingly. "The important thing is to think positively. I always do. Who can remember last year's problems? Everything will turn out all right, you'll see."

The old man took out a disgraceful handkerchief and blew his nose. "You're right, David," he said, snuffling. "I must think positively."

On the drive back home, Rita asked, "What were you and Gevalt talking about while I was having my picture taken?"

Rathbone laughed. "The poor old man thinks his wife has a boyfriend. A hulk with a tattoo."

"Can't say I blame her. What would you do if you found out I had a boyfriend?"

"Couldn't happen," David said. "If I can't trust you, who can I trust?"

56.

The previous day's tapes were delivered to Anthony Harker's motel every morning at about seven A.M. He listened to the first run-through while he was shaving. He found he was listening to but not hearing the personal portions, much as one might look at something without seeing it. He closed his mind to the intimate murmurs and cries; they had, he kept assuring himself, nothing to do with him. He was interested only in names, dates, hard facts.

On Saturday morning, January 27, he heard Rita and David discussing a visit to Gevalt. Then Rathbone joked about not informing his clients before he decamped, and Birdie Winslow was mentioned. That rang a bell with Harker; Rita had given him that name weeks ago, but he had never followed up on it.

He made himself a cup of instant coffee and chewed on a stale bagel. Then he went to the office, planning to put in a full day. Work was the only relief he could find from brooding on what was tearing him apart: those murmurs and cries that had nothing to do with him.

He found a note on his desk from the night duty officer. It was a message from Henry Ullman in Boca: Please call him ASAP. Harker popped an antihistamine capsule, and phoned.

"It's on." Ullman reported. "Bartlett called Mulligan last night. He's going to make a deposit at the bank on Friday, February second, at noon. Got that?"

"Got it," Tony said. "Next Friday morning at noon. Hank, you handle the collar. I'll get some warm bods to you early on Friday to help out. Two men be enough?"

"Plenty," Ullman said. "I don't expect Bartlett to turn mean. What about the other bank officers involved?"

"We'll scoop them up later. I'm hoping Bartlett will make a deal with us. Then we'll have corroborative evidence for Mulligan's confession. How's the little man acting?"

"Believe it or not, I think he's excited. It's probably the most dramatic thing that's ever happened to him."

"Except for those Saturday night parties."

"Yeah," Ullman said, laughing. "The Great Toilet Tank Capers. He'll never forget those."

Harker now had a date and a time, D day and H hour, and could begin firming up the destruction of the Palace gang. But before he got to work on schedules and personnel deployment, there was something he wanted to do first: He looked up Birdie Winslow in various telephone directories and finally found her in Pompano Beach. He was startled to discover she lived less than a half-mile from him.

Before he called, he pondered on his best approach. If he told Winslow the truth about her "financial planner," she'd probably scream bloody murder, demand all her funds back from Rathbone, and tip off the shark that the law was closing in. Harker decided to play it cool.

"Birdie Winslow?" he asked.

"Yes. Who is this?"

"My name is Anthony Harker. I hate to bother you, but I've been considering employing a money manager, and David Rathbone is one of the possibilities on my list. Mr. Rathbone has provided me with a list of his clients so I can check his track record. I was hoping you'd be kind enough to spare me a few moments. I'm in your neighborhood, and I promise not to keep you long."

"Well," she said, "I planned to go shopping today, but I guess I can spare a little time. How soon can you be here?"

"Twenty minutes," Harker said. "Thank you very much—uh—is it Miss or Mrs. Winslow?"

"Mrs.," Birdie said. "And your name is Harder?"

"Harker. Anthony Harker. I'm on my way, Mrs. Winslow, and thank you."

She turned out to be a buxom matron, a bit blowsy in Harker's opinion. She was wearing a black gabardine suit, and both jacket and skirt were too snug. Like many overweight women, she had legs which were exceptionally shapely, the ankles slender. But the scarlet patent leather pumps didn't help.

She was pleasant enough, got him seated in an armchair, and offered him a drink which he declined. She sat on the couch, but even at that distance he could smell her perfume, a musky scent he thought much too heavy for this woman and this climate.

Her apartment was as overstuffed as she, with too much of everything in lurid colors and clashing styles. Near the door, he noted, was a stack of matched luggage, so new that the manufacturer's tags were still tied to the handles.

"Mrs. Winslow," he started, "I appreciate your seeing me on such short notice, and I'll try to make this as brief as possible. As I told you on the phone, I'm planning to hire someone to handle my investments, and naturally I want to learn as much as I can about the person I select. If I ask questions you'd rather not answer, please tell me and I'll understand. Believe me, I have no wish to pry into your financial affairs. I'd just like to know whether or not you can recommend David Rathbone as an asset manager."

"Oh, ask anything you like," she said blithely.

"Could you tell me how you happened to meet him and become his client?"

She thought a moment. "Why, I believe it was Ellen St. Martin who introduced us. Ellen is the real estate agent who found this apartment for me, and she suggested David was the perfect man to take care of my finances. After my husband died, I just couldn't handle all the investments he had made. And then I had the insurance money, of course. Ralph left me very well fixed, I'll say that for him. Then I met David and was quite impressed with him."

"You investigated his record?"

"Oh yes. I spoke to several of his clients, and they all were very enthusiastic about what he had done for them. Why, he had increased their investment income forty or fifty percent a year."

"And has he done as well for you?"

"He certainly has! I think my net worth has increased at least that much since I've been with him, and that's been less than six months."

"Remarkable," Harker said. "Do you receive monthly statements from Mr. Rathbone?"

"I surely do."

"And monthly statements from the brokers he deals with? Confirmation slips on your trades?"

"Oh no," she said gaily, "none of that. David said it's just unnecessary paper. After all, everything's included on his monthly statements."

"Uh-huh," Tony said. "When you started with Mr. Rathbone, I suppose he had you sign some documents. A full power of attorney perhaps, or a management contract."

"I know I signed some papers, but David said they weren't

important, and I could get my money back from him whenever I liked."

"You didn't ask if Mr. Rathbone is registered with the Securities and Exchange Commission or the Florida Department of Securities?"

"No, but I'm sure that if he's supposed to be registered, then he is. You could ask him."

"Of course, I'll do that. Did he ever mention if there was an insurance policy in effect to protect your account from fraud or theft?"

"No, the subject never came up. But as long as David will return my money whenever I ask, there's no need for an insurance policy, is there?"

"No," Harker said, realizing this woman was hopelessly naive, "no need. Mrs. Winslow, would it be too much if I asked to see your most recent statement from Mr. Rathbone? I'd like to get some idea of the type of investments he prefers."

"I don't see why not," Birdie said, rising. "You'll see that David is making me lots of money."

The statement she brought him was, he noted, a computer printout. But that didn't mean a thing. It was a perfect example of GIGO: Garbage In, Garbage Out. The statement listed several Certificates of Deposit at Texas and California banks Harker had never heard of. All were allegedly paying over thirty percent. But the bulk of Mrs. Winslow's wealth appeared to be invested in the Fort Knox Commodity Trading Fund.

"This Fort Knox Fund," Tony said. "What is that?"

"Oh, that's something David heard about through close friends on Wall Street. He got me in on the ground floor, and it's just made oodles of money."

"But what exactly *is* it?"

"I'm not sure, but I think they buy and sell things. You know, like wheat and corn."

315

Harker nodded and stood up. "Thank you very much, Mrs. Winslow. You've been a big help, and I appreciate it."

"I hope I've convinced you that David is really the best in the business. Everyone says so."

"Well, he's certainly high on my list," Harker said. "I expect to be having a long talk with him very soon." He started to leave, then paused at the stack of new luggage. "Planning a trip, Mrs. Winslow?" he asked, smiling.

Unexpectedly she giggled like a schoolgirl. "Well, if you promise not to tell anyone, I'm taking a long vacation in about six months—with David!"

Harker kept the smile frozen on his face. "That sounds like fun," he said. "Seems to me that you and Mr. Rathbone have more than a business relationship."

"He's a *divine* man," she said breathlessly. "Just *divine!*"

Tony nodded and got out of there, not knowing whether to laugh, curse, or weep.

The moment the door closed behind him, Birdie Winslow picked up the phone and called David Rathbone.

57.

On Monday, January 29, Suarez and Fortescue had lunch at the Tex-Mex place Manny had discovered. They ate cheese enchiladas, rice, refried beans, tortillas, guacamole salad, tacos, nachos, plenty of hot sauce, and two beers each. As they devoured this stupendous feast, they had their notebooks open on the table and exchanged skinny on Ernie the bartender.

"Full name Ernest K. Hohlman," Suarez reported. "Claims to be forty-four. Divorced. Got a young daughter. They live in a condo up at Lighthouse Point. Ernie was on the force in Manhattan. He came down here about five years ago and went to work at the Palace Lounge. When I called the NYPD, they said he resigned, but I finally got hold of a landsman who was willing to *hablilla* for a while. He says Ernie was allowed to resign quote for personal reasons unquote after he was caught shaking down crack dealers."

"Pension?" Fortescue asked.

"*Nada.* But he owns his condo, drives a white Toyota Cressida, and has almost fifty Gs of CDs in the bank. Neat for an ex-cop and bartender."

"You have a gift for understatement," Roger said. "Well, I talked to all my snitches and my snitches' snitches, and I've got a pretty good idea where Ernie's gelt is coming from. The guy is a world-class hustler. I mean he's into *everything:* books bets and peddles pot, coke, stolen credit cards, and merchandise that 'fell off the truck.' Also, he pimps for a young call girl, a real looker. His daughter."

"That's not nice," Manny said.

"No, it's not," Fortescue agreed. "I think that maybe after we finish this heartburn banquet we should go visit Ernie and point out the evil of his ways."

"How we gonna handle it? You wanna try the good cop–bad cop routine?"

"Nah," Roger said. "He was a cop once himself; he'd recognize the plot. Let's both just be nasty."

"Hokay," Suarez said. "I can do nasty."

They drove over to the Grand Palace in Manny's Ford Escort. It was then almost three o'clock, and there was only one parking valet on duty. He was a young black who looked like he could slam-dunk without jumping.

"Let me talk to him alone for a few minutes," Fortescue said, and Suarez nodded.

They waited until the Escort was parked, and the valet came trotting back. Roger drew him aside.

"A moment of your time, bro," the agent said, and showed his ID.

The youth raised his palms outward. "I'm guilty," he said. "Whatever it was, I did it."

Fortescue smiled, took a morgue Polaroid of Termite Tommy out of his jacket pocket, held it up.

"You do this?" he asked.

"Jesus!" the valet said. "He looks dead."

318

"If he isn't," Roger said, "he must be cold as hell in that icebox. Ever see him before?"

The boy studied the grisly photo with fearful fascination. "What happened to him?" he asked.

"He died," the officer said patiently and repeated, "Ever see him before?"

"Yeah, he was around a few times. Drove an old beat-up truck. We called him El Cheapo because he always parked his heap himself."

"That's the guy. Did you work on New Year's Day?"

"Nope. There was only one valet on duty that day. Al Seymour. I was home and I can prove it."

"That's good," Fortescue said. "Now I won't have to goose you with a cattle prod."

The youth was horrified. "You don't really do that, do you?"

"All the time," Roger said, motioning to Suarez. "This job has a lot of fringe benefits."

They entered the Palace Lounge through the side door. There were three men drinking beer at one table, and a middle-aged couple working on whiskey sours at another. The only other person in the room was the man behind the bar. He was reading a supermarket tabloid. He put it aside when Roger and Manny swung onto barstools.

"Yessir, gents," he said, "what's your pleasure?"

"Mine's pussy," Suarez said, and turned to his partner. "What's yours?"

"A boneless pork loin with yams," Fortescue said, and displayed his ID.

"The sheriff's office?" the bartender said. "I know some of the guys there. They stop by occasionally. What division you in?"

"Community relations," Roger said. "This is my partner, Manuel Suarez. Your name is Ernest Hohlman?"

"That's right. Everyone calls me Ernie."

319

"Uh-huh. Did you work here on New Year's Day, Ernie?"

The bartender stalled a beat. "Sure I did," he said finally. "Got paid triple-time because of the holiday."

The agent placed the morgue photo of Termite Tommy on the bar. "Know this guy?"

Ernie glanced at it. "Nope. Never saw him before in my life."

"That was queek," Suarez said. "Wasn't that queek, Roger?"

"Quick?" Fortescue said. "Sheet, it was fuckin' instantaneous. Take another look, Ernie. A nice long look."

The bartender stared. "Dead?" he asked.

"Couldn't be deader," Manny said cheerfully. "Ever see him when he was alive and kicking?"

"No, I don't make him. Listen, this is a busy bar. Maybe he stopped by once for a drink. You can't expect me to remember every customer."

"Did he stop by on New Year's Day?" Suarez said.

"I don't recall him being here."

"That's odd," Fortescue said. "The parking valet on duty that day, Al Seymour, says this guy was here."

"Maybe he was, maybe he wasn't. I can't swear to it either way. You men want a drink? On the house?"

"No, thanks," Fortescue said. "We never drink on duty, do we, Manny?"

"Never," Suarez said. "Against regulations."

"David Rathbone a customer of yours?" Roger asked suddenly. "One of your regulars?"

"Mr. Rathbone?" Ernie said cautiously. "Yeah, he stops by occasionally. Hey, what's this all about? If you could tell me, I'll be happy to help you any way I can. I used to be a cop myself. In New York."

"Yeah, we heard about that," Suarez said. "I wouldn't want to be a cop in New York with all those crack dealers running around with Uzis. How come you left the NYPD, Ernie?"

"I just got tired of the cold weather up there."

"Cold?" Manny said. "I thought maybe it was because it was too hot. So David Rathbone was in here on New Year's Day?"

"He could have been. I really don't remember. Hey, those guys are signaling for another round of beers. I gotta go wait on the customers."

"Go ahead," Fortescue said, "but don't try to make a run for it. The place is surrounded."

"Very funny," Ernie said.

By the time he returned behind the bar, the two officers had decided to lean a little harder.

"We're going to level with you, Ernie," Fortescue said. "After all, you used to be a cop so we know you'll cooperate."

"Sure I will," Ernie said.

"So we'll tell you some of what we've got. The clunk in the photograph was a two-bit con man who went by the moniker of Termite Tommy. We know he was here on New Year's Day. That night someone stuck an ice pick in his right ear. We're talking homicide, Ernie. We also know David Rathbone was here on New Year's Day. Now all we want to know is whether or not Rathbone and Termite Tommy met, maybe had a drink together, maybe talked awhile."

"I don't remember," Ernie said.

"Oh Ernesto," Suarez said sadly. "You are not cooperating, and you *promised.*"

"Listen, I can't tell you something I don't remember, can I?"

"Try," Fortescue urged. "Surely you recall how Rathbone got drunk that evening and you had to call his woman to come get him. You remember that, don't you?"

Ernie wiped the top of the bar with a rag, making slow circles, not looking at them. "Well, maybe he had a few too many," he said in a low voice. "Yeah, now I remember; he got smashed."

"But you don't remember his meeting with Termite Tommy?"

They waited, but Ernie was silent.

"Why you protecting this guy Rathbone?" Suarez demanded. "He's your brother or something? You talk or you don't talk, he's going to take a fall. But you don't talk, you fall right along with him."

"Me?" Ernie said indignantly. "Take a fall? What the hell for? I haven't done anything illegal."

Manny sighed. "Tell him, Roger," he said. "Tell him the good news."

"Well, first of all, Ernie, is the problem of your making book. That's not a capital crime, I admit, but you gotta agree it's illegal. And then we got the grass and coke you been peddling. Not pushing it exactly, but it's available here just for your friends—and from what we hear, you haven't got an enemy in the world. Then we have the stuff that 'fell off the truck' and the stolen credit cards. That adds up to quite a total, wouldn't you say, Manny?"

"Oh yeah," Suarez said. "Years and years."

"Now we haven't dotted all the i's and crossed all the t's on these things," Fortescue said to the bartender. "You've been a cop; you know the drill. We get a squeal or pick up a tidbit from a snitch, and then we go to work, turning over rocks to see what's underneath. That means pounding the pavement and ringing a lot of doorbells. You could save us all that time and trouble."

Suarez tugged at his sleeve. "The *puta*, Roger," he said.

Fortescue snapped his fingers. "Right, Manny," he said. "Thanks for reminding me. That hooker you're running," he said to Ernie with a bright smile. "Your daughter. We'll have to pick her up and take her in for questioning, of course."

"The gossip sheets will love it," Manny said. " 'Ex-Cop's Daughter Accused of Soliciting.' On local TV, too."

Ernie had listened to all this like a spectator at a tennis match, his head turning back and forth as each agent spoke. But when his daughter was mentioned, he froze and stared directly at Roger.

"Listen," he said hoarsely, "maybe we can make a deal."

"I don't see why not," Fortescue said.

58.

Simon Clark imagined that having decided to flip from the side of the law to the side of the lawless, he might suffer guilt or shame. But he discovered that converting from a U.S. assistant district attorney to a south Florida shark was no more painful than switching jobs, going from one corporation to another.

All it entailed was redirecting his energies and talents. His skills at organizing, managing, setting goals and achieving them—all that was still important. Even more crucial was his courtroom experience, the ability to convince and manipulate witnesses, judges, and juries. He called this "human relations," and he knew how vital they would be in his new business.

Best of all, of course, was that he would now be self-employed, and no longer have to play the degrading game of office politics. To be one's own boss—that was exhilarating but scary. If the profits of success were to be all his, so would be the losses of failure. Still, he was convinced the risk-benefit ratio was in his favor.

On Tuesday evening, January 30, he sat at a florid imitation of a Louis Quinze desk in his new condo and worked on his accounts: cash on hand, debts, expected income. He figured he could squeak by for six months without cutting a deal. But he was confident that long before his funds were exhausted, he would be flush with Other People's Money, and on his way to becoming wealthy.

He had already made progress. He had learned, for example, that his real estate agent, Ellen St. Martin, would be willing to introduce him to potential mooches in return for a finder's fee. And he found that one of the best places to meet and cozen pigeons was at public seminars on investing hosted by legitimate stock brokerages. And, of course, to get him started, he had that copy of Mortimer Sparco's Super Sucker list.

He was reviewing the list when his phone rang, and he knew that if it wasn't a wrong number, it was either Nancy Sparco or Ellen St. Martin. It was Nancy.

"Hi, big man," she said breezily. "Feel like having company?"

"At this time of night?" he said. "How come?"

"Because my jerko husband is out playing poker with his crummy pals and won't be home till midnight."

"All right," Clark said, "come on down."

"Don't I always?" she said. "Be there in a half-hour."

He had discovered her favorite drink was Pimm's Cup No. 1 with seltzer and a lemon slice, and he had stocked the makings. He had a drink ready for her when she arrived, and was working on his second gin and bitters.

"I'm glad you called," he told her. "I've got something for you."

"An erection?" she said. "Just what I wanted."

"Even better than that," he said, and took two envelopes

325

from the desk drawer. He handed the thin one to her. "Twenty-five hundred for the Super Sucker list." He thrust the plump one into her hands. "And twenty-five thousand for your new business."

She opened the flaps frantically, and when she saw the green, she just squealed.

"Oh you sweetheart!" she cried. "I love you, love you, love you!"

He watched, amused, as she counted the money with nimble fingers. Then she looked up, still amazed.

"You got your stake back from Morty?"

"Uh-huh."

"How did you manage that?"

"Oh, I just persuaded him. He listened to reason."

"Bullshit," she said. "You must have held a gun to his head. But I don't care how you did it; it's a whole new life for me."

"Listen," he said, "don't stick all that money in your bank account. If a cash deposit is ten grand or over, the bank's got to report it to Uncle Sam."

"I know that, dummy. Don't worry, I'll spread it around. Then it's ta-ta, Morty."

"You're moving out on him?"

"You bet your sweet ass. By this time tomorrow, my hubby will be frying his own calamari. I always hated that stuff."

"Where are you going when you leave?" Simon asked.

She shrugged. "Probably check into a motel temporarily until I can find a decent place."

He drained his drink and mixed himself another. "How about moving in with me? Temporarily. I've got an extra bedroom."

She looked at him shrewdly. "Expect me to pay half the maintenance, utilities, and food bills?"

He was offended. "Of course not," he said huffily.

She patted his cheek. "Simmer down, sport," she said. "I'm willing to pay my own way. But if you want to take it out

326

in trade, that's okay, too. Tell me something: What are you going to be doing while I'm setting up my new business?"

"Setting up *my* new business. I told you I'm going to join the game."

"I thought you were just blowing smoke."

"No, I meant it. I'm going to become an investment adviser."

She looked at him doubtfully. "Don't you need a license for that?"

"Nope. Anyone can call himself a financial planner or a money manager. You don't need a license to steal. All you need is a plentiful supply of mooches. When you get your escort service organized, maybe you'll be able to steer some marks my way."

"Of course I will, honey. After all you've done for me . . . Hey, let's celebrate our new careers with a bang."

She tugged him by the hand into the master bedroom, a flossy place. She stripped down swiftly. She was wearing white nylon panties with a red heart embroidered on the crotch.

"See?" she said. "I've got a heart on, too."

She flipped down the top sheet, then suddenly stopped.

"Wait a minute!" she yelled.

She ran into the living room, came back with the two envelopes of money. She dumped them around to make a green, crinkly layer, then threw herself naked on top.

"I've always wanted to do this," she said throatily, and rolled around, burrowing into the money, eyes closed, mouth open, almost panting with pleasure.

Then she opened arms and legs to him, and that's how they screwed, on a bed of cash.

59.

At noon on Tuesday, David Rathbone drove over to Bartlett's home on Bayview Drive in response to Jimmy's phone call. The two men sat in the Bentley in the driveway, and Rathbone lighted a cigarette.

"You're smoking too much," Bartlett observed.

"And drinking too much," Rathbone added. "So what else is new? Why the hurry-up call?"

"I'm making a deposit at the Crescent in Boca at noon on Friday. Mitchell Korne says it will be more than a million."

"Wow," Rathbone said. "And you can quote me on that."

"I think we can safely take out two hundred grand," Bartlett said, "and replace it with our funny money. Providing the German can print that much by Thursday night."

"Printing isn't the problem," Rathbone said. "It's getting the stuff at the last minute, while the bills are still in one piece. Print it up too soon and we'll have a sackful of shit. How about this: I'll drive up to Lakeland first thing tomor-

row morning and tell Weisrotte we want the queer by late
Thursday afternoon. Then on Thursday, I'll drive back to
Lakeland again to pick it up."

"That's a lot of driving."

"For two hundred thousand I'd drive to LA and back."

"All right then," Bartlett said, "let's do it your way. You
get the stuff to me by late Thursday, and we're in business.
I haven't read anything more about Termite Tommy, have
you?"

"Not since that first story. It just fell out of the news. I
guess the cops figure he got drunk and drove into the canal.
They have more important things to worry about than the
accidental death of a lush."

"Of course," Bartlett said.

Rathbone drove back to the town house and went directly
to his office. He jotted some numbers on a pad. Two hundred
thousand dollars. Deduct the German's fifteen percent and
Bartlett's forty. That left Rathbone with ninety thousand
clear. He grinned at that. Not bad for two trips to Lakeland.

He was working on his personal ledger when the office
phone rang, and for a moment he was tempted to just ignore
it until the caller gave up. But then he figured it might be
Bartlett wanting to add more details on the deal. He picked
it up.

"David Rathbone Investment Management."

"David!" Birdie Winslow said, and her laugh was a trill.
"How nice to catch you in. I've been calling and calling."

"I've been awfully busy, Birdie," he said. "How have you
been?"

"In seventh heaven," she said, "dreaming about our trip. I
can't begin to tell you all the wonderful things I've bought.
Luggage and dresses and hats and shoes and just everything."

"Why not," he said. "You deserve it."

"But that's not why I called. I just wanted you to know
that I think I've won you a new client."

"Oh?" he said, suddenly cautious. "How did you do that?"

"Well, you know that man you gave my name to, that Anthony Harker, he stopped by last Saturday and asked a lot of questions about you and if I was satisfied with your services, and of course I said I was, and I think by the time he left he was convinced that you were the right investment adviser for him. He said he was going to have a talk with you. Have you heard from him yet?"

"Anthony Harker? No, not yet."

"Well, I'm sure you will. I showed him my last statement, and he was just amazed at how much money you were making for me. I told him you were the best in the business, and everyone said so. Aren't you proud of me?"

"I certainly am," he said. "Thank you for the recommendation."

He finally got her off the phone and sat awhile, staring at his big green safe. Then he dragged out his telephone directories and looked up the name. No Anthony Harker in Lauderdale, Boca Raton, or Pompano Beach. He sat back and lighted another cigarette with hands that were not quite steady. He recalled what Irving Donald Gevalt had told him, and wondered if Anthony Harker was interested in McGuffey first editions.

He left for Lakeland early Wednesday morning, January 31. Rita was still asleep, so he scribbled a note saying he'd return in time to take her to dinner and maybe stop by the Palace for a few drinks with the gang.

It was a cool, crisp morning, but he knew it would warm up later. He didn't wear a suit, just linen slacks and an aqua polo shirt with a bolo tie, the clasp set with a thirty-carat emerald-cut blue topaz.

He drove with the windows down; the new world smelled sweet and clean. But he was in no mood to enjoy it; all he could think about was what Gevalt and Birdie had told him. Live like a jackal, he told himself, and you develop an animal instinct for danger. And right now he had the feeling he was being stalked, but by whom and for what reason he could not fathom.

So intent was he on trying to puzzle it out that he was not aware of how fast he was driving until he was pulled over by a state trooper on Highway 27.

"Know what you were doing?" the officer asked, writing in his pad.

"To tell you the truth I don't," Rathbone said with a nervous laugh. "My wife's having our first baby in a hospital in Lakeland, and I'm in a hurry to get there."

"Nice try but no cigar," the trooper said, handing him the ticket. "I clocked you at eighty, at least. Take it easy and maybe you'll live to see your first kid."

"I'll do that," Rathbone said, and then, after the officer went back to his car, "Up yours!"

He was in Lakeland by noon and was happy to find Weisrotte reasonably sober. He told the printer he wanted two hundred thousand in fake 100s by late Thursday.

"Zo," the German said. "And when my share do I receive?"

"Early next week," Rathbone promised. "You can count on it. You're the most important man in this operation, Herman, and we want to keep you happy."

"Goot," Weisrotte said, and insisted Rathbone have a glass of schnapps with him before leaving. It was caustic stuff, and David wondered if the printer used it to clean his presses.

On the drive home he tried to convince himself that he was foolish to worry; the guy at Gevalt's could have been a rube hoping to buy forged ID at an old-book store, and Birdie's Anthony Harker could have been a legit investor looking for an adviser. But none of that really made sense, and Rathbone felt someone closing in on him, a faceless hunter who came sniffing at the spoor, hungry for the kill.

He was pulled over again for speeding; same stretch of highway, same trooper.

"How's the wife?" the officer asked, writing out the ticket. "Have the kid yet?"

"Not yet," Rathbone said with a sick smile. "False alarm."

"Uh-huh," the trooper said, handing him the ticket. "Have a nice day."

He was in a vile mood by the time he got home, but after a vodka gimlet and a hot shower, he felt better, reasoning that he had been in squeezes before and had always wriggled out. The important thing was to keep his nerve.

The sight of Rita helped lift him out of his funk. She wore a tight miniskirt of honey-colored linen and an oversized nubby sweater with a deep V-neck that displayed her coppery tan and advertised the fact that she was bra-less. Her gypsy hair swung free, and when they sauntered into an elegant French restaurant on the Waterway, she made every other woman in the place look like Barbie.

They did the whole bit: escargots; a Caesar salad for two; rare tournedos with tiny mushroom caps and miniature carrots; Grand Marnier soufflé; and chilled Moët.

"This is living," Rita said. Then: "Why are you staring at me like that?"

"Ever hear of a man called Anthony Harker?" he asked.

She fumbled in her purse for a cigarette and signaled the hovering waiter for a light. "Nope," she said. "The name rings no bells with me."

The bill arrived, and Rathbone offered his stolen credit card. It went through without a hitch, and he gave munificent cash tips to the waiter and maître d'.

They drove to the Palace and found everyone partying up a storm at the big table: Trudy and Jimmy Bartlett, Cynthia and Sid Coe, Frank Little, Ellen St. Martin, and, by himself, Mort Sparco.

"Where's Nancy?" Rathbone asked him.

"The bitch walked out on me," Sparco said glumly. "This afternoon while I was at work. Took most of her clothes, jewelry, and a bottle of extra-virgin olive oil I've been saving."

"Don't worry about it," Rita consoled him. "She'll be back."

"Damned right," Mort said. "Where's she going to go? She'll be lost without me."

Rathbone went to the bar for drinks, but Ernie wasn't on duty; Sylvester, a waiter from the dining room, was filling in as bartender.

"Where's Ernie?" David asked.

"Called in sick, Mr. Rathbone. Hasn't worked for the past two days. He wants you to phone him. Here's his number. He said to be sure and tell you to call him from outside, not from here."

"Okay," Rathbone said, stuffing the scrap of paper into his pocket. "Now let me have a couple of brandy stingers."

"What's a stinger?" Sylvester asked.

Rathbone went behind the bar and mixed the drinks himself.

It was the kind of night he needed. He caught the bubbly mood of the others, and his premonitions disappeared in the noise, jokes, laughter, chivying, and just plain good fellowship of these splendid people. When he and Rita departed a little after midnight, they waited, hand-in-hand, for the valet to bring the Bentley around, and they sang "What'll I Do?"

Theodore and Blanche had left a light on downstairs. They had also left the air conditioning turned so low that the town house felt like a meat locker. David switched off the air and opened the French doors.

"I'm going upstairs and change," Rita said.

"Go ahead," Rathbone said. "I'll pour us a nightcap, and then I have to make a phone call."

333

He brought two small snifters of cognac from the kitchen and placed them on the glass-topped cocktail table. Then he settled down in one corner of the big couch and used the white phone on the end table. He took the scrap of paper from his pocket and punched out the number.

"Ernie?" he said. "This is David Rathbone."

"Hiya, Mr. Rathbone. Where you calling from?"

"From my home. Why?"

"I just didn't want you to call from the Palace. The phone there may be tapped. My own phone probably is. I'm not home now. I'm staying with a friend."

"Ernie, what's all this about? Why should the Palace phones be tapped? Or yours?"

"Listen, Mr. Rathbone, two cops from the sheriff's office came to see me at the Lounge on Monday. I thought at first they were a couple of clowns wanting to put the arm on me for a contribution—if you know what I mean. But it was more than that. They showed me a picture of a dead guy they said went by the name of Termite Tommy. The picture had been taken in the morgue. This Termite Tommy had been wasted. Someone stuck an ice pick in his ear."

Rathbone leaned forward and picked up one of the brandy snifters. He took a deep swallow, then held the glass tightly.

"They wanted to know if this guy had been in the Lounge on New Year's Day. I told them I didn't remember. But they said they knew he had been there; one of the parking valets had seen him. Then they asked if you had been there at the same time, Mr. Rathbone."

David finished the cognac, put the empty glass on the table, picked up the other one.

"I tried to cover for you, Mr. Rathbone, really I did. But they knew all about your passing out and how I had to call Rita to come get you. Now how in hell did they know that?"

"I have no idea," Rathbone said hoarsely.

"Well, they knew, all right. They kept asking if you had

talked to that Termite Tommy, if the two of you had a drink together. Mr. Rathbone, you've always treated me decent so I got to level with you. Those jokers knew all about my little sidelines, so I'm talking a deal with them. Or rather my lawyer is. I'm sorry, Mr. Rathbone, but my ass is on the line. If they want to throw the book at me, I'm liable to end up doing heavy time. I've got to cooperate with them. You can understand that, can't you, Mr. Rathbone?"

David gulped down half of the second brandy. It caught in his throat and for a moment he was afraid he might spew it up. He swallowed frantically again and again. Finally it went down, burning his stomach. Then:

"What did you tell them, Ernie?"

"Just that you were there at the same time as Termite Tommy. That the two of you had a drink together and talked awhile. That's all, Mr. Rathbone, I swear it. Oh, I also told them about those two bums who were having a beer at the other table while you and Termite Tommy were talking. Remember those guys? The cops want me to go through the mug books and see if I can make them. Maybe they're the skels who used the ice pick."

"Maybe," Rathbone said.

"Anyway, I wanted you to know what's going on. Ordinarily, I wouldn't gab about any of my customers—you know that—but my balls are in the wringer and I've got to make the best deal I can. You can appreciate that, can't you, Mr. Rathbone?"

"Sure, Ernie. It's okay. No great harm done."

"I'm glad to hear that. I just didn't want you to think I was a rat. I wish you the best of luck, Mr. Rathbone."

"Thanks, Ernie," David said. "The same to you."

He hung up and finished the second cognac. He took the empty glasses back to the kitchen and started to pour new drinks. He stopped suddenly, remembering. At least Ernie hadn't mentioned his passing a white envelope to Termite

Tommy or how he, Rathbone, had gone into the men's room and had been joined there by one of the thugs.

Perhaps Ernie hadn't seen either incident. Or had witnessed them but just didn't recall. Or did recall them and hadn't told the cops. Or had told the cops and wasn't admitting how much he had blabbed.

But it really didn't matter, Rathbone concluded. The important fact was that he had been seen in the company of a homicide victim shortly before the murder. Sooner or later, he knew, the cops would come looking for him.

First Gevalt, then Birdie, and now this. . . . For one brief instant he thought it might be smart to run at once, that night. But he immediately recognized it as stupid panic. Even if the cops came around in the morning, he could stall them for a day or two. He could tell them he had met Termite Tommy quite by accident in the Palace Lounge on New Year's Day. They had been casual acquaintances. They had a drink together, wished each other Happy New Year, Tommy left, and that was that.

The cops might not buy the story, but it would take time and a lot more digging before they discovered Rathbone was holding out on them. And by the time they tied him to the Corcoran brothers—if they ever did—he'd be long gone.

His need to stall the fuzz, even for a short while, was obvious: He couldn't run until Bartlett's deposit on Friday was a done deal. Jimmy would take his forty percent, and David would pocket a cool $120,000. Screw Herman Weisrotte! If that drunken Kraut wanted to sue in Costa Rica for his fifteen-percent cut, lots of luck! But there was no way Rathbone was going to run before he made that marvelous score.

He carried the fresh drinks into the living room, feeling up again. Rita was coming down the stairs barefoot, wearing the yellow terry robe he had given her the first morning she awoke in his bed.

"You okay, honey?" she asked, looking at him closely. "You look like something the cat dragged in."

336

"I was a little shook," he admitted, "but I'm better now. That phone call—an old friend of mine up north just died."

"Ah, too bad. What did he die from?"

"Cancer," David said. "Sit down and drink your drink. There's a lot I want to talk to you about."

She curled up alongside him on the couch, and he put an arm about her shoulders.

"How soon can you be ready to leave?" he asked her. "I mean leave the country for good."

"I told you," she said. "Give me twenty minutes."

He laughed and hugged her. "You're a wonder, you are," he said. "It won't be until after this Friday. It all depends on when I can book a flight for us. But let's figure early next week—okay? Now listen carefully: I'm driving up to Lakeland tomorrow and may not be back until late in the evening. I'll leave you two grand in cash, and I want you to go out to Gevalt and pick up your passport. Got that?"

She nodded.

"Now on Friday afternoon, you and I are going shopping. I have charge accounts at Burdines, Jordan Marsh, Lord and Taylor, Macy's, Saks, and Neiman-Marcus. Make out a list of everything you want. We're going to charge up a storm at all those stores."

She turned her head to look at him. "And we'll be gone before the bills come in—right?"

"Right! So forget about the cost. Just buy everything you want."

"But what'll I need—fur coats or bikinis? Where are we going?"

"Costa Rica," he said. "A climate a lot like Florida's. Even better. I have a ranch down there you're going to love. It's out in the country, but not too far from the beach or the city. Plenty to do, plenty to see. And you already *habla* Spanish."

"Oh God," she said, "it sounds great. I'll bet they have wonderful plantains."

"And fantastic melons," he said. "The place is a paradise."

He picked up her drink and led her upstairs to the bedroom. She took off her robe, sat on the edge of the bed, watched him undress.

He knelt on the floor at her feet. He pressed her bare knees together and leaned his chin on them, his eyes turned upward to her face.

"I've got to tell you something, Rita. I've been a grifter all my life, and loving you is maybe the first straight thing I've ever done. It's a super feeling."

She clasped his face, lifted his head gently.

"Come to mommy," she said.

60.

On Thursday morning, February 1, Anthony Harker listened to the previous day's tapes in his motel room. Then he packed all the reels in a battered briefcase and lugged it to the office. He finally decided Crockett had to know. He wasn't going to dump the problem in his lap, just present the evidence and tell Crockett what he planned to do. He owed the chief that much.

Crockett was already behind his desk, as trig as ever in his vested suit with a neatly knotted polka-dotted bow tie. He listened closely as Harker ran through the checklist on his clipboard.

"Roger Fortescue will drive up to Lakeland tomorrow morning in time to be there by noon. He'll arrest Herman Weisrotte. Two Secret Service men will provide backup.

"Henry Ullman will collar Bartlett at the Crescent Bank in Boca at noon. He'll be assisted by FBI special agents.

"Manuel Suarez will take Sidney Coe. Manny will lead a

squad from the Fort Lauderdale police. In addition to Coe, all the yaks will be booked.

"I figured Simon Clark would bust Mortimer Sparco's brokerage, but Clark asked if he could pick up Irving Donald Gevalt instead. That's okay with me, so I arranged for an SEC team to hit the brokerage. They know what to look for.

"The DEA will coordinate their raid on Frank Little's warehouse. At the same time they arrest Little, they'll grab all his customers they've been able to identify.

"I'll lead a team from the Broward County Sheriff's Office against David Rathbone's town house. The warrants authorize his arrest and seizing whatever records we can find in his private office.

"Ernest Hohlman, the bartender at the Palace Lounge, picked out two ex-cons from the mug books who might be involved in the murder of Termite Tommy. They're Brian and Thomas Corcoran, brothers, with rap sheets as long as your arm. Heavy stuff like armed robbery and felonious assault. There's a warrant out for both of them right now.

"I should warn you, sir, that some if not all of the assisting agencies are sure to rush to the newspapers and TV cameras as soon as the operation goes down."

"That's all right," Crockett said. "There'll be enough glory to go around, and we don't want any for this organization. We may need the cooperation of those people in the future, so let them get their headlines. Have you been able to keep a lid on all this?"

"I think so," Harker said. "There have been no leaks that I know of."

Lester Crockett leaned over his desk, clasped his hands, looked directly at the other man.

"Tony," he said, "you haven't mentioned Rita Sullivan. What part have you planned for her?"

Harker hoisted his briefcase onto Crockett's desk. "Sir," he said, "I've been providing you with abstracts of the tapes from David Rathbone's home. Now I think you better listen to the complete tapes. I know what must be done, but you should be aware of my reasons."

Crockett nodded. "If you feel it's that important, I'll do it now. Is there a machine available?"

"Yes, sir. In the bullpen. I'll have it brought in here."

He wasn't summoned back to Crockett's office until late in the afternoon. The reels were stacked on the chief's desk. He motioned Harker to a chair and stared at him.

"You should have told me sooner, Tony," he said quietly.

"I wasn't sure. Not absolutely sure. She could have been playing her role."

Crockett shook his head. "I was afraid of something like this. And so were you."

"No! I didn't expect anything like that to happen."

"I think you did," Crockett said, "but perhaps you wouldn't admit it to yourself. If you were sure of her, you would have told her about the taps on Rathbone's phones and the bugs inside the house."

Harker was silent.

"I'm sorry, Tony," Crockett said. "People do turn sour, you know. And sometimes the best. Will you handle it?"

"Yes, sir. Before noon tomorrow. What's the most we can offer her?"

"Immediate resignation for reasons of health. Nothing on her record, but never another job in law enforcement. Oh God, what a fool!"

"Rita?" Tony said. "Or me?"

Crockett looked at him sadly. "Both of you," he said. "But perhaps 'fool' isn't the right word. 'Victim' is more accurate."

"Mooches," Harker said bitterly.

61.

Friday morning, February 2.

It was a squally day, no sign of the sun, ripped clouds
scudding before a northeast wind. There were spatters of
rain, an occasional zipper of lightning, thunder rumbling in
the distance like an artillery barrage.

It must have poured during the night; streets on the way
to the office were flooded, and a royal palm was down across
Federal Highway. Tony Harker splashed through puddles to
a coffee shop, but his stomach was churning and he ordered
a glass of milk and dry rye toast.

He wondered why he felt no exultation. He was bringing
a complex investigation to a successful end, but he had no
sense of satisfaction. In fact, this final day was almost anti-
climactic. He saw it as cleaning up after a wild party: a mess
of cold cigarette butts, empty bottles, stale food, and broken
glass. Nothing left to do but throw out the garbage.

His first call was to the sheriff's office, requesting that two
plainclothesmen be sent in an unmarked car to stake out Da-

vid Rathbone's town house. They were to collar Rathbone at noon if Harker hadn't shown up.

He spoke to Manuel Suarez and Simon Clark, and gave them final orders. He called Henry Ullman in Boca to make certain there was no last-minute hitch in their plans. There was no way to reach Roger Fortescue; Harker assumed he was on the road en route to Lakeland. He called his contact at the DEA and was assured everything was on schedule.

Finally, at 9:10 A.M., he called the office of the Fort Knox Commodity Trading Fund. He was connected to an answering machine, and hung up. He called every ten minutes after that with the same result. He had resolved that if he couldn't contact Rita at the office by eleven o'clock, he'd call her at the town house and run the risk of Rathbone's answering the phone.

But at 10:20, she answered the office phone. "The Fort Knox Fund," she said perkily. "Good morning."

"Harker here," he said. "You alone?"

"Yes."

"I've got to see you right away. It's important."

Silence for a beat or two. "Will it take long?" she asked finally. "We're supposed to go shopping this afternoon."

"No, not long. An hour at the most."

"All right. Where?"

"My motel," he said. "I'm leaving now."

He hadn't devised any scenario or even decided in what order to say the things that had to be said. So he'd have to wing it, and he wasn't much good at improvising.

She came into his motel apartment wearing a clear plastic slicker over a peach-colored jumpsuit. Her wind-tossed hair was glistening with mist, and she was laughing because the flowered umbrella she carried had turned inside out. She tossed it into a corner and stripped off her raincoat.

"Let's move to south Florida," she said, "where the sun shines every day. Got a cold beer for me?"

"No," Harker said, and she whipped her head around to

343

look at him. "Sit down," he told her. "I'll make this as brief as possible."

She sat, crossed her legs, took out a pack of Winstons. She slowly went through the ceremony of shaking out a cigarette, lighting it, inhaling.

"What's up?" she asked quietly.

He was standing behind an armchair, gripping the top. But he found his knees were beginning to tremble, so he paced a few steps back and forth.

"I promised to tell you before we moved on Rathbone. I'm telling you now. We're taking him today."

"Oh?" she said, inspecting the burning tip of her cigarette. "When?"

"Noon."

"Thanks for giving me so much advance notice," she said, making no effort to hide the sarcasm. "Who's going to arrest him?"

"I am. With men from the sheriff's office. The town house is staked out right now. Did Rathbone ever tell you where he might go if he left the country?"

"No, he never said."

Harker laughed, a harsh sound that sounded phony even to him. "Not a word about his ranch in Costa Rica? Close to the beach and city? The two of you leaving early next week? But first let's go shopping and charge up a storm."

She reacted as if he had struck her across the face. Her head flung back, tanned skin went sallow; she stared at him with widened eyes, trying to comprehend.

"Bugs!" she finally spat out. "The place was bugged!"

"And the phones tapped," Harker said.

"And you never told me?" she cried. "You prick!"

He sat down heavily in the armchair, suddenly saddened because despite what she had done, her first reaction was to accuse him.

"It's all a can of worms, isn't it?" he said. "I've learned that logic doesn't always work with human beings."

344

"What makes you think you're a human being?"

"Oh, I'm human," he said. "I'm just as fucked-up as everyone else."

But she wouldn't let it go at that. "No," she said, shaking her head, "you're vindictive, malicious. You're getting your jollies out of busting David, aren't you? Big deal! That guy's just a con artist who's ripped off a few rich people, and you've gone after him like he's a serial killer. He'll never spend a day behind bars, and you know it. He'll get himself a sharp lawyer. He'll make full restitution—and he's got the money to do it. He'll promise to straighten up and fly right, and he'll get off with a wrist tap. You'll see."

"I told you a dozen times," Harker said, "and you wouldn't listen. Rathbone's been doing more than stealing pencils from blind men. In addition to a dozen financial felonies, we've got him on drug dealing. What did you think the Fort Knox Fund was trading? Their commodities were cocaine, heroin, and marijuana. And we've got him on counterfeiting and bank fraud. Why do you think he made all those trips to Lakeland? It was to pick up packages of the queer printed by an ex-con up there. And we also want him on suspicion of being an accessory to murder. When he got drunk in the Palace Lounge on New Year's Day, he had just fingered a guy who was later found dead in a canal. Someone had stuck an ice pick in his ear. So much for your poor, misunderstood con artist who's going to make restitution and dance away whistling a merry tune. In a pig's ass he will!"

She had listened to this diatribe with lowered head. Now she looked up, and he was shocked at how old she appeared.

"Are you telling me the truth, Harker?" she asked.

"It's the truth," he said. "That bastard is going to do hard time."

"He's beautiful," Rita said in a low voice. "You know what they'll do to him in prison?"

"I know," Harker said.

She pulled herself from the chair and began to walk about

the room hugging her elbows. She was silent a long time, and he glanced at his watch to make certain time wasn't running out.

"David's got a lot of puppy in him," she said finally, speaking in a monotone as if thinking aloud. "He likes to be petted and played with. And sometimes spanked and told what a bad boy he is. Prison will kill him."

Harker said nothing. She stopped pacing and stood before him, looking down, hands on her hips.

"Can we cut a deal, Harker?" she asked him.

His expression didn't change. "What kind of a deal?"

"You said you wanted to marry me. Did you mean that?"

He nodded. "I meant it."

"I'll marry you," she said, staring at him, "and do my damnedest to be a good wife. In the bedroom and in the kitchen. I won't cheat on you, and I won't leave unless you kick me out. For that you let me make a call right now. David's smart enough to get away. He'll duck the stakeout, go out a back window or through the pool area. Just let me phone him. If he doesn't make it, I'll still keep my part of the deal."

Harker felt like weeping. "You must really love him," he said.

"Love?" she said, almost angrily. "What's that? Poets and songwriters know all about it, but I don't. Sure, I have affection for him, but that's a small part of it. Mostly it's guilt for having conned him. It's knowing I helped put him away, and realizing I'm going to live with it till the day I die."

"You've helped put villains away before. Did it bother you?"

"No," she said, "but this is different. He said he was going straight with me, and it turned out to be a scam. What does that make me?"

Harker didn't answer.

"Well," she said, "time's getting short. Do you want to marry me? Have we got a deal?"

"No," he said.

She looked at him with a gargoyled grin, all twisted and ugly. Her hands clenched, knuckles white. She was trying to hang on, but it didn't work. She broke and collapsed into the armchair, black wings of hair covering her face, shoulders rocking back and forth. What moved him most was that she wept silently, no sobs, no wails, just soundless grief.

He relented then and went looking for something to drink. The only hard stuff he had was a bottle of Popov. He poured it over ice and brought one of the drinks to her. He took her hand and pressed her fingers around the glass. The feel of her velvety skin still had the power to stir him.

He sat down in his chair again, took a gulp of his drink, watched her. Her body finally stopped shaking. She straightened, jerked her head back to get hair away from her face, drained half the glass of vodka.

"Why did you do it?" he asked her. "You don't have to answer, but I'd really like to know. Was it the loving?"

"Part of it," she admitted, taking a deep breath. "And part was the way he treated me, like I was the most valuable thing he had ever owned. And part was the lush life. David really knows how to live."

"What kind of bullshit is that?" Harker demanded. "You talk like it's a special talent. Everyone knows how to live. All you need is money."

She smiled wanly. "That's what David always said. His favorite expression. Well, he had the money."

"Sure he did. But look how he made it, and look where it got him."

"So you've got me on tape," she said. "Am I going to be charged?"

"No," Harker said. "There'll be no charges. You'll be allowed to resign for reasons of health. Nothing on your record. But no more jobs in law enforcement. Crockett okayed it."

"So he knows, too?"

Harker nodded.

"Anyone else?"

"No, just Crockett and me."

She sipped her drink and stared at him. "Why didn't you tell me about the bugs and the taps? Was it because from the first you were afraid I'd turn?"

"That's what Crockett thinks," he said, not looking at her. "But I don't think that's the whole reason. I think part of it was jealousy. Listening to you and Rathbone in bed together was like pounding on a wound."

"You were right," she said. "You *are* fucked-up. What's going to happen to me now? What'll I do?"

Harker shrugged. "I'm not worried about you," he said. "You'll find another David Rathbone. Or another me," he added.

She finished her drink, and with it her breezy courage returned. "And what about you, kiddo?" she said. "No more fun and games with me on motel sheets. That was the best loving you'll ever have."

"I know."

"You'll get your allergies back," she jeered. "And your nervous stomach and your sun poisoning."

"I'll survive," he said, not certain he would. He glanced at his watch. "After twelve. They've taken Rathbone by now."

They fixed her umbrella, and he locked up and accompanied her down to their cars. They faced, not knowing whether to shake hands, kiss, or knee each other in the groin.

"Will I see you again?" she asked.

He looked upward, hoping for an omen: the muddy clouds parting and a shaft of pure sunlight striking through to bathe them in gold. He saw only zigzags of lightning splitting the sky, heard only the growl of far-off thunder.

"Will I?" Rita persisted.

"Maybe," Tony said.

FIC   Sanders, Lawrence
SAN
           Sullivan's sting

$19.95

6/90